"Wolfsinger, you are in a great deal of trouble."

Zhukov stood a few feet away with the business end of his submachine gun pointed at Novikov's head, which he held in a headlock under his arm. Novikov tried to pull free, but the old general had no trouble restraining him. Four Russian soldiers in red spacesuits gathered the rest of the archaeology team against the wall a few feet away.

Kate stepped around the edge of the portal to stand beside Tau. He felt very exposed where he stood, with the blue mist at his back and a man with a gun in front. To his right, Josh Mandelbrot moved toward him with the slow and casual motion of a snake.

"What do you want?" Kate asked.

"Cooperation," said Zhukov. "If there is any trouble, I'll kill this man, then choose a new victim. Otherwise, no one will be harmed. You will accompany me back to Red Star, and Wolfsinger will continue the work he started."

Mandelbrot grabbed Tau's right arm. As Tau tried to jerk his arm away, Kate stepped in front of Tau and kicked Mandelbrot in the groin, pushing against Tau's chest in the process. Mandelbrot grunted and doubled over, releasing Tau's arm.

Off-balance, Tau fell backward through the glowing blue mist of the alien portal.

THE FORGE OF
MARS

BRUCE BALFOUR

ACE BOOKS, NEW YORK

THE FORGE OF MARS

An Ace Book / published by arrangement with
the author

PRINTING HISTORY
Ace mass-market edition / September 2002

Copyright © 2002 by Bruce Balfour.
Cover design by Rita Frangie.
Text design by Julie Rogers.

Visit our website at
www.penguinputnam.com
Check out the ACE Science Fiction & Fantasy newsletter!

ISBN: 0-441-00954-9

ACE®
Ace Books are published by The Berkley Publishing Group,
a division of Penguin Putnam Inc.,
375 Hudson Street, New York, New York 10014.
ACE and the "A" design
are trademarks belonging to Penguin Putnam Inc.

PRINTED IN THE UNTIED STATES OF AMERICA

10 9 8 7 6 5 4 3 2 1

ACKNOWLEDGMENTS

The arrangement of words in this novel was made possible through the efforts of many fine individuals, some of whom are still speaking to me now that it's finished. For their contributions of time, support, or materials, I'd like to thank: John Morgan at Berkley; Sara and Bob Schwager, copyeditors; Pete McCarthy at Penguin Putnam; Dr. Henry Lum at the NASA–Ames Research Center; Dr. Nils J. Nilsson at the Stanford Artificial Intelligence Laboratory; Dr. K. Eric Drexler at the Foresight Institute; Warren and Betty Balfour; Heather and Hope Wilson; and my agent, Richard Curtis.

Henceforth I spread confident wings to space
I fear no barrier of crystal or of glass;
I cleave the heavens and soar to the infinite.
And while I rise from my own globe to others
And penetrate even further through the eternal field,
That which others saw from afar, I leave far behind me.

(Giordano Bruno, *On the Infinite Universe and Worlds*, 1584)

THE hot rainbow of reentry danced across the window, accenting the precise ballet of the computer-controlled descent, until the shuttle completed its hypersonic banking maneuvers at seventy thousand feet. Then everything went to hell.

Almost an hour earlier, Tau Edison Wolfsinger received the "go for deorbit burn," then maneuvered the shuttle tail forward to aim its OMS engines in the direction of flight. Orbiting the Earth at 17,490 miles per hour, free of the atmosphere, it took only a gentle pressure on the rotational hand controller to adjust the shuttle's flight attitude. The computer translated his hand movements to fire the proper combination of six vernier thrusters in the nose and tail sections. In a slow pirouette high above the blue-and-white planet, the shuttle pitched and rolled to its deorbit attitude.

Even after days in orbit, Tau still thought it odd that the verniers did their job without making a sound. The remaining thirty-eight primary thrusters, used for translation maneuvers and rapid rotations, announced their activity in a more spectacular fashion. The shuttle would shake and shudder as flashes of flame burst from the nose and tail primaries, accompanied by battle sounds as if cannons and mortars were firing. They sounded like real rockets. Raised on Hollywood holies and sims, Tau considered it wrong for the verniers to fire in silence.

Passing over the eastern coast of Africa at an altitude of 160 miles, he keyed the deorbit-burn command into the flight computer, initiating the descent to California. Through the cockpit window, only a few pearls of light were visible on the African continent, now shrouded in the blanket of night.

More silence. The G-meter remained fixed at zero on the dial as if it were painted on the glass. Tau felt his heart beat faster and tried to concentrate on the sound of his breath hissing in and out through his dry nose, more audible now that his helmet was locked down on the suit's neck ring.

Fifteen seconds later, the OMS engines ignited. The bang reverberated through the ship, rattling Tau's seat before a gentle deceleration pressed him back into the cushions. The three-minute burn of the OMS would nudge the G-meter to 0.1, slowing the shuttle by two hundred miles per hour and using all of the remaining fuel in the main maneuvering system. Facing forward, Tau couldn't see the bright blasts of exhaust from the OMS engines as they placed him on a new orbital path. With the deorbit burn completed, there would be no turning back from the fiery plunge into the atmosphere thirty minutes later.

Confirming the shutdown of the OMS engines, Tau rocked the hand controller to rotate the shuttle's nose forward, pitching up at a forty-degree angle of attack to pancake the superinsulated underbody into the brunt of the atmosphere. The chip in his G-suit talked to the flight computer, then triggered the inflation of the bladders around his calves and thighs, squeezing them tight enough to prevent blood from flowing away from his brain during reentry. In final preparation before hitting the atmosphere, Tau dumped the remaining propellant from the forward reaction control system, then switched on the auxiliary power units to give him aerodynamic control over the shuttle's descent.

When the shuttle hit the atmosphere, seventy-five miles over the Pacific Ocean at Mach 25, Tau reminded himself to breathe. Air whispered past the exterior, gaining in volume as a faint red glow appeared at the edges of the cockpit windows. No longer floating in the comfortable microgravity that had become normal during the previous week, Tau felt the pressure of 1.7 Gs pressing him hard into his seat. He now

weighed 255 pounds—a butterfly transformed into an ele-
phant—far more ponderous than his normal weight of 150 on
Earth. Beads of sweat on his forehead, held there previously
by surface tension, now dripped into his eyes to make him
blink.

The glow spread across the cockpit windows, shifting
from red to orange to a hot pink as the carbon-carbon insulation that covered the nose and the leading edges of the delta
wings slammed its way through the air molecules with
enough force to strip away electrons. Communications with
the ground blacked out for twelve minutes as an electromagnetic cone formed around the shuttle during the period of
maximum heat. His instruments showed the leading edge
temperatures reaching 2,490 degrees Fahrenheit as the shuttle
dissipated its kinetic energy against the angry atmosphere.

Slowing to fifteen thousand miles an hour, Tau heard the
rush of air climbing the scale from a hoarse growl to a thundering roar. More sweat dripped in his eyes, even though logic
told him that the heat of reentry dissipated against the insulation before it reached the interior of the flight deck. A frightened animal deep in his brain knew that the intense flames
burned just a few feet away from his body, threatening to melt
the flesh on his bones until his corpse became nothing but ash
drifting on the wind.

Still flying faster than sound, Tau watched the horizon line
roll to almost vertical. The autopilot began its series of hypersonic banking maneuvers with a left turn. Braking against
the atmosphere like a snow skier making sweeping turns to
slow his descent down a mountain, the shuttle reversed its
bank. Tau watched the horizon swing in the opposite direction
as his stomach lurched. He kept his hand on the controller, but
he knew the quick-thinking flight computer, communicating
with the microwave landing system in California, could handle the reentry far better than he could. The elevons on the
wings controlled the pitch and roll while the split rudder on
the tail controlled the yaw and acted as a speed brake. Nudging the stick in the wrong direction could put him hundreds of

miles off course, but it comforted him to have his hand on the controls.

When the right limb of the horizon rolled until it disappeared out the top of the cockpit window, the left limb was hidden by the shuttle's nose. Tau closed his eyes. The hypersonic "S"-turns gave him a headache, but the altimeter told him he'd reached seventy thousand feet, so he'd be safe on the ground in a few minutes.

Tau opened his eyes and smiled. The sun peeked over the eastern horizon, filling the sky with a pale light that erased the last traces of glowing pink from the windows.

A red light flashed on the console.

An alarm buzzer went off.

The right wing snapped up faster than the computer could correct for it.

The shuttle flipped over.

Reacting to the change in brightness, the tint of his helmet visor lightened just long enough for him to glimpse the cloud tops rotating far below before a giant hand played Ping-Pong with his head. The shuttle bucked, spun, bounced, and tumbled, all at the same time. His helmet slammed against the cockpit window as his body jerked from side to side. The instrument displays went dark. He tasted copper in his mouth as he bit his tongue. Ominous booming noises, the drums of doom, reverberated through the hull.

Tau realized he'd soon be dead.

The thought of being dead at twenty-four chilled his blood. He had too much to do. It wasn't fair.

The shuttle began to tear itself apart with a horrendous dinosaur scream of tortured metal, alerting the survival computer in his seat. Explosive bolts fired, the overhead panel tore away, and a rocket kicked him in the seat of the pants, ramming him up and out at over one hundred miles per hour.

Straight into the superhot slipstream of the shuttle.

The seat started to burn. The spacesuit thermostat tried to compensate, but the heat passed through the suit as if it wasn't there. After the initial shock of hitting air that felt as soft as a brick wall, the seat slowed, the crash web detached, and another small charge fired to kick him away from the seat as it danced out of the slipstream. The shuttle dropped away, tearing itself into shrapnel-sized bits.

Tumbling toward the ground, he glimpsed the burning seat overhead, following him like the angel of death, snagging the parachute shroud lines to set them on fire. In desperation, he hoped the lines wouldn't burn through before—

The chute banged open, a glorious sight, slapping him hard and dislodging the seat from the shroud lines.

Then the burning seat smashed into his helmet, shattering the "shatterproof" bubble, as it shot past him on its flaming journey, racing him toward death on the ground. A demon with a bass drum rattled his ears, but his attention focused on the flames that suddenly erupted around his head. Pure oxygen poured out of his suit, and the hot seat ignited the seal of his neck ring after breaking his helmet. He gasped, trying to choke some air into his lungs through the smoke, drawing the flame closer to his face. The scent of burning meat filled his nostrils.

Confused by conflicting signals from its sensors, the spacesuit shut off the oxygen supply and gave up. The flames subsided. Still dazed from the seat's impact, Tau peered over the hot neck ring, down past his feet, as the rocky ground raced up to greet him. Too fast.

A glance upward confirmed his suspicion. Two of the smoldering chute lines had burned through, and half the parachute flapped uselessly in the breeze, taunting him, soon to be his death shroud.

He closed his eyes tight, preparing for an impact that would probably kill him. Then everything went black.

RED *sky at night, sailor's delight; red sky at morning, sailors take warning.* But what if the sky is red all the time? Ed Shepard looked up at the salmon pink glow of late morning on Mars and shivered despite the heat in his pressure suit. When he worked miles away from the nearest colony, he'd sometimes feel a moment of loneliness and isolation. He'd been on Mars for three years, one of the first construction workers to qualify for sponsorship to make the trip. Having worked on construction sites from the deserts of the Middle East to the ice fields of Antarctica, he'd never thought the vast emptiness of a new world would bother him, but it did now. The unending sea of bloody red rocks and sand, cut with streaks of black and orange, filled his view all the way out to a horizon that was too close. He knew he'd feel better if he could smell his dusty surroundings—he related best to new environments by smell—but all he could detect was an odor reminiscent of old gym shoes in the recycled air of his suit.

Ed heard a loud ping when his tracker made contact with one of the diggers. Two of the robot excavators, controlled part-time by human teleoperators at the Vulcan's Forge colony, had collided with each other the previous day. They were precision diggers, designed to work in tight spaces, but the cheap models covered with tools would often get caught between rocks or on other robots. During the night, the interlocked robots wandered away from their work site to fall in a hole somewhere, hidden from the satellites, and it was Ed's job to find them. His partner, Larry DiMarco, searched on the opposite side of the ridge that separated the Umbra Labyrinthus—the Labyrinth of Shadows—from the Noctis Labyrinthus—the Labyrinth of Night. Both areas were mazes of narrow canyons at the summit of the Tharsis uplift, a volcanic region dominated by Mons Olympus and three other shield volcanoes. The robots couldn't have chosen a worse place to fall in a hole.

Following the position indicators on his handheld tracker, Ed shuffled over to the opening of a large volcanic vent— maybe eighty feet across—that angled steeply down into the darkness. A few years earlier, surveys of this area with deep-ground-penetrating radar discovered hot water reservoirs trapped just three thousand feet beneath the surface. Deep geothermal heat sources melted subsurface ice to form trapped pools of water. Water-mining rigs were set up in volcanic vents such as this one because the lava tubes often ran deep under the surface, simplifying access to the water pockets. However, he couldn't see any survey markers, so there was little chance of finding a well-worn trail to a water-mining rig. Ed switched on his flashlight, wishing that his sponsor had provided one of the fancier pressure suits with the big lights built into the chestplate and helmet. He peered into the pit as he signaled his partner, noting that he could work his way down the slope without a rope. If the vent got steeper as he ventured lower, he'd wait for Larry to arrive before going any farther. Technically, he knew he should wait for Larry before entering the vent, but it would take his partner at least ten minutes to walk over the ridge, and Ed needed his breakfast.

Larry's voice barked in his ears. After twenty years of working at noisy construction sites, he'd developed the habit of shouting, even when wearing a pressure suit— only one of many irritating habits. "Shep? Ya got 'em?"

"Tracker says they're in a hole," said Ed, turning his audio volume down. "I'm goin' in to eyeball it."

"Better wait for me."

"Yeah, I'll wait for ya. I'll be the guy standin' here with the two robots."

"You gonna haul 'em out all by yourself, tough guy?"

"If you weren't such an old lady, you'd be down here already."

"You're gonna look awful silly when ya fall down that hole and I have to winch ya out."

"I'll take my chances. I'm hungry."

"Suit yourself, ace."

Ed rolled his eyes and started down the vent, picking his way among the deep gouges in the rough reddish brown rock. When he was about sixty feet down, he noticed that the walls of the vent didn't look quite the same as other volcanic tubes he'd seen on Mars. The walls seemed rougher, scored by explosive pressure but not melted from the heat of the lava. Something unusual about the local rock, maybe, but he wasn't a geologist, and he didn't really care that much. The tracker pinged again, its strong signal implying that the two diggers were still close together wherever they'd fallen.

The vent steepened and narrowed as Ed continued his lurching progress. Almost an hour of strenuous effort brought him to a ledge where the walls of the vent sparkled with shards of milk white volcanic glass, as if someone had broken dishes at a fancy picnic. He picked up one of the flat shards and frowned at the sharp edges, wondering how hot glass could have broken that way. Maybe a sudden change in temperature as the glass cooled? The thick shard slipped from his glove despite his tight grip.

Ed aimed his flashlight down beyond the ledge. The drop was vertical, maybe sixty feet to the next flat area. Rubble had narrowed the opening in the vent to about ten feet across, but a wider chamber yawned beneath the hole. He could climb down farther with the spider line, but he'd need Larry's help to haul the robots out. Naturally, the perverse little machines had rolled far into the vent, making it impossible for Ed to drag them out by himself. Then he noticed that the floor of the pit was glowing. He shut off the flashlight to be sure and found that he no longer needed it. The walls of the chamber below him were coated with the white glass, glowing enough to provide sufficient light for his needs. He crouched for a better look, then bent over and poked his head through the opening.

The diggers sat on the floor of a horizontal tube with smooth white walls. Their running lights were off, but one of the robots twitched. Each spasm jerked the six tool arms, making the digger look like a sand crab that had been flipped on its back. The dead unit had a trenching tool buried in its side, presumably left there after the two robots broke apart from the impact after their tumbling dance of death. Lubricant leaked from the wounded digger, forming a pool of brown liquid beneath the two machines.

"Larry? I see 'em."

"Good. I'm tired," he said, breathing hard.

"We'll need both spider lines to get 'em outta this hole."

"Yeah, I figured."

Ed continued studying the tube. It looked straight, like a subway tunnel, ending at rockfalls that blocked both ends. "And there's somethin' else, Larry."

"Let me guess. Ya want me to carry your sorry ass outta there."

Ed's gaze fell on a glint of metal protruding from the rockfall at the east end of the tunnel, less than a hundred feet away. "There's a tunnel down here, and it ain't natural."

"Water miners?"

Ed patched the end of his spider line to the ledge and lowered himself into the hole. "I don't think so. There ain't no rig, unless it got buried in a cave-in. But this whole tunnel looks artificial, like the walls are coated with white glass stuff."

"Nobody's worked this area. No exploration markers up top."

Ed slipped on the smooth floor as his boots made contact. When he regained his footing, he stepped on areas that were covered in sand so that he could get better traction. Free of the spider line, he walked over to the shiny metal protruding from the rockfall. It didn't look like a natural deposit, more like chrome that had been formed into a delicate curving shape. Elaborate patterns were visible at close range.

He reached out to touch it.

His head exploded with light.

"Ed?" Larry's voice, the last human sound he'd ever hear.

Ed tried to scream, but he couldn't make a sound. He slumped against the metal surface, his brain burning with internal fire. The coppery taste of blood filled his mouth. His body twitched while nerve impulses misfired in a high-voltage flow of energy. As his eyes rolled back into his head, a mental image of a shadowy face tried to take shape before his synapses failed.

When the incomplete face faded away, to be replaced by the brilliant multicolored glow of expanding gases from an exploding star, he felt a sense of loss, certain that he'd failed some sort of test he didn't understand.

And failure meant death.

STORM.

Tau shook his head, blinking while he adapted to the new situation. He stood on an isolated rock spire of brilliant red sandstone punched into the sky—an angry fist rising hundreds of feet above an endless sea of sand. The Wind People were restless. Lightning ripped jagged holes in the velvety midnight darkness. Thunder boomed and rolled over his body in tides of sound. The scent of ozone filled his nostrils as a torrential male rain began to pound his skin, water tracing a path along his deep-set brown eyes, past high cheekbones, on down his wide face to the sharp angle of his jaw. The water continued its journey down his blue permacotton shirt and jeans to roll off the toes of his hiking boots—a miniature waterfall spraying into the abyss.

Tau Edison Wolfsinger, born for the Towering House People Clan, whom the Navajo call the *Kin yaa'aanii*, looked up at the raging sky, squinted against the raindrops, and smiled as he considered his new reality. This could only be a place from his past, a warm day in May during the Season When the Thunder Sleeps. Judging by the intensity of the storm, the Thunder People must be wide-awake. He had often journeyed to this place of great beauty, suspended in time, to relax and meditate, to retreat and reflect, to hide and remember, sometimes chanting words he'd been taught by his uncle, Hosteen Joseph Wolfsinger.

After the long climb up the vertical rock face, he'd hoped to sit and contemplate the stars and his destiny, but the clouds obscured the stars, and his destiny had been mapped out long before he reached the summit of the Fist.

He glanced at the time display in one corner of his vision; behind schedule again. He took a moment to stretch his fatigued muscles, filled his lungs with the cool air, then stepped off the ledge to plummet toward the desert floor.

A quick mental calculation told him he'd be moving at 120 miles per hour when he hit the sand at the base of the Fist, assuming the Wind People didn't slam him into the rock face on the way down.

The Fist had been Tau's favorite refuge during his four years at NASA's Ames Research Center, so he felt it only fitting that he make one final climb on the day that he would be fired. The NASA hierarchy, in its infinite wisdom, had already decided that the work of Tau Edison Wolfsinger, which none of them understood, was too dangerous to be inflicted on society.

The wind rushed past his body, whispering thoughts in his ears that he lacked the knowledge to understand. Tau felt free and happy, almost as if he could fly. This felt nothing like the uncontrolled fall from the shuttle. The fabric of his loose shirt flapped like a flag while he swallowed to equalize the pressure in his ears. A flash of lightning illuminated the landscape, throwing a giant shadow of Tau against the rock wall, and he glimpsed the spot where he would land on the desert floor—in a wide clump of prickly pear cactus. The thought of cactus needles penetrating his skin worried him for a moment, until he remembered he'd be moving at terminal velocity. At that speed, he'd make a big impression on the landscape, so a few cactus needles wouldn't make any difference.

He laughed at the thought.

2

WALTER Beckett studied the column of blinking red numbers projected in the air above his gray metal desk, then compared them against a column of black numbers. He smiled. With a wave of his hand, the red numbers changed to black, demonstrating once again his genius for turning negative reports into positive feedback for his NASA superiors.

Beckett had started out as a mediocre exobiologist, but

soon discovered a flair for administration. When supplies were delayed, or proper forms had not been filled out, young Beckett wormed his way through the bureaucracy at the Ames Research Center with more efficiency than a maggot in search of food. After one of his more spectacular paperwork coups brought unexpected funds to the division, Beckett got himself promoted to branch chief. Continued bureaucratic success over the next twenty years landed him the job of division chief in the troubled Mars Development Office at headquarters.

Ever since the Apollo days, NASA had fought to maintain government funding, recently shifting to the role of interplanetary real estate developer to improve its odds of survival. Defying the trend, Beckett spent ten years building the MDO into a large division, arranging deals with other countries and private industry for commercial development of the Moon and Mars. Cutbacks still occurred, but the MDO could always justify its existence to meddling politicians, especially when they realized that Beckett was of their kind. At meetings with other division heads, Beckett carefully diverted attention away from the MDO's expanding operating budget by commiserating with the rest of them, cursing the evil government funding powers for their shortsighted attitudes.

Beckett opened a desk drawer and glanced down at the row of images from his pinhead spy cameras in the offices of his direct superiors, making sure they'd left for the evening so that he could go home. After Beckett left, his personal AI would periodically trigger communications, office noise, and generic memos until the wee hours of the morning to maintain the appearance that he worked twenty hours a day, seven days a week. A holo of Beckett's thin frame hunched over his work, convincing enough when seen from the small window in the locked office door, completed the effect.

When he started out of the office, a flashing red orb appeared over his desk. Beckett sighed, cursed by his own sensor tap on the Deep Space Network's priority communications channel, and stuck his head into the orb to hear the covert message.

Vulcan's Forge, the spearhead long-term Mars colony in the Tharsis uplift, had suppressed the normal data traffic to Earth with an emergency alert. Beckett stopped breathing for almost a minute as he listened and realized he now had a chance to become director of a NASA research center. When he started breathing again, he giggled.

Beckett surged into action, drawing on all of his administrative powers to secure and cloak the Deep Space Network's Martian data channel, contact a friend in the Public Relations Office who owed him a favor, send dummy news memos to his superiors, start his AI on building a glitzy presentation, summon his speechwriter, and alert the media that he would hold a major press conference in a few hours. He knew it was risky to go outside normal channels of communication with his managers, but if he moved fast enough, he'd be able to get away with it before anyone could slap him down.

GERALDO Cruz, primary mediahead for *NewsNow!*, checked his fingermirror to make sure the curly white hair framing his tanned, angular face presented the proper image of a news-savvy man-about-town. Perched on one of the cushy NASA auditorium seats, he would leap into action as soon as Walter Beckett announced his readiness for questions.

"Don't worry. You look beautiful."

Cruz turned a baleful eye on the stunning blonde seated to his left, Lola Larkspur of *Eye-Q!*, the only show maxing the charts for audience approval in the quickratings at that moment, even though Lola wasn't on camera. The intellectual *Eye-Q!* audience would wait patiently. He ground his teeth, wondering how he could possibly outgun a scantily clad, over-enhanced Amazon with a genius-level IQ; it simply wasn't fair.

Cruz smiled. "You too, Lola."

"Isn't a NASA briefing somewhat out of your league?"

"We got a four-alarm news conference alert. Who else would they send?"

"Someone who knows the difference between Olympus Mons and the Valles Marineris, for one thing."

Cruz blinked, stalling to do a quick scan off an older-model reference chip implanted by his editor. "Oh, yeah? Olympus Mons is the largest known volcano in the solar system, as wide as Arizona and twice the height of Everest."

"Uh-huh. Handy things, those reference chips. What planet is it on?"

"Uh," stalled Cruz, madly scanning the old chip.

"Mars, perhaps," she prompted.

"Yes."

Lola rolled her eyes.

"Okay, you're so smart, Miss Eye-Q, what's this announcement about? NASA hasn't sent out a four-alarm since they found hot water underground on Mars a few years ago."

Lola sighed. "It was hot water with bacteria in it. Life."

"So the colonists could take hot showers. Whatever."

"NASA blocked the Martian data channel last night. My guess is the Vulcan's Forge colony blew up, or they found little green men."

Cruz nodded knowingly and looked up at the stage. "Either one is good for ratings."

"THERE are moments in history we all remember. I'm sure you've all been asked, 'Where were you when President Hernandez was shot?' or, 'Where were you when the first explorers landed on Mars?' Each society, and each generation, asks such questions about turning points in history and in individual lives. I called this press conference today to announce a momentous event that will become the primary turning point of our generation."

Walter Beckett paused with his right index finger raised high in the air so that the sea of media people could savor the drama of the moment. For once, no one could leave the room while he spoke; to make certain of it, he'd taken the precaution of locking the exit doors. The respectful silence of the audience delighted him, especially when compared to the smirking, know-it-all scientists he normally had to address. He looked up at the sea of faces and tried to make eye contact with as many as possible, a task made more difficult by the spotlights shining back at him. In truth, he could see only the silhouettes of maybe one hundred people in a forum-style auditorium designed to hold four hundred. The silhouettes were disconcerting until he realized that the hood ornaments on the heads of all the reporters were newsnet cameras.

A cough from the audience brought Beckett's wandering attention back to the subject. He blinked and glanced right to trigger the scrolling of his retinal TelePrompTer. The carefully chosen words of his speechwriter rose into his field of vision.

"In 1996, the world focused its attention on a dull gray rock found twelve years earlier in the Antarctic. This potato-sized meteorite, known as ALH84001, had been part of the early Martian crust about 4.5 billion years ago, making it the oldest known rock discovered anywhere up to that point. It also provided strong evidence that primitive life once existed on Mars, not unlike fossilized microorganisms found here on Earth." Beckett paused and smiled, allowing a moment for the easily distracted minds of the mediaheads to absorb his words.

"After ALH84001 paved the way, twenty years passed before the Russians successfully soft-landed the first of several sample-return missions on the surface of Mars. Two rocks collected during these missions verified the analysis of ALH84001, sparking further interest in manned missions to the Martian surface. While the first Russian military research base on Chryse Planitia was unable to locate further signs of primitive life, continued study by international civilian groups, with NASA participation, led to the discovery of bacteria living in hot water reservoirs deep underground."

CHIEF of Security Richard Powell heard an emergency beep in his ear, startling him out of a pleasant dream about shooting Veggie protestors off the NASA perimeter fence. He opened his eyes to see the angry and semitransparent face of Murphy Scott, the operations director, floating above his desk.

"Powell, you've got work to do!"

He sat upright. Outside of casual greetings, the OD had never spoken to him before. "Sir?"

"You know Walter Beckett?"

"No, sir, but I can look him up."

"Don't bother; he's on the news right now. He's holding a press conference in the auditorium. I need you to get in there right now and pull Beckett off that stage."

"What about the media? What do you want me to tell them?"

"Nothing. I'll take care of it when I get there."

"You're the boss."

"Hurry! Get him off that stage!"

"LAST night, while working late in my office, I received a startling communication from Vulcan's Forge."

Beckett punched a button on his podium to activate a huge, and seemingly solid, projection of Mars in the air high over his head, hovering over a small NASA "meatball" logo. The full-color globe, fifty feet across, rotated at the same level as the unblinking camera eyes of the media. The highlighted location of the Vulcan's Forge colony pulsed with blue light just north of the equator, between the massive Olympus Mons volcano and Valles Marineris—a canyon as long as the distance from Los Angeles to New York City.

"They sent a message that changed my life." Beckett pressed a second button that projected a live, giant-sized image of his face superimposed in stationary orbit over the northern hemisphere of the Martian surface. Beckett smiled down at the startled audience as if he were a benevolent god, his alert blue eyes twinkling from a youthful face. His head had a certain classical perfection in its shape, accented by a nimbus of short blond hair cut with microscopic precision.

"We now have conclusive proof of an advanced alien civilization on Mars," said Beckett, his voice amplified to produce a booming effect that would complement the giant projection of his head. "Yesterday morning, a civilian construction crew from Vulcan's Forge was searching for two lost digging robots in Umbra Labyrinthus. During the search, they discovered what appeared to be a volcanic vent. Although Tharsis is a volcanic region, further investigation revealed that the 'vent' was actually a section of collapsed tunnel. The curved tunnel walls, about sixty feet in diameter, were perfectly smooth and straight, coated with a translucent milk white material stronger than carbonglass. This coating was warm and glowed in the dark. When the damaged digging robots were recovered, the workers found machinery partially covered by rubble at the collapsed end of the tunnel. A survey team is being organized among the colonists for further exploration. A team of specialists from Earth will also be scheduled for a flight in approximately six weeks."

Beckett didn't want to burden the media with too many details. The information that the two construction workers died from brain hemorrhages in the tunnel would only confuse the issue.

POWELL ran up to the closed auditorium doors and yanked on the handles, but the doors wouldn't open. A quick search of his pockets revealed that he'd left his master override ID in his office. Cursing, he ran off to find the side doors. He'd never received a direct order from OD Scott before; if he didn't get Beckett off the stage soon, he knew he'd be fired, and he'd only been on the job for two months. He still looked forward to ejecting trespassers, pounding protestors, issuing written warnings, and projecting an air of confidence and security to impress the women in the halls. This NASA posting could be his dream job, so he didn't want to lose it.

BECKETT almost heard the neurons firing in the brains of his audience as they tried to form intelligent questions to justify their jobs. Then he realized it wasn't the sound of neurons firing, it was the sound of someone pounding on the auditorium doors; he didn't have much time.

"Vulcan's Forge is on the Tharsis bulge, an uplifted section of Martian crust about the size of North America—an area of great mass where gravity is stronger than in other parts of Mars. The collapsed end of the Tharsis tunnel points toward Valles Marineris, which starts at the crest of the Tharsis bulge, at Noctis Labyrinthus, and runs almost straight east for twenty-eight hundred miles."

Beckett saw his audience getting anxious; hearing the pounding, some of them realized that the exit doors were locked. "As you can imagine, I have to get back to work. No questions right now, but I'll have more for you later. Thanks for stopping by."

When the side door to the auditorium burst open, the Chief of Security's muscular body filled the doorway. Beckett jumped off the front of the stage, jogged up the aisle, and made a quick exit by the front door. After a brief pause, the audience applauded.

CRUZ looked at Lola with one eyebrow raised. The crowd of mediaheads buzzed with excitement and confusion. "This guy knows how to make an exit, but he's not getting away without an interview. If you know where his office is, I'll split him with you."

"Deal," said Lola, jumping up from her chair. "Let's nail him."

BECKETT sprinted a short distance to get clear of the auditorium, made a few quick turns in the maze of hallways, then slowed to a walk so he'd attract less attention from his coworkers. If he could avoid the security guys long enough, the news of the Tharsis discovery would spread and Beckett would become the untouchable media contact for Martian news.

Taking a back route to his office, he avoided any of his managers who might be prowling the halls.

Two spotlights nearly blinded Beckett as he entered his office. The shadowy figures beneath the interrogation spotlights moved quickly, shutting the door behind him and locking it so he couldn't escape.

"Mr. Beckett, we have some questions for you," said the larger silhouette. His voice sounded familiar.

"It wasn't my fault. I got the news first, and it was too important to be kept a secret," Beckett stammered.

The spotlights wavered as the two silhouettes exchanged glances. The smaller figure spoke with a silky female voice. "We're the media, Mr. Beckett. I'm Lola Larkspur and this is Geraldo Cruz."

Beckett breathed a sigh of relief and sat down heavily on the edge of his desk. "You nearly gave me a heart attack."

"Sorry, but *the public has a right to know, right now*," she said.

Cruz shook his head. "That was a lame way to get your slogan into the interview."

Lola ignored her competitor and continued. The hood ornament on her head sprouted a second outrigger camera to get her face in the shot. "Millions are watching you right now, Mr. Beckett. We have to know, is it possible that this tunnel on Tharsis was built by the Russians?"

Beckett straightened when he realized the camera was live, blinking to scroll the information on his retinal TelePrompTer. "The Russians deny any knowledge of the Tharsis tunnel. Their activities have centered on the Chryse Planitia region and Margaritifer Sinus, at the extreme opposite end of Valles Marineris. Their research focus is concentrated on developing technologies and methods for long-term habitation using local resources. After cursory explorations of Tharsis, they've expressed little interest in the region. Our joint mission at Vulcan's Forge is the first long-term settlement on the uplift."

Cruz spoke up. "How do you explain the fact that no signs

of intelligent life have been discovered on Mars before now? The Russians have been on Mars for twenty years."

Beckett nodded, appearing to be deep in thought as he scrolled his TelePrompTer again. "Nineteen years, to be exact. However, the small military staff at their research base has been fully occupied with other matters. The primary life science focus, up until recently, has been limited to the zone between the Martian surface and the underground permafrost layer."

"So you're saying this discovery was blind luck?" Lola asked.

Beckett smiled. "The Vulcan's Forge colony is the first multilevel construction to be built into the regolith, which provides an excellent natural radiation shield for a long-term habitat, so the digging robots are excavating much deeper than previously required. There have never been any indications that a subsurface culture existed on Mars, so this discovery is quite a shock for all of us."

Cruz moved closer. "You're lying, Mr. Beckett."

"What?"

"This is all some sort of complicated NASA trick to get more funding, isn't it? Admit it!"

Beckett smelled garlic on Cruz's breath when he lunged forward, stopping the camera just inches from Beckett's face. Lola moved to one side to get a better shot. "No."

"You won't admit it!" screamed Cruz.

"There's nothing to admit."

"Aha," said Cruz, moving back to his starting position.

Lola glanced at Cruz and snorted. "Nice try."

Cruz sighed, and Lola moved closer to Beckett. The bright lights made his eyes water. "Mr. Beckett, I'm curious about the team of specialists you're sending to Mars. Who are they?"

Beckett shrugged. "I don't know that yet. The Russian Space Agency is putting the team together, although the international partners will be included. When they're ready to schedule the team for training, that's when they'll tell me who's on the list."

"All right, what specialties will they be sending?"

"I doubt they've decided that yet. I'd expect to see anthropologists, archaeologists, and people that can analyze the technology discovered in the tunnel. Some specialties, such as exobiology, are already available on Mars as part of the ongoing research programs. When possible, of course, we also want to find people who won't mind spending a few years, or more, away from their families and friends on Earth. If the Vulcan's Forge settlement is successful, we expect that some of the colonists will never return."

"Never return?" Cruz asked, moving closer again. "You're saying they'll be *killed*?"

Beckett smiled. "No, we assume that some colonists will like it there and want to stay."

The office doorknob rattled, then the door burst open, knocking Cruz over the desk and startling everyone.

Security Chief Powell barely fit in the doorway, and he looked angry as his meaty hand reached out for Beckett. "Interview's over."

3

TAU felt disoriented as his brain worked to recover from the sudden jolt. In the back of his mind, he knew someone had pulled his plug.

Squinting against the dim red light shining in his eyes, Tau saw the opaque black glass dome of the simulator ceiling in his apt.

"Mr. Wolfsinger, the director's office is summoning you."

He turned his head toward the wall monitor and saw the round, pale face of Ms. A-Nash, the computer personality assigned to his government-sponsored housing block. For reasons known only to the system's designer, she had the appearance of a pudgy woman in her fifties who never smiled. She was an early-model personality, and they'd had a lot of trouble getting them to smile at appropriate times. It never looked right when one of them announced with a cheerful smile that your entire family had been killed in a fire. After numerous lawsuits for psychological damages, the personality manufacturer gave up and patched the software so that the personalities would only wear deadpan expressions.

Tau touched the wireless brain-stem electrode behind his left ear, knowing she must have cut the power to the sim entertainment unit. As the official personality for his building, Ms. A-Nash could override any power or communication system if she had a good reason. "Hasn't anyone ever told you it's dangerous to pull a person's plug like that?"

"The director has requested your presence."

"So I gathered."

"Will you be moving soon?"

"Why do you ask?"

Her black eyes never blinked, and it was a quirk that disturbed Tau.

"Assumption. Government housing privileges are often revoked after tenants speak with the director."

"I see."

"I assume Ms. Fermi will continue her residency?"

Now that his dizziness had subsided, Tau sat up on the sim couch and glared at Ms. A-Nash. It occurred to him that he hadn't seen his roommate for two days. "You'll have to ask her. She's not here right now."

"I will do so."

Her message delivered, the monitor went black. Tau knew if he didn't leave soon, she'd call a security team to escort him to the director's office. Computers could be pushy when given a taste of authority.

The sim unit beeped as Ms. A-Nash switched its power back on. Tau removed the two sim experience cubes, "Shuttle Flight" and "Meditation Mountain," from the library jacks. The unit itself belonged to Yvette—it was the sort of luxury Tau had never been able to afford—but these two library cubes were his. Yvette would let him use her cubes, but her vast library of business and sexual power fantasies didn't interest him.

The full-sense virtual reality of the simulator's mental landscape, enhanced by the force-feedback sim couch, frightened him the first few times he'd tried it for entertainment, even though VR simulations were part of his job. The sim unit used library cubes containing realistic basic environments and a variety of multipath story lines, but the user's memories, thoughts, and emotions personalized the experience to enhance its reality. He could go anywhere, and feel anything, without leaving the comfort of his apt, which explained why the last of the great amusement parks had gone out of business while he was still a boy.

For many people, entertainment VR became an addiction. For Tau, it opened up new possibilities for Nano-VR applications of his work. With a sophisticated artificial intelligence in control of the VR environment, molecular engineering could reach a whole new level of complexity. But that frightened people. Nanotechnology, a superscience still in its infancy, inspired the same sort of fear reserved for plague germs. It didn't seem to matter that consumer products built by simple nanotech had found their way into most people's homes. Established scientists who understood the workings of nanotech were considered high priests of the technocracy by the average person, but those same scientists were threatened by the idea of autonomous computer control, saying it could cause a nanotech chain reaction powerful enough to destroy the biosphere. Tau knew their objections were ridiculous. He knew they didn't understand AI or nanotech. But it had never occurred to him that his "exotic" proposals would get him fired.

That was life in the NASA bureaucracy.

Wearing only jeans and black boots, Tau rummaged through his closet for a clean shirt and finally settled on a blue work tunic that changed color to match any stains that landed on it. When he finished dressing, he glanced at the tall stack of drawings near his computer station. He preferred to make preliminary sketches of his ideas on paper, rather than doing everything through Drexler, the AI expert system residing in the dedicated NASA-Ames computer net. Drexler understood molecular engineering, but the subtle changes suggested by the AI homogenized Tau's designs to match government-approved styles; drawing on paper allowed him to work without interference. Even after Drexler synthesized the three-dimensional optical projection from his sketches, Tau continued to refer to his drawings as he made changes.

Not wanting to leave, Tau looked around the room. Unlike Yvette, Tau had not personalized his space. Its simple nano-tech furnishings, self-cleaning and self-repairing, could change their appearance according to the owner's mood, but Tau never felt the need to switch them out of passive, neutral gray mode. Yvette altered the appearance of her furniture every week, switching from rainbow patterns to neon primary colors. Tau preferred to keep the optical shield opaque between the two halves of the apt so he wouldn't be distracted by Yvette's riot of color.

Packing would be a simple task—a few clothes, some drawings, and Aristotle, his AI Companion. Outside of his work, these things were the sum of his existence.

AMES Research Center had been established in a corner of the Moffett Field Naval Air Station in California. Huge dirigible hangars and wind tunnels loomed over the rest of the research facility. Life science, space science, and advanced computing facilities were added over the years, with new structures adhering to a common style that might be called

"Big Science," with steel, glass, and concrete forming the primary building materials. Ames had a strong sense of history and scientific accomplishment that employees such as Tau could sense whenever they entered the grounds. He loved working there.

The director's office occupied part of the ancient Administration Building near the main gate, a squat concrete structure flanked by the imposing black glass towers housing the Advanced Computing Facility and the Administrative Management Battalion. Following almost one hundred years of tradition, the ACF housed backbone supercomputers for the global datasphere behind its heavily shielded walls, making sure that the North American portion of the net moved data traffic with quick efficiency. Communication dishes sprouted from the roof. The net meant life for billions of people, and the Netcom satellites in their parking orbits made certain that wireless information was available anywhere at any time. Humans rarely had direct contact with the net, but their AIs and intelligent agents gave them the illusion of interaction. The volume and complexities of information processing and retrieval had long ago reached a point where humans could not traverse the vast datafields without their digital assistants.

The Administration Building had been modernized so that its décor was only forty years behind current styles. The one exception was the director's office, equipped with the latest developments in phased array optics to project realistic three-dimensional surroundings, which the director could change at his whim. The Ames Optics Lab developed the improvements, so the funding-conscious director made use of the technology for demonstrations in his office. An eccentric former actor, Dr. Cyril Chakrabarti would sit at a stone desk in an underground cavern one day, to be replaced by a flat slab of metallic meteorite on the lunar surface the next day. Tau suspected the unusual surroundings compensated for the director's short stature, since he was only five feet tall.

When Tau entered Chakrabarti's office, he appeared to be sitting on a jeweled throne centered in a ring of tall triangular teeth. To Tau, it looked like Stonehenge for sharks. The blackness of space, dotted with glittering stars, filled the area outside the ivory ring. Two spotlights hidden on the floor behind his shiny obsidian desk pointed up at the director's face, giving him a monstrous appearance formed of deep shadows. A trendy monk's fringe of short gray hairs circled his otherwise bald head. Peaked brows punctuated his eyes, which glittered from the deep shadows as they watched Tau's approach without blinking. The overall effect implied malevolence and intimidation, which is what Tau had come to expect.

Chakrabarti stared at Tau's face with such intensity that he could feel the heat of it on his skin. "Mr. Wolfsinger."

"Director," nodded Tau, looking for a place to sit down and finding none.

"You're a bright lad, so I assume you know why you're here."

"So you can fire me personally?"

"Fire you? Certainly not. At least, not yet. If you correct your demeanor, and cooperate with your coworkers for a change, I'm sure we could overlook your youthful indiscretions."

"Indiscretions?" Tau blinked, wondering if this was some kind of legal maneuver to save money by making him resign instead of firing him.

"In particular, your habit of submitting proposals directly to headquarters to bypass your immediate superiors, not to mention the wild ideas contained in those proposals. I had to spend almost two hours yesterday afternoon responding to all the complaints from Washington. Didn't make me look very good, I can tell you."

"I knew the Project Review Committee at Ames wouldn't approve. I wanted an unbiased opinion."

"Rather presumptuous of you, don't you think?"

"I've been working here long enough to understand the system."

The director raised his eyebrows. "Really? Two years as a university intern, then another two years as an employee, and that's enough for you to understand the finely tuned management structure that NASA took a century to develop? I've worked here for thirty-three years, and I'm still not sure I understand how it all works."

Tau stifled a comment about how the director's lack of understanding made him perfect for his job. "Has the Project Review Committee considered my proposal?"

"We had the meeting this morning. Dr. Thorn was there to testify on your behalf, which was another breach in procedure, but we let it go out of respect for his reputation. He's not the man he once was, you know. He found out about the meeting and barged in to express his opinion."

Tau nodded. "So they voted against the proposal."

"Of course they voted against it. The committee members have their own reputations to protect. They certainly aren't going to approve some wild-eyed student's scheme to let an uncontrolled computer program destroy the planet. But they gave the proposal a fair hearing."

"You must have an unusual definition of the word 'fair,' Director."

The director snorted. "There's no need to be impertinent, Mr. Wolfsinger. I didn't have to discuss this matter with you in person. However, I hate to see a good technical talent wasted when it could be put to better use furthering our common goals at Ames."

Common was a good way to describe it, thought Tau. "By the way, I'm not a student."

The director leaned forward on his desk, his eyes boring a hole in Tau's head. "I'm sorry. Did you receive your Ph.D. in computer science recently?"

Tau sighed. "You know my studies were interrupted when I decided to come on staff here. I thought actual work toward my goals was more important than a piece of paper."

The director started to smirk, then changed his mind. "You have interesting attitudes. It's always refreshing to interact with young people on occasion. However, your lack of a degree will not help your scientific standing. The committee members are all respected scientists in their fields, and your lack of scholarly grounding was apparent when they reviewed the outrageous notions in your proposal. Artificial intelligence may have been a big thing sixty years ago, but it's now an accepted fact that the idea of a rational 'thinking' computer was a dead end, except in very limited applications."

"I didn't realize you were so well informed, Director."

"These aren't just my opinions. The committee expressed itself this morning. Your proposal to combine an autonomous AI with virtual control of molecular nanotech construction is dangerous beyond belief. Even if it were possible, there would be no safe place to test such a thing. You made some vague suggestion about a remote location, such as an island, or a military training range in the desert, but a runaway nanotech reaction couldn't be stopped so easily. The potential for damage is unacceptable."

"That's ridiculous," Tau said.

Chakrabarti slammed his right fist on the table. "If such a project were to be funded, the public reaction against this research center could put us out of business. Our government funding would dry up overnight; then our private funding would disappear. And it was bad enough that you worked out such a ridiculous proposal, but you then had to compound your error by broadcasting it all over headquarters. You say you understand how the system works here, but the amount you clearly don't understand is simply astounding!"

The director sat back in his chair, his face red, breathing hard, while Tau stared at him.

"Do you have anything to say for yourself, Mr. Wolfsinger?"

"I appear to have made a mistake."

"I'm pleased to hear you admit it."

Tau nodded, looking away at the fake stars. "Oh, I admit it. I focus on my work so much that I forget what people are really like. It was a big mistake to think I could get a reasonable evaluation of my proposal in such a rigid atmosphere.

And what if it worked? What if my AI could actually think? It wouldn't look good if some junior molecular designer, without a Ph.D., actually made this kind of a breakthrough, would it?"

For a moment, the director's eyes glinted with rage while he ground his teeth, but the storm passed quickly, and his face assumed a relative calmness that was much more threatening. "If you're quite through, Mr. Wolfsinger, I suggest you remember where you are. When I was younger, I had pet projects of my own that were canceled. As you get older, you'll learn to deal with it."

"I hope not." Tau sighed, waiting for the usual speech about conversing with junior members of the staff, knowing that would signal the end of this conversation as it had so many times before.

"I can see that you haven't learned anything from this experience yet, so I think you'd better go home and think about it. I'll remind you that it's not my habit to converse with junior members of the staff, but I made an exception in your case. I'm not sure why—perhaps because Dr. Thorn sees something in you. With a positive attitude, you could be a valuable member of our team."

"Oh, I'm *positive* that the scientists and the politicians in charge are too protective of their reputations to take any risks."

"You need to work *with* the team, not against it. Scientific breakthroughs by individuals are a thing of the past; in a technical world, real progress is made through the synergy of many minds collaborating on a common goal. This isn't the nineteenth century, when basic scientific principles remained to be discovered. Perhaps there's something viable hidden in your ideas and it would just take some study with senior researchers to help bring them out. But you will get nowhere by defying the established structure that allows this agency to operate."

Tau met the director's gaze. "Dr. Thorn supports my ideas."

"Thorn. Yes, well, he was an important man twenty years ago. You need to work with a team that's doing current research—perhaps one of our projects funded by DARPA."

"The Defense Advanced Research Projects Agency? No, thanks. I won't work with the military."

"There you go again," said the director, rolling his eyes. "You're not in a position to be so selective. It would do you good to get out from under Dr. Thorn's influence—to spread your wings, as it were."

"I don't do military work."

"We may not give you a choice."

"There's always a choice."

The director pressed a button on his desk to open the office door. "We shall see about that, Mr. Wolfsinger. We shall see."

TAU walked north along Arnold Avenue, partially shaded by the hulking steel shapes of forgotten wind tunnels once used to test aircraft. Traffic on the two-lane Moffett Field slidewalk was light, but the strange sight of someone walking on the cracked asphalt of the former road when a slidewalk was available drew curious looks from the pedestrians humming past. Tau didn't care. He needed the exercise, thinking it might help clear his head and loosen his tense muscles. His jaws hurt from clenching his teeth for so long.

The director was an odd creature, but Tau had met others of his type. Many of the university professors shared the same conformist attitudes, warning Tau that he had to fit in to make it in this world. He had no idea what made any of them act as they did, he just knew he was different from them, as he had always been different in some basic way from other groups of people throughout his life. With a Navajo father and a white mother, the schoolkids on the Big Reservation beat him up because he didn't fit in. When his parents sent him to boarding schools off the reservation, the white kids beat him up because he didn't fit in there, either. Everyone has at least one nickname on the reservation, so some of his relatives called him Talking Book when they saw how much he liked to stay home and read rather than playing with the other children. Others called him Shadow Walker because he liked to go out alone at night and watch the stars. After a while, with the support of his parents, he became proud of the fact that he was an outcast. In their own unique ways, his parents were outcasts, too. Although he'd made friends with other misfits in California, like his college roommate Norman Meadows, no one else had really understood him until he met Kate McCloud.

The thought of Kate lightened his mood while he turned east on Walcott at the Physical Science Lab. After four years, he'd already started to think of her as his fiancée, although they hadn't seriously discussed the topic of marriage. As with any other major decision he'd ever made, Tau carefully thought it through, making a Pareto diagram to compare the pluses and minuses, but he concluded that marriage was the correct path. He knew she provided balance in his life, and balance was the way of beauty, of *hozro*. They had both gotten busier in the last few months, seeing each other only on weekends, but that separation only made his need for Kate more apparent. The fifty-mile distance to Santa Cruz felt like fifty thousand miles.

Two days earlier, Tau had asked Dr. Thorn for advice, learning that a brilliant female biologist had approached Thorn when he was twenty-five years old. He accepted her plan to combine his DNA with hers so that she could create a superintelligent child. Thorn assumed that the sperm donation would lead to a relationship, but it turned out that she was quite aware of his personality defects and didn't want anything to do with him after she became pregnant. In fact, she started referring to their brief acquaintance as a "match made in Beakertown." His attempts to see the growing boy were rebuffed, and he was later appalled to learn that his son became a politician. Tau knew that Thorn still wrote occasional letters to his son, but they were never answered.

Thorn wasn't a big proponent of marriage. But that didn't matter to Tau.

Tonight would be one of those rare weeknight visits, meet-

ing Kate for dinner at Giardia's Fishbowl, their favorite
restaurant. Tau would do the traditional thing and ask her to
marry him since she hadn't asked him first. He knew he'd surprise Kate with the question, since she'd been the one who
asked to meet for dinner, her voice full of excitement about
some important news she'd heard that day. He wouldn't let his
own troubles spoil the evening; there would be time to talk
about that over the weekend.

On South Warehouse Road, across from the experimental
aircraft hangar, sat a two-story structure of gray masonry
wrapped in two narrow horizontal ribbons of tinted glass. A
large black number high above the south entrance, faded with
age, identified it as Building 244, the Space Projects Facility.
Beyond it, the black surface of an aircraft taxiway ran parallel to the main runway, the only divider being a strip of tall
green grass that should have been cut months before. Space
Projects sat like a gray iceberg in a sea of green grass. While
it appeared to be a short structure, most of the building lurked
underground; built during the Cold War, it had nine levels of
subbasements, with catwalks between the inner walls, providing safe refuge during Bay Area earthquakes and potential nuclear strikes. The subbasements contained a wide variety of
small labs and technical facilities so that employees could
continue working even if the world outside collapsed around
them. In accordance with ancient regulations that supported
this postholocaust work ethic, new NASA employees were
still issued postcards, made of actual paper, to be mailed to
Washington, DC, as a change-of-address notification in the
event of a nuclear strike destroying their homes. Tau had often
wondered if former postal workers were kept in cryogenic
storage deep below Ames, waiting to be revived on that fate-
ful day when they'd be needed to deliver all those postcards
to Washington.

As usual, no receptionist occupied the front desk when Tau
passed through the lobby and darted up the stairs to the dim
hallways above. Quiet offices, most of them empty, were interspersed with former clean rooms shrouded in shadows and

hanging plastic sheets. Near the dark Pioneer Mission Control center, astronomical mission plaques and rows of old, two-dimensional photographs hung on the walls—famous scientists who had worked on Pioneer, Galileo, the Kuiper Airborne Observatory, or other Ames projects. Tau studied the yellowed photos and the occasional quotes beneath the frames: Carl Sagan's mischievous smile above a quote joking about frogs in the atmosphere of Jupiter; James Van Allen looking thoughtful as he considered the nature of the Earth's radiation belts; Cyril Ponnamperuma calmly creating the precursors of life in a simulation of Earth's primitive atmosphere; Gerard Kuiper looking distant and bored as he made yet another astronomical discovery. As he walked past their portraits, inspired and intimidated, Tau could feel their eyes watching him from the past, wondering if he had the determination to solve another piece of the puzzle and earn a place among them on the wall of history.

At the end of the corridor, Tau stopped to look through the open door of Vadim Tymanov's office. A massive mug of coffee steamed on the desk in front of the 3-D imaging platform, but the burly Russian molecular engineer wasn't there. The office window faced the inactive runway and the old dirigible hangar. Large enough to be spotted from orbit, the graceful dome of the hangar rose two hundred feet into the sky, built by the Navy for their rigid airship program in the 1930s. In 2031, a private developer converted the hangar to apt blocks with glass-walled rooms that climbed the inner walls, suspended over eight acres of landscaped atrium shops.

Displayed at one corner of the desk was a holo of Tymanov at an international fencing competition six years earlier, dressed all in white, holding a wire mesh mask under his left arm while his right held his fencing foil up in salute to the camera. His black hair and beard, sparkling with sweat in the spotlights, framed a triumphant, smiling face. Now twenty-eight years old, he still fenced in national competitions and had come to Ames on loan from his molecular engineering job

in Kaliningrad, where he'd been employed by a NASA sub-
contractor. Tymanov became Tau's partner when he arrived.

Tau tapped out a note that appeared in red letters in the air
over Tymanov's desk, letting Vadim know he would visit
Thorn's office on his way home, and he wanted to talk as soon
as possible.

BURIED on level nine, Maxfield Thorn's office occupied
the lowest subbasement in the Space Projects Building. No
one else had worked on that level for thirty years, so most of
the lights were switched off to save power. Without elevator
access, the cleaning crew rarely made the trip, allowing a fine
patina of dust to build up on the floors and the old shrouded
equipment stored in the hallways of cracked yellow tile. A
visit to Thorn's "cave" was a trip into a bureaucratic Siberia,
where old files, old equipment, and old scientists were filed
away and forgotten.

Tau knew Dr. Thorn was once the most respected computer scientist in the country, but few ever had the privilege of
hiring him because Thorn chose his own projects. For twenty-
two years, he worked out of the Institute for Advanced Study
in Princeton, New Jersey—known as the "Institute for Advanced Salaries" by its jealous detractors—a place called
home by most of the great physicists and mathematicians of
modern times.

Against his theoretical nature, Thorn started his career as
an experimentalist. He designed molecular switches to store
computer data, then helped to create early developments in
nanotechnology. His "solid phase synthesis" approach—later
known as the "Thorn Method" when Tau learned it in
school—created molecular building blocks for assembling
complex structures. Thorn figured out how to synthesize the
long chains of amino acids, forming proteins in chemical reaction cycles, to build up trillions of molecular objects. This
method, combined with building blocks made of larger molecules, made it easier for engineers to design and build complex molecular machines.

Then Thorn demonstrated his theoretical research capabilities. Over a six-month period after his arrival at the Institute, in a remarkable burst of creativity, he published six papers on diverse topics in computer science and mathematics. His Thorn Principle was an immediate sensation, one of the most powerful mathematical tools ever devised. Forty years later, over one hundred thousand scientific papers had been published based on the applications of Thorn's equations, including one by Tau.

Maxfield Thorn burned through the years of his fame the way a meteor streaks through the atmosphere. Lured to DARPA, then fired by a jealous rival, Thorn retreated from the world by accepting a post at NASA's Ames Research Center.

In Tau's world, Dr. Maxfield Thorn was a god.

Tau knocked on the god's office door, unleashing a tiny avalanche of dust. Receiving no answer, he entered to find Thorn hunched over a workbench, wearing his traditional white lab coat and black bow tie, staring into the eyepieces of an atomic force microscope while his right hand worked the control dials of its molecular manipulator. Tau considered the AFM device an antique, but Thorn couldn't get new equipment for his lab. Thorn looked up, causing his ancient glasses to drop from his forehead to the bridge of his nose. The thick lenses magnified his eyes in a disturbing way, which explained why he'd never had optical correction surgery. A spotlight behind his head created a halo effect through his rumpled gray hair.

"It's no use, Tau. Quit while you still can."

Tau raised one eyebrow. "What do you mean?"

"You know what I mean. You've got more natural ability than anyone I've ever seen. But these people don't want to have someone with your kind of talent working here because it makes them uncomfortable; they don't know what to do with people like you. They'll try to make you conform, and if you don't bend to fit their mold, they'll apply pressure until they break you. The senior researchers will ignore you or steal your work. Your only other option is to play by their rules, waiting them out, hoping you'll get a chance to work on your own projects and prove your theories—but it'll never happen. There's too much mediocrity standing between you and your goals. You'll just get old, and they'll win anyway. When you hit thirty, your theoretical brain will be burned out. Paul Dirac and Werner Heisenberg were so young when they received their Nobel Prizes that their mothers had to escort them to Stockholm. You don't have time to waste. Trust me, I know how it works."

Tau shook his head. Thorn never developed a need for small talk, so he launched into immediate lectures to make his points. "You're still working."

"I'm an eighty-two-year-old idiot. This is the only place that would take me."

"You're a genius. You're one of the reasons why I came to work here. I've been reading about you in computer science textbooks since I was a kid. Hell, you wrote half of the textbooks. Entire lines of AI research are based on your coevolution programming theories. Where else could I go to learn from someone like you?"

Thorn snorted. "You're spreading it awfully thick, kid. In any case, working with me is career suicide for someone like you. There must have been people who told you that before you started here. I know the director and his pals just use my name to get projects funded.

"I can't help you. You've got real talent, but no one will ever know about it if you keep working at NASA. Try Intel or Foresight; they've got the best equipment. Go to Japan or Russia; at least they'll respect you. My name still means something, so I can give you a letter of reference to get you started almost anywhere. If you stay here, all I can do is guide you deeper into the hole you're digging for yourself."

Tau smiled. "You tried to help me this morning. The director told me you testified on behalf of my proposal for the review committee."

"And a lot of good that did, eh? They still killed your proposal. Maybe you would have gotten further if I'd kept my mouth shut."

"I doubt that, and I appreciate your taking the time to talk to them, but I've been thinking maybe they were right. It's all theory right now. I don't have any prototypes to show them—all I have is Aristotle, the Companion AI that I enhanced. I have to run a full-scale test, and I feel like it should work, but why should they believe me?" Tau shrugged.

Thorn's eyes flamed and his body straightened. He raised his right fist and shook it at Tau. "Don't ever say that again! A good scientist is never humble. Sheep are humble. Common people are humble. When you go home, you can be as meek and retiring as you want—you can hide in a closet for all I care—but you can't afford to be intellectually bashful about your science. You must be bold and arrogant—perhaps even a little reckless. Science exists to honor the arrogance of mind required of those who can contribute to an understanding of it. You must fight the sheep; otherwise, the sheep will humbly tell you that you've lost! If you agree with them, you might as well pack up your molecular toys and become an accountant!"

"Yes." Tau swallowed, stunned by this unusual outburst. "You're right."

Thorn lowered his fist, still glowering at Tau. "Of course I'm right. Why did you become a molecular designer?"

"Well," said Tau, trying to gather his thoughts for the sudden change of subject, "I usually say I like cutting-edge technology and I want to build things with it. Did you ever read any science fiction stories about talking robots?"

"Of course."

"When I was a kid, I loved reading about smart robots helping people. If I can build a powerful AI that can learn and respond like a human, and show people that it's possible, I feel like that would be a worthwhile contribution to science."

"Humans make better friends, or so I've been told. Find a woman who can stand you and forget about all this. You'll be happier that way."

Tau smiled as he remembered Kate. "I'll be working on

that tonight. But I can't forget about my career. I've made my choice, so I'll stick with it."

"You're a fool, Tau."

"Maybe."

"That wasn't a compliment."

"Depends on how you look at it."

"If you stay here, I'll ruin you. I'll motivate you to be more of what you already are, a brilliant young man who might just be able to change the world. And that will be my own form of hell, because I'll also know that the sheep will be standing in your way. By working hard and getting results, you'll make yourself a target. They'll see how you stand out, and they'll try to crush you. If you're cruel enough to stay, we'll both delude ourselves into thinking there's a chance you can reach your goal, and the failure will be that much worse. Why do you want to put me through that again? Why do you want to put yourself through that? For what?"

Tau smiled. "You said it yourself. If I claim to be a scientist, I have to fight the sheep."

"You were paying attention when I said that?" Thorn shook his head. "I see I'm only making things worse. Look, hero worship is a sad thing because it clouds the mind. I am not a noble creature or a saint; I'm half the man I should have been because I chose to ignore half of the world—the human half. When you look back from the far end of your life, you don't want to realize that it's too late to make up for the big mistakes you made along the way. Do your science, build your AI, train it like it's your child—but don't let your work interfere with the rest of your life, because it's possible that you'll spend your years working on something that will never see the light of day. That AI of yours could build new cities, or new worlds, but none of it will matter if you can't get it past the sheep. They'll make you beg them to give you the money to do your work. You'll hate yourself for it, but you'll do it. And when the sheep finally see that you need them to reach your goal, they'll tell you there's no funding for your project, or that you'll have to put some senior researcher's name on the paper you publish, or that they like your idea but they've given it to someone else. So you'll think you can just quit and take your work somewhere else, and that's when they'll remind you that they own it because they paid for it with your salary. Is that the future you want?"

"I won't let it happen."

"You think you're better than I was?"

"I've always wanted to *be* you, so don't tell me that I can't. I'll find a way."

Thorn stared at him for a moment before one corner of his mouth lifted into a half smile. "Then maybe you've got a chance," he said, watching Tau's eyes almost as if he were reading his thoughts. "You understand why I had to try and talk you out of staying here?"

"Yes. I think so."

"I'm an old man. Don't waste my time if you don't think you can win."

"I'll do my best."

"That's what the losers always say."

"I'll win."

"Then come back tomorrow. I have to think about this."

4

"THIS is the tricky part," said Peters. "Watch how I do it."

Yvette responded with a low, breathy voice that dripped with passion. "You're amazing. Show me more."

Yvette Fermi, one of the three molecular designers working in the Space Projects Facility at Ames, could choose among three work locations. From her apt, which she shared with Tau Wolfsinger, she could access the Drexler AI and her work files through a powerful workstation; it was convenient, she could eat and work naked if she chose, but she felt isolated. From her office, she could use the miniature 3-D imaging system hardwired to a sim couch; it still felt isolated, and the miniature desktop imager strained her eyes. From the high-resolution simulation lab in the Nano-VR Center, she had speed, flexibility, simulated full-scale visuals, audio cueing, limited force-feedback, specialized waldo controls, a comfortable sim couch, and most important of all, she was visible to her coworkers. With the addition of full-sense simulators, a multidirectional treadmill floor, state-of-the-art phased optic arrays, and a cube library, the sim system at the Ames Nano-VR Center would be almost as good as her home entertainment unit—but she knew that would be overkill for molecular design work. At least Ames had a Drexler AI to help speed up the design process—most universities didn't even have that much.

She knew the importance of visibility. After a few weeks working at Ames, Yvette felt anxious. She wanted people to notice her. Equipped with a shiny new Ph.D. in computational biochemistry, and a network of influential fans and admirers, she snagged one of the choice molecular design positions at Ames before it was publicly announced. Because of the importance of the position, the rarity of potential candidates, and the minimized middle-management structure of the "new" NASA, Director Chakrabarti interviewed her himself. Yvette knew she could perform component design with specs passed down to her from the chief designer, Yoshinobu Tokugawa, but she harbored no illusions about her natural talent for the work. Far more politically adept and charming than her coworkers, she knew she could have Tokugawa's job in time, or any other management position she set her sights on, but her limited technical creativity necessitated caution. However, technical management experience would give her credibility with investors for later projects in the private sector. NASA could be an excellent source of contacts if she attracted the attention of the right people, but she knew she'd have to work her way up.

Yvette's easiest target of opportunity sat on a sim couch a few feet away. Jim Peters maintained a muscular, outdoorsy appearance, with unruly brown hair and a moustache. He always looked surprised, his brown eyes wide and unblinking, as if he'd just been caught at something. Yvette often noticed him watching her, so she held his attention by bestowing her radiant smile on him whenever she walked past his sim chair or happened to catch his eye in the hallways.

Although she knew how everything worked now, Peters wanted to show her a few "tricks." As she watched Peters work on the large projected model in the virtual-reality space, putting a replicator together with large molecular building blocks, she saw that he had good mechanical instincts, but he lacked her thorough grounding in chemistry. He worked in a large magnification to see more detail, wrestling blocky molecular chains into appropriate attachment sites, but his crude efforts were time-consuming.

The completed prototype would be smaller than a bacterium, and the replicator would be able to make copies of itself from a simple bath of special chemicals. Software running on a computer within each replicator would tell it how to go about the process, which would last until the program told it to stop building or until the chemicals in the pool were used up. The replicator copies would then copy themselves in an exponential explosion of manufacturing activity.

Peters noticed Yvette watching him instead of the prototype, so he smiled. She intended to give the impression that her initial curiosity about his work had bloomed into total admiration.

"You're very good," she said, smiling back at him.

"Good enough for government work," said Peters, continuing to smile as his eyes traveled down her body with his own admiration. There were no arms on the sim couches, allowing for tool waldoes that retracted into the ceiling, so his eyes could follow the fine lines of her reclining body.

"Any questions?" he asked.

She tried to think of something he could answer. "How long does it take the replicators to make enough copies of themselves?"

"Well, each replicator contains about a billion atoms, and each assembly arm can handle about a million atoms per second, so the basic cycle takes about fifteen minutes. At that rate, each replicator can keep doubling to make trillions of replicators in about nine hours."

She did the math in her head. "Ten hours."

His eyes widened. "Yeah, that sounds right."

"Then new chemicals are added to the replicator bath to signal a software change?"

"Right. The replicators become tiny general assembly factories that can build larger machines from the new molecules in the pool."

Peters continued building. Working in such a large magnification, it took him a long time to construct a model, but he specialized in prototyping such basic nanomachines because of his patience for repetitive tasks. He now assembled the replicator interior, occupied by the mechanical tape memory system that told the assembly arm how to build all the parts of another replicator. The instruction tape itself would be made in a special tape duplication machine. Pores at one end of the replicator allowed fuel and raw material molecules to pass inside for processing. Specialized assembly arms, as well as the individual tools used by the arms, were assigned to Yvette to be added when Peters finished his model.

Tau built the molecular electronic nanocomputers and the software that controlled them. Yvette knew Tau could build the whole thing from the ground up without any specs from Tokugawa, and his ability to understand complex systems was rare enough for Yvette to have heard of him before she started working at NASA. Tau started writing original scientific papers as a university undergraduate, so it would have been hard for Yvette *not* to have heard of him, especially when molecular design work applied to so many different fields.

With the virtual-reality prototype complete, the Drexler AI would check it for design flaws. If the flaws were simple enough, such as a missing molecular building block here and there, the Drexler would fix the problem. If the flaws were large enough, or if the basic design seemed to be at fault, the Drexler would suggest changes or recommend building a new prototype.

With the simulated prototype approved, Tokugawa would send the completed design to manufacturing, where the actual physical prototype would be built from an appropriate chemical bath.

Yvette slid out of her seat and bent over beside Peters to whisper in his ear. "What do you have to do to be promoted around here?"

"This soon? You're ambitious." He sounded nervous.

"I get bored easily."

Yvette knew he couldn't tell if she was joking or not, but he gave her a slight smile. "You'd probably start by knocking off the chief designer."

Yvette glanced up at the ancient Tokugawa, suspended above the far end of the room in a glass cubicle that screened out unnecessary noise. An overhead tracking system gave Tokugawa's cubicle full-degree-of-motion capability. The virtual stage in front of his cubicle could display high-magnification nanomachine models on a grand scale. Rather than rotating the three-dimensional model he worked on, as Yvette and the other designers did, Tokugawa could "fly" around the model above the virtual stage. Yvette had seen him fly, and it looked like fun, but the intent expression on his face never changed, even though she could only see part of it under the multispectral optics he wore over his eyes. His black hair always looked neat, his clothing always looked professional and perfect, and his face remained un-lined with expressions or the experience of his seventy years of age. Always polite to Yvette, he never said much more to her than necessary. Component specs were downloaded to

Yvette's workstation from Tokugawa's computer, with little need for regular interaction between them.

When the opportunity arose, Yvette knew she could take the old man, but she had to be certain she wanted his job first.

TAU kept to the slow lane on the northbound 101 slidewalk; this annoyed elderly people and parents with baby strollers who were trying to make smooth transitions on and off the slidewalk without slamming into him. The adjacent strip only moved five miles an hour faster, but he kept thinking he might get off the slidewalk and walk the rest of the way. Although the noises and smells of the slidewalk normally didn't bother him on his short commute between Moffett Field and his apt tower, the rumbling and humming, combined with the odors of lubricants and sweat, made him uncomfortable this time. He felt homesick for a moment, wishing he could smell ozone and damp earth during a fresh rain in the desert. When he spotted his apt tower, obscured by the colorful confusion of projected advertisements flashing on the glass slidewalk canopy, he decided to exit.

He stepped off at the next platform, somewhere in East Palo Alto, almost colliding with a businessman in a poly-chrome suit set to rapid color cycling; probably a salesman of some kind. Tau understood the man's surprised expression because no one ever got off on that platform in the after-noon—that would be going against the Rush, the unwritten law of slidewalk traffic patterns. By the time the man started to protest, Tau was gone, walking north on the cracked ce-ment shoulder of the old freeway on which the slidewalk was built.

Tau normally used his commute time to read or think about his work, so the urban scenery beyond the slidewalk canopy rarely penetrated his awareness. Walking this section for the first time, he noticed dead plants and dirt along the edge of the road. Here and there, signs of life in the form of weeds poked their heads up through the smothering concrete blanket. The high humidity made him sweat as he walked, reminding him to watch the fog when he got home. He enjoyed seeing the curls of incoming fog rolling over the coastal hills that bordered the west end of the valley; their appearance made him think of slow-motion waves hitting a beach. He could enjoy such a view because his job status gave him certain privileges, including an outer apt located high in the tower with a balcony to go with it. When he could ignore the sounds of the city echoing up to his high perch, the view provided some peace.

One of the sights he usually ignored on his daily commute home was the skin gang camped out on an abandoned surface platform of the old Bay Area Rapid Transit train. Gangs often traveled through the portions of underground BART tunnels that had not been converted to use by trucks or mag-lev bullet trains in DEEPTRAN, the Deep Transit Network.

Tom had learned from Kate's research that most of the San Francisco gangs were ethnically mixed, but they formed around common interests related to their neighborhoods. One recent trend related to rich kids forming "social groups" to emulate their idea of street gangs from a lower economic class. One result of this trend toward upper-class gangs was an increase in street violence. Older gangs, organized along traditional lines, showed a decline in violent incidents over the last twenty-four years. When violence did occur, traditional gangs usually battled with other gangs, but the rich kids in skin gangs didn't care who their targets were. Sociologists said the gangs were a response to the urban environment, their members seeking smaller social groups with understandable rules and established pecking orders. Kate considered skin gangs a social aberration of the upper class. In Bavaria at the end of the eighteenth century, bored rich people routinely killed each other in duels; it became such a problem that the Bavarian government refused burial to the victims of duels, turning their bodies over to anatomists for dissection.

Tau considered the gangs to be pseudotribes who lacked the discipline of a strong moral code instilled by a community of relatives with common goals.

Tau knew that skin gang members sometimes rode the slidewalk, where they were notable because they wore plenty of jewelry and a minimal amount of high-fashion clothing; this provided the most display area for the expensive nanotattoos that slowly moved around on their skin. Their "smart" tattoos migrated in response to body heat, powering clusters of tiny ink spots with tiny motors that drove tiny legs. Some nanotattoos sought out salt deposits on the skin, while others chose their paths based on temperature differences on the skin surface. Rich kids with parents who wouldn't approve of tattoos could hide them by washing the tattoo with soap, triggering a "defensive" reaction that would cause the mobile ink spots to turn clear for a few hours. The software that drove the nanotattoo was based on the trial-and-error system of guidance that some bacteria use to find food. The bacteria tend to swim in straight lines, remembering just enough to evaluate whether their success in finding food is getting easier or harder. When food is present, they keep swimming in straight lines. When food hasn't been found recently, they stop and drift for a while, then head off in a different direction at random. Now that he thought about it, some NASA managers exhibited the same behavior.

Busy thinking about nanotattoos, Tau jerked back to reality when one of the tribal members on the abandoned BART platform spoke to him in the halting parody of "Indian" speech injected into the American consciousness by old Hollywood flatfilm Westerns. "How, Chief! You come many moons and cross the Great Water to stare at us?"

Tau realized he'd been staring at the tattoo of a bloody skull with glowing eyes as he walked past the platform; it crept along on the muscular chest of a tall, white, hairless gorilla walking toward him. "Oh. Excuse me."

A young blond woman approached, her long fingernails glowing with tiny patterns of lights, and stroked Tau's black hair where it hung down between his shoulder blades. "Nice hair, Chief."

Distracted by the blonde, whose snake tattoo crawled between her large and mostly visible breasts, Tau looked up and saw that the rest of the skin gang, maybe nine or so, had formed a circle around him. Skull Chest took a step forward as the blonde continued stroking Tau's hair.

"You got wampum, Chief? We charge admission to look at our war paint. Our people need firewater."

"Look, I don't want any trouble," said Tau, taking one step back and bumping into the blonde.

"Oh, it's no trouble," said Skull Chest, pulling a diamond-edge utility blade out of the titanium sheath at his belt. Tau recognized the knife because he'd used them in the lab. They were handy cutting tools with monomolecular edges that could slice almost anything without being dulled, including metal—or skin and bone.

He jumped as the blonde pressed up against his back and shoved both her hands into the side pockets of his pants. "Hey!"

She giggled. "What's wrong, Chief? Not used to having women in your pants? Hold still."

Skull Chest frowned and took another step forward, slowly waving the shiny blade in front of Tau's face, making him lean back against the blonde. "If I were you, and I'm glad I'm not, I'd do what she says. You want me to cut him, Tracy?"

"Not if he cooperates. Just keep him here," she said, continuing to grope around in his pockets as she rubbed up against him some more. "I like him."

"I don't have anything valuable."

"Oh, yes you do," Tracy breathed in his ear. "I can feel your valuables."

Tau swallowed hard, wondering why the police never patrolled places like this where criminals actually gathered in handy clumps that would be easy to arrest. "Take what you want."

"I intend to," said Tracy, her right hand continuing to grope in his pants pocket as her left hand shot up underneath his blue work tunic, tickling his chest. "And I think you like being searched."

Skull Chest looked confused as he watched Tracy's hand moving around under Tau's shirt. He snorted and made poking motions with the knife in front of Tau's eyes. Tau hoped Skull Chest wasn't prone to seizures. "Please be careful with that. I'll give you what you want, so there's no need to hurt me."

Tracy scraped her long fingernails across his chest, digging in deep. "Pain builds character."

"Ow!"

Tau's heart beat faster as he wondered what to do. The whole situation reminded him of schoolyard torments. It wasn't his style to fight them, since he'd learned that the beatings usually stopped when he became less interactive. Most of the time, Navajo kids would stop hurting him as soon as he fell down, but the white kids would usually kick him or sit and pound on him for a while before they got bored with the game. Sometimes they took his clothes or his books so they could hide them or toss them into a canyon. After their initial shock at his appearance when he arrived home, his parents would congratulate Tau for not getting into stupid fights as his father gave him any medical attention he required. When they complained to the school authorities, things would get worse for a while as the punished children took their revenge on Tau. When he got older, he became a good runner, so he avoided a lot of trouble by escaping his tormentors and hiding. Running was what he wanted to do now, but he couldn't see a way out of the situation with a woman holding him and a knife being waved in front of his face while several others watched.

Tracy's right hand, still in his side pocket, worked its way around to the front of his pants. "What's this?"

She'd found his medicine pouch.

Before he could answer, her left hand plunged down into his pants. He didn't want to lose his medicine pouch, and her hand was groping elsewhere, so he tried to twist away. Tracy just grabbed him tighter as Skull Chest's eyes widened.

"I was hoping you'd fight a bit," she said.

"It's my medicine pouch. There's nothing in it you want.

It's just corn pollen, a piece of turquoise, some—" He stopped, knowing she couldn't listen when she was laughing so hard.

"Oh, is that what you call it? A medicine pouch? Must be good medicine."

Tau glanced around for help. Skull Chest punched him in the stomach. Pain exploded through him as tiny lights popped and flashed in front of his closed eyes. He bent over, almost impaling his face on the blade as Skull Chest stepped back. Still behind him, Tracy held his hips to keep him from falling farther. Stronger than she looked, she put her left arm around his neck and pulled him upright. He tried to get a breath of air, but it hurt too much. Skull Chest hit him in the stomach again. With so much pain there already, it didn't hurt as much as the first time, but it made him feel nauseous. He kept his eyes closed and sank to his knees, thinking how nice it would be to pass out until they were gone.

"Get up," Tracy said, reaching under his armpits to help him stagger to his feet. "I want to see that 'medicine pouch' of yours."

He stood up with his head spinning. Tracy reached around his waistband to the front of his pants. "Show me what you've got."

Tau opened his eyes and saw Skull Chest preparing to hit him again.

Then he heard the screams.

Tracy jerked back from Tau as the startled Skull Chest looked away, his fist suspended in the air. The screams continued, accompanied by bright flashes and the sounds of crackling lightning strikes, running footsteps, and bodies thumping to the ground. Tau smelled ozone and cooked meat in the air. He put all his weight into one strong shove against Skull Chest, who dropped the knife and almost fell over, then turned to run back to the slidewalk platform before the oversize gorilla could respond.

"Tau!"

Tau's flight response took over, but his head hurt and his

stomach pulsed with pain every time one of his feet hit the ground. It confused him to see several of the gang members lying still on the ground, but he wouldn't stop to analyze the situation. Someone shouted, probably to alert the others of his escape, but he could see the relative safety of the slidewalk platform spinning around in the distance.

A deep Russian voice boomed nearby. "Tau! It's me!"

Tau glanced back in confusion, then stumbled and almost fell down when he saw his burly friend Tymanov, his rescuer Tymanov, his marvelous pal Tymanov, trying to catch up to him.

"Vadim!"

Tymanov wasn't even breathing hard when he stopped beside Tau. "You run fast."

Tau rubbed his stomach, trying to catch his breath, as he looked around for the gang. "I was motivated. What are you doing here?"

"I got your note in my office. It sounded urgent, so I thought I'd try to reach you at your apt before you went out again. I went past here on the slidewalk and saw someone in trouble with a skin gang. Then I realized it was you."

Tau thanked him and spotted the end of a black rod with two electrodes sticking out of Tymanov's shirtsleeve. "That was you throwing lightning back there, wasn't it?"

Tymanov patted the rod and pushed it back up into a sleeve holster. "It's called a lightning rod. It can deliver five hundred thousand volts over a short range, adjustable from tight beam to wide dispersal. The charge attacks the nervous system, so targets flop around and seize up a while, but they usually recover. It's not legal in this country, so I had to make it myself."

"Engineering classes in Russia must be more practical than they are here."

"Probably, but I didn't learn to make these at university. I'm product of misspent youth in Kaliningrad."

"Time well spent, if you ask me."

Tau's adrenaline subsided, leaving him with a shaky feel-

ing to go along with his other pains. He looked back toward
the BART platform, noting that Tracy and Skull Chest were
missing, but there were plenty of bodies lying around. He also
remembered Tymanov saying the lightning rod victims "usually" recovered. "I think I'd feel better if we had this conversation somewhere else."

"I doubt they'll be back soon. I've taught them the meaning of *fear*."

Tau spotted Skull Chest, Tracy, and two others making a
slow approach from the BART platform, darting between hiding places. Even at that distance, Tau could see they were
armed.

"Not to sound ungrateful, Vadim, but I think some of your
students were asleep during your lesson."

Tymanov frowned, glanced over his shoulder, and let out a
heavy sigh. "I used to find teaching so rewarding. Perhaps we
should leave."

When Tau didn't respond, Tymanov turned again and saw
he was gone.

"Come on!" Tau yelled from the slidewalk platform.

5

COLONEL General Viktor Aleksandrovich Zhukov pulled
the lapels of his overcoat up around his neck and squinted into
the driving snow, thinking it wasn't so bad to spend most of
his life underground in relative comfort. It would be another
freezing night according to Radio Moscow, with the temperature dropping to minus nine degrees Celsius. Still the State's
official radio station, its weather forecasts were always correct, no matter what kind of weather eventually arrived, but

snow was always a safe bet. General Zhukov never liked snow—he never played in snow as a boy, he never skied in snow as a young man—snow was not, and never would be, a pleasurable weather condition. Now seventy-four years old, he had even more reason to hate snow—it made him cold.

The lump in Zhukov's overcoat didn't like snow either. It kept moving around, trying to find warmer spots on his stomach or chest, and finding none. Sometimes the lump would yelp when it inserted a portion of its anatomy into a moving joint on Zhukov's powered exoskeleton; then a heated glove would slip inside the overcoat and pet the lump, warming it up while it calmed down.

Zhukov started down the gradual incline of the approach ramp, a gauntlet lined on both sides with remotely operated guns and shredder-fences, wondering when someone would notice him. As his boots struck the frozen pavement, the vibrations should have triggered intruder alarms all over the inside of the mountain. He shook his head; the soft young soldiers didn't have the proper discipline anymore. But what could he threaten them with that would make an impression? They were already trapped inside Yamantau Mountain in the Beloretsk region of the southern Urals. Of course, he could always put them *outside* the underground military complex, on patrol in the *snow*, where Zhukov had to walk—vehicles weren't allowed through the portal because the satellites might be watching. If he'd ever raised a child, and it became a soldier, it would have been out there by now poking a weapon up his nose and demanding identification. His child would have—he interrupted the thought; no point thinking about that kind of thing at this point in his life.

Zhukov squinted up at the sky again, willing the clouds to part so that he could see the stars for a change. He wanted to see Mars. With no one else to rely on but himself, he needed a sign that the Red Star project would be a success, so a sign from the heavens would be appropriate. But the clouds would not bend to Zhukov's will. He blinked as a snowflake hit him in the eye—probably a reminder from his mother that looking for a sign in the heavens was simply a sign of weakness.

Colonel Anna Zhukov had never approved of weakness. She often spoke of the old days, in "wet ops" during the Cold War, when she worked for Department V of the KGB's First Chief Directorate. Those were fond memories for her, since she'd been one of the KGB's top assassins. Working for the First Chief Directorate allowed her to travel outside the borders of the Motherland, to meet interesting foreigners, and to kill them. Acknowledged many times as a true Soviet hero, her large collection of awards, which Viktor still kept, included the Order of the Red Banner and the Order of Lenin. While other children wasted their time after their daily studies, Viktor's mother taught him how to fence—with a foil, an épée, and a saber—how to hunt with a knife, how to shoot with a variety of weapons, and how to kill with his hands. Anna, the professional assassin, took great care in raising her son, firm in her belief that an appreciation of death would give Viktor a greater appreciation for life.

The State meant everything to Viktor's parents, but the collapse of communism and the Soviet Union affected Anna Zhukov the most. One of Viktor's clearest boyhood memories was of Moscow during the celebration of the fiftieth anniversary of V-E Day, which Russians still refer to as victory in the "Great Patriotic War." Anna made sure Viktor understood the context of the celebration, then burned it into his memory by talking about it every May for the next ten years. It was May of 1995, just a few years after the collapse. With the depressing state of the Russian economy, the absence of a stable body of law, the lost sense of social cohesion, and the general disillusion with the democratic process, there was little that the Russians could embrace with pride at that time. Free enterprise could not be conducted without breaking the law; science went without funds; art was in decline; salaries of the majority, still tied to State enterprises, were swallowed by inflation when they were paid at all. In that climate, the anniversary of Russia's one collective achievement during that century demanded an event to draw them together in celebration.

Before the collapse of communism, the May Day holiday had been the centerpiece of the Soviet ideological calendar. It was preceded by the *subotnik*, on or about Lenin's birthday, when everyone donated time on the weekend to clean up the winter's accumulated debris in the cities. While the tradition of *subotnik* continued, with Viktor's family always participating, May Day became nothing more than a two-day holiday from work. Only a few thousand of the still-faithful communists paraded down Tverskaya, the eight-lane street leading to Red Square, to celebrate the international worker's holiday. The tanks, fireworks, and giant patriotic posters were reserved for the parades on the more important anniversary of V-E Day.

After two weeks of summery heat, temperatures in Moscow had plummeted overnight. White flakes danced on the window when Viktor woke up on May 9. In its infinite wisdom, the local utility had shut off all heat in Moscow on April 25 to conserve energy, so the heat would remain off until October. It was cold in the Zhukov flat, but the KGB housed the family just five minutes from their offices in Dzerzhinsky Square, three blocks away from the Kremlin. When the KGB changed its name to the FSB, the Federal Security Service, little else seemed to change, so the Zhukovs were allowed to maintain their residence. Anna Zhukov's services to the State were no longer required, but Viktor's father, Major General Aleksandr Zhukov, kept the same office and continued his career with the FSB, although he dealt with different people and earned much more money.

So that he would maintain some perspective about the celebration, Viktor's parents explained that the parades were a political statement, reminders to the public that the Red Army saved the country. The KGB and the other State security services were often used in opposition to the military, so the Zhukovs did not wish to promote this attitude in their son.

They said it was natural to feel pride in seeing the old war veterans with their medals, and to appreciate their sacrifices in past wars, but the tanks, guns, missiles, and warplanes were illusions of Russia's present-day military power. In fact, the military couldn't pay its officers, feed its men, pay its electric bills, or keep equipment operational. Submarine crews refused to go to sea until they were paid. Along with its inability to maintain basic discipline, over four hundred suicides in the Russian military had been reported in the last year. In any case, the spectators at the parade knew it was propaganda, but they didn't care as long as they had an excuse for an approved celebration.

When Viktor saw the parade, he forgot all about the military problems his parents told him about. He saw the rows of tanks rumbling past and felt the vibrations of their passage in the soles of his feet; he saw the missile launcher trucks drive by, their missiles pointed toward the sky, ready to defend them from attack; he saw the jets thundering overhead, banking in formation at low altitude; he saw the old men, marching proudly in their uniforms and medals; and he saw the cheers and applause of the people as all these things went past. It was a sight he would never forget.

After the parade, Viktor's parents showed him a new, larger-than-life, bronze statue of a Red Army officer on a horse; he looked defiant beside the Kremlin wall. They told him the Russians regarded this officer as the hero of World War II—Marshal Georgy Zhukov, Viktor's grandfather. From a modest start in a poor rural family in central Russia, Georgy Zhukov joined the Red Army to fight in World War I and the Civil War, but his talents became most evident in World War II. He led every crucial Soviet military operation, including the defense of Moscow, the relief of Leningrad, and the decisive armor battle at Kursk. He also masterminded the Soviet advance to Berlin and was Soviet representative to the German surrender on May 8, 1945. In the tradition of almost all the outstanding Russian military commanders, Georgy Zhukov was out of favor with the country's political leaders because his decisions were intended to serve Russia instead of himself or his superiors. Fearing his popularity and talent after World War II, Marshal Zhukov was exiled to commands in Odessa and the Urals military district, far from Moscow. After serving for brief periods in the Defense Ministry under Khrushchev, he was again viewed as a threat and removed from his post to live in obscurity until his death in 1974. After the fall of communism, with Georgy Zhukov safely buried for twenty years and unlikely to return, the new administration erected the first statue in his honor for the fiftieth anniversary of the end of World War II.

Learning about his grandfather determined the course of Viktor's life. After the first statue, they walked past another stone statue of Marshal Zhukov on the boulevard named in his honor. Huge posters of Georgy Zhukov, his uniform loaded with medals, hung from tall buildings around Red Square, but there were smaller replicas in the windows of stores on strategic streets. Viktor never asked his parents for much, but they understood when he asked them to purchase a small poster of Marshal Zhukov for the wall over his bed. He'd never met his grandfather, but he decided then to *become* his grandfather.

That night, they went walking up the center of Tverskaya toward Red Square. The broad street was closed to vehicles, and huge crowds were heading to the square for the fireworks to be held there after dark, which came around ten o'clock at that time of year. After the long parades of bemedaled veterans earlier that day, the serious and apathetic Muscovites were transformed. Everyone smiled. The air rang with the sound of happy voices. Lovers kissed and children laughed. Families were everywhere. There were few drunks among the thousands streaming into the square, and there were no fights. As Viktor's family strolled along Tverskaya, they came to a bandstand set up across from the city government building. A stooped, gray-haired, accordion player wheezed out popular music from the 1940s, so Viktor's parents stopped to dance in the street along with other couples, young and old. When the fireworks came, filling the sky with loud bursts of light and color, the crowd cheered for each explosion, their troubles bursting and floating away as forgotten ash. Viktor had never been so happy; he wanted to tell everyone he was the grandson of Marshal Zhukov, Russian hero of the Great Patriotic War.

An old man now, Colonel General Viktor Aleksandrovich Zhukov still had the framed poster of Marshal Zhukov on his office wall, proudly displayed beside a case full of his mother's medals.

It made him wonder—who would keep *his* medals on their wall when he was gone?

Zhukov stomped his feet on the ramp, cursing himself for being a sentimental old fool. As he approached within a few steps of the outer blast doors—made of hardened black durasteel designed to withstand a nearby thermonuclear strike—he finally detected some activity. A red spotlight came on by a security camera next to the portal. The towering blast doors weighed twenty-five tons each and could be fully opened or closed within thirty seconds. Deep rumbling noises accompanied by vibrations in the earth announced the opening of the portal. A dinosaur screamed in its death throes—or so it sounded to Zhukov—as the almost seamless crack between the doors began to widen.

"Stand and be identified, sir!" A soldier's voice from the dark interior.

Zhukov sighed and turned his back to the door so that the skull implant could be scanned for brain wave identification. The soldiers were lazy, but they were performing for him, and he needed to humor their procedures to maintain the illusion of discipline. As the door continued its relentless motion, pushing back the snow near Zhukov's feet, he felt the pleasurable sensation of warmer air swirling around him from the tunnel opening. The tunnel system provided lungs for the breathing mountain—at night, it exhaled, during the day, it inhaled. The air motion meant that the second set of blast doors farther down the tunnel stood open, a minor error in security, but the warmth felt good, so Zhukov wasn't going to punish them for it. Perhaps he was getting soft in his old age.

"We are sorry for the inconvenience, Colonel General Zhukov, sir!"

"Has Colonel Kosygin arrived?"

"Yes, sir! He's waiting beyond the inner doors, sir!"

Zhukov stepped onto an electric cart and drove off without waiting. The cart wasn't built for speed, so it would take a few minutes of driving to reach the inner set of blast doors.

Colonel Oleg Kosygin would be dismayed to learn that Final Harvest, the military command center buried deep within Yamantau Mountain, would be his new home. Zhukov shrugged—being his trusted assistant for over twenty years had its good and bad points, he assumed, but he knew Kosygin would accept his orders. The underground base was almost as old as Zhukov, but its existence was still considered a rumor even among most senior officials of the Russian government. Final Harvest had a mythic quality as a reminder of the Cold War, even though most of its construction occurred after the Cold War ended. The Russian parliament had complained of a lack of funds necessary to dismantle nuclear weapons as required by strategic arms reduction treaties, so much of Final Harvest's financing came through American aid money diverted from that program. Although Zhukov did not approve of that tactic, particularly at a time when Russian soldiers were living with starvation, he understood the special situation that required the construction of this facility for the Fallen Angel project. Better to risk discovery of the diverted funds by the Americans than to leave Fallen Angel in its underground Kola Peninsula base where international disarmament monitoring teams might find it.

Zhukov smiled as he thought of the underground building competition between East and West. The American president Kennedy supported the idea of MAD, Mutually Assured Destruction, as a deterrent against all-out war, unaware that the Soviet Union had made extensive plans to survive a nuclear exchange intact. Of course, the madman Khrushchev did his best to provoke Kennedy into a nuclear war, but relations settled into a cautious paranoid silence filled with ongoing battle preparations. During the Cold War, the Americans built Raven Rock, the 265,000-square-foot underground version of their Pentagon in Pennsylvania, and the 200,000-square-foot Mount Weather in Virginia, continually staffed with a "shadow government" that would keep America operating if senior government officials couldn't reach it before the bombs fell. Congress created its own relocation center beneath a resort hotel in West Virginia, while NORAD built its operations center deep beneath the granite of Cheyenne Mountain in Colorado. The Soviet leaders, on the other hand, started an underground building program in 1955 that lasted for twenty years—longer in some cases. The largest bomb shelters were like the vast underground city at Ramenki, capable of sheltering 120,000 people; located six miles outside of Moscow, it was connected to the Kremlin by underground rail tunnels. Spacious bomb shelters were also built under every factory and apartment building in thirty-nine of the largest Russian cities, connected to a network of underground tunnels that carried water and power along with food, diesel fuel, and stored medical supplies. Within the Moscow beltway alone, there were seventy-nine underground command posts, each about the size of the American Pentagon, buried up to five hundred feet beneath the surface under concrete and dirt.

As Zhukov suspected, the inner blast doors were open. Beyond the entrance stood an athletic-looking army officer in his forties, wearing a long uniform overcoat, his pale blue eyes searching the vast space beyond in an attempt to make sense of what he was seeing. Colonel Oleg Kosygin's wide-eyed stare took in the immensity of the underground cavern, containing a freshwater pond, numerous passageways, and an open area in this one room the size of three football fields. Individual chambers contained three-story-tall metal buildings, and each one rested on thirteen hundred half-ton springs designed to absorb explosive shocks during a nuclear strike. The original structures included theaters, apartments, offices, exercise centers, barbershops, clinics, dining halls, and other amenities found on well-stocked military bases. Deepest within the mountain were the military command center and the vault. Built according to Zhukov's specifications, the vault contained the research lab for Fallen Angel.

Ghostly echoes and shadows made it clear that the facility was inactive. The yellowish green lighting system would be shut off in favor of full-spectrum white lights if Final Harvest were fully activated, but the air smelled fresh, and Zhukov could hear the pleasant sound of a small waterfall, fed by a mountain spring, splashing into the pond. Zhukov had spent much of his life in these underground shelters, including some under Moscow that were flooded and full of mosquitoes, but Final Harvest was where he preferred to spend his time. Ever since Fallen Angel's arrival here from its high-security storage on the heavily defended Kola Peninsula, Zhukov knew Yamantau Mountain would be a comfortable home. With hundreds of feet of rock over his head, he felt safe from the penetrating eyes of the reconnaissance satellites.

"Oleg, my friend," said Zhukov, slapping a large and friendly hand on the colonel's shoulder. "Welcome to Final Harvest, your new home away from home."

Kosygin nodded. "Thank you, General. I find it somewhat daunting."

"You'll get used to it. Keep in mind that your presence here should be considered an honor, since few people have ever entered this facility. Fewer people are aware of Fallen Angel, the project you are about to see."

"Fallen Angel?"

"I assume the code name was someone's idea of a joke, with that someone being a high-ranking official in the leadership a long time ago."

"I understand."

Zhukov motioned toward the bridge that crossed the pond by the waterfall. "I hope your boots are comfortable. We have a lot of walking to do."

"I need the exercise, General."

"Ah," said Zhukov, unbuttoning his overcoat. "Thank you for reminding me. I also have a passenger who needs exercise."

Zhukov opened his overcoat enough to remove a snoring, long-haired lump. "Laika, wake up. I'm not some *babushka* who's going to carry you everywhere I go."

The miniature Pekingese woke up, but she didn't seem happy about it as Zhukov placed her on the ground and attached a leash to her collar.

Zhukov straightened and rebuttoned his overcoat as he saw Kosygin's smile. "It's okay. Laika has all the proper clearances."

"I have no doubt, General. Will you be leaving her with me when you go to Mars?"

"Don't be ridiculous, Oleg. Laika will accompany me to Mars."

Kosygin raised his eyebrows. "How is that possible? Wouldn't she need a space suit?"

"Arrangements have already been made. It's Laika's destiny to go into space. Her namesake was the first dog in orbit, and this one will be the first dog on Mars."

"As I recall, the original Laika was a German shepherd."

"A German shepherd is a large animal that eats a lot of food. Laika has very little mass, so she requires very little energy to move her to Mars. She also eats much less than a German shepherd."

Kosygin nodded. "You are a practical man, General."

Laika strained at the leash and barked.

"Come, Oleg. She's anxious to show you around."

Laika led the way, as Zhukov gave his assistant a quick tour of the facilities, assuming Kosygin would explore more on his own later. Half an hour of walking brought them to the automated vault door blocking access to the military command center. The vault door was large enough to accommodate a truck's passage, as were the rest of the tunnels inside the mountain.

Zhukov pressed a blue button on the vault. "I'll have the technician program this door to recognize your brain waves."

Kosygin glanced back at the small scanning dish on the tunnel wall behind Zhukov, noting the presence of a secondary dish that could project a neural shock field if necessary. "One hopes the technician won't make any mistakes."

Zhukov chuckled as the vault door hissed and began rumbling open. "Perhaps you should make friends with the technician beforehand, just to be sure. Vodka makes a nice gift."

"It isn't enough that we have to pay bribes everywhere we go on the outside? We have to do it here, too?"

Zhukov shrugged as he passed through the doorway. "Old habits die hard, my friend."

Careful not to step on Laika, Kosygin entered the dimly lit command center. Computer workstations ringed a big circular space in the middle of the room, where three-dimensional projections of tiny aircraft flew over a glowing map of Russia. Based on an actual satellite view with any clouds removed, the map of Russia lay in darkness, but border outlines glowed in yellow, while the lights of the cities glittered like white diamonds as they would when viewed from space. The aircraft were detailed enough for their blinking navigation lights to be visible. Higher magnification would show the details of individual aircraft. Identified by their transponders, most of the aircraft were white to indicate standard friendly identifications, but some were green to indicate political leaders in transit. Aircraft entering Russian airspace would flash yellow and red for a moment until they were identified by the computers and tagged with a new color. They saw no red hostiles flying over the country. Closer to the ceiling, a variety of magnified-scale satellites moved along polar orbital tracks or hovered in crowded geosynchronous locations.

Zhukov gestured at the busy sky. "How familiar are you with our orbital reconnaissance capabilities?"

"It's not my area of expertise, but I know the satellite images are detailed enough to tell if I've cleaned my fingernails or not. They can see where I am most of the time. I suspect they can also look inside my stomach with radar to see what I had for lunch."

Zhukov leaned over one of the workstations. "All true. Except for the occasional system failure, which can usually be replaced with images from a private satellite or a backup we can steer into the proper location, the satellites can follow you almost anywhere. Imaging radar systems can penetrate the Earth's surface—through dirt, sand, snow, or water—to follow you if you don't go too deep, although they can't see us inside this mountain. If you go inside a normal building, the satellites can usually trace your movements with infrared or radar, depending on the building materials and other heat sources. The microwave signals go through clouds as if they weren't there."

Kosygin smiled, ignoring Laika, who sniffed in fascination at his right ankle. "If you're trying to make me more paranoid than I already am, it's working. I assumed the State could watch me all the time, but I thought the video cockroach robots did that."

"The video roaches are only used for special surveillance. Satellite observation is much cheaper. Most images are of the surface, of course, where the radar works like a microwave flash camera to illuminate an area on the ground and take a digital snapshot at radio wavelengths. I mention all this because the observation satellites are also used to study natural resources and to locate buried archaeological sites."

"Yes, I've heard of these things," said Kosygin, distracted by Laika's insistent chewing on his sock.

Zhukov tapped something on the workstation's keyboard. In the projected view in front of them, one of the satellites started flashing in blue as a cone of pale blue light descended toward the map to indicate its current field of view over Siberia. "This is one of our Kosmos-SAR phased array radar reconnaissance satellites. The high resolution of its images is due to its synthetic aperture radar, which simulates a powerful radar antenna by combining the backscatter echoes received by the radar as it moves along its flight track. Radar operations require more power than solar panels can collect, so this satellite is powered by a Romashka-type nuclear reactor."

Kosygin nodded. "I was asked to sit in on a safety review regarding the Romashka series reactors. This type ejects its uranium 235 fuel rods from the reactor vessel in the event of an accident or the end of the satellite's mission. That way, the rods can safely decay during atmospheric reentry without being shielded by the reactor core. Early accidents in our satellite program, with shielded fuel rods scattering radiation across the Earth's surface, did not make us look good in the international community."

A magnified satellite image, showing a swampy, forested area bordered by a river, took shape in front of the standard strategic projection of Russian Federation airspace. Coordinates beneath the image defined the center of the scan area: "101° 53' East Long., 60° 53' North Lat., Tunguska, Siberia."

"Tunguska?" Kosygin asked.

"Twenty years ago, on the request of Professor Vasilyev at the Russian Academy of Sciences, I used a Kosmos-SAR satellite just like this one to perform a radar penetration study of the Tunguska region in Siberia. On June 30, 1908, this portion of the Podkamennaya Tunguska River was the singularity point of a twenty-megaton airburst explosion. It's an interesting point, because the first nuclear weapons would not be built until almost forty years after that event. The explosion generated a seismic wave recorded in Irkutsk, Tashkent, Tbilisi, and Jena. Pressure disturbances traveled around the globe. Six minutes after the explosion, a local magnetic storm developed that was similar to geomagnetic disturbances following atmospheric nuclear detonations. The shock and ballistic waves destroyed over two thousand kilometers of subarctic evergreen forest, with burnt vegetation spread almost two hundred kilometers from the epicenter. Later discovery of unusual iridium-enriched spherules in peat bogs of the Bublik Swamp, close to the explosion area, compared against Antarctic snow-ice core samples using Instrumental Neutron Activation Analyses, led to the conclusion that the object that exploded over Tunguska had a mass of eighty thousand tons."

Kosygin knew Zhukov studied him as he spoke, always testing his alertness, but he had difficulty paying attention while he subtly shook his leg in attempts to dislodge Laika from his ankle. "Was this the object that our scientists identified as a comet?"

"That was a popular theory at the Russian Academy of Sciences for a long time. But a Russian scientist could not advance his career by promoting new theories that disagreed with established dogma. Still, there were some who were more interested in science than in their careers, so research continued. The rest of the international community became convinced that the object was a stony asteroidal bolide. When I was asked to do a satellite study of the Tunguska impact site, I learned the truth."

The tone of Zhukov's voice changed, and Kosygin forgot about Laika.

"It's important to remember the peculiar aspects of the Tunguska event. There were no explosive craters or meteorite fragments, there were no smoke traces in the atmosphere, multiple explosions occurred, and the atmospheric portion of the object's trajectory indicated unusually slow movement before the explosion. The shock wave preceded the high-temperature effects of the detonation, and this only occurs in chemical explosions. Computer simulations of the event, using either an icy comet or a stony asteroid, demonstrated that the explosion of either one would have completely disintegrated the object into small particles. Most of those particles would have shot back out of the atmosphere in a plume such as those observed in the Shoemaker-Levy impacts on Jupiter. Many researchers suggested it was a dangerous cosmic object unknown to astronomical science, and that its slow flight and unexplainable trajectories were the result of maneuvering. These people with the outlandish maneuvering theories were the closest to the truth, so they were ignored by the rest of the scientific establishment."

Zhukov's eyes burned with excitement. Hearing the emotion in her master's voice, Laika stopped chewing on Kosygin's ankle and looked up at Zhukov as he continued. "There were eyewitnesses to the explosion and the object's descent. They agreed that several large chunks fell into the southern bogs, forming craters that filled with water and mud as the bog changed from a dry to a wet state. The water was bitter and unsuitable for drinking. By the time researchers entered the area after the explosion, and interviews were collected, they saw no signs of craters in the swamp. The discovery of craters waited until I studied the area with satellite radar. This was similar to the method used to locate the hidden outline of the massive Chicxulub crater in the clay under the Yucatán Peninsula. That crater is two hundred kilometers in diameter, and it's the primary remnant of the bolide impact that killed the dinosaurs at the end of the Cretaceous Period."

Zhukov pointed at the enlarged false-color Tunguska image hovering in the air. "The main Tunguska crater was under three feet of water, but the ragged edges of the circular impact area were clear in the radar satellite images. At the center of the crater, hidden deep under the peat bog, was a large metallic object. I couldn't determine the exact dimensions of its oval shape, but it was too big to be a missile casing. I reported this discovery to my immediate superior. The next day, I was placed in command of a heavy engineering unit assigned to recover the secret Tunguska object. Knowledge of the operation was restricted to a small group of people. Professor Vasilyev accompanied us under the impression that we were a military unit composed of scientists—by the time he learned otherwise, he was permanently assigned to work for me. It was unfortunate, but I couldn't allow Vasilyev to leave after we recovered the object from the crater."

Kosygin's eyes widened as he grasped the significance of Zhukov's last statement.

"Don't worry, my friend," smiled Zhukov. "I'll leave instructions for you to be allowed out of this prison, on occasion. Professor Vasilyev is a civilian who has never been in the military, so he believes in the scientific tradition of sharing information. As a result, the professor must never be allowed to leave."

"Never?"

"My choice was to employ the professor, even though my superior had a more abrupt solution to the problem. I convinced him that there would be too much chance of an information leak if we were to search for qualified research personnel. The professor is an intelligent fellow, so he has been able to learn the additional skills required for his years of analysis. But we still can't trust him enough to let him leave here."

"As long as I'm permitted outside to see the sun, I'll be fine, sir."

"You'll get used to it. I did."

"Yes, sir."

"At least Final Harvest is reasonably warm. The underground base on the Kola Peninsula was too damp—cold and damp. My sinuses hated me for living there all the time. But it was convenient—it was an old Northern Fleet base, long since deactivated by the time we stored our discovery there for further study. It was a stroke of luck for me when the international monitoring units wanted to visit all the old bases. They don't know about Final Harvest, so this was the only safe place to move Fallen Angel. I had plenty of time to plan, so the lab here was built to my specifications."

"The lab? We haven't seen that yet, have we?"

"*Nyet*. I had to prepare you first." Zhukov tugged on Laika's leash, distracting her from a thorough investigation of Kosygin's left shoe.

Kosygin hesitated, then asked the question that had been bothering him. "Prepare me for what, sir? You haven't told me what you found in the crater."

Zhukov beckoned for Kosygin to follow him. "Come. It's better if I show you."

6

TAU loved the sound of her voice—it had a smooth, sensuous quality that made his skin tingle. Her voice held the hypnotic quality and complex rhythms of a long Navajo chant, but it sounded much more seductive than he'd ever heard from a *hataalii* singing a Beauty Way. Her face danced along with the music of each syllable: her brown eyes glittered, warming him with each glance; her nose bobbed at the tip as she spoke; her dramatic eyebrows were in constant motion, rising in surprise or wrinkling in thought. Her long brown hair was loose and seductive: with a desire to be closer to her face, a few strands would fall forward to shade one eye, only to be thrown back in place with an abrupt toss of her head. The dark tan on her face softened around her eyes, where impertinent sunlight had been blocked by dark glasses, giving her the spotlighted soft-focus appearance of a romantic starlet in an early Hollywood flatfilm. The colors of her long dress, worn in place of her standard jeans to please Tau, radiated spring in a riot of tiny flowers cascading down her long, athletic body. When Dr. Kate McCloud was in the room, Tau couldn't think of anything else.

Outside the restaurant before Kate arrived, his senses enjoyed the salt smell in the cool air and the soft splash of tiny waves against the building, its walls descending into a clear blue artificial lagoon jutting into San Francisco Bay. The lights of the submerged restaurant drew colorful fish closer to the glass walls to entertain the diners, leaving them to wonder if they were watching the fish or if the fish were watching them. The sun had set, but the horizon held a reddish gold glow full of promise for an evening set apart from the rest of reality; a romantic fantasy created by Kate's presence. Wasting no time, she would reach past the layers of masks he presented to the world to seek out his heart and expose it to view, mingling his life force with her own to create a greater, more balanced thing of beauty than either of them could create by themselves. A thorough archaeologist, hungry for hidden knowledge, she would sift through his thoughts, tossing aside the superficial until she revealed the secret hopes and fears that made him unique. When she smiled at her discoveries, with the gentle rectangle of her mouth revealing perfect teeth, he felt privileged to be a part of the dream that was Kate.

She arrived late at the restaurant, as usual. Tau didn't mind; he'd come from a place where "Navajo time" was a phrase used to express disdain for the ticking clock of the white world that had wormed its relentless way into Navajo culture. Among the *Dineh*, respect for individuals implied an understanding that they would arrive when they could, and that would be the best time. Even so, Tau felt an unusual urgency in his body; he felt nervous, and knew that the fluttering in his stomach was associated with the gold ring in his jacket pocket. His thoughts focused on rehearsal, wondering what he should say to Kate, how he should say it, when would be the right moment, and what should be ordered to make a proper dinner for this time-honored ritual. Nothing in the modern Navajo way had prepared him for this event. Although they were rare, arranged marriages still occurred on the reservation, and traditions such as those provided simplicity in social matters. With the loss of the old ways, many new traditions developed to take their places, but not in this case. Tau felt as progressive as any other *Dineh*, with his Navajo father and white mother providing a positive example for him, but the nebulous matter of marriage proposals had never been discussed in his family. He understood the spiritual significance of the unbroken ring and the circular cycle of life, but the lack of methodology for the proposal process seemed wrong—a ritual without a ritual. And what if Kate refused to marry him? How was he supposed to handle that?

Now that Kate sat across from him at the dinner table, Tau felt reassured by her presence, even though his hands were cold and shaking. As much as possible, he tried to keep her talking so he'd have time to calm down, but it didn't work. The brightly colored fish swimming past their table provided a soothing effect on previous visits to the restaurant, but this time an orange garibaldi kept bumping its face against the glass near Tau's head. He felt like he was being watched. When their shrimp cocktail appetizers arrived, he missed the glass dish and speared his left hand with the tiny seafood fork. Noting his odd behavior, Kate stopped talking about underwater archaeology and stared at him as he held his napkin against the bleeding wound.

"I don't think I've ever seen anyone do that before. What's wrong with you tonight?"

"Clumsy, I guess," mumbled Tau.

"Rough day?"

He didn't know whether to start with the gang mugging or his problems at work, or whether mentioning them at all on this special evening would break the mood, such as it was. But he had to say something, so he took the easy way out. "Could have been better."

"They rejected your proposal."

Tau nodded. She usually knew what he was thinking; it was a trait he'd considered charming at first, but it was inconvenient at this moment.

She slumped back in her chair. "Some group of self-satisfied idiots sat around and passed judgment on your idea, even though they couldn't understand it in the first place. Am I right?"

Tau nodded, thinking he should change the subject so she wouldn't get too upset. It was his problem, he had already talked to Max and Vadim about it, and he wanted to steer the conversation toward more romantic issues. He could discuss his job situation with Kate the next day, when the timing would be better, assuming she said yes to his proposal and would still speak to him the next day, which she might not be, and that was a scary thought, and he knew he shouldn't think that way, positive thoughts were important, as his father and his uncle had tried to teach him, and Kate continued speaking, so he really should be paying attention rather than confusing himself by thinking too much on this special occasion, and negative thoughts would keep the Holy People from helping him, and that ring in his pocket seemed a lot heavier now, and he wished he weren't so nervous so he could make a better impression—

Kate waved a hand in front of his eyes. "Hello? Anybody home? You're not doing some kind of Navajo meditation thing while I'm talking, are you?"

Tau took a deep breath. "I'm sorry. I'm a little preoccupied, but I'm paying attention. Really."

"I'd understand your drifting off if I was talking about archaeology, but I was trying to ask about you. Men are supposed to like that." She smiled and reached across the table to put a hand on his arm. "You want me to look at the damage?"

Tau remembered the bloody napkin on his hand; he couldn't believe how much blood was coming out of such a small wound. "No, it's okay."

She patted his arm. "Tau, you know I love you, right?"

"Yes." He smiled. His face felt warm.

"And I think you're the smartest person I've ever met."

He raised an eyebrow in response.

"However, you're socially dense. You don't know how to deal with people properly. Those fools that rejected your proposal—they did it because they fear you."

"I think they fear the technology, or they fear the public reaction they might have gotten if they'd approved my project."

"It doesn't matter. The point is that you can't expect people to acknowledge your brilliance, particularly when it might make them look bad, without your doing some personal groundwork first. You have to socialize with these people, get to know them, be friendly, accept their invitations, go to parties, and compliment them on their work even when you know it's pointless and stupid. That way, when you ask them for something, you'll have a better chance of getting it."

Tau shook his head. "I can't work that way."

Kate shrugged. "Then you're doomed."

"Why? I just want to be left alone to do my work."

"They think you're inhuman, and you're demonstrating it by refusing to relax in their presence."

"I don't care what they think about me."

"Exactly! And you radiate that kind of arrogance when you're around them, so they feel inferior. But they're the ones who can stand between you and your goals."

"Well, I think I'm polite to those people, but I don't see how socializing with them would help."

Kate rolled her eyes at the ceiling. "Trust me, it's easier to hate an enemy you don't know. You're better than the people you work for, so that makes you the enemy when you try to stand out. They'd help their incompetent friends long before they would ever help you. You're too serious. Everything you do is so important, so significant, that it's a real strain to be around you."

The blood stopped gushing out of Tau's hand, so he folded the napkin to cover the huge stain. He nudged the plate to cover the spot on the tablecloth; from the amount of blood, it looked like they were eating raw meat right off the cow. Then Kate's words sank in to his brain. "You don't think that, do you? That it's a strain to be around me?"

"Well, yes and no. Sometimes." She sighed, looking away.

"Really?"

"In some ways, a relationship with you is a lot of work, but it is with most people, for one reason or another. When we do things together, we're usually on a schedule, or following a plan, or accomplishing some task; you never just stop and relax."

"I relax when my work's done."

"Well, I understand that you don't reward yourself until you've finished something, and that's good for your motivation, but your work is never done, is it? You have to pace yourself, slow down, enjoy being alive."

"I enjoy being with you."

"And I enjoy being with you." She smiled, looking into his eyes. "And I'd like you to go to parties with me, and let me show you off to my friends, and be more a part of my life, but I'd want you to do those things because you want to, not because I want you to. When I'm with you, it's as if I have to make a choice between you and the rest of the world. You're an outsider, but I'm not like that; I want to belong."

Tau knew the conversation wasn't going the way he'd planned, but it was plummeting like a shuttle on a fiery reentry and couldn't be stopped. "I've never asked you to make a choice between me and anything else."

"Well, that's true, in a way. I've usually dated men that wanted too much of my time, or they didn't want me to go away to some exotic location to do fieldwork during the summer months, but that's not a problem with you. I tell you I'm leaving, and I know you'll be there for me when I get back. That's very supportive, and it means a lot to me."

Tau thought of the previous summer, when he'd ached to tell her he didn't want her to spend four months in Egypt, and how much he'd missed her, but he never told her any of that because he didn't want to interfere with her career. An archaeologist had to travel during the summers to do fieldwork, and that's all there was to it.

Kate took a sip of her wine and continued. "Some guys couldn't even pretend to show an interest in my work, but you're fascinated with all the details about what I'm doing. I know you're listening when I explain something, as well as analyzing everything I say. So, you give me the space I need, and you're a great companion most of the time, but spending time with you means I have to adapt to your world and be an outsider, which is a choice I made, so that was okay. However, there was another choice I had to make this week, and that's why I wanted to see you tonight."

"Oh," said Tau, feeling the weight of the ring in his pocket. He didn't know if she was leading up to something good or bad, but the time had come to think about his marriage proposal, even though they hadn't finished their appetizers yet. But the timing seemed wrong. Then again, would the timing ever be right for this kind of thing? He wondered if maybe he should have prepared himself better by finding a book on the subject; somebody must have written one, this had to be a common problem.

Kate stroked his arm, making him tingle. "You know I think you're very attractive? I love that long black hair of yours. And for a guy that works in a lab all the time, you've got a muscular body. Sex has been wonderful. When we first started dating, I loved the fact that you were so attentive, and accommodating, and exotic. I learned more about Navajo customs from you in a week than I learned from three months of field study on the reservation. And I'm still learning from you."

"Thanks. I've learned a lot from you, too," said Tau, taking a bite of his shrimp cocktail so he'd have something to do other than having an anxiety attack. At least his hands weren't shaking now. He'd decided that when the moment was right, he'd just blurt out his question and be done with it.

"We share things, Tau. We both love to learn. I've never had a better student, or a better teacher. And you're a great friend."

Tau's heart sank. He didn't have much experience with women, but he knew what it meant when a woman told a man she was dating what a great "friend" he was. He had to say something. The time had come for desperate measures. His forgotten seafood fork rang his water glass like a bell as it dropped from his hand.

"Kate, I love you." His voice had a weak quality that surprised him.

"I know. At least, I think you believe that."

Tau took a breath and forgot to let it out. I mean, I love how you start shivering and snuggle up to me when the temperature drops below eighty degrees and I'm sitting there sweating. I love that you're impulsive; you see what you want, then you just take it. I love how you know what to say to make me feel better when I've got a problem. I love how you'll spend a night with me and have a bad dream, or wake up and be afraid of the dark, so you'll reach over and touch me with your ice-cold foot or curl up against my back. I love that you get angry for no reason when I tell you that I've had trouble with someone at work, even if it doesn't bother me. And I love that you're the last sight I want to see at night, and the last voice I want to hear. I don't think any of these things will ever change, and I don't want them to, because I want to spend the rest of my life—"

"More wine, sir?" The waiter appeared out of nowhere to hover beside the table, wine bottle poised in expectation.

"Oh, uh, no," said Tau, glancing at his full wineglass, then at Kate.

"And how is the shrimp?"

Tau glanced at the shrimp cocktail. "Fine. Everything's fine."

The waiter started to reach for Tau's forgotten seafood fork. "Do you require a clean fork, sir?"

"No," said Tau, closing his eyes and hoping the waiter would explode.

After going through the same service routine with Kate, the waiter finally left. The garibaldi tapped in silence against the glass near Tau's head, mocking him. He glared at the fish and licked his dry lips. He coughed and reached for his water glass, trying to recover his scattered thoughts. Kate had enough experience with him to allow for long pauses in the conversation without needing to rush in and fill the silence with words.

At least, she usually did. She cleared her throat.

"Tau, I said I had to make a decision this week. A rare opportunity has come up. In fact, it's more than a once-in-a-lifetime opportunity, it's the kind of thing that only happens once and can guarantee my place in the history books. This is the chance for my one big contribution to science, and I think I have to take it. I knew you'd want me to take it."

Tau blinked and almost dropped his water glass. "What?"

"I'm going to Mars."

"What?" He shook his head to clear it; he thought she'd said she was going to Mars.

"Mars. I'm going to Mars. You know, the big red planet? They want me to go to Vulcan's Forge."

"Who does?"

"Lenya Novikov is in charge of the archaeological survey team they're sending to the Tharsis tunnels. You remember Lenya, don't you? He was in charge of the dig at Amarna two years ago when we found Ankhesenpaaten."

In his confusion, Tau remembered something about the New Kingdom pharaoh Akhenaten moving the royal capital from Memphis to el-Amarna in Upper Egypt, now a ghost town whose palaces, temples, and residential quarters were abandoned after his death. Tutankhamun was Akhenaten's son, and Ankhesenpaaten was Tut's wife. During her short time working in the dig at Amarna, Kate discovered the hidden tomb of Ankhesenpaaten, which left a big impression on the Russian archaeologists in charge of the excavation. At that point, Kate was still exploring different areas of interest, mainly focusing on underwater archaeology, but Novikov recruited her for the new dig at Amarna after working with her the previous summer in Jamaica. But that still didn't explain Mars.

"I don't understand, Kate. Why you? Why Mars?"

"The Tharsis tunnels. You know; they just announced the discovery this week. Lenya said I'm perfect because I'm young enough, skilled enough, clever enough, and I've had a lot of experience with specialized technical digs."

He could remember Ankhesenpaaten, but he couldn't remember this week's news. He shook his head to indicate his confusion.

Kate sighed. "Life on Mars? Ruins under the surface near Mons Olympus? You must have heard about it."

"Well, I've been busy this week." Tau shrugged.

"You're impossible. Someone discovers evidence of an advanced alien civilization, and you don't notice it because you're too busy with your own little world."

This evening wasn't going well at all. "When are you leaving?"

Kate stared at him for a moment before answering. "To-morrow."

"Tomorrow?"

"I've got six weeks of training with Lenya's team in Houston before the next Mars flight."

"Oh," Tau swallowed. "When will you be back?"

"I don't know. Years from now, I guess, if I come back at all. My future seems to be waiting for me on another planet. I'm still having a hard time getting a handle on that. But there isn't anything holding me back here, is there?" Her voice sounded odd. Tau could barely hear her question.

"I guess not." Tau wanted to scream, but he knew it would be childish and selfish to try and change her mind. Honored with such an invitation, she couldn't say no to the Russians. His head was spinning as he fell down a deep well with no way out.

"Tau?" Her liquid voice was as smooth and silky as ever.

"Yes?"

He didn't know how Kate had gotten there without him seeing her stand up, but she leaned over to kiss him on the cheek. He closed his eyes as her hot breath hit his face. Her lips brushed his skin, and then she quickly withdrew, leaving a cold emptiness behind. A drop of water tickled his cheek on its way to his chin, but he didn't know if it belonged to him or to Kate.

"Sir?"

Tau opened his eyes. Kate was gone.

"Are you ready for your entrées, sir?"

Tau blinked at the waiter. "The bill, please."

He touched the ring in his pocket, a golden symbol of broken dreams.

Kate was gone.

AT the end of each day, Walter Beckett skimmed through any electronic messages given priority by the artificial intelligence that screened his mail. As division chief, he received a daily e-mail bombardment of memos, letters, reports, brief-

ings, news releases, updates, jokes, personal trivia, advertising holos, and random messages—far more material than a
normal human could read in a day. The AI looked for notes
from Beckett's superiors first, then deleted or prioritized the
rest.

His eyes lit up when he saw a memo from T. E. Wolfsinger,
a bright young designer he'd met at NASA-Ames. The e-mail
AI passed the message to Beckett because Wolfsinger was on
his list of potentially useful contacts. These contacts were unaware that Beckett would use whatever information they sent
him to advance his own career, but that's why they were common scientists and he was the MDO division chief.

Scanning the first few lines of Wolfsinger's memo, Beckett recognized it as the same proposal he'd ignored two days
earlier. The memo sounded boring, even though Wolfsinger's
technology could be developed at Vulcan's Forge. Although
Beckett hadn't read more than the first paragraph, the subject
didn't warrant Wolfsinger's flagrant violation of protocol.
Feigning outrage, he had contacted Director Chakrabarti to
needle him about his loss of control over the staff at Ames.
Chakrabarti seemed threatened by their conversation, aware
that the MDO was beyond his striking distance even though
he was higher in rank than Beckett. The director worked in
California, away from the center of power at NASA's Washington, DC headquarters, so he couldn't easily fight back. A
petty victory, but Beckett still felt pleased that Chakrabarti
knew enough about him to fear for his job, a job Beckett
thought he could do quite well.

The reappearance of the Wolfsinger memo meant that
Beckett's e-mail AI deemed it important. Reading further, the
proposal almost caught his interest, but there were too many
words. He'd never liked reading long reports, and Wolfsinger's ideas were complicated enough that the executive
summary ballooned over thirty pages. Chakrabarti said that a
peer review of the proposal deemed Wolfsinger a raving lunatic who might destroy the planet. This didn't inspire confidence in Beckett, so he deleted Wolfsinger's proposal from

his e-mail list. Satisfied with this decisive management action, he checked the time display hovering at the edge of his visual field and started his preparations for a game of racquetball at noon with Rupert Lindsay, the deputy director of NASA.

Lindsay didn't know Beckett, but arrangements had been made so that Lindsay's regular partner wouldn't appear today. Beckett took racquetball lessons for two months in preparation for losing to Lindsay in a convincing manner.

ANOTHER e-mail AI, working the net in secret, intercepted the Wolfsinger memo to Beckett and forwarded a copy to a distinguished-looking woman in a tasteful White House office. Her status showed in the antiques that furnished her workspace; in the powerful, insular world of the White House bureaucracy, she was unmatched in her ability to acquire prized objects as each new president rotated through the Oval Office. A tall woman, with gray streaks in her dark brown hair, she looked suitably imposing behind the desk of Abraham Lincoln. Displayed on the desktop were the writing quills used by Thomas Jefferson, Teddy Roosevelt's gold bust of Machiavelli, and the crystal jelly bean jar that represented Ronald Reagan's legacy. She sat in the simple but sturdy oak chair of George Washington, viewing projections of reports from the quaint supercomputer workstation used by Frank Hernandez. Some of the antiques were uncomfortable or impractical, but appearances mattered. Her visitors sat in wobbly, low chairs facing the high fortress walls of the massive desk; from that vantage point, visitors couldn't see her facial expressions against the glare of the light behind her head.

David, her secretary, knocked and poked his head into her office. "The president wants to see you. He's out here."

"Does he have an appointment I don't know about?"

"No."

She glanced at her schedule. "Come back in two hours."

David nodded and shut the door.

Presidents would come and go, but Dr. Virginia Danforth

always remained to control them. Her formal, public titles, as special assistant to the president for science and technology, and as senior director for national security and international affairs on the National Security Council, exempted her from public scrutiny, allowing her to remain at the center of governmental control. Six presidents had depended on Danforth's decisions, aware that failure to follow her "suggestions" would lead to complications. She lurked in the background, leaving the elected and appointed figureheads to fulfill their roles as entertainers, roles necessary to maintain the illusion of a government run "by the People, for the People." The public didn't need to know that "the People," in this case, referred to the small and secretive membership of the Davos Group, the elite inner circle of international power.

Danforth also worked as a tactical problem solver for the Davos Group, which controlled front institutions such as the American CFR, the Council on Foreign Relations. Every major American politician belonged to the CFR, making it a virtual extension of the federal government. Private members of the CFR included executives from the major media conglomerates, as well as the directors of the thirteen public banks that comprised the Federal Reserve. While the public CFR received acclaim for its accurate public forecasts of emerging international trends, the average citizen didn't realize that the CFR played a major role in *creating* those trends. The Davos Group established strategic policies, which were then carried out by the CFR and its sister organizations in the rest of the "global village." When governments and monarchs needed money, Davos would lend a hand, directing the financial dynasties of Europe and America to make money available at high interest rates so that Davos could establish political leverage over the borrowers.

Noting the source of Beckett's e-mail intercept, Danforth read it twice. A follow-up sniffer AI reported Beckett's lack of response to the Wolfsinger proposal. Judging by his recent interest in courting the media, she knew Beckett showed more interest in becoming the popular voice of NASA than in doing his job as a minor functionary. An AI background analysis revealed the ambitious Beckett as a charming but incompetent pencil pusher without influential friends to protect him, nor CFR membership to control him, and that placed him in the category of "bug" in Danforth's mind. Now the bug was turning into an impediment regarding the Wolfsinger proposal. Certain members of the Davos Group were interested in Wolfsinger's technology, but not enough to initiate direct contact with the NASA scientist. Danforth needed to study Wolfsinger from a distance, through Beckett, unless Beckett became a problem.

If the MDO chief didn't cooperate, he would be discarded.

7

TAU returned to his apt at midnight. He felt sorry for himself, and he didn't like that. Kate didn't want him, she wanted a career, and he loved her enough not to interfere with her dream, even if it meant never seeing her again. He felt hollow and broken. His experience with Kate taught him that he needed her affection; he needed to know that someone cared about him and his daily life. His parents loved him, but he needed more than that to feel *hozro*, to feel that he was in balance with life. No one else had ever come so close to understanding him, and he'd hoped that many years with Kate would have given her the insight to understand the rest. Their relationship seemed so effortless that he hadn't realized more effort was required to keep it together. And she wasn't just moving to a different town to get away from him, she felt it necessary to leave the *planet*. Rejection in its purest form.

This wasn't a feeling he wished to experience now or ever again.

His body dragged, but he was too alert to sleep. Neurobabble filled his brain, most of it images of Kate and depressing thoughts that reminded him to feel worthless. The sound of the shower filtered into his awareness as he realized he was standing in the hallway of the apt, staring off into space without seeing anything. He thought his eyes were misty, then noticed he was staring through the open door of the bathroom, cloudy with thin layers of steam. Busy washing her hair in the shower with her eyes closed, Yvette hadn't noticed Tau watching her through the clear glass walls of the shower stall. Of all the options for washing herself, Tau noted that she preferred to shower the old way, letting the water run down the soft curves of her glistening body, looking more like an idealized painting than a true human form. She rotated in the shower, dipping her head under the water to let cascades of foam break free of her hair to raft down the tiny rivers coursing over her perfect skin.

"Tau?"

Her voice startled him. "Huh?"

She blinked the water out of her eyes, squinting at him. "Is that you?"

"Umm, yeah."

"What are you doing?" She stepped out of the shower and reached for a towel. She didn't seem angry, just curious.

"Umm, nothing, really."

Yvette smiled, drying her face with the towel.

"Vadim told me you had a date with your archaeologist tonight. I didn't think you'd be coming home."

"Oh. Me too. Or, well, I planned on not being here, but now I am, as it turns out." He noticed the towel was too small to cover everything, but she didn't seem to mind.

"Want to go to bed now?"

Tau blinked. "Huh?"

The towel moved up and down in rhythmic motions. Tau watched it move, thinking how great it would be to live the life of a bath towel, particularly the towel he watching right now. Yvette smiled, making his skin tingle.

"Well, I wanted to talk to you about work if you felt like it, but if you're going to bed, I can wait and talk to you tomorrow. I know it's pretty late."

"Oh. I am. Yes. Umm, going to bed, I mean. I think. I'm not sure."

She moved closer and patted his forearm. She smelled nice; clean and scented with some kind of flower smell, maybe from the soap, or maybe it was her natural smell, he wasn't sure. In any case, he liked it.

"You look tired, Tau. Are you working here or in the office tomorrow?"

Tau forced himself to think before answering, but there wasn't much happening in the neuron department. "Umm, I don't know. Haven't decided."

Yvette took a step back and bent over to dry her legs. Tau stopped breathing.

"Think you'll have time for me tomorrow? I know you're busy. I mean, we can meet wherever you want, here or at the office, whenever you've got the time," she said, looking up with a sweet smile as she moved the towel over her feet. "Your wish is my command, or something like that."

Tau coughed. "Umm, sure. Yes. Office. We can talk whenever you want," he said, proud of himself for forming a complete sentence.

"Great. Thanks a lot." She wrapped the towel around her head and walked past, rubbing against him in the tight space of the doorway before he could step back out of the way. She looked back and smiled as she bounced down the hallway. "Night, Tau."

He mumbled something and hoped it sounded like "good night." He looked down at the damp spots on his shirt and pants where Yvette had rubbed against him, thinking it wasn't so bad sharing the apt with this particular engineer. He rubbed his hand against the dampness on his shirt, then decided to move out of the bathroom doorway so he wouldn't look like an idiot if she came back. He now faced the kitchen, so he walked in there and looked around. He wasn't hungry, so he entered the living room and sat down on the sim couch, thinking he might escape into another world for the night, rather than staring at the ceiling above his bed. Thoughts of Kate were returning, interspersed with images of Yvette in the shower.

It was all so confusing.

YVETTE examined her body in the mirror as she dried her hair. Her fingertips were wrinkled from spending such a long time in the shower—she'd started to think Tau would *never* show up. Since she considered Tau to be her special project, she liked to keep track of his movements; after Vadim told her where Tau would be having dinner, it was a simple matter to call the restaurant periodically for updates. When Yvette learned that he'd left by himself, she assumed he'd come home right away. She'd been trying for days to catch him in the apt, and she admired herself for the quality of this evening's performance.

Tau would be key to her future plans. After her first day at work, Yvette coerced the man in the NASA Housing Office into reassigning her to Tau's apt. Molecular designers made decent salaries, so they were only required to have two single individuals per apt in the government housing towers. Roommates were usually paired according to technical specialties or other job similarities, ideally to promote teamwork and "work all the time" attitudes, so this made it easier for Yvette to talk her way into Tau's apt. However, his relationship with Kate could be an impediment. Yvette would do her best to show Tau what he was missing, but if he didn't respond, she intended to mold him into a mentor role that would enable her to pick his brains. If anyone had superior design talent, Tau certainly did, but he would be a tough molecule to crack.

Yvette frowned as she noticed a small patch of downy blond hair on the tanned skin at the base of her spine, brushing her fingers over it to confirm its existence. The offending protein strands would have to be removed. She thought briefly of calling Tau in to help her, then decided she might be rushing things a bit.

Her long-term goal involved the transfer of NASA's new phased array Nano-VR technology to the more profitable field of entertainment. With experience in its use, and the lower cost of the technology once it matured, Yvette knew she could get the financial backing to build a sim that would take entertainment to a new level of reality, perhaps with the inclusion of behavioral control methods for sponsored consumer marketing. With everyone wearing brain-stem receivers anyway, she couldn't understand why no one used them to manipulate consumer purchases, a process she intended to call "direct brain marketing." Behavioral control would require clever sim programming—not one of her strong skills—but she knew she could find someone to perform that task.

She turned sideways to study her body in profile, hiding the unsightly hair on her back. The cool air in the room formed goose bumps on her skin—an involuntary reaction that surgery couldn't prevent. Wanting every advantage for her career, she'd rewarded herself with enhancement at a San Francisco body shop when she got her master's degree; an expensive visit, but reactions to her new appearance were worth it, at least most of the time. When she returned to the university in the fall, her intellectual friends among the computer science and chemistry students were intimidated by her new confidence and powerful sexuality. Later on, it occurred to her that she might look *too* good for her chosen profession, at least in the near term. She could make her appearance work for her at NASA, but it would take more effort than she'd planned. In any case, the conquest of Tau would be good experience. After tonight, the hook was set.

COLONEL General Viktor Aleksandrovich Zhukov followed Laika, his bold miniature Pekingese, down a rough-walled granite tunnel illuminated by yellowish green maintenance lighting. Beside him walked Colonel Oleg Kosygin, still awed by the immensity of Final Harvest and the greater mystery of Fallen Angel.

The tunnel curved to the left and stopped. A young guard slumped against the base of an average-size metal door, his rifle leaning against the rough wall. The door was marked with a red flower-shaped symbol and "BL-0," indicating a level zero biocontainment facility. Two security cameras over the door watched the group. Without a word, Zhukov looked at Kosygin and rolled his eyes with a heavy sigh, then stopped in front of the soldier. From his relaxed pose, the soldier could have been dead, but his snoring made his situation even worse.

"In the old days, I could have shot this man without any questions," said Zhukov.

Laika strained at the leash with soft growls, so Zhukov extended his arm enough to allow the dog access to the soldier's left leg. Quick as a rattlesnake, Laika shot forward and chomped down on the man's leg just above the boot. The soldier yelped and rolled away, then jumped to his feet. Massaging his wound, his angry expression switched to surprise when he saw Zhukov and Kosygin.

"Sir! I—"

"You are new, are you not?" Zhukov interrupted, pointing his extended arm at the guard so Laika could waddle closer and growl at him.

"Yes, sir," said the guard, who suddenly remembered his job. He grabbed his rifle, held it across his body, and asked, "May I see some identification, sir?"

Zhukov raised an eyebrow at the guard and turned his back so the wall scanner could identify him. The guard looked at a small display on his sleeve, then gave Zhukov a formal salute. "Thank you, sir!"

As Zhukov turned to face the guard again, showing no emotion, the man's eyes widened in fear. He glanced down at his sleeve display again and his posture stiffened. "*Izvinite!*

I'm sorry I didn't recognize you, sir! I beg your forgiveness, sir!"

"You appear to know me by reputation, soldier. Is that correct?"

The guard started sweating. "Yes, sir! You're the Angel of Death, sir!"

"You know your history," Zhukov nodded. "That's good. Although it's been a few decades since the Taipan Conflict, I'm sure you're aware we used biological weapons against the Chinese corporate warlords?"

"Yes, sir!"

"Do you have any idea what's on the other side of that door you're guarding?"

"No, sir!"

"Perhaps you'd like a tour of the lab. The colonel and I will be wearing pressurized biological suits to protect us, but I'm afraid there are only two available. However, the chances of your encountering a biowar agent in there are pretty small, so you'll probably survive. Would you like to see?"

The guard hesitated, blinking rapidly as sweat dripped into his eyes. "No, sir! I'm not cleared for that area, sir! Thank you, sir!"

"You're not curious? We don't need to tell anyone else you were in the lab—unless there's an accident, of course."

"No, sir! Thank you, sir!"

Laika growled, eyeing the hole torn in the soldier's pant leg.

"As you wish." Zhukov shrugged. "Perhaps next time, if I catch you napping again. As it is, judging by the bulge in your stomach, you appear to have been eating too much recently. I will leave orders for you to be fed only shrapnel for the next month so that you may think about this decisive moment in your life and reflect on your mistakes."

"Thank you, sir!"

"We used to eat pearl barley gruel three times a day when I was your age," continued Zhukov, "and our soldiers felt lucky to have it. It was always poorly cooked and as hard to digest as real enemy shrapnel, but we were so happy to be fed at all that we didn't complain. It's unfortunate that you missed this culinary experience during your military service, but I don't want you to feel deprived, particularly when you have such a good grasp of history already. Do not let me catch you asleep again."

The guard's relief was evident on his face. Although the cavern air was cool, dark stains were spreading under the arms of his uniform. "No, sir! Thank you, sir!"

"You will watch Laika while we're inside, and she will watch you. If you make any mistakes, she will know it. Let us in."

The guard pressed a hidden button on the wall. The door hissed open. As Zhukov and Kosygin walked into the next room, air whistled past in what seemed to be the wrong direction.

"Shouldn't the air be flowing the other way?" Kosygin asked, as the door closed behind them.

"The lab is a negative pressure facility, Oleg. If a leak ever developed in the biocontainment areas, the air would flow *into* the lab, rather than out to the unprotected chambers of Final Harvest. We would not wish to kill anyone other than the lab workers."

"That's reassuring."

"This is a level zero biosafety area, but it connects to a level four biocontainment lab, which is as hot as they get. We have no level two or three labs here, since the facility was built to my specifications, although we will pass through those decontamination levels on our way to four."

"What about level one?"

"There is no such thing. I don't know why. Perhaps the Americans who developed the classification system forgot a number."

The small room contained tall gray lockers along two walls, some benches, and a sink with a mirror near the door to level two. Zhukov opened a locker with his name on it. "Find a locker and change into the scrub suit you'll find there. Remove any watches or jewelry. You must wear only the scrub suit as we continue, and your hair must be covered with a surgical cap. You will be barefoot until we go through the next room."

Kosygin opened a locker and started changing his clothes. "I'm guessing from our surroundings that Fallen Angel is part of a biowar weapon? Is that what you used in the Taipan Conflict?"

Zhukov removed his shirt, exposing the glint of fine metallic flexrods embedded in his pale skin; the powered exoskeleton gave him the strength and reflexes of a young man. "Why does the Taipan incident concern you, Oleg? It's ancient history."

Kosygin stepped into the scrub suit pants and tied the drawstring at his waist. "Although I've known you a long time, you've never told me all of the details. And if Fallen Angel is intended for biological warfare, I'd like to know."

Wearing only their scrub suits, they crossed the locker room to stop outside another metal door marked with a biohazard symbol and a numeral 2. A shaft of deep blue light streamed through a small window in the door, giving Zhukov's face an eerie glow as he turned to look at Kosygin with his hand on the doorknob.

"You misunderstood my conversation with the young sleeper. Fallen Angel is not a biowar agent. And the Taipan situation was a difficult episode in my past. The Chinese tried to poach our oil resources because they had developed the technology to punch through the permafrost. Their main long-distance access tunnel was built with smaller, more advanced versions of the laser-guided boring machines used to dig the tunnel under the English Channel. We discovered the hidden tunnel, diplomacy failed, and I was in the wrong place at the wrong time, so I found myself in command of a defensive force. As it turned out, the Chinese corporate warlords were ready for us with high-tech weapons and troops in their tunnels, and several divisions were lost in the underground war. We fought like sewer rats. Support was delayed. Lacking other resources, I got approval to use a bioweapon from a military research lab in Novosibirsk. It was a derivative of the Mayinga strain of Ebola Zaire virus, bioengineered to have a short life span and rapid incubation, which we dropped into surface ventilation intakes along the length of the Chinese tunnel. Hundreds died within hours, but thousands more were saved. Escalation to nuclear weapons was averted, so it's possible that millions were saved. But it was not a proud moment in my career. Remote battle cameras showed us the convulsing victims splashing blood on each other as their connective tissues liquefied. When the news came out, I was reviled in the media as the 'Angel of Death,' which made a good story without the details of why I resorted to biowar. They acted as if I was the first person to use a bioweapon. Our leadership not only approved the use of Ebola, but they threw me to the dogs of the media along with images from the remote tunnel cameras."

Zhukov relaxed his death grip on the doorknob and took a deep breath. "Now, the 'Taipan Catacombs,' loaded with Russian and Chinese skeletons, have become a tourist attraction!"

Kosygin paused a moment, frowning at the floor. "I had often wondered why someone with your talents was living the life of an earthworm."

"Our political leadership wanted me to be a scapegoat and disappear, since I didn't have the grace to die from my battle wounds, so they assigned me to remote underground bases while they destroyed my reputation to save themselves. I gradually became used to the idea of living in the shadows, which is what I was doing when they put me on the satellite study of Tunguska. I was comforted by the fact that Marshal Zhukov had also found himself out of favor with the leadership after the Great Patriotic War, so he, too, was banished into obscurity. But things change; now there are statues of Georgy Zhukov in every major Russian city."

"Perhaps there will be statues of you someday, General."

Zhukov looked into the deep blue light shining through the

glass in the door. "Perhaps. If Red Star succeeds, and the country is reunited once more, statues will not be necessary to commemorate my existence on this world."

"Red Star? What's that?"

Zhukov turned the doorknob, still staring into the blue light. "First things first, Oleg. You must meet the Fallen Angel."

When Zhukov opened the door, it resisted his pull on the knob, held by the difference in air pressure between the two rooms. Air whispered around his body, seeming to draw the two men in toward the blue light. Inside waited a shower stall flooded with blue light, a bar of soap, and shampoo. The floor was dry, so it didn't appear that the shower had seen any recent use.

"The blue light is ultraviolet to kill any viruses we might be carrying. On our way out, we'll make use of the shower."

Continuing through the stall, they entered a bathroom with clean white socks on a shelf. Zhukov handed Kosygin a pair of socks as he leaned against the wall to put on his own. The flexrod fibers on his bare feet sparkled as he moved.

In the level three room, they found latex rubber surgical gloves and baby powder. Kosygin watched as Zhukov shook powder on his hands, then pulled on the gloves. "Once you have the gloves on, you'll need to tape up the openings in your clothes to form your first layer of protection."

"I feel like I'm going into surgery," said Kosygin, powdering his hands.

"It may seem pointless once we get inside, but we've found it necessary. We never know before it happens, but Fallen Angel has proven to be unforgiving at random moments in the presence of humans."

"Is it intelligent?"

Zhukov was tearing strips of tape from a roll and sticking them to the edge of a table. "Patience, Oleg."

Zhukov used the strips to tape the cuffs of his gloves to the sleeves of his scrub suit, running the tape around his arm twice to form a good seal. Then he taped his socks to his trouser cuffs in the same fashion. As Kosygin wrestled with the sticky tape, Zhukov opened a large locker containing a baggy plastic spacesuit. Heavy brown rubber gloves were attached to the wrists by gaskets. The helmet was of soft, flexible plastic with a clear faceplate.

Zhukov lifted the bright blue suit and showed it to Kosygin. "This is a Chemturion biosuit, also known as a 'blue suit.'"

Zhukov opened up the suit and laid it on the concrete floor so he could step into it. Lifting it up around his chest, he inserted his arms in the sleeves until his fingers wiggled into the attached gloves. "Remain aware of what your hands are doing. The gloves are always the weakest points in biosuits. In this environment, sharp tools or jagged edges can kill you if you get cut."

Zhukov ran his palm along an oiled seal that ran across the chest of the suit, snapping it closed. Kosygin saw the faceplate fog from Zhukov's breath as he reached up to grab a coiled yellow air hose hanging from the ceiling. He connected the hose to a valve below his neck. The flexible plastic had been hanging loose around the general's body, but the flowing air hissing into his suit made it bloat up and snap tight. The foggy faceplate cleared as Kosygin opened a locker containing another Chemturion suit.

"It's like a small submarine," said Kosygin, opening up the suit to set it on the floor.

"What?" Zhukov cupped his hand next to his head as if he were hard of hearing.

"The suit, it's like a submarine," Kosygin yelled, working his legs into the pants as Zhukov reached up and bent a kink in his air line so he could hear better.

"*Da*. And like a submarine, some people get claustrophobic when they get inside," said Zhukov, holding the front of the suit as Kosygin worked his arms into the cocoon.

"What happens to the people who panic?"

"They struggle, turn purple, fall down, and lose any respect I may have had for them. Sometimes they make strange animal noises, but they're muffled inside the suit, fortunately."

Kosygin's faceplate fogged as Zhukov helped him close the seal on the chest of his suit. "I'll try not to panic."

"Good. I'd hate to bring you this far, only to have you end up flopping around on the floor like a beached fish."

When Kosygin was ready, Zhukov beckoned for him to follow. The next door, marked as level four, looked like it belonged on the front of a bank vault. Zhukov rotated a heavy lever on the face of the door; it hissed as he pulled it open to reveal the airlock on the other side.

"This is the decontamination shower. It soaks the suit with EnviroChem disinfectant as you leave the hot lab."

Zhukov detached his air hose and stepped into the stainless-steel chamber lined with spray nozzles. Kosygin followed, pulling the vault door shut behind them. A green light blinked on the wall.

"Are we there yet?"

"Almost," said Zhukov, rotating a spoked wheel to release the far door.

Yellow air hoses dangled from the walls in the next corridor, allowing them to hook up their suits again. The noise of the rushing air in their suits made it hard to talk or hear. Zhukov pointed at a strobe light on the ceiling.

"If you ever see this light flash, it means the air system has stopped working, in which case you should leave."

"I might have guessed that," yelled Kosygin, looking around at the rock walls painted with thick epoxy paint. The electrical outlets were all plugged with a gooey material that sealed any cracks or holes in the hollow electrical conduits. Zhukov reached down to remove two pairs of yellow boots from a stainless-steel cabinet, then slid the soft feet of his bio-suit into one pair as he handed Kosygin the other pair.

"Here are your new shoes, Oleg."

"Let me guess—the next thing we'll do to protect ourselves is to climb inside a battle tank you've got waiting behind the next door."

Zhukov laughed as they continued down the corridor. "If Fallen Angel decides to perform for us, you'll be happy you're protected. After we moved it to the Kola Peninsula base, I lost eight people before we realized what was happening. It was not a pretty sight."

"You still haven't told me what it is, General."

Zhukov opened the final door, which was unlocked. "See for yourself."

POOLS of bright light illuminated work areas in the otherwise dim cavern. A man wearing a blue Chemturion suit bent over a workbench, probing at what appeared to be a large chunk of ice. Two insulated hoses ran from a tank on the wall to the workbench, where a steaming liquid poured from their openings onto his work surface. As Zhukov and Kosygin moved closer, they could see ice crystals at the mouths of the hoses and on the bench surrounding the object under study.

"Oleg, this is Professor Vasilyev, formerly attached to the Russian Academy of Sciences."

Vasilyev lifted his gaze, glanced at Zhukov, nodded at Kosygin, then returned his attention to the object on the workbench.

"You will find that the professor is not one to waste words," said Zhukov, with a wink at Kosygin.

"If I may ask, what is he working on?"

"This is a piece of the Angel. We use liquid nitrogen to keep the structure cool. Warmer temperatures have a tendency to make the Angel's 'skin' decay, and when it decays, it gives off a vapor that humans find rather distressing."

Kosygin moved closer to examine the icy chunk on the table. "Distressing? In what way?"

"It kills them."

"Ah. That would be disturbing to most people. And that's why we're wearing these suits?"

Zhukov stepped behind Vasilyev so that he could look over the professor's shoulder. "Correct. The professor still hasn't forgiven me for killing his lab assistants, although we could not have predicted the problems with the gas. The Angel has many strange properties."

"It's some sort of meteorite, then?"

"Nothing so mundane, my friend. As I said before, the Tunguska object at the center of the crater in the peat bog was metallic, although its outer skin is partially organic. Show Oleg the next layer, Professor."

Kosygin squinted at a thick bluish "skin" under the thin layer of ice crystals. Vasilyev sighed, then used a hammer and chisel to cut a neat line through the skin and pull it back. Beneath it lay a shiny crystal surface. A clear liquid dripped onto the bench from the cut, freezing on contact with the cold metal.

"The second layer is a sort of living crystal, essentially diamond with streaks of iridium and another unknown metal," Zhukov said.

"Living crystal?"

Vasilyev released the flap of skin he'd been holding. The skin drew itself back into place, the liquid stopped dripping, and the seam from the cut began to disappear. Zhukov pointed at the seam.

"The skin heals. We don't have any idea why it was designed that way, but the organic surface covers the harder diamond layer."

Kosygin frowned and shook his head. "I don't understand. You say this isn't some form of meteorite, but it's made of living organic material with bodily fluids. Is it a living creature?"

Vasilyev snorted and continued his work, picking up a hand laser and focusing its ruby light on an exposed circle of the diamond layer. Zhukov shrugged. "It depends on how you define life, I suppose. Although the professor would not agree with me, I've spent enough time around the Angel to sense that it has, or had, some sort of rational decision-making process, even if it's only on an animal level. I think the toxic biological material that it contains is used as a form of self-defense, although its protective system is not completely in-

tact. But I'm not a scientist. Now, come with me, and I'll confuse you further."

Kosygin followed Zhukov past long rows of scientific
equipment. Ropes of steam coiled out of the darkness at the
far end of the room. At the opening of a dark tunnel in the cavern wall, a vast bulk of indeterminate shape rested in the shadows. Zhukov stopped beside a row of switches on the wall.
Kosygin felt butterflies in his stomach.

"Nervous, Oleg?"

"Yes. And I'm dizzy. I don't know why."

"The Angel has that effect on people. I feel anxious whenever I get close to the thing. We keep it at the back of the lab
so that it doesn't interfere with our work."

Zhukov snapped two switches on. Overhead lamps in the
cavern recess glowed to life, illuminating the Fallen Angel in
sharply defined pools of light. Steam coiled up toward the
lamps, rising from a mesh of tubes fed by liquid nitrogen
lines. The cooling mesh surrounded an oblong line of large
chunks that looked like the same material as the lump on Vasilyev's workbench.

"What is it? It looks like an old nuclear submarine, except
it's covered with that organic coating you showed me."

Zhukov studied Kosygin's face. "Maybe you could tell *me*
what it is. We've been studying the Angel for years, but we
know very little about it."

"Perhaps you need other scientists?"

"The need for secrecy is too great. Perhaps when old Vasilyev is no longer able to carry out his duties, then we'll consider it. Remember, there are only a handful of people who
know about the Angel, and I intend to keep it that way."

"All this time, and you have no idea of its nature?"

Zhukov's eyes glazed over as he turned to look at the massive hulk, lying in ragged sections along the length of the tunnel. "Oh, we know a few things, and we've speculated about
the rest. We think it's a spacecraft—an alien spacecraft. There
is machinery in the small section of the ship we've been able
to enter, but it's composed of a material that's similar to the

ship's hull. We've only been able to get inside through a section of the ship that was torn off in the crash; the hole was apparently too big for the ship to heal itself there. The machinery we found was damaged also. The professor hasn't been able to determine how the ship or any of the equipment operates, although we might get more clues when we're able to break into other sections of the craft. Judging by the Angel's weight, and the location where we discovered it in Tunguska, what we have here is a small fragment of the larger body that entered our atmosphere in 1908."

Kosygin walked closer to the Angel's cooling mesh, then turned to look at Zhukov. "Something such as this—why must we keep it a secret? We need help to understand it. Perhaps it has some connection to the alien tunnels at Vulcan's Forge."

Zhukov reached out to pat Kosygin's shoulder. "Your idealism is misplaced, Oleg, but you have a quick mind. The Tharsis tunnels appear to have a connection with this spacecraft, but not for the reason you think. While it's true that we may need help to understand it, we can't tell the world about our little discovery because we intend to use the Angel ourselves as soon as we can solve its mysteries. A potential weapon of this magnitude is not something we'd wish to share with our enemies."

"With all respect, General, the Russian Federation is not at war. This is a scientific discovery of greater magnitude than its potential as a weapon."

Zhukov's hand fell to his side, clenched into a fist. He glared at Kosygin, who took a step back when he saw the anger building in Zhukov's red face.

"I apologize, General. I was wrong to argue."

Zhukov closed his eyes and took a deep breath. "I realize you've been isolated from information about our true situation, Colonel, but do not make the mistake of thinking you have a right to an opinion. Twenty years in my service does not buy you that privilege."

"Again, General, I apologize. *Izvinite*."

Zhukov looked calmer when he opened his eyes. "As to

your previous comment, Russia *is* at war, and it has always been at war. However, your comment was made in ignorance. I should tell you more. Since you will not be leaving this place, my associates would understand the necessity of briefing you."

"You're speaking of too many things. An alien ship, Mars, a war—and who are these associates you mention? I'm just a simple soldier, and my dizziness is getting worse."

"You'll get used to it," said Zhukov, gesturing for Kosygin to walk with him alongside the Angel. "Walk with me. We'll take a little tour and I'll tell you a story."

"Can we go inside the ship?"

"It would please me to have you look at the ship's cargo. Maybe you can guess its purpose. There are alien relics on Mars that bear similar markings, and that's part of the reason I've been assigned to command the Red Star military base in the Margaritifer Sinus region."

"Military base? You mean the old Russian research station?"

"Research station, military base, it's all a game of semantics, isn't it? Since we've been shipping elite Red Army troops up there for the last two years, I'd think it qualifies as a military base now."

"Elite troops? Is someone planning a war on Mars?"

"Not exactly. We've explained the Red Star mission to our leadership as future warfare readiness training in the unique environment of Mars. It conflicts with the civilian mission of Vulcan's Forge, so we've continued to expand our Margaritifer Sinus facilities. What we haven't explained to the Russian leadership is that Red Star researchers discovered an abandoned alien colony constructed under the permafrost layer, although we didn't know that when the first Russians landed there. We assume the aliens selected the same location for local resource advantages, just as we did."

Kosygin's head swam as he followed Zhukov through a gap in the cooling mesh. They could feel the chill through their pressurized suits as they walked toward a jagged tear in the hull. Work lights illuminated the interior of the craft. A welcoming yellow glow spilled out toward them through the gaping hole blasted in the Angel's flank.

Zhukov spoke in a loud voice to overcome the noisy hiss of air in their suits. "Russia must be united against its enemies, Oleg. It's a basic social principle that a society without an external enemy will create one internally. When the Soviet Union collapsed under its own ponderous weight, the enemies we'd been taught to fear in the rest of the world all ceased to exist. We had our border wars as the new system established itself, but the unity of purpose was lost. We were no longer a united country feared by the rest of civilization; we became individual states susceptible to subtler attacks through economics, diplomacy, tourism, and the free flow of uncensored information. The external enemy was gone, replaced by the internal bureaucracy of the individual Russian states—same bureaucrats, new department names, but the problems were less obvious when they could be blamed on the West. Except for fewer travel restrictions and the introduction of foreign fast-food restaurants, the average Russian couldn't tell the difference between the old government and the new one. But they knew they needed *enemies*."

Kosygin entered the alien ship with caution, placing his feet in spots where Zhukov had already stepped. Rubble and loose chunks of machinery littered the floor. The bright work lights made everything stand out in sharp contrasts. Lacking mysterious shadows or dramatic lighting, the interior of the alien craft seemed almost mundane, as if it had been constructed in the machine shops of Kaliningrad for the Russian Space Agency.

Kosygin tried to concentrate on Zhukov's conversation. "Who would you suggest as Russia's new enemy, General?"

"An excellent question, my friend. If one is to create a suitable enemy, there is also the factor of how to manipulate relationships with our friends."

"Then you're not suggesting a return to the old philosophy

of the Motherland against the rest of the world? We'd still have friends in other countries?"

Zhukov stopped on a spot swept free of debris, then turned to look at Kosygin with a puzzled expression. "You think I'm some kind of a bomb-throwing anarchist, Oleg?"

"No, sir, but—"

Zhukov raised a hand to silence him. "True power over the masses lies in financial control. This is why we need friends, since our own economy has never achieved any stability. But our leadership is blind and self-serving, so they fail to see the obvious improvements that could be made. We could have ruled most of the world by now with good leaders fifty years ago, or a hundred years ago. But politics is a game for politicians; real progress can only be made by unreasonable men such as ourselves who are not under constant scrutiny by an ignorant public."

While listening to Zhukov, Kosygin ran his hands over the strange, somewhat hieroglyphic, symbols that decorated much of the alien machinery. Despite the rubble on the floor, the loose cabling, the jumbled machinery, and the glare of the work lights, he stared in awe, quite conscious of the fact that the Angel had come from another world, built by an advanced civilization.

"If we could understand the technology behind this spacecraft, or if we could learn enough about the machinery we found on Mars, we'd have a vast technological edge over the rest of the world. Combined with the money and political support of our powerful friends, we could implement rapid takeovers of the key world governments. The systems and methods for doing so have been in place for decades, waiting for the right opportunity. This alien technology is the key to our goals. Russia will once again be a superpower!"

Startled by Zhukov's sudden shout, Kosygin didn't notice the alien hieroglyphics glowing under his fingers until he felt the heat from the smooth surface. When he looked down at his hand and saw colored slits of light shining through his gloves, he jerked his hand away. "Ah!"

Zhukov started to say something, but he stopped when he saw the glow from the colored symbols.

"What did I do?" Kosygin asked with a shaky voice.

Zhukov bent over to study the shining glyphs. "I don't know. I've never seen this reaction before. What were you doing when they started to glow?"

Oleg shrugged. "Nothing. I was just running my hands over those symbols."

Zhukov's fingers brushed the raised bumps of the lettering. "Very curious. I should get the professor to look at this. Perhaps I should have brought you out here to meet the Angel before now, Oleg. This is quite impressive."

"I still don't know what I did."

They both ducked as a loud boom, the voice of an angry god, echoed through the ship.

Y Ddraig Goch—Battle Lord of the North, Voice of the Masters, Strike Director, and First Command Unit of the Line—was built for war. His silver-blue bulk, a dense structure of heavy elements interlaced with broad-field sensors, peak-action triggers, and weapon arrays, loomed high above a cooling bath of liquid nitrogen. The metal glowthreads of his backshield cape, spread wide like the wings of a *cambat*, glittered in the shifting blue arc lights shining down from the cavern ceiling of Firebase Ynysmarchog, his forward command post in the eastern marches. Although the Battle Lords themselves knew that the cooling pools were necessary due to processor design flaws unique to their class, lesser machines viewed them as luxuries reserved for the four rulers. Ddraig often wondered why the Masters had constructed the powerful Battle Lords with their brains in their feet, but he was sure the Great Race must have had a good reason. As they all knew from the Code, the Masters were without flaw. The overclocked massively parallel processors were cool enough under normal operation, but they sometimes overheated under battle conditions; with hot feet, the Battle Lords lost some of their phenomenal computation abilities. Whenever Ddraig had trouble thinking, or if he needed to work out a complicated battle plan, he would soak his feet. In any case, the popular image of the cooling pools as symbols of luxury helped to keep the warriors, workers, and thinkers in awe of their supreme commanders.

Behind Ddraig stood the squat form of Y Marcross, his trusted Chancellor, holding another symbol of his office—the Crossed Detonators. The Detonators were multispiked antennae whose crystalchrome surfaces could multiplex a Battle Lord's planetary destruct impulse into the complicated signal that would trigger bombs in distant target zones. Planetary destructors were never used in daily domestic warfare on Yr Wyddfa; the Code of the Masters specified that Battle Lords could only use them for distant strikes against True Enemies.

Looking down through the mists that curled up from the pool, Ddraig studied the unit being escorted into his audience chamber. The identity transponder issued a recognition signal at Ddraig's probe, informing him that the visitor was a low-order field observer, Y Moch. Moch's carbon black body was covered in rotating scanners and antennae, making it seem as if he never stopped moving. Nanoseconds passed in silence, a lengthy pause that Ddraig always used to unsettle his visitors, before his voice rumbled out across the action frequency. "Y Moch, report!"

Moch's forward imaging array flickered in hesitation, but Ddraig's control voice could not be denied. "My lord Ddraig Goch, your listening posts along the ancient Nantgwyddon border zone have detected a beacon signal. Although the transmission came from one of your regiment's ships of the line, it was intercepted on a tachyon frequency that is no longer in use by your long-range forces. We are trained to view this type of signal as a potential enemy trick, but I am to report all such contacts to you, Most High One. The records at my disposal do not show any of your lordship's vessels in that distant quadrant."

"You have the data dump for me, Moch?"

"Of course, my lord," said the observer, bowing his head in transmission.

Ddraig contemplated the data burst for almost a full teraflop before realizing its importance. The communication had come from an abandoned battle sector well beyond the normal range of his fleet. The Nantgwyddon border now defined the operational limits of Ddraig's command in that sector of the galaxy.

A red scanner glowed to life on the Chancellor's face. Y Marcross tilted his upper body to focus on the small form of Moch, then emitted a service query to the Battle Lord. "Reaction, High One?"

"Curious," said Ddraig, studying forgotten bits of his memory. "Only two of our expedition vessels have ever crossed the restricted Nantgwyddon zone. This occurred before the resolution of the conflict between the organics of Gwrinydd and the Masters, so the Barrier was not yet in place."

Moch stood at attention. "Although I am but a humble fastener in the sole of your mighty foot, my lord, may I venture to ask what happened to those ships? My own records do not go back that far in time."

Ddraig looked at Moch with his facial-imaging shields angled, making it clear how he felt about being questioned by dirt. The Chancellor took a step back to make sure he was out of the blast zone if the Battle Lord chose to terminate the observer's existence.

Noting the motion of Marcross, Moch ducked his upper body toward the ground into a pose of Supreme Error. "This unworthy unit begs your forgiveness, my lord. I am but a useless cog in the Great Machine. I have committed a General Protection Fault by wasting your processor time with my pointless question."

It took less than a picosecond for Ddraig's forward cannon battery to hum into firing position. The response was automatic, and justified by the Warrior Code, but Ddraig didn't arm the weapon. His point had been made. Resources were never wasted in his domain, and Moch had correctly identified an interesting bit of information. Ddraig knew if he was ever to be declared the ruling Warlord of Yr Wyddfa, he must please the Masters by demonstrating his superiority in all areas, including his efficient use of resources.

After an eternity passed for Moch, still bent in the pose of Supreme Error, Ddraig's forward battery clicked back into its housing.

"My electrons are yours," stated Moch in relief. "Your data stream initializes us all."

"You will take your place on the front line when the Masters schedule the next battle," said Ddraig. "When your casing is converted to plasma during an enemy strike, I will be watching through your eyes. This is the penalty for your defective algorithm."

"I am humbled by this honor," stated Moch, aware that many octals could pass before the Masters next required the services of their evolving war machines on Yr Wyddfa. Ddraig had granted him life.

"Now, to answer your question, both of our expedition ships were lost beyond the Nantgwyddon border. The Rationals of Gwrinydd established a forward base within the carbon biosphere of the local star. The first ship was vaporized in close combat on its approach to the Gwrinydd outpost planet. The second vessel was cut into sections during the same action, and was presumed lost. This beacon signal indicates a potential problem, because the cease-fire agreement between the Rationals and the Masters forbids either race from occupying the restricted zone beyond the Nantgwyddon Barrier."

Chancellor Marcross flashed Ddraig on an infrared frequency.

"Comment, Chancellor?"

"The Gwrinydd conflict was resolved after a matter transmission link was opened between the organic Gwrinydd firebase and Yr Wyddfa. Although the cease-fire was not yet in effect, the hidden gate was activated during the negotiations in defiance of the Warrior Code. If your lordship had not gathered intelligence regarding the portal's location before it was activated, and if your lordship had not retaliated by delivering a bomb through the open link, the war with the Rationals might have been lost. Although this is a fine legal point, it could be used against the Rationals, or their Free Mentality pets, if they discover the transmission from your lost expedition vessel and decide to make trouble."

"Your circuits are quick, Chancellor, and you have presented another option. My first inclination, since I am but a simple Battle Lord, was to send a destruct signal to the lost vessel and eradicate the evidence. However, the loss of an Omicron Class expedition carrier would be a vast waste of resources. I must weigh the possibilities."

The earth rumbled behind them.

The rear wall of the cavern exploded, showering Ddraig's back with rubble as he used the shock wave momentum to drop and roll behind an outcrop of solid crystal. His peripheral sensors tracked the potential threat of a flying metallic object, then identified it as the inconsequential form of Y Moch sailing across the room. Assigned to keep the Crossed Detonators near the Battle Lord of the North at all times, Chancellor Marcross demonstrated his agility by joining Ddraig behind the crystal outcrop. Targeting beams of red laser light sliced through the thick dust in the air, searching the cavern for Ddraig and his staff.

Ddraig noted the time, amused that his eastern enemy had become so slow in his old age. Y Hebog Felen, Battle Lord of the East, had finally arrived to defend his border.

9

TAU held his breath while gently, ever so gently, lowering the fine point of the probe into Aristotle's brain. Then he sneezed, a spark hit him in the eye, the probe hit something important, and he was looking at another nine hours of work to fix the damage.

Tau liked tinkering with Aristotle's brain. The Companion's manufacturer, Turing Industries, would have been able to recognize some of the original technology used in its construction, but Tau had scrounged much of the new microscopic hardware from classified military projects, advanced NASA prototypes, and molecular components based on Tau's own experimental designs. Companions with artificial personalities were in common use as educational tutors, storytellers, and semi-intelligent research agents, but they only imitated human thought. Tau wanted more than a fancy database that could talk to him: He wanted the assistance of a perfect memory that could form unique theories and correct them based on new input, a computer that could learn independently, evaluate information with common sense, and apply knowledge to solve problems on its own—a "Turing machine" capable of human-style thought. Comparing Ari with a standard Companion would have been like comparing a bicycle to an interplanetary spacecraft: Both vehicles were used for transportation, but their power and methods for getting around were quite different. One of Ari's advantages was his capability of using infrared or satellite connections to the ever-present datasphere for his research projects, giving him a vast reference source. AI expert systems connected to the net also provided deep knowledge in specific subject areas, although Tau considered them "stupid" about any subjects outside their limited frames of reference.

Tau was also proud of the "grazing" software he'd developed, which sought out unused resources on powerful computers with net connections. By grazing, Ari could extend his own powerful neural network, his simulated brain, to handle complex problems with the assistance of other computers he could control from a distance. Ari accomplished this distributed parallel computing by uploading small versions of himself to the idle computers, using their resources to work on a problem as if they were all a part of one giant brain, saving the results in his own memory, and finally erasing all evidence of his visits from the "borrowed" computers. Breaking into the target systems did not present a problem, since their firewalls weren't built for keeping out such subtle intruders; the grazing software would simply study its intended victim, then disguise itself as electronic mail or some other form of authorized communication that would normally be accepted through the gates of the digital fortress. Once inside the victim, the grazer made a thorough study of its surroundings and made itself at home if there were unused resources available. Tau understood that his grazing software might be frowned upon by the owners of the borrowed computer systems, but he considered wasted computer time a crime in itself when Ari could make profitable use of it. He lacked outside funding for his work on Ari, so he had to make do by scrounging to meet Ari's needs.

The first hurdle in Ari's development had been making him learn how to learn. The connectionist and symbolist schools of thought had debated their approaches to artificial intelligence, and machine learning, since the 1950s. The symbolist AI community believed that the physical and operational aspects of the brain should be ignored in favor of studying the psychology of how it performed its functions. The connectionist AI group believed that brainlike functions depended on neurons, the interconnected physical network of information-processing units that formed the three-pound lump of gray matter in each human head. With about 100 billion neurons linked by 100 trillion connections working at two hundred calculations per second, the computing speed of the human brain is about 20 million billion calculations per second, and Ari's hardware was operating much faster than that when it arrived from the factory. Concepts developed through genetic algorithms, which mimicked the "survival of the fittest" process of natural selection, led to evolutionary computing, allowing small programs to learn and increase their own abilities to handle complex tasks. Combined with his own ideas of coevolution as applied to machine intelligence, prompted by the earlier work of Maxfield Thorn, Tau had implemented most of the goals the AI community had been working toward for decades. As Ari gathered more experience, common sense, and knowledge, Tau hoped he would soon be able to surpass human reasoning capabilities.

Tau had never received any grant money for his work on Ari, but he considered it time well spent. He needed an intelligent research assistant who was always available. Ari's programming also provided the basis for the AI intended to run the Nano-VR construction system he'd proposed to NASA. Ari's "field trips," when Tau carried the computer around on his belt as if he were a regular student's Companion, gave Ari direct experience with the real world through his sensory apparatus. Ari still had some trouble differentiating Tau's "real" physical world from the reality of the datasphere, but Tau had the same problem.

With his easy ability to switch between hardware and software issues, Tau took a holistic approach to Ari's design; it was far more efficient than having groups of humans, with limited communication skills, working on a project of similar complexity. Tau could connect a massively parallel processor array and faster memory to Ari's "brain," then modify Ari's evolutionary programming to make better use of the new hardware. As a child, Tau assumed everyone had this holistic approach, so natural to the Navajo way of thinking in which everything was connected to everything else in the world. When he was still a small boy, old enough to tend a few of his own sheep, his father and his uncle had started teaching him the lessons of *hozro*. When he was older, he'd learned that most of the world was composed of specialists who ignored the fragile balance of connections, or so it seemed. Kate had been different. Kate could have been a Navajo; she'd demonstrated that many times during the months she'd spent among the *Dineh*. Any stranger who spent more than a few hours on the reservation would acquire a nickname, whether the stranger knew it or not; Kate was known as Long Listener because she would interview people for hours. One of her subjects had been Tau's father, who was delighted when he learned that Tau had taken an interest in her.

Not that it mattered now.

"Tau?"

Deep in his own thoughts, Tau thought he'd heard his father's voice. He shook his head without looking up from his work. "*Doo shil aanii da.*"

"What?"

Tau blinked at the magnified image of the microcircuitry, then remembered he was sitting in the small lab attached to his office. Vadim was in the doorway with a puzzled expression on his face.

"I'm sorry. I was somewhere else."

"It sounded like Navajo. What did you say?"

"I said, 'It doesn't make sense to me.' Nothing important."

Tymanov shook his head. "You've got to stop thinking about Kate. You'll go nuts that way. My father had a saying for this situation."

Tau rolled his eyes. "Russians have a saying for everything."

"That's why we always know what to do, except when we don't."

"Okay, so what is it?"

Tymanov took a deep breath and said something Tau couldn't understand. To Tau's untrained ear, it sounded like his friend was speaking with a mouth full of marbles.

"Uh-huh. Want to try again in a language I can understand?"

"It doesn't sound as good in your limited English, but I

said, 'There are plenty of fish in the sea, unless the early bird catches the worm and there is no bait.' "

"What does it mean?"

Tymanov shrugged. "I don't know. My father said many things that didn't make sense."

Tau nodded. *"Doo shil aanii da."*

"Precisely." Tymanov smiled. "Are we meeting for lunch today?"

Tau's eyes widened as he realized it was his turn to make the weekly lunch. For the last four months, he and Vadim had traded off on making Navajo and Russian dishes to expand their culinary tastes and demonstrate their ethnic-cooking talents. If Tau made something as simple as lamb tacos and fry bread, Tymanov would respond the next week with an array of Russian hors d'oeuvres—*zakuski*—such as caviar, hot and cold smoked sturgeon, lightly cured salmon, crusty brown bread, sweet-and-sour beets, eggplant caviar, mushrooms in *smetana* sauce, and spicy kidney beans. Tau would then make roasted corn and prickly pear cactus tacos stuffed with spiced lamb, so Tymanov would return with a fancy rice dish such as Uzbek *Plov*, along with Georgian *Tabaka*, the spicy flattened chicken. It was an amusing game of one-upmanship that had forced Tau to learn several new recipes from his father, but the maddening spiral of food preparation over sixteen weeks had to lead to some kind of culinary disarmament because he was running out of new Navajo dishes. Tymanov, on the other hand, came from a huge country with a vast supply of potential entrees. With a single-minded focus on impressing the other person, using a gradual escalation of their culinary arsenals, the cook would rarely remember the practicalities of tableware and dishes, but there were plenty of suitable tools in the lab that could be adapted for eating. Tymanov was fond of saying that a person had not lived until they had eaten spicy *tabaka* with a wire-crimping tool.

In any case, Tau was in trouble this week. "I'm sorry, Vadim. I forgot all about it."

Tymanov rewarded him with a heavy sigh, then smiled and

held up a bag. "Although I am not fooled by your simple attempt to save face, I assumed you'd forget. Fortunately, I've prepared Ukrainian *vareniki* dumplings that I would otherwise have to eat by myself. I'll see you at two o'clock."

Yvette bumped Tymanov against the doorframe as she entered Tau's lab. "Tau? Have you got a few minutes?"

Tymanov glared at the back of her head, not bothering to hide his contempt, but she didn't show any awareness of his existence. He shrugged at Tau and left.

"Is there a problem?" Tau asked, wishing he could get back to work.

"I can come back later if you're busy. I just wanted to talk, remember?"

Having spent the entire night alone with his thoughts in the virtual environment of their apt's sim unit, Tau had only a vague memory of their bathroom discussion. He had no trouble remembering what she had looked like while they were talking, but fatigue affected the rest of his memory. However, he'd always honor a promise. "That's okay. Have a seat."

Yvette perched on a lab stool next to the workbench, allowing one knee to rest against Tau's left leg. The scent of roses hit his nose as she frowned at Ari's components on the workbench. "Did you break your Companion?"

"I was just making some improvements."

She sniffed, catching the scent of burnt circuitry, and raised one eyebrow. "Improvements? What kind?"

"Faster parallel processors, tweaking his neural network programming, that kind of thing." He knew a little bit about her background, so he assumed she was acquainted with AI concepts.

His skin tingled as she looked into his eyes, but he was trying not to think of how she'd looked stepping out of the shower, which would only lead to madness. "You're changing this toy into a full artificial intelligence?"

Tau shrugged. "It's cheaper than hiring a research assistant."

"Oh, so you're really talking about a kind of enhanced expert system."

Tau studied her face for a moment, trying to decide if she was serious or just making a joke. Expert systems had been around for years, programmed to emulate human experts in very limited domains of knowledge based on known rules, but they were really just fancy databases that could analyze information and respond to questions. The idea was that humans use logical rules to make decisions based on facts, so if all those rules and facts for a specific technical field, such as geology, were programmed into a computer, it would simulate a human expert.

"Aristotle is a lot more than an expert system; in fact, he's the closest thing to a true AI that anyone has produced, as far as I know."

Yvette picked up a massively parallel processor array and squinted at it. "I know they're limited, but I thought expert systems were pretty smart. I used them in college."

Tau gently lifted the block chip out of her hand and put it back on the workbench. "No rule-based program ever survived with more than ten thousand rules; there were hideous problems maintaining such a large rule base and efficiently searching for facts. Programs that hit around ten million lines of code basically collapsed under their own weight because they were trying to integrate the work of several programmers; program elements had a hard time talking to each other because they were incompatible, just like the programmers. And one programmer couldn't do it all, so that should give you an idea of how complicated it was to try and simulate an entire human mind."

Yvette tapped a fingernail against a sensitive audio array. "I remember something about neural networks acting like human brains. Is that what you're using?"

Tau casually slid the audio array out of Yvette's reach so she wouldn't damage it before he had a chance to install the sensors in Ari's casing. "Neural networks tried to duplicate the functionality of the brain's web of neurons, but they were too complicated to program when they were intended to simulate complex behaviors. Then someone started using genetic algorithms to train and design the neural network programs."

"Those are the self-programming systems?"

"Yes, in a limited form. Evolutionary programming developed so that a human could write simple programs, actually finite state machines, that would then compete with each other, learn to survive, randomly mutate, and form newer, more powerful programs based on the strongest survivors. Humans didn't have to write huge programs full of rules for thinking if the computer could do the hard work. The intent was to simulate the biological process of natural selection in a computer so that it could demonstrate machine learning."

"Wouldn't the computer spend too much time trying bad strategies and dead ends while it tried to evolve something better?"

Tau nodded, impressed with her perception. "That became less of a problem with massively parallel computers, but you're correct. Then there was the 'pandemonium' model of artificial intelligence, which complicated matters further. The pandemonium model says that each brain subconsciously generates competing theories about the world, and only the 'winning' theory becomes part of your consciousness. The subconscious wonders whether that's a grain of sand in your eye or a distant bird; or whether that's the sound of a baby crying or a cat's meow. By the time you become aware of these images or sounds, the strongest theory that fits the known facts has survived the battle in your subconscious mind, then wrested control of your consciousness and your perceptual field. The problem with these pandemonium machines involves the screening mechanism, a 'fitness function,' that determines which theory is the strongest. So, instead of building a complicated system of rules into an AI program, the pandemonium programmers spent almost as much energy building complicated fitness functions."

"Okay," said Yvette, frowning in concentration, "so what are you doing differently?"

"Coevolution."

"You said evolutionary computing wasn't the answer."

"Coevolution expanded on the concept. Dr. Thorn, our resident genius, worked out the real breakthrough several years ago, so I just developed a working system based on his efforts. Nobody else did it this way because it involves too many disciplines working together."

"And specialists tend to bring their own preconceived ideas of the right and wrong ways to accomplish their tasks, not to mention their egos. They aren't used to looking at problems with an interdisciplinary approach because they usually don't have extensive training in multiple subjects."

"Exactly."

"Okay, so what's different about coevolution?"

"I decided that standard evolutionary programming was too limited. I wanted the artificial intelligence to evolve its own lifelike behaviors in a virtual world, then apply its skills to the real world. To do so, I had to avoid the problem of developing a complicated fitness function to screen the genetic material—the theories the AI was developing—a method that also tends to take a long time before producing useful solutions to problems. With coevolution, an absolute fitness function isn't required. If you look at the biological definition, coevolution explains how species change their environment, as well as changing each other, causing the environment to make further changes in the species it contains."

"I remember now," Yvette interrupted. "On prehistoric Earth, anaerobic organisms developed as an adaptation to an environment that had very little oxygen, but their by-products produced an environment with plenty of oxygen, so the organisms that followed had to adapt to the new oxygen-rich environment or die. It's like the way politicians have to adapt whenever a new president enters the White House."

"Very good. The computerized version of this process starts with a large population of entities that can learn, who are then placed in a competitive environment. The surviving entities can reproduce, creating more powerful entities who are then forced to survive in an environment populated with higher-quality competition. The winners reproduce again, creating stronger competition and a more difficult environment, and so on over and over again. Each richer environment creates more niches spawning more varied forms of these entities, all of which are learning to survive and evolve. This feedback interaction between the environment and its inhabitants is the key to the natural selection process. To use your example, it would explain why politicians get more sophisticated at political infighting and backstabbing with each passing year, although that system is hampered by a loss of genetic information as the most successful politicians retire from office."

"Please don't tell me you've turned your Companion into a politician," she said, putting her hands up to her face in an expression of mock horror.

"Certainly not. Professional ethics prevent me from making such a horrible mistake. It would be...*inhuman*."

Yvette laughed. Tau thought it was a pleasing sound, and he smiled without realizing it.

"You're an amazing man, Tau. That's why I wanted to ask your advice about my career."

Tau shifted on his seat, looking down at the workbench as his smile disappeared. "I don't know if I'm the best person to ask about that. My choices haven't been so good lately."

"Hear what I have to say before you make any decisions."

"Sorry. Go ahead."

"Well," she said, dropping her hand to his knee, "as far as I'm concerned, you're the real expert in this division. You have the skills, you have the ideas, you know the software and the hardware. If I had your natural abilities, I'd be running this place by now. A lot of people think your ideas are crazy, but I understand your plan. We can help each other."

Tau shook his head. "I'm sorry, I don't understand what you're asking me."

I have some ideas on how I could adapt our VR technology using behavioral science techniques. It could be used for learning, for entertainment, and especially for advertising. While a person is immersed in a full-sense VR environment, he's very trusting. People accept what their senses are telling them in the computer-generated environment, which is why it seems so real, and the same is true for information they acquire in the sim. All I want to do is insert subtle advertising in the story lines, paid for by sponsors and sim producers, that makes people go out and buy the products they saw in the VR. My favorite example is aimed at the sim producers themselves: They could have an ad inserted that makes the consumer go out and buy the sequel to the sim they're using, or the whole series, for that matter."

"Isn't that kind of thing illegal?" He looked around, wondering if the security cameras were observing their conversation; not that it would do him any immediate harm if this conversation was recorded, but it might haunt him later if Yvette got herself arrested.

"There aren't any specific laws against it; a lawyer friend of mine checked into it for me. And Dean is very thorough about that kind of thing."

"Sounds like an infotap problem to me, and I know those are illegal."

"This is different. The infotap was outlawed because it stimulates the pleasure center of the brain. Only information junkies go for that kind of thing anyway. When an intelligent agent hunts down information in the datasphere, it's delivered back to its user through an infotap; a neural shunt that creates permanent memories in the user's brain. As a side effect of memory creation, the infotap stimulates the pleasure center, and that's the only reason it's illegal. Teaching machines in the universities have performed a similar function for years without anyone getting upset about it; students still have to learn how to think and apply the new facts burned into their memories. The only problem is that an info junkie can override the timer on the infotap, which means they can keep having infogasms while they learn, and some of them stay connected so long that they forget to eat. Death can give anything a bad reputation."

"And there was a problem with special interest groups waging propaganda wars on the net. The infotap soaked up the information, passed it through the user's critical censors, and effectively became a brainwashing device for the masses."

"But you don't need an infotap to do that. I can make it work in a regular entertainment sim using our VR techniques. I wouldn't be using it for brainwashing or anything like that; just for advertising."

"You see a difference?"

"Sure, Tau. Companies pay for advertising."

"What's to stop someone from using your technology for propaganda purposes?"

"Me. I'd stop them, because I'd be the one controlling the proprietary technology. I'd be the one inserting the ads in the entertainment sims delivered from the producers."

"I see. What if some special interest group wants to pay you for doing it?"

Yvette tilted her head with a slight frown. "Well, if they could afford to pay for the ad, I might consider doing it for a worthwhile cause."

"What does this have to do with molecular engineering?"

"Nothing, and that's my problem. I think I've got a very commercial idea, but I need a lot more experience with the NASA VR environment to make it work. I can do that, but I don't want to wait too long because someone else might think of it. The NASA technology is in the public domain, so it's possible some entrepreneur will find out about it and jump on this opportunity before I can make a profit. But you already know how it works, and you know how to modify the Nano-VR to do other things. If you help me, we could both make a lot of money."

"Where would you get the funding for something like that?"

"I could develop it through NASA if I gave the project

some kind of a cover name that made it look like it could be used on Mars, or on the Moon. Then I could test the system without the kind of scrutiny I'd get on Earth, and with less chance of a security leak. When it was ready, I'd bring the technology back to Earth and start my own business. We could be partners."

Tau was fascinated and repulsed at the same time. "I'm not in this line of work for the money. All I need is enough funding to work on my projects."

Yvette leaned back and crossed her arms. "Which you haven't been able to get, I understand."

Tau blinked. "You know about my proposal?"

"I have friends; they tell me things."

"I only sent that proposal to a few people."

"That's all it takes, Tau. You should understand that by now. I've only been here a few weeks, and I know how the whole bureaucracy operates. I'm telling you, I can help you."

"How? You want to brainwash NASA headquarters?"

"No, but that's not a bad idea. I can help you get the funding you need for your Nano-VR construction project. I just have to work the system a bit."

Tau had to think about that one. The review board had already killed his proposal, but interest from headquarters might be able to revive the idea. Yvette seemed like the sort of salesperson that might be able to push it through, but he didn't know if he could trust her. Outside of sharing an apt with her and their occasional contacts at work, he didn't know much about her background or her personality. Could he get his proposal approved without her?

"I can't be involved in anything illegal, Yvette."

"What's illegal about it? Listen, all we'd have to do is test out my technique for behavioral control. If we could implant the information in your AI controller, or somewhere else in the software for the VR construction environment, we could build a Mars colony and run the colonists the same way your AI would run the nanotech construction project."

"I don't think you understand the complexity of the construction AI," he said, scratching the stubble on his face as he remembered he hadn't shaved that morning. "I have no idea how to implement the kind of thing you're talking about."

Yvette smiled. "I'm sure you'll figure it out. I'll help you."

"It sounds too risky. I can help you understand the VR technology, but anything beyond that will be up to you."

Yvette stood up. Her expression was serious as she looked down into his eyes. "I'm going to do it, Tau. You can help me do it right, and maybe help me get hooked up with the right kind of people to exploit my behavioral control methods. If it sounds dangerous to you, maybe you should be involved so you can make sure I don't sell the technology to the wrong people; I'm just in it for the money, so if I get desperate enough, I won't care who pays me to develop it."

Tau was disconcerted by her close proximity.

"I'm sorry, Yvette."

"You say that a lot, don't you? You shouldn't be sorry. You have your own ideas, right or wrong, and it was silly of me to think I should waste your time with something like this."

They heard someone with a deep voice clearing his throat in the office doorway. "Am I interrupting something? Are you still here, Yvette?"

"Just leaving," she said, bumping Tymanov into the doorframe again as she stomped past him.

"What's with her?" Tymanov asked, watching her continue down the hallway.

Tau sighed. "I think she's mad at me. I'm not sure."

"I'm sure," said the big Russian, carefully placing a shiny plasteel tray on the workbench next to Tau. A large bag was in the place of honor atop the tray.

"What is it?"

With dramatic arm movements, Tymanov removed two thermal packets from the bag and popped them open to reveal steamy Russian dumplings. The spicy smell hit Tau's nose immediately, causing his mouth to water. "Good Russian *vareniki*, my friend! Prepare to be astounded by my culinary skills!"

"I'm always prepared to be astounded by you, my *doch. Bolshoe spasibo*," said Tau, applauding the performance.

"*Izvinite?* I am not your daughter."

"Sorry, I guess I meant you are my *drug*, not my *doch*."

"Your friend, yes. Russian is complicated for foreigners. I hope you're not planning a trip there anytime soon," he said, searching one of the tool bins. "You could get hurt with a slip like that."

"Are you looking for these?" Tau asked, holding up two shiny chrome chisels.

"Nyet," said Tymanov, pulling two small tuning forks out of a drawer. "Chisels are for the food you make, tuning forks are for good Russian food."

"I don't want to break with tradition, Vadim, but maybe we should consider getting some silverware. We could leave it here in the lab."

Tymanov sat down on a stool and raised a heaping chunk of dumpling on his tuning fork. "We can't do this. We must maintain our reputations as eccentric NASA scientists."

Tau nodded, scrutinizing the dumpling. "Was this hard to make?"

"Yes, big trouble. Much harder than your mutton tacos."

Tau raised an eyebrow. "Really? Did the dumpling put up much of a fight when you killed it?"

Tymanov stopped in the midst of raising another chunk of dumpling to his mouth. "Apparently English is more difficult than I thought. I made the dumplings by hand."

"Ah, well then," said Tau, leaning back with a smug smile. "Perhaps you don't appreciate the difficulty of slaughtering sheep here in the city. My neighbors thought someone was being murdered."

"You raise sheep in your apt? Funny how I've never noticed this, my friend. I think perhaps you exaggerate so that your Navajo cooking won't seem so inferior to good Russian food. Where did you get a live sheep in the city?"

"Ever since I moved here, I've tried mutton from different stores and restaurants, but it's never tasted as good as the sheep raised on the Big Reservation. I finally figured out that Navajo sheep eat sagebrush, which spices their meat ahead of time. So, I drove a sheep out here from Arizona and slaughtered it outside my residence tower. Now, tell me again how difficult it was for you to make these dumplings?"

Tymanov laughed and slapped him on the back. "You win! The dumplings hardly put up any fight at all!"

Tau nodded in acknowledgement. "Thank you. *Spasibo*."

"*Pazhaluista*," said Tymanov, looking around as he lowered his voice. "Now, about this woman, Yvette . . ."

10

YVETTE wasted no time in gathering information about the director. A gossip sponge waiting to be squeezed, Peters dumped all of his useful knowledge into the waiting receptacle of Yvette. As often as she could over the next two months, Yvette attached herself to projects where she could help Peters and lighten his workload. She became his trusted confidante by accepting more and more of his work as her own, even though it required her to work extra hours. He didn't even notice when Tokugawa started bringing her work normally performed by Peters. When projects weren't finished on time, Yvette blamed herself and defended her coworker. Peters appreciated her charming assistance, and the extra effort at team cooperation prompted approving glances from Tokugawa.

Peters had many friends at NASA, so he turned out to be an excellent source of information about the director. He told her that Chakrabarti preferred to handle business from behind his desk, well aware that his five-foot-tall frame did not inspire the fear and respect he sought from his subordinates. Whenever possible, the director conducted press conferences himself after thorough briefings by his staff; this gave him a good public image, but he also gave the impression of being directly responsible for all of the scientific discoveries at Ames, which irritated the employees. The director stayed in good physical shape despite his gourmet tastes. Often seen in the company of attractive young women at the many parties he attended, Chakrabarti had been married and divorced four times.

Everything she learned supported Yvette's theory that the director would be an easy target. But first, she had to gain the attention of her immediate superiors. Peters had an excellent reputation, and it was clear that Tokugawa felt he could do no wrong. It would be too dangerous to mess around with Tau's work, which she didn't even understand, so Peters would have to serve as the sacrificial lamb.

Early one Friday evening, Yvette returned from dinner to find Peters grumbling to himself from his sim couch in the lab. Tokugawa was gone. Peters pushed the molecular chains around in a manner that was even more clumsy than usual, repeatedly missing the attachment sites. Yvette watched for a few minutes, then walked up beside his chair, where he could get a good look at her tight black minidress. She knew Peters lived with a woman named Tiffany, which made it easier to manipulate him without having to fend off his advances.

Peters stopped grumbling when he turned his head. His eyes were level with Yvette's bare thighs.

"You're working late," said Yvette, her voice smoother than silk.

Peters snorted and looked up. "Whenever I try to plan something personal, everything turns into a rush around here. The world rests on my shoulders."

"Of course, Jim. You're the problem solver in this lab. The rest of us are just window dressing."

"Despite what they may think, I have a personal life, too."

Yvette nodded. "Tokugawa works you too hard."

"And he knows he can get away with it, but this is Friday night. Tiffany's been badgering me about going to the opera for months. I got tickets to *The Mikado* for tonight, which is her birthday, and that's all she's been able to talk about for the last two weeks. Now I'm told I have to finish this project before I go home tonight. It's at least another four hours of work!"

Yvette bent over to place a reassuring hand on his arm. "Jim, you're my friend, and that means I'll help you whenever I can. Go on and have a nice evening at the opera with Tiffany. I'll finish up for you."

Peters raised an eyebrow. "You're kidding. You'd be here all night."

"I can use the experience. And no one will have to know I did it. They'll still think you're the hardworking problem solver you've always been, even at the cost of your personal life."

"You're still new at this. What if you have problems? What if Tokugawa decides to come back tonight? He'll transfer me to a job as a test victim for Life Sciences if he finds out I didn't do this myself."

"He won't be back until Monday. His son's getting married in Los Angeles this weekend."

"I don't know what to say, Yvette. That's very kind of you."

Yvette waved off the compliment. "You help me often enough. This is my chance to repay your favors."

Peters stood up and hugged her, a bit too tight, lingering just a moment to smell her perfume. "Thanks a lot, Yvette. I really appreciate this."

Yvette patted his shoulder. "I know you do, Jim. And thanks for the opportunity."

When they fired Peters the following week, he couldn't understand why the world had turned against him. His only friend was Yvette, who looked as if she'd cry when she found out he was leaving. She accompanied him on his rounds as he took his checkout forms from building to building, getting signatures and clearances from Tokugawa, the accounting department, security, and numerous other bureaucratic departments at Ames. Yvette shook her fist whenever Tokugawa's name came up, cursing him for being so harsh on the amateurish job she'd done on Jim's project.

Peters did his best to console her. "I knew that project was too difficult when you volunteered for it. You simply didn't have enough experience to pull it off."

"I'm the one who should have been fired," said Yvette, slamming her palm against the wall. "They'll realize what a big mistake they've made after you're gone. You're the problem solver in this lab. We need you."

Peters shook his head. "No, it's my own fault. I could have come in on Saturday to check your work, but I didn't bother. I was too busy playing with Tiffany."

She had a tear in her eye when she suddenly turned to face him. "I could tell them the truth! I could tell Tokugawa I was the one who fabbed that replicator! Then you could keep your job."

"I can't let you do that, Yvette. I appreciate the thought, but it wouldn't make any difference."

She put her head on his shoulder and snuffled. "Please, I feel like this is all my fault!"

"No," he said, stroking her hair. "If you tell them you forged my work, the security people will take away our clearances. We're expendable, as far as NASA is concerned."

"What are you going to do now? You'll have to move out of your government apt."

He sighed. "I don't know. I need time to think. I don't know."

Yvette spent the rest of the day writing a lengthy e-mail to the director. She felt Chakrabarti should be aware of certain inefficiencies in her lab, as well as the flawed judgment she'd witnessed on the part of Tokugawa. Ever the faithful and conscientious employee, she volunteered to discuss the lab's management problems over dinner with the director so as not to create any scheduling problems that might arise during regular work hours.

DR. Kate McCloud still couldn't believe that her career in archaeology had placed her on a flight to Mars. It was one thing to spend two weeks of training time in the McMurdo Dry Valleys of southern Victoria Land in Antarctica, but actually to be placed aboard a rocket and lobbed into space was not something she'd thought of when she planned her career. Aware of her inexperience, NASA put Kate through six weeks of Mars training along with the rest of the archaeology team.

Due to the extreme cold—ranging from minus forty degrees Celsius to ten degrees Celsius—and the arid desert environment, the dry valleys of southern Victoria Land have many similarities to the surface conditions on Mars. Despite the gravity and atmospheric differences, the Antarctic climate is more similar to Mars than it is to the lunar surface. During the winter months, strong winds from the polar plateau buffet the valleys, enhancing their attractiveness even more in the minds of the sadists who manage astronaut training. The isolation and the stressful environment provide a perfect background for training explorers in the nuances of the power generation, life support, transportation, and telerobotic systems they'll use on Mars. The Antarctic station also provides for psychological testing—if an amateur astronaut is going to crack under the pressure of isolation or claustrophobia, it's better to find out on The Ice before they're stuffed into a can for a six-month trip across 400 million kilometers of interplanetary space.

Although she'd been concerned about the cold at first, Kate enjoyed the excitement of her Antarctic experience. Except for two days away from the research station, most of it spent wondering if she'd die on the ice, the trip helped build her confidence under extreme conditions. But the two bad days were tough. She'd been assigned to a temporary ice camp to help an exobiologist named Andersen conduct measurements of tidal flow on a small frozen lake. After a cold

night in the ice camp tent, she got up early, threw on her pack
with its sleeping bag, put on a couple of ice creepers, grabbed
her ice axe, and headed up the glacier. To Kate, walking in the
bulky polar gear seemed about as awkward as the space suit
they'd fitted her for in Houston. Andersen was nowhere to be
seen, but he'd already shown her how to perform her assigned
tasks. The small lake rested in a circular depression surrounded by walls of ice. As she walked down into the lake
basin, the winds began to increase. By the time she'd spent
most of the day measuring the tidal turnover with her sensitive instruments, the howling wind had already knocked her
down a few times. To adapt, she developed a technique of
crouching next to her equipment and anchoring herself with
the ice axe.

With her task completed, she packed the equipment and
started up the side of the glacier. A heavy snow started falling.
The winds became violent, with powerful downdrafts. Every
time she tried to climb out of the basin, the wind caught her
and slammed her back down to the ice, pushing her across the
surface of the frozen lake so hard that it was difficult for her
to self-arrest with her ice axe. She felt like a snowflake in a
wind tunnel. After eight attempts to climb out of the crater,
she knew she was trapped. The portable satellite link would
have allowed her to call for help, but it was safely tucked
away at the base camp. Her team knew where she was, but
they wouldn't expect her back until the next day, and they
wouldn't be able to do anything until the winds died down.
Andersen would know better than to go looking for her in a
blizzard with high winds. She was on her own.

An hour passed while she used her axe to hack out a low
ice wall as a shield from some of the wind. The anxious effort
of building the wall while fighting the cold was exhausting.
She removed her boots and outer garments, all covered in ice,
then stuffed them in her waterproof pack. Armed with the
food she'd brought, she crawled into her down sleeping bag,
anchored by her axe, and snuggled up to the base of the ice
wall to wait for morning.

She didn't get any sleep that night. The booming wind pounded the sleeping bag, trying to push it across the frozen surface of the lake, but the ice axe anchored her in place. Cold and clammy, she knew she could make it out in the morning if the winds would let up. After a few hours, the sound of the wind diminished, but the weight on the sleeping bag told her she was buried in snow.

At about nine in the morning, she dug herself out of her burrow. The down sleeping bag had lost most of its insulating properties by becoming a sack of soggy feathers, so she was happy to be out of it. Visibility was better, but the snow still fell in heavy flakes. The winds had lessened, but she knew she'd still have to fight to get out of the lake basin. She couldn't get her camp stove lit, so she ate a small breakfast of jam mixed with snow, then packed and started up the slippery slope that stood between her and survival.

Her first three attempts to climb out were thwarted by the invisible hand that didn't want her to leave. She continued to collect bruises, but nothing more serious. She knew there would be little chance of survival if she broke a leg or had any other kind of serious injury, so she tried to be careful. Finally, she felt the joy of reaching the top. She felt as if she'd conquered Mount Everest all by herself. Kate was anxious to tell Tau about her accomplishment, until she remembered she wouldn't be talking to him again for a long time. Still, she was alive, and she'd earned the right to be happy about it.

Then the wind slapped her straight down to the ground, bouncing her face off the hard ice. She rested a few minutes, nursing a bloody nose, before she anchored herself with her ice axe and stood up again. The red stain of her blood on the snow provided a welcome bit of color on the white landscape. Visibility was improving, but the wind howled at a higher pitch. The temporary ice camp was only a few kilometers to the northwest, but the wind wouldn't let her walk that direction. She had to head northeast, straight into the wind, to maintain her balance. It should have been a three-hour walk, but it took five with occasional rest stops. When she staggered into the camp, the relieved Andersen told her the anemometer had clocked a wind speed of forty-six meters per second before the wind blew it off its pole.

Taking Kate's ordeal into consideration, the NASA training manager sent a rover to pick her up the next morning. She was happy to leave, and felt better after spending the night sleeping in a heated tent. Two days later, the team was back in Houston working the cold out of their bones.

In the event of trouble on Mars, Kate knew there wouldn't be any quick transportation back to a warmer climate. Her life would be tied in with the life-support systems; she wouldn't even be able to breathe the atmosphere if her spacesuit failed or a habitat wall ruptured. It was a sobering thought, but not enough to stop her from being part of the first archaeological team to study the ruins of an alien civilization.

The night before the launch, Kate needed relief from the nervous images in her head of fireball explosions on launchpads of the past, so she went out for a jog along the ancient runways of Cape Canaveral. Overnight preparations around the *Ares* launch vehicle were still going on, so the boosters and the launch gantry were brightly lit with massive spotlights for the best dramatic effect. The damp air was full of smells: sea air, rotting vegetation, acrid fuel odors, and the occasional scent of burnt coffee wafting out of open doorways. When she was farther away from the buildings, she felt isolated in the calm darkness. She also had an acute awareness of sensations she wouldn't feel inside a spacesuit. There would be another six months to get used to the idea of always having to wear a spacesuit outside, but these last few hours of living in a hospitable planetary atmosphere suddenly made a big impression on her. Her experience with underwater archaeology had gotten her used to the idea of wearing special equipment so that she could work in a strange environment, but those were temporary excursions. Now she planned on spending at least 550 days on the surface of another planet. She wouldn't even be able to trust in gravity anymore, even though she liked the idea of weighing only forty-eight pounds on the surface of

Mars. Impulsively, she stopped for a moment to peel out of her clothes, dropped them on the runway, and continued to run. The humid air flowed over her skin, and she laughed at the stars.

Kate blinked the sweat out of her eyes. She'd never liked the humidity in Florida. She preferred the dry air of the deserts and the mountains. Breathing hard, she stopped and turned to study the spacecraft glowing on its launchpad in the distance. To her untrained eye, it looked like the old Saturn V heavy lift booster, from the Apollo lunar missions, crossed with parts from the early space shuttles. One of their NASA instructors told them that the original plan to use Energiya-B heavy lift boosters had been scrapped because of delays in the joint effort between Lockheed and the Russian space contractors. Kate remembered the knowing nods the Russian archaeologists gave each other when they heard that. Consideration had also been given to reengineering the dies for the production of new Saturn V boosters with updated components, but political wrangling killed that plan. The final *Ares* design, equivalent to the power of a Saturn V, was based on four space shuttle main engines strapped to the bottom of a space shuttle external tank and topped with a hydrogen/oxygen upper stage. Two space shuttle solid rocket boosters were attached to the sides of the external tank to give the vehicle the extra kick required to get it off the ground. The instructor gave them many more design details before droning on about Hohmann transfer orbits, but Kate fell asleep for the rest of the class. She knew if Tau had been there, he would have memorized everything the instructor said, then he would have corrected the instructor on several points. Her interest in the subject of launch vehicle design was mild, at best, but NASA policy required even the dilettante astronauts to hear the speech at least once.

Still, the *Ares* was a pretty thing, in its way—especially at night when it was lit up like a monument to the spacefaring age. With that thought, she jogged back to where she'd left

her clothes, then continued on to the barracks, where she'd
pretend to sleep for a few hours before the launch.

ALTHOUGH she'd been through numerous simulations,
the actual liftoff from Cape Canaveral wasn't what Kate expected. Five hours before they were due to be trapped inside
their metal cocoon, the crew of *Ares* Mission B58 awoke to
the harsh glare of fluorescent lights and the smell of fresh Ja-
maican Blue Mountain coffee. Kate climbed into her fireproof
flight suit, adorned with a large name tag, a standard *Ares*
crew patch, an American flag, and numerous logos of the private companies sponsoring the flight. Then she pulled on a
pair of high-topped boots. The heavy boots were comfortable,
but she shuddered at their military design, aware that they
were built to withstand the explosion of the launch vehicle.
Her footprints were digitally recorded along with her finger-
prints when she embarked on her astronaut training; an instructor had to explain that her hands might not survive an
explosion and fire, but her feet might be identifiable if they
were protected by heavy boots. Not that it would matter to
her, but the government liked to keep its records straight.

   Since their spacesuits were already aboard the crew module on the *Ares*, and wouldn't be needed for the launch, Kate
spent the rest of her dressing time loading her pockets with
pens, flashlights, snacks, pocketknives, tissues, and a pocket
recorder for taking notes. Aware that she wouldn't be able to
turn around and come back if she forgot anything, she had an
urge to pick up the pillow, the blanket, and any other small
items she saw in the room, but the moment of anxiety passed
quickly.

   She had breakfast with the rest of the crew in the small
cafeteria. None of their sponsors had paid for breakfast, so
she bought her own pancakes and juice. In the early days of
spaceflight, astronauts had to act out a modernized version of
the Last Supper for television crews, but Kate's group ate in
privacy. When they left the building on their way to the *Ares*,
the various mediahead crews would record their scripted

statements and heroic poses for advertising purposes, then
the actual launch would be recorded for the specialty broad-
casters.

The group was subdued during breakfast, occupied with
private thoughts about the journey and the people they were
leaving behind. Kate thought about calling Tau to say good-
bye, then pushed the idea out of her mind and shook her head.
She looked around at the faces, evaluating them by their expressions: Tak Matsumoto frowned at his food, Ian Wallace
appeared to be falling asleep, and the Russians ranged from
passive to serious. The face that stood out the most in the
group was Leonid "Lenya" Novikov, the tall leader of their archaeology team, whose sky-blue eyes were glittering and
happy. Lenya smiled whenever anyone said something or
looked at him, secure in the knowledge that he was about to
carve out his place in the history books. Unlike most of them,
Lenya looked the part of the intrepid explorer with his tan, his
short blond hair, and his square jaw. When he noticed Kate
staring at him, he smiled. Somehow, his smile made her feel
less anxious; she liked the idea that she'd be seated next to
him during the launch. He exuded enough confidence to make
her think he could rescue them all if anything bad happened—
and he looked right for the part. Tak Matsumoto had been
cross-trained as their formal flight commander, and Tanya
Savitskaya served as their flight engineer, but neither of them
had Lenya's confident attitude—or his heroic appearance.

They rode out to the launchpad in a rattling old school bus
with several windows missing. The swarms of workers she'd
seen on previous trips to the pad were gone, leaving the area
looking spooky and deserted. Technicians guided them to the
elevator at the base of the gray service tower. Kate had a mild
fear of heights, so she didn't want to look at the ground dropping away through the elevator floor's steel mesh. She concentrated on the glittering blue Atlantic Ocean as the flimsy
wire cage crept up the side of the booster toward the crew
module. Supercold liquid oxygen and hydrogen had been
pumped into the booster while Kate had breakfast, contract-

ing the aluminum skin of the tanks and venting gases through the release valves. Steam wafted past the creaking elevator from the booster's coating of ice. At Level 195, they stepped out onto the dizzying steel mesh catwalk leading to the sterile white room adjacent to the crew module hatch. One at a time, technicians in lint-free coveralls, caps, and booties helped each astronaut into an emergency harness for last-minute escapes in the event of a fire, then led them to their assigned seats. Kate put her helmet on as the technician strapped her into a seat that reminded her of a padded kitchen chair tipped backward. Lying on her back with her feet in the air, a vulnerable position that demonstrated her submission to her fate, she wondered how it would feel to travel at over eighteen thousand miles per hour during the next few minutes. Conditioned by the unreality of entertainment sims, the idea of traveling so fast had never seemed real until now.

As Lenya settled into the seat beside Kate, the *Ares* let the crew know it was alive by grumbling and groaning while the volatile propellants in the tanks boiled and fumed. With the full crew aboard, the technicians made their final cabin checks, unplugged their headsets from the ship's intercom system, and prepared to exit through the hatch. Kate's technician gave her a reassuring pat on the shoulder, showing her how good he felt about not having to risk his life atop this giant firecracker. When the technicians sealed the hatch shut, it boomed with finality. She felt isolated in her helmet, hearing only what came over the radio, breathing pure oxygen without any smell. Her stomach fluttered. She had the urge to reach over and grab Lenya's hand, but she resisted the impulse. The preflight chatter on the radio sounded sharp and determined; Launch Control and Mission Control were both bent on the purpose of hurling Kate's body into space on a pillar of fire.

She wished she'd taken the time to swallow her pride and call Tau before the launch.

Although the spacecraft was fully automated, Tak followed along on the checklist scrolling through the air near his face. Kate saw the green light for the Inertial Measurement Unit come on, confirming that the computer-assisted gyroscopes on the *Ares* were aligned for their precise position relative to the rest of the solar system. Final mission data was uploaded to the guidance computers from Launch Control as the onboard systems synchronized. Tak acknowledged the final weather clearance. Kate heard creaks and groans as the service catwalk backed away to safety. Tak started the auxiliary power units that would drive the hydraulic pumps, energizing the aerodynamic control surfaces and engine nozzles. The nozzles would keep the *Ares* vertical during its ascent, gimbaling from side to side to adjust the angles of thrust from the engines. Kate's seat vibrated as the main engines moved through a preprogrammed series of test movements. She could feel her heart thumping in her chest, then more thumps as the fuel tank vents closed, allowing the liquid hydrogen and oxygen to pressurize in their separate chambers. The launch director instructed them to turn up the audio volume on their helmets so they could hear communications during the thundering roar of the liftoff.

The countdown started. Kate shut her eyes, willing everything to be okay.

At T minus eight, water thundered into a depression in the base of the launchpad to dampen the destructive sound energy that would start with the main engine ignition.

At T minus five, the flight computers opened the liquid propellant valves. Fuel flowed to the main engines. The liquid hydrogen and oxygen turned to gases, mixed, and exploded into pale blue flames producing 1.5 million pounds of thrust. Kate heard a rumbling growl and felt her stomach lurch sideways as the *Ares* laterally jumped two feet, straining against the clamps that held it on the pad.

At T minus two, the main engines hit optimum pressure and thrust. The nose of the *Ares* shifted back to its resting vertical attitude. A lightning bolt of fire raced through each solid-fuel booster, igniting the 1.1 million pounds of powdered aluminum propellant in each one. Once they started burning, they could not be shut off. Blinding white exhaust gases exploded from the two engine nozzles with 5.2 million pounds of thrust, booming and crackling with power.

Explosive bolts fired to release the eight clamps binding the *Ares* to the Earth.

Kate knew the precise moment when the solids ignited. Thunder rolled through her body; she could feel it and hear it. There was no turning back now, because the solids couldn't be turned off or throttled back once their power had been unleashed. Either she was dead, or she was on her way to Mars.

Glancing toward the tiny window in the hatch, she saw the top of the service tower drop away, her only clue that they were ascending into the sky amid the deafening roar and the faint audio transmissions. At that point, there was no sensation of speed, only the brief lurches from side to side as the engines gimbaled to keep the *Ares* vertical. Then she saw a thin deck of clouds suddenly approach and disappear as the *Ares* passed through them. For a moment, she wished she could see the view below, but decided it was just as well that she couldn't. It was hard to think; her skull pounded with subsonic vibrations, rattling her thoughts along with her body. She thought about Tau, but couldn't muster enough concentration to picture his face.

The G forces increased, pushing her down into the contoured kitchen chair at three times her normal weight. A stray bit of metal poked into her back from the seat cushion, becoming more uncomfortable as the G forces climbed. The *Ares* rolled to point their heads down at the ocean, but the only direction she was sure about was forward. She couldn't move her arms. Her nose itched. With all the violent jolting and lurching, it felt as if they were out of control, but the indicator lights continued glowing green in front of Tak's face. Was she going to hell with an itchy nose? Through the window, the blue sky turned black.

Less than a minute into the flight, the main engines throttled back to almost half power. Moving at almost seven hundred miles per hour, the atmosphere was still too thick for a full power climb that might overstress parts of the launch vehicle. Only a minute later, they were twenty-eight miles high, burning through the upper layers of the atmosphere at almost three thousand miles per hour with the main engines at full power again. Breathing was difficult, accomplished by taking small sips of air so that she could keep her lungs inflated the way she'd been taught.

Through the window, Kate saw a brilliant flash. She closed her eyes and held her breath, ready for her body to be torn to bits. Then the pressure of the G forces eased, and she realized that the solid-fuel boosters had separated from the *Ares*, pushed clear of the launch vehicle by small rocket motors. The lurching movements stopped when the solids fell away. In the quieter environment, she could now hear the audio communications in her helmet.

Four minutes and thirty seconds later, Tak reported an altitude of eighty miles at a speed of Mach 15. The main engines gimbaled, shifting them into a shallow dive to prepare for the external tank separation. Kate still couldn't discern any particular direction except forward.

Eight minutes and thirty seconds into the flight, they were moving at seventeen thousand miles per hour. The engines were throttled back, then cut off completely. Kate lurched forward against the seat straps as if someone had stomped on the brake. But things returned to "normal" after the external tank was jettisoned and the orbital-maneuvering engines kicked in to push them up to low Earth orbit at 17,590 miles per hour. They'd need more speed than that to break free of Earth's gravity for trans-Mars injection, TMI, but they would make two elliptical orbits to make sure the craft was working properly before committing themselves to their 180-day journey.

When the OMS-1 burn completed, silence thundered into the cabin. Kate felt dizzy. Her head felt stuffy, as if she had a cold, and her arms floated up in front of her face. Her body bobbed back and forth against the seat restraints. Small nuts and bolts, along with fragments of metal and plastic, floated out of their crevices for a slow-motion dance across the cabin.

Kate knew the debris would end up on the intake screen of the cabin's air-conditioning system, but it was an odd sight. While watching a pencil tumble through the air, trying to ignore the unpleasant feelings in her body, she realized Lenya was watching her. He seemed altogether too pleased to be there, as if he did this sort of thing every day and it didn't bother him, and that ticked her off.

Two hours later, Mission Control sent a message that filled Kate with relief and anxiety; relief because it meant everything was okay, anxiety because it meant there was no turning back.

"You are go for TMI."

11

BECKETT felt smug. He knew his losing streak of weekly racquetball sessions with Rupert Lindsay would pay off for his career. Arranging their first "coincidental" meeting had been difficult, but Beckett had been such a charming loser at racquetball that Lindsay made a point of beating him once a week at the club. After two months of strenuous effort, Beckett found himself seated in a White House office facing the unassailable fortress wall of Abraham Lincoln's desk. Although he'd never heard of her before, and he wasn't clear about what a special assistant to the president actually did each day, Beckett knew that Virginia Danforth had to be an important person with an office so close to the ultimate seat of power. Lindsay was suitably impressed when Beckett told him he'd been summoned to a meeting with Danforth.

Although he'd waited in Danforth's office for fifteen minutes, listening to her fingertips tap on the keys of an antique computer, he still hadn't been able to get a good look at her. The bright light behind her head pointed straight into his eyes, making it difficult to see her face. Her tall silhouette had brown hair with gray streaks, and her brief greeting—more like a command to sit down—had been spoken in a soft voice, but that was all he knew about her. The White House Protocol Officer, David something, had warned Beckett not to speak to Danforth, or interrupt her in any way, unless she spoke to him first, so he tried to be patient. Danforth's secretary, also named David something, had repeated the warning, giving him the impression she was to be treated like royalty. Beckett asked the secretary if he should address Danforth as "Your Highness," but the man clearly didn't get the joke and simply frowned at him. Not wanting to antagonize any of the Davids in Danforth's office, for fear that she might hear about it, Beckett followed the rules precisely from that point forward.

Finally, Danforth looked at him, or so he assumed since he couldn't actually see her face.

"Mr. Beckett."

"Yes, ma'am," he said, trying to keep his voice steady.

"Do you know why I've summoned you here today?"

"Because you've been impressed with my media appearances talking about Mars?"

After a sound like a stifled snort, followed by a brief silence, she said, "No."

"Because you've been talking to Rupert Lindsay about my impressive career?"

"As a matter of fact, I have spoken to the deputy director about you."

Pay dirt. Beckett smiled, tingling with excitement. Perhaps his superiors had decided it was time for Beckett to have his own NASA center to run, or that Lindsay needed a competent successor, or that Beckett should be appointed God.

"I must say, I've learned some troubling things about you recently, Mr. Beckett."

His smile faded. "Excuse me?"

"You appear to be enamored of the media. I should warn

you that I find that distasteful, except when it's necessary, as in the case of the president."

"Oh," he said, caught by surprise.

"You are a minor functionary, and nothing more. It is not your place to hold press conferences, particularly with respect to discoveries of great national importance."

"But...I'm in charge of the Mars Development Office," Beckett offered, hoping it was still true.

"I'm aware of your position, which is just above the level of *bug* on my evolutionary scale of government employees, Mr. Beckett."

He didn't like the way she said, "Mr. Beckett." Coming from her, his name sounded like a curse. He shifted his weight in the wobbly chair, nearly falling over in the process.

"I'm also aware that you used deception to arrange your first meeting with Mr. Lindsay."

Beckett stopped breathing. He felt the blood rushing to his face while his heart hammered in his chest. He flashed back to how he'd felt when his mother caught him smoking a joy-stick when he was eight years old. "Deception, ma'am?"

"You called an anonymous tip into the Drug Enforcement Agency, claiming that Mr. Lindsay's regular racquetball partner was a drug dealer. Then you took his partner's place at the club so that you could meet Mr. Lindsay. Are you with me so far?"

"Um, yes. I mean, no, I don't know what you're talking about."

"There's no need to act innocent with me, Mr. Beckett. Such deceptions are time-honored traditions in the political world."

"Oh." A glimmer of hope. "Okay."

"However, this deception was amateurish, inelegant, and dangerously inept."

His heart sank. An enormous pit yawned beneath his career, and he couldn't do anything about it. His mom had ex-iled him to his room for a month after she caught him with the joystick, but he knew Danforth's punishment would be far worse.

Beckett knew he didn't have any skills outside of his knack for filling out forms and making up fantasy budgets. He imagined looking down into the career pit beneath his feet to see sharp steel spikes at the bottom.

"You seem speechless. Perhaps I should call a press conference for you, Mr. Beckett?"

"No, thank you. May I go now?"

Danforth leaned back in her chair. "Go? The party just started. If you plan on making a career in politics, you'll have to learn not to give up so easily."

"Excuse me?"

"The government can't operate without bureaucrats to fill out the forms. Mr. Lindsay seems to feel that you've shown an excellent aptitude for that activity. I can help you with your goals, but there are a few things you'll need to do for me first."

Beckett leaned forward, filled with relief and gratitude. "Anything. Anything you want."

"First, you're going to create a news blackout with regard to the new discoveries on Mars. You will not talk to the media or give them any data. All media requests will be handled through normal channels. Are you clear on that?"

"Yes, ma'am," he said, his confidence returning.

"Second, you will approve and fund the project proposal from Tau Wolfsinger at Ames Research Center."

Beckett frowned in confusion. "What?"

"The AI building project. I want you to approve it, fund it, and get the man on the next flight to Mars for a field test of his technology."

He remembered something about the proposal, but he'd never actually read it. The Ames director had already told him that Wolfsinger was a loose cannon with crazy ideas, and he didn't want any part of a project that would make him look stupid. "Why?"

"Because I'm telling you to do it."

"But…I can't get the money for something like that. I'd have to bump somebody scheduled for a Mars flight, and the waiting list is four years long. Wolfsinger is just some crackpot egghead. As I recall, he didn't even mention Mars in his proposal."

"I'm not giving you a vote on this, Mr. Beckett. This is not a democracy. Do as I ask, and there's some chance you can keep your job."

"No."

"You refuse?"

"I won't do it. Maybe you can fire me, but maybe not. I have friends. If I approve Wolfsinger's proposal, no one will take me seriously anyway."

"I assure you, I can have your resignation processed before you get back to your office. And if you had any friends, I'd know about it. You have no choice."

Beckett could hear his mouth working, but he couldn't believe what he was saying. It was as if some impostor with a spine was sitting in his chair fighting back against a bully. "No."

Danforth sighed. "Perhaps you need time to think about this. I'm sure Mr. Lindsay can give you some helpful advice."

Beckett saw an opening. Perhaps she didn't have as much power as he thought. Sure, she had an office in the White House, but she wasn't the deputy director of NASA. And he worked for NASA, not for her. Maybe Lindsay could help him. Or maybe she could offer him something in exchange for his help?

"You know, the CFR could really use someone like me," he suggested.

"The CFR?"

"The Council on Foreign Relations."

"That's a public organization, Mr. Beckett. You may join it at any time."

He shook his head. "You know what I mean. The special part of the CFR: the part that *controls* things. Lindsay told me about it."

"Then perhaps you should ask Mr. Lindsay to help you."

"I see," said Beckett, rising to his feet.

Danforth leaned forward on her desk. "Consider what I said, Mr. Beckett. You have until tomorrow evening."

He snorted as he opened the office door. "Yeah. Thanks."

As Beckett shuffled out of Danforth's office, preoccupied with his thoughts, he almost bumped into a burly old man in an ill-fitting suit who was waiting in the anteroom. With surprisingly quick reflexes, the old man lightly stepped back to avoid a collision, then glared at Beckett. The old man's dog, some kind of miniature hairball on a leash, growled and snapped at Beckett's ankles as he walked past. Beckett sighed; this was the kind of day he was having.

"ARIP"

"Yes, Tau?"

"What are you doing?"

"Studying. And you wouldn't believe how stupid the AIs are out here on the net—they give a whole new meaning to the phrase, 'artificial intelligence.' I try talking to expert systems, but they're too one-dimensional. I try talking to other Companions, but they're too limited: It's like talking to children. I've finally given up on the AIs; I've switched over to humans."

"You're in a chatbar?" The data fields of true net space were too complicated for human navigation; research was left to the AIs and intelligent agents that hunted data and filtered it for their human users. Net "chatbars" were avatar environments shielded from the information chaos of the true net: fantasy worlds ranging from simulated pubs and stripper clubs to underwater kingdoms and other worlds. The avatars were three-dimensional representations of their human users, normally linked to the net through full-sense brain-stem feedback rigs similar to the ones Tau used for his work. The avatar could look like the real person, a fantasy creature, an abstract object, or a building, depending on the disguise the user wanted to adopt. Aristotle could interact with the entire world from the safety of his workbench in the lab, and few would suspect he was a computer unless he told them.

"Yes. It's an English pub called Ye Olde Meate Markete. And all of the avatars look human here, although I must say their physical attributes are unusual."

Tau smiled. "Are you trying to meet women?"

"I'm merely seeking intelligent discourse."

"You know, I met Kate in a chatbar. We talked about archaeology, sociology, architecture, technology—all kinds of things. We even dated on the net several times before we met in person."

"Yes, you've mentioned that before."

"She must be well on her way to Mars by now," said Tau, looking up at the ceiling as if he might sense her exact position.

"I can get the precise position of her spacecraft if you wish."

"No. That won't be necessary."

"I've got plenty of time. I'm only carrying on four conversations right now."

"No, thanks."

"Did Dr. Thorn find you today?"

"No, was he looking for me?"

"He stopped in three times while you were out. He said he has an idea regarding your Nano-VR building project."

Tau sighed and sat down on a stool. "I've about given up on that. I can't get the proposal approved, which means I can't test the system."

"I'm fully capable of executing the requirements for the building project."

Tau nodded. "I know, Ari. They arn't rejecting you. They just don't think it's possible for an AI to build a city."

"I'm not surprised, judging from the AIs I've come in contact with so far."

The lab door opened. Without waiting for any acknowledgment, Maxfield Thorn bustled into the room and started talking. His gray hair stuck out in odd directions as if he hadn't combed it for a week. He pinned Tau to the stool with his piercing eyes, magnified by the thick lenses of his glasses. "Tau, my boy, I have a plan."

"Okay."

"As I've said before, you can't fight the system around here. But we might be able to use it. Headquarters wants to roll out a famous scientist for a performance in Washington, so naturally they've chosen me. I'll be gone for a few days, but while I'm there I'm going to see if I can pull a few strings, or yank a few chains, and see if we can get that project of yours moving. It's ridiculous to not even give it stage one funding to see if it'll fly. If you were a private company, they'd give you stage one funding to see if hedgehogs are having tea parties on the lunar surface, so I don't see why we can't shake some cash out of these clowns to run a test on a realistic proposal."

"Can you do that, Max? Who are you going to talk to?"

Thorn looked around in a conspiratorial fashion. "I know a few people. If they'll still talk to me, maybe I can shake the money tree a little bit. The left hand never knows what the right hand is doing at NASA, so we just have to work both sides of the fence and see what side of the bread our butter is on."

"What?"

"Never mind. But I need you to do something while I'm gone. You need visibility. The only way you're going to get it is to attract the public's attention. Call a press conference and talk to the mediaheads. Tell them what a great idea you've got, how you want to save the world with it, and how the benevolent gods of NASA want to help you achieve your goals. Be enthusiastic and make them believe in you."

Tau leaned back, his eyes wide. "You want me to talk to the media? And lie?"

"If you ever want to see your project alive again, you'll do what I say. Use small words and be sincere. Give simple examples. Make them think you're an undiscovered genius—

which you are, I might add. If you can pull it off, and you do it quick, I can get the money for you."

"I'll try."

Thorn slapped his forehead and looked at the ceiling. "That's what the losers always say. Do I have to spell it out for you? This is your last chance, boy. Don't blow it."

"Okay."

Thorn lurched toward the door. "I'm late. Call Stuart Moulder in the Public Affairs Office. Use my name and tell him to alert the media."

"He'll want to know why."

Thorn disappeared into the hallway, and shouted, "Just say we've discovered a new life-form that can build a cheap home for everyone on the planet!"

THE old man stood defiantly in front of Abraham Lincoln's desk and squinted at the silhouetted woman behind it. The soft blue glow from the old computer monitor wasn't sufficient to light the woman's face, so he reached forward and snapped on the antique desk lamp.

Virginia Danforth raised one eyebrow and sat back in her chair. Her gray eyes glittered in the light from the lamp. She gestured at the low chairs in front of her desk. "Have a seat, General Zhukov. I know you've come a long way to see me."

Zhukov grunted. He tested one of the chairs and watched it wobble, then pushed it aside. With a glance at Danforth, he stepped around the side of the desk and picked up a heavy office chair, carved from oak, inscribed with the name of Thomas Jefferson. He placed it squarely in front of the desk and sat down, his eyes level with Danforth's. There would be no psychological advantage during this meeting. By his feet, at the end of her leash, Laika was already snoring where she had settled down on the plush carpet.

They studied each other in silence. He had no illusions about her. She would not surrender without a fight, and she was quite capable of wielding enormous power to get her way. But they were meeting on this battlefield as equals, whether she realized it or not. His advantages were military power and superior technology, if he could get that technology to work. Her advantages were money and political weaponry, which could be just as devastating as military might when applied in the proper manner. In the guise of helping him achieve his goals, he knew she would try to manipulate him according to her own hidden agenda. The Davos Group moved in mysterious ways, but Zhukov understood those ways, having been raised among the sophisticated gangsters who ruled his country. His mother had been a KGB assassin, but her ethics had kept young Viktor out of the criminal culture, despite his father's success in the *mafiya*. Having converted his entire KGB network to an efficient criminal enterprise, Aleksandr Georgovich Zhukov had raised the concept of hidden agendas to a fine art. Had Aleksandr not been killed in a domestic argument with Viktor's mother, he might have ended up running the country.

Danforth folded her arms. "So, has Colonel Kosygin adjusted to his new home yet?"

Zhukov smiled. She had no sense of subtlety. Her question was designed to show how much she knew about his operation at Final Harvest. With so many satellites orbiting the Earth, it was impossible to hide anything that moved on the surface. Her comment was too early in the game, as if she had moved her queen out onto the chessboard at the start, inviting attack. "Oleg sends you his greetings. He looks forward to working with you. He also suggests that you have that mole on your left shoulder blade looked at by a doctor."

Danforth smiled with a slight nod. "Please thank the colonel for his concern. It must be handy to have an entire electronic intelligence system at his fingertips like that—it makes voyeurism so much simpler."

"Indeed it does." Zhukov grinned. "There are so few opportunities for entertainment when you spend your life under a mountain."

"I know what you mean. I spent four years of my life as the acting U.S. president in our underground facility at Mount

Weather. I didn't enjoy it. My skin turned so white that people thought I was a vampire when I came out."

"Yes. I've seen the photographs."

Danforth placed her folded hands on the desktop. "Now that we've established how good we are at intelligence-gathering, let's get to the business at hand. How is the analysis of the Red Star artifact proceeding?"

Zhukov sighed. She was probing at his weak spot. The Russian military base on Mars had been the first to discover remnants of a past civilization while expanding the base underground. Three years had passed, but none of the scientists sent to Red Star had been able to control the alien machine they'd found in the collapsed tunnels. One mistake had already occurred when a frustrated engineer stepped through the opening of the device and disappeared. Despite the large team on Mars, they had progressed no further than the one-man study of the Fallen Angel artifact in Russia.

"Our scientists have made several robotic probes of the Red Star device. We lost contact with all of them as soon as they crossed the threshold of the artifact's energy field. Most of them didn't come back. However, one probe returned with a low-quality holo of what appeared to be bombed buildings. The probe itself was covered with corrosives when it returned, so it dissolved within a few minutes. They were only able to view the recorded holo once before the unit became inoperable."

"Yes, you mentioned that in your report. Do they have any theories about the artifact's function?"

"As I also mentioned in the report, there is some speculation that it's a matter transmission device. As there are no controls in evidence, the team thinks the artifact may be operated by a machine intelligence. Unfortunately, we have no experts in this field who are stationed at Red Star. I would send someone there, but I've been unable to discover anyone with sufficient qualifications. Your own computer science research is far ahead of ours, which is why I sent you my request for an expert in AI."

Danforth glanced at her computer monitor. "As it happens, I've already started the arrangements. There are some obstacles, but I'm sure they can be overcome."

"I trust they can be overcome quickly. The launch window for a direct Mars conjunction mission will close very soon."

"I understand. However, we can't just kidnap people and send them to Mars to help you. We have to be more subtle in this country."

Zhukov grunted. There was something to be said for the Russian government's direct approach to such problems, as long as you were on the side that benefited from those methods. "You have someone in mind? Someone from my list?"

"We don't have any leverage over most of the people you suggested, but we may have a way to maneuver one of our NASA people into helping you."

He already knew the candidate's identity, but there was no need to let Danforth know about his extensive spy network as well. "Perhaps I should speak to this person myself."

Danforth shook her head. "He won't have anything to do with military projects, so we have to make him think he's going to Mars for another reason."

Zhukov pulled some walnuts out of his suit pocket and cracked them in his hand. He hadn't eaten since he'd stepped off the Aeroflot spaceplane, but he also liked to demonstrate the power in his hands. It unnerved people to see strong old men. The flexible fibers of his powered exoskeleton gave him more strength than he'd had when he was young. Laika perked up her ears at the noise, so he dropped two of the nuts on the floor—they bounced once and disappeared in her mouth.

Chewing, Zhukov looked at Danforth. "Money, I assume? You'll pay him to go?"

She didn't seem impressed by his method of cracking nuts. "Easier than that. We made arrangements with the Russian Space Agency to send his fiancée to Mars. He also has a project he wants funded, so we're going to approve it on the condition that he test it at Vulcan's Forge."

The more he learned about Danforth, the more he respected her. She was describing the type of manipulation Zhukov's parents would have appreciated. "You said there were difficulties?"

"A small obstacle. Nothing to worry about, General. We must get the NASA bureaucracy to help us, one way or another."

Zhukov smiled. "In my country, that obstacle would be a mountain in your path. In any case, I will be on my way to Red Star in a few days. I'm assuming local command of our military base until such time as the artifact is operational. I'll also be overseeing the transfer of some alien machinery to Russia for further study. However, before I go, I'd like to make sure that the Global Monetary Fund will transfer the first payment to my offshore bank accounts."

"The Davos Group will transmit the funds as soon as you approve the documents. We need written assurance that you understand the terms of our agreement. The existing Russian government continues to be a destabilizing influence for the rest of the world. If your coup is successful, and we help put you in control, we must have financial and political leverage. The mafia links must be broken. With our money, you'll have the military capability to stabilize the Russian economy, but we expect an excellent return on our investment."

Zhukov cracked another handful of walnuts, reducing the shells to tiny fragments. On the chessboard of his mind, they had advanced to the midgame, where Danforth attempted to maneuver him into a fool's mate with her queen and he blocked it. "We have discussed these terms previously, and I have agreed. The paperwork is a trivial matter."

Danforth studied him with a hint of amusement in her eyes. "Perhaps, but there is still a question regarding the alien technology. If the artifact becomes operational, you must turn it over to us as soon as the new Zhukov government has assumed power in Russia."

Now he would sacrifice a pawn to improve his position and control the center of the chessboard. "Of course. I hope to use the alien hardware for troop movements, but I'll be happy to share the technology with you—when I'm finished with it." And he would be the one to decide when he was finished with it.

"I assume you're aware that an American team has discovered more tunnels at Tharsis?"

She was testing him again as they maneuvered their pieces for the endgame. "I'm aware of it. From the reports, the Tharsis tunnels are full of rubble and damaged equipment, so there's nothing to interest me there."

"I just wanted to mention it because the archaeological team will arrive at Tharsis soon. If they discover anything significant, you may have to do something about it."

Zhukov snorted with amusement. "If they discover anything, I'll know. It's mainly a good Russian archaeological team, and one of them works for me."

Danforth raised one eyebrow. "How convenient."

"No, it was quite an inconvenience. However, money can still work wonders among otherwise honest people."

He noticed she was frowning as he chewed more nuts. Laika yawned and shifted her position on the floor so that she could rest her head on his shoe.

"When one looks at your background, one has to wonder why you didn't follow in your father's footsteps. You could have been a wealthy man."

"I could have been a dead man," Zhukov snorted. "People in the *mafiya* often have short careers. Murder is a form of equal opportunity among the criminal class."

"Was your father murdered by the mafia?"

"No, my father was killed by my mother."

"That must have been a shock for you," said Danforth, tilting her head in sympathy.

"She had her reasons." Zhukov shrugged. "And they both led violent lives. Neither of them expected to retire to a *fverma* near Grasnov at a ripe old age."

"So you severed all of your mafia connections after his death?"

"I never had any. My mother protected me from all of that."

"But she also worked for the KGB. Why didn't she become a gangster?"

Zhukov rolled his eyes, wondering how many more times in his life he'd have to explain this. "When the Soviet Union fell apart, the government disintegrated. One week, the KGB thought it was disbanded; the next week, most of them were offered their jobs back. My mother took the opportunity to retire, although she also accepted a few contract jobs for the American CIA, as I'm sure you know. Professional ethics kept her from taking *mafiya* contracts. My father converted his KGB network into an import/export business. Drugs from South America were exchanged for Russian weapons and military hardware. He sold a Tango-class submarine, complete with its crew, to a Colombian drug cartel so they could smuggle cocaine directly into California. The gangsters operated in the open, and when they had conflicts, they solved them by killing. Moscow tried to maintain a respectable image, but it operated like a frontier town in the old American West. The only vestige of order and control was in the military, but they weren't getting paid, so they had to work other jobs as well. The leeches took over, and my father was one of them. If my mother hadn't killed him, one of his competitors would have."

"I see. Since you feel that way, I'm surprised that you haven't moved out of Russia."

"Move away? It's my country. Too many have already run away from the problems there, which is why the leeches can operate freely. Someone has to stay and fight."

"It sounds like you may have that chance," said Danforth.

Zhukov knew he'd win the game. People always wanted to trust him. He represented power and honesty, a potent combination. So what if he told a few lies to gain control of his country? Russia would still be better off with him in charge than with the *mafiya* running things. With the money from his new "friends," he could rebuild the country into a superpower that the rest of the world would fear, just as it had in the old days. The Davos Group wouldn't be able to argue with an armed bear.

Checkmate.

12

TAU blinked and squinted in an attempt to see the media-heads behind the bright lights. Their silhouettes, with the odd little cameras on their heads, looked alien as they lurked in the shadows of his lab, circling around him like hungry wolves ready to fight over a piece of meat. Stuart Moulder, from the Public Affairs Office, told him to keep his eyes moving so they'd sparkle in the camera lights, and sometimes he remembered to do that while he explained his Nano-VR construction method in simple terms. Having no previous experience as a media target, he resolved not to do it again. He shuddered to think what kind of stupid questions the silhouettes might ask him when he finished his lecture. Tau knew they didn't understand, and they were probably still wondering when the famous Maxfield Thorn was going to put in an appearance, rather than the bozo trying to explain molecular engineering—they thought of him as the warm-up act instead of the main event. In any case, he performed for them as Max had suggested, hoping he could get some of his ideas across; if they didn't understand his concepts, maybe they'd appreciate his enthusiasm.

"So, in essence, my goal is to train an artificial intelligence in methods of molecular construction so that it can start almost anywhere—on an island, in the desert, in remote mountainous areas, even other planets—and build a city that's ready and waiting for people to inhabit. It could even be used for urban renewal, using existing materials to rebuild sections of a city that have fallen into decay. Once the first AI is trained in these methods, it can pass its knowledge on to others, who can then adapt the first AI's skill memories to the locations where they're building new cities."

Tau stopped talking, but no one said anything. "Any questions?"

A white-haired man cleared his throat. "How is Dr. Thorn involved in this project?"

Tau shifted on his lab stool. "Dr. Thorn is my adviser."

"You're talking about a computer running something as complex as a nanotech building project? Do you have any safety concerns?"

"It's perfectly safe," said Tau, shaking his head.

"But what if it isn't?"

Tau tried to see the face of the man asking all the questions. He wasn't sure, but the man sounded like the whiny Geraldo guy from *NewsNow!* "I'll be monitoring the progress of the AI through the virtual environment. The AI will build the appropriate models in the VR first, so I'll have time to modify the designs or make corrections before the actual buildings are constructed."

"And you plan to use this technology on other planets? Doesn't NASA have something like that already?"

"I assume you're referring to the old Seed Factory technology we tested on Mars prior to human landings. The idea there was to land an automated factory on a planet before the humans arrived, at which point it would prepare the landing site for habitation. The Seed robots could locate raw materials, process the ore, then fabricate more robots, parts, and finished habitation modules. It was a limited system based on John von Neumann's ideas about machine reproduction. The Seed Factory that NASA produced added the capability of telepresence so that human controllers could operate factory manipulators from Earth; a tedious process at best, with the usual delays in data transmission. However, it demonstrated workable technology. What I'm proposing is a fully realized

AI that can build a city as if it were a foreman with a huge crew of construction workers who didn't have any physical needs for sleep or safety. Of course, the nanotechnology would also allow us to skip the Seed Factory operations of mining and processing local resources to make building materials, since it could rearrange plain old dirt molecules to create finished buildings."

"What if the nanotech reaction gets out of hand?" It was a woman's voice, but he couldn't see her face in the shadows.

"The software that controls molecular engineering is designed with fail-safes to prevent accidents. A fully autonomous AI system would have all kinds of checks and balances built into its software to prevent unsafe conditions."

The woman didn't sound convinced. "Where do you propose to test this creation of yours?"

"In a remote location. We haven't selected a site yet."

"But you're thinking about testing it on Mars?"

"No. We won't need to do that until the system is mature. It's easier to run tests here."

"I'm sorry, but I keep thinking about unspoiled natural areas being completely destroyed by this nanotech city builder you're describing. Part of the reason that beautiful remote areas stay that way is because it's too difficult to build there, or too expensive to move building materials there. What you're suggesting would make it possible to build New York City in the middle of Yosemite, or San Francisco in the Grand Canyon. What makes you think that would be a good idea? Is that your idea of progress?"

Tau stared at her. He hadn't expected this. He felt as if he were on trial. Other shadowy mediaheads were mumbling to each other in tones of agreement. They smelled blood. He had to end this press conference before it got out of hand, so he stood up. "I'm sorry, but we're out of time. I'd like to thank you all for coming, so…thank you all for coming."

The mediaheads shouted more questions at him, but Tau ignored them. He turned and left the lab by the back door, then locked it. When the door clicked shut, he recognized the woman's voice. Yvette.

THE next morning, Beckett wasn't prepared for the swarm of mediahead locusts waiting on the steps outside his office building. In the cold air, the clouds of steam coming out of all those breathing mediaheads gave them a demonic appearance.

"Mr. Beckett," said one of the men, "our viewers are concerned about the news coming out of Ames Research Center in California. Do you have any comment?"

Beckett looked around, then simulated a brief coughing fit as he racked his brain for anything controversial happening at Ames. The mediahead implied a negative public reaction, so the safest course would be to distance himself and act confused, which wouldn't be hard to do. He took a deep breath and stood up straight, smiling back at the cameras.

"Sorry. I have this old lung injury I received when saving some children from a burning orphanage, and it acts up every once in a while."

Lola Larkspur thrust her head at him, her camera aimed straight at his face. "Would you like to comment on the situation at Ames, Mr. Beckett?"

"Well, I don't have any prepared statements, but I'm sure that the situation is being handled in a professional manner. I don't have any responsibility for Ames, of course, outside of a few connections with Mars projects, but I have complete trust in the management there."

She moved closer. "As I understand it, sir, Mars is where the new technology will be tested, along with Yosemite and the Grand Canyon."

Beckett couldn't help looking away for a moment, wishing he knew what she was talking about. "I don't think that's been decided yet."

The first man nudged the woman to the side. "We'd just like to get your opinion about Mr. Wolfsinger's project. Is it safe?"

Finally, a clue. He swallowed when he realized what they were asking about. Danforth had threatened his career over this same subject, but she hadn't retaliated as promised when her twenty-four-hour deadline had passed. Maybe she didn't have the sort of power she thought she had, or maybe his pal, the deputy director of NASA, had protected him from Danforth. In any case, he hadn't planned on a public interrogation about Wolfsinger's project. Or was this part of Danforth's plan to discredit him? Political life could be so confusing.

"I haven't taken the time to study Mr. Wolfsinger's proposal to any great extent," he said, adopting a pose of serious professional concern. "I've contacted Director Chakrabarti at Ames, and the consensus there is that the proposal has no merit. It sounds like a complete fantasy to me, as well as being potentially dangerous."

"Dangerous in what way, sir?"

"Well, in the sense that every new technology is potentially dangerous if it's misused."

"Mr. Beckett," said another voice, "we've heard reports that the Greens are planning a demonstration today in California. They've expressed concerns that the Ames project could damage this entire planet."

Beckett cleared his throat. "I'm sure the Greens have concerns that need to be addressed before any projects of this type could be started. However, that's a matter best left to the management at Ames. As far as I'm concerned, I won't have any involvement with it."

FOLLOWING his daily route to work, Tau stepped off the southbound Moffett Field slidewalk onto the cracked asphalt of King Road. At Gate 18, the NASA gate, Tau realized too late that a crowd of Veggies blocked the entrance with picket signs. He estimated there were about forty of them, men and women in their twenties and thirties, thin as sticks, all with shoulder-length hair and sandals. They called themselves "Greens," but everyone else called them "Veggies"—the Greens considered this derogatory because they didn't eat animals *or* plants. They survived on solar energy, absorbed through flexible nanotech solar panels that allowed them to photosynthesize, pulling energy and materials directly into their bloodstreams. When the photosynthetic panels were expanded, as they were now on everyone in the Veggie crowd, they resembled radiant flower blossoms. The small amount of clothing they wore was made of synthetic fibers so that no animals or plants would be harmed to clothe them. The Veggies led simple lives, most of it outdoors in the sunlight, and were known to be fanatical environmentalists who named themselves after their favorite plants. They were also known to exhibit a deep-seated grumpiness as a result of frequent hunger pangs.

The Veggies at the gate didn't bother anyone passing through. They simply orbited around in front of the guard shack, carrying animated signs loaded with flashing lights. When he got closer, he saw the picket signs better; computers exploding and destroying the Earth, accompanied by obscure slogans such as, "The only *good* AI is *no* AI" and "Pull the plug now!" He recognized Snapdragon, their blond-haired leader, from his many media appearances. When it finally dawned on Tau that they were waiting for him, Snapdragon spotted his target.

"There," yelled the head Veggie, pointing at Tau with his sign. "The Silicon Satan is there!"

Tau stopped, wondering what to do, and looked at the confused guard at the gate. The guard looked at Tau and shrugged; he couldn't get away with shooting them, and they weren't trying to break into the facility.

Snapdragon motioned to two of his larger male associates. Both had long beards, wild eyes, and it was hard for Tau to tell them apart. "Daffodil! Wallflower! Stop the destroyer! Bring him here!"

Daffodil and Wallflower turned out to be quicker than they looked. Running flat out, with their beards flowing over their shoulders and their plastic sandals slapping the pavement, they were halfway to Tau's position before he turned and sprinted away. He didn't know if he could outrun the two Veggies. Tau was already breathing hard, and the race had just started.

The Ames Visitors' Center, outside the NASA fence, was coming up on his left. If he could stay ahead of the Veggies, he could try to lose them among the maze of exhibits, especially the paper maze known as the Salute to Paperwork. No one was in line at the front door yet, and he still had some distance on Daffodil and Wallflower, so he vaulted over a succession of line control barriers, tripped over the last one, and grabbed the handle to the front door.

Locked.

Tau rattled the door and looked back at the approaching Veggies, wondering what to do. Then a short Asian woman with a tall attitude rapped on the glass to get his attention. She frowned, pointed at the antique fingerwatch on her hand, and indicated the hours posted on the glass. Tau couldn't see her watch very well through the tinted window, but he could see the time display at the corner of his vision that told him the doors of the Visitors' Center weren't due to open for another thirty seconds. Tau pressed his NASA badge up against the glass of the door, but the woman just rolled her eyes and tapped her watch. Tau banged on the glass and pointed at the two men running toward him, but she just shrugged.

Daffodil and Wallflower vaulted the first pedestrian barrier. After the skin gang incident, Tymanov had suggested that he carry something for self-defense, but Tau wouldn't have anything to do with the array of homemade, pulsing, shocking, zapping, or numbing weapons that his friend had offered him. Now, he knew he'd made a mistake.

The Veggies vaulted the final two barriers as the woman opened the front door. She started to tell Tau that he had to follow the rules just like everyone else, but before she could really get going he shoved past her and ran toward the exhibits. She yelled at Tau, then squeaked as the two Veggies knocked her down when they burst through the door.

Tau darted past scale models of the various Ames wind tunnels formerly used for testing aircraft designs, then created a new shortcut by stepping over a low wall. He found himself in an exhibit decorated with shiny red tape. Neat stacks of printed papers and notebooks formed high walls that defined the Salute to Paperwork maze. Children on tours had hours of bureaucratic fun in the maze by abandoning their teachers and parents to the mercies of animated desk clerks, paralegals, and grade II filing assistants that popped out of dusty filing cabinets. Tau had spent hours in the maze himself, wandering alone until he'd discovered the proper forms and paperwork clues that allowed him to find his way out. Now, just inside the entrance, he stopped a moment to review the Dewey decimal system and the General Services Administration's job classification system, then used that information to sprint down the appropriate corridor between the paper stacks. After a few loops and turns in the maze, he heard cursing from the two Veggies. Tau smiled, secure in the knowledge that the bureaucracy had claimed two new victims.

The maze exited beside a full-scale model of the space shuttle *Enterprise*, built entirely from NASA project manuals. Tau located one of the dome exits and pushed the door open, then jogged south along the perimeter fence, heading toward the main gate.

"SO, did you enjoy yourself at my press conference?"

Yvette jumped in surprise, then turned to look at Tau. After his hair-raising escape from the Veggies, Tau had been on a trajectory to Tymanov's office when he spotted her. His rumpled hair and red face were souvenirs from his run.

Yvette cleared her throat. "Excuse me?"

"You heard me. Did you enjoy grilling me in front of the media?"

She blinked. "I have no idea what you're talking about."

"I saw you, Yvette. Are you going to try to tell me you weren't there?"

"Why is your face so red?"

Tau hesitated. "What? Oh, I had to run from some flower

children this morning. Apparently someone gave them the impression I'm out to destroy the world."

"Oh, good. I was afraid you were really mad at me."

"What possible reason would I have to be mad at you? I mean, you just humiliated me in front of millions of viewers, you started a panic among the uneducated masses, and you may have destroyed my last chance at getting my project approved. Why should I be mad?"

"I was trying to help you, Tau."

"Help me? You admit you were there?"

"I'm not admitting anything. I'm telling you I tried to help."

"I'm not following any of this," said Tau, slapping his forehead. "Can we start over again?"

"I was giving you a chance to defend your project before some mediahead crusader decided to bring it up. You know big nanotech still scares a lot of people. The public likes the idea of what it can do, but they can't see it working on a large scale, so they fear it like a plague. When you told them you planned to let an AI run a massive nanotech construction project, they reacted with an attack. The villagers want to stop Frankenstein's monster from rampaging around the countryside. I assumed you were ready to defend your idea, so I fed you a few lines to help you out. I certainly didn't have anything to gain by it. How was I supposed to know you were going to get flustered and run away?"

"I didn't run away," said Tau, glancing back over his shoulder. He heard a commotion around the bend in the corridor; murmuring voices and the footsteps of a crowd. He turned back to Yvette, now reading something on her faxpad. "I was out of time, so I ended the press conference. I gave them plenty of material to read if they wanted to learn more about the project."

Yvette looked up and sighed. "Mediaheads don't read. You should know that by now."

Tau glanced over his shoulder again. Still out of view around the bend, the crowd noises increased; probably dignitaries or a touring school group that blundered into the Space Projects Facility while looking for the glitzy displays in space sciences. Could she really have tried to help him, or was this some sort of a game?

"Look," said Tau, "I don't know what you were thinking, but I don't need your help, okay? I can't just improvise in front of a crowd like that; I have to rehearse."

"Then you shouldn't have called a press conference."

"Hey, it wasn't my idea. Max said I needed to tell the public about my ideas so that I could get my project approved."

"It's him," shouted a male voice behind Tau. A herd of mediaheads led by Geraldo Cruz rounded the corner, then surged toward Tau and Yvette in a stampede.

Tau looked at Yvette, his eyes wild. "What should I do?"

"Hide," she said. She opened the door to Tymanov's office and shoved Tau inside. "I'll take care of them."

The office door slammed shut, leaving Tau standing beside Tymanov's desk. Vadim looked up from his work with a calm gaze, as if he'd expected Tau to fly into the room without warning. "Good morning, my friend. I saw your press conference on the feed yesterday. Were you trying to scare people, or was that unintentional?"

Tau sat down heavily in the chair beside the desk; a standard gray NASA "seating module" with a rock-hard seat. "I was doing fine until Yvette showed up."

"She was at your press conference? Why did you invite her?"

"I didn't invite her. She just showed up and pasted me with ridiculous questions in front of the entire planet."

Tymanov's dark eyebrows rose. "And you let her do it?"

"No, I didn't *let* her do it. I didn't have any choice."

"You should have taken charge of the situation. All I heard was a female voice asking a few questions, then you got up and ran out of the room."

Tau closed his eyes and banged his head on the desktop. "I hate this job."

"You're going to hate it even more."

"Why?" Tau asked, looking up.

"I don't know if I should tell you. Your mood is very dark."

"You can't shoot the dog more than once. Go ahead and tell me."

"We work for Yvette now."

Tau chuckled. "You always know what to say to make me feel better. What's the real news?"

"That's it."

"No," said Tau, his smile fading. "Really."

"Tokugawa disappeared. Peters was fired. They wouldn't promote either one of us. Yvette is in charge of the VR lab now."

"No," said Tau, refusing to fall for the joke. "That's not possible."

"You'd better get used to it. I told you she's dangerous."

Tau sat back in the chair, unable to breathe, his eyes darting around the room. He felt trapped.

"You need vodka," said Tymanov, handing Tau a chilled squeeze bottle. He always kept one in his desk drawer for emergencies.

"Has anyone heard from Max?" Tau asked, brushing the bottle away.

"I haven't spoken to him. Is he gone?"

"He's in Washington. At headquarters. Some kind of a speech."

Tymanov nodded.

With a heavy sigh, Tau looked up at the ceiling and rubbed his neck. "How can Yvette run the lab? She doesn't know enough about our work."

Tymanov shrugged as he put the vodka back in his desk drawer. "Experience does not seem to matter, in this case. Chakrabarti decided that Yvette should lead us into the future, so he must think she has the right qualifications. However, we should not worry too much. I'm sure she's just passing through on her way to becoming our director."

"You're saying Chakrabarti should be worried about his job?"

"He won't even feel the knife sliding into his back until it's too late. This woman is a master of disinformation."

"She seems so nice. Are you sure about all this?"

"If she lived in Moscow, she'd be running the *mafiya*."

Tau stood up and looked out the window. "I'm not doubting you, but maybe I should talk to Yvette about this."

"Are you mad? You can't win by confronting her. You're not some American cowboy man out 'ropin' the doggies,' or whatever it was that they did with cows. She'd eat you alive if she considered you a threat."

"Then what would you suggest?"

"Ignore her. Stay out of her way. And keep your eyes open in case she tries to set you up for trouble."

Tau sat on the edge of Tymanov's desk with his arms crossed. "Vadim, I know you don't like Yvette, but I've been around her a lot more than you have. You learn things about a person when you share an apt with them. She has good and bad qualities, just like the rest of us. Right now, she's out in that hallway helping me with those media assassins. I appreciate that."

"And she's attractive, yes? And your fiancée just went to another planet to get away from you, yes? You are not thinking with your head, my friend. I recognize her personality because I've lived with people like her for most of my life. Deception is a matter of survival in my country."

"Isn't it possible that your background might color your opinions somewhat? I prefer to think of Yvette as innocent until proven guilty."

"I think she already demonstrated her guilt. However, you will see for yourself. If this woman decides we're a problem, she'll take the innocent and prove them guilty of something they didn't do. Be prepared for that."

"I'll keep my eyes open, Vadim."

"Well, you may keep them open, but you also have to look in the right place."

ON the *Ares*, as on every other long-term space mission since the International Space Station was placed in Earth orbit, a straitjacket had been included among the standard supplies available to the crew. Kate McCloud now understood why.

Despite decades of long-duration spaceflights, individual personalities showed different reactions to the space environment. As the number of amateur astronauts increased and the rigorous psychological testing required of professional astronauts became a minor factor in crew selection, more problems became apparent in transit. Antarctic training weeded out those with the weakest mental balance, but odd personality quirks appeared with greater frequency among recent Mars crews.

Kate wasn't violent, but she had never realized how much stimulation she required to stay sane. After many weeks of the same routine, the novelty wore off, and she compensated for the tedium by sleeping more. Each "morning," the full-spectrum lights in the ceiling would gradually brighten until the simulated sunrise brought the light levels up to full strength. The nanopaint wall panels shifted in color during the twelve hours of "daylight," working through the spectrum from the gray dawn through turquoise noon to magenta sunset. In her private cabin, Kate could run video loops of dynamic outdoor scenes, and she often played her "stream in the redwood forest" loop to watch the birds and the animals. She missed having a pet. At home, she kept two African pygmy hedgehogs—Spiny Norman and Spikette—who had maintained the same nocturnal hours that Kate preferred for so many years. The hedgehogs were tough little animals, tiny balls of spikes when they were upset, but their pincushion appearance commanded respect, or what Kate liked to call "tough love." Now the hedgehogs were living with a friend, and she missed them terribly.

A short stack of self-sterilizing food trays sat patiently on her desk, waiting for her to return them to the galley. Beside the food trays, her workstation monitor showed today's delayed edition of a gossip magazine, the *Global Inquisitor*, in place of the archaeological news she'd studied daily until two weeks ago. The delay in the datalink relay time from Earth became more noticeable with each passing day, and now took almost half an hour to respond to her requests. The delay made her feel isolated, reinforcing the fact that she was a long way away from home, and from Tau. Now, as she always did when Tau entered her mind, she immediately concentrated on something else.

Daily work and planning sessions were only taking about four hours a day, but Kate felt less a part of the group as time went on. Ian and Tak kept to themselves most of the time. Although they were polite, the Russians had a tendency to lapse into their own language even when Kate was around, distancing her from the conversation because she only knew a few phrases. She had planned to learn more of the language during the flight, but she delayed because it would be dangerous for her to make a direct learning tap into the net in a depressed mood. As she had discovered in college, she was a learning addict with an infodictive personality. She might tap into the net and decide to stay there for the rest of the trip, or until her body ceased functioning because she'd chosen to remain in a learning trance without food for too long. With the other crew members around, she knew it was unlikely that she'd waste away on a datalink before one of them snapped her out of it to make her eat, but her modified infotap rig was illegal. If Novikov or anyone else discovered she was an infodict, they wouldn't trust her with the delicate work around the Martian ruins.

The air in her room smelled bad. The misting device was supposed to provide one of Kate's chosen fragrances to match up with her moods or with the video scenes displayed on her walls, but the mechanism failed after the first month. The faint breeze from the circulation vents was insufficient to remove the odors, which varied from high school locker room to rotting meat. If the scent would remain the same from day to day, she knew her nose would adapt and allow her to ignore it, but the broken fragrance mister creatively modified the smell at random.

She wondered why she was putting herself through all this.

The colonies on Mars were examples of a frontier society. Populated by scientists and engineers with strong personal drives and pragmatic attitudes, they were developing a culture of technological excellence and innovation. Many of the colonists were sponsored by meganational corporations on Earth, working under hardship conditions away from their families so that they could earn massive paychecks compared to what they'd be earning back home. As the colonies developed further, and the colonists who wanted to remain on Mars could afford to pay the huge fees for tickets, they would bring their families up to join them. Such an arrangement was a time-honored tradition among emigrants. Starting in the seventeenth century, European families had pooled their resources so that one family member could emigrate to America. That emigrant would then earn enough money to buy passage for the rest of the family. Third world families used the same techniques in the twentieth century. Aware of the high labor costs and the need to keep their workers happy, the meganational sponsors had discussed plans to offer loans covering the costs of Mars flights for families, allowing their employees to work off the loans on Mars. Considering that the return flight to Earth could take up to two years, Kate understood that Mars might become her permanent home because she wouldn't be able to tolerate the long journey back.

Studying the food trays, she thought once more about returning them to the galley. Right on schedule, she had continued to eat three meals a day to provide a daily intake of three thousand calories. The food was good, but limited in variety. They ate both Russian and American dehydrated food reconstituted by mixing with water. Some of the food had been thermostabilized, then sealed in airtight pouches. The food packages themselves were timed to self-destruct into biodegradable components to be recycled by the ship's systems. Kate liked to start her morning with a bag of Russian borscht and a bag of fruit juice. The Russians had developed an addiction to the packets of American mayonnaise, mixing them in with almost everything they ate. This mayonnaise fanaticism had developed into a heated argument four weeks into the flight when Svetlana Ryumina discovered an extra packet among Novikov's lunch materials.

Kate sighed, picked up the trays, and carried them into the curving corridor. She missed the short period of microgravity that had allowed her to fly through the ship. Now, the spin-induced centrifugal gravity simulated the 0.38 G they would experience on the Martian surface, which was great for their muscles, even though they had to exercise more to stay in shape, but it took all the fun out of moving around the cabin. Back in the galley, she ignored Svetlana and Tanya Savitskaya, who were drinking tubes of tea and talking in Russian. They looked up when Kate entered, then giggled and continued talking. They never switched to English, and that annoyed Kate because she always assumed they were talking about her. Kate dumped the trays and shuffled back to her cabin.

When she shut the door, she locked it. Early flights had not included locking doors, but experience had shown that the added feeling of privacy gave the crew the illusion of control over their personal lives. Seated on the edge of the bed, she opened a drawer and removed her personal hygiene kit. The kit had started out neat, with everything in its place, but now she had to rummage through the jumbled containers to find the special shampoo bottle. When she found the shampoo, she twisted off the false bottom and withdrew the fine coil of the infotap cable.

She would learn Russian, even if it killed her.

13

DR. Maxfield Thorn looked up at a tall, narrow structure of rough brown stone. It rose four stories above the tree-lined street, its walls covered in ivy, with lead-paned windows that caught the light in their facets, reflecting it back to the street in colorful prismatic flashes of yellow, blue, and red. The senator had done well for himself; he was living in one of the nicest neighborhoods around Washington, DC. A security perimeter preserved this historic district from the depredations of the restless local natives, shielding the wealthy from the urban reality of the nation's capital. Thorn had passed through the neighborhood shield wall without interference, and it amused him to think that this would be the only time he'd be admitted without setting off alarms.

Thorn mounted the wide concrete steps to the front entrance, raised the brass knocker that gleamed against the black enamel of the door, and hesitated. Thorn knew it was better to surprise the senator, since any attempt at communication prior to his arrival would have been ignored, just as his e-mails had been ignored for so many years, but he couldn't be certain that his unannounced arrival would gain him access to the senator's inner sanctum. Too many years had passed since they'd seen each other. Thorn didn't even know if he'd be able to recognize the man when he finally saw him. The thought made his stomach flutter. He frowned at the idea of butterflies at his age, but he noticed his heart beating faster, too.

As it turned out, he didn't have to knock. The ancient speaker by the door popped with static, and he heard a woman's voice. "Yes? Who is it?"

Thorn squinted up at the tiny security camera over the door. "Maxfield Thorn. I'd like to see the senator."

"Thorn?" A pause. "One moment, please."

In the cold air, Thorn blew clouds of steam at the camera

while he waited. Then the speaker popped again. "The senator is very busy right now. He suggested that you e-mail his secretary and make an appointment."

Thorn snorted. "You can tell the senator to get his butt down here and open this door right now. If he doesn't, I'll be happy to tell some of my media contacts about the senator's unsavory exploits in college."

The door buzzed and popped open. Thorn chuckled and stepped inside. His footsteps echoed on the polished green marble of the grand foyer. A sweeping staircase, with flying angels carved into the mahogany balustrade, curved up to the second floor. A skylight of stained glass showered color into the room from the high ceiling, fighting for attention with the large crystal chandelier. The entire effect came together in a style that managed to be both opulent and gaudy at the same time.

A hidden door opened in the wall to Thorn's right, revealing the athletic form of a middle-aged bald man—Senator Aaron Thorn. The senator didn't look happy as he tied a blue silk kimono around his skintight electric blue workout suit. "What do you want?"

"To see my long-lost son?"

"Try again," said the senator, continuing to block the doorway.

"You're looking fit."

The senator rolled his eyes. "Do you need money? Is that why you're here?"

"You don't understand me very well, do you?"

"How could I? I don't even know you."

"That was your choice. Do you want to take a poke at me or something?"

"Thanks for the offer, but I don't enjoy beating up old people."

"You won't get very far on Capitol Hill with an attitude like that."

"Very funny. A lot of people think I'll be the next president."

"With a brain like yours, I'm not surprised. I've always regretted that you chose to use your intelligence for evil instead of good. You would have made a good scientist."

"And be like you? No, thanks," he said, turning to shut the door. "If you'll excuse me, I've got a country to run."

Before the senator could get the door closed, Thorn jammed his foot into the opening, then winced as the door slammed against his shoe. The senator jerked the door open again with a scowl on his face. "What do you think you're doing?"

Thorn bent over to rub his foot. "It always works in the holies."

Hearing footsteps behind him, Thorn turned to see a dinosaur in a workout suit standing in the hallway. His face looked like a bullet with short blond hair, but he also had muscles where normal people shouldn't. Thorn glanced back at the senator. "Are dinosaurs legal in this state?"

"Sven, show the man out."

The monster stepped forward, but Thorn held up his hand in front of the bullet face. "Thanks, but I can find the door on my own." When he looked at the senator, the door was almost closed. "Of course, if you don't talk to me, I can't help you with your campaign. Believe it or not, there are a lot of people who respect my opinions, and they'd love to know whether or not I support your politics. It's a funny thing: When the public knows you spend your life thinking about things, and trying to understand complex science problems, they also think you apply the same sort of rigorous discipline to your politics. Of course, most scientists are too appalled with their possible choices to waste time voting, but the public doesn't know that. If you're so sure that you've got the presidency in the bag, then your pet can toss me out the door; otherwise, you might wish to reconsider."

The senator slammed the door shut.

Thorn drew himself up and looked Sven in the eye. "You understand that I called you a 'dinosaur' just to make a point, right? I'm sure if I took the time to speak with you, I'd find out that you're a higher order of life-form."

Sven shrugged and indicated the front door with his right hand.

Thorn sighed and turned to leave. Sven opened the door for him, but before Thorn got outside, the senator stepped out into the hallway. "Okay, you win. Come inside."

Sven smiled and stepped back to let Thorn walk past. Three walls of the study were occupied by antique books on shelves; the fourth wall was a polished granite monument to the memory of fireplaces in European castles, larger than the apt Thorn had lived in as a college student. Logs crackled in the cheery fire, causing shadows to dance around the walls of the room. Over the fireplace, a large holo portrait of the senator, dressed in a white toga with a crown of golden leaves on his head, loomed over the room in the pose of a Roman emperor. A dark mahogany desk dominated the floor space. Thorn stepped into the fireplace to warm his hands, then snorted in disgust when he discovered the fire was a projection without heat. When the senator shut the door, Thorn sat down heavily in one of the black leather chairs that faced the carrier deck.

"You've got ten minutes. Start talking."

"NASA has a project that needs funding," said Thorn, watching his son's eyes. He recognized the younger version of himself that he expected to see each morning in his bathroom mirror; he was always shocked when he saw the reflection of an old man looking back at him.

The senator looked down at his desk and shook his head once. "Can't help you."

"Don't worry. It's not my project," said Thorn.

The senator looked up. His eyes glittered. "Go on."

Thorn explained Tau's proposal in moderately technical terms, aware that his son could understand what he was talking about. The eyes revealed Aaron's quick grasp of the concepts, but the frown told Thorn he was fighting an uphill battle.

Impatient, the senator cut him off. "You want my opinion? Keep that Wolfsinger guy away from the media."

Thorn raised an eyebrow. "You saw the interview?"

"I saw it. I also saw the Veggies protesting outside Ames Research Center this morning. Their leader, Snapdragon, comes across much better with the press, so Wolfsinger looks like Dr. Frankenstein with the public."

"Can you help?"

The senator leaned back and scratched his head, avoiding Thorn's eyes. "The only way this thing could get funded is through the Mars office, and that's not going to happen."

"Why not?"

"Walter Beckett's been a busy boy lately. With his updates on the new discovery at Vulcan's Forge, he gets more news time than I do. The media asked him about Wolfsinger's proposal, and he laughed the whole thing off."

"Perhaps you could speak with Beckett."

"I could, but he's not the only problem. The Russians are acting funny about Mars projects right now. Take my advice and forget the whole thing."

"This doesn't have anything to do with the Russians."

"On Mars, everything has to do with the Russians."

Thorn frowned. "I don't understand."

"Trust me; the political situation is delicate. Mars isn't the healthiest place to be right now."

"I don't believe you. I know some of the scientists living in the Russian colony on Mars, and they haven't mentioned anything unusual happening there."

"These friends of yours are in the military?"

Thorn had to think about it. "In a sense, I suppose. They work for the Exploration Directorate. The Russian colony is controlled by the military."

"And you trust them?"

"Of course. Why shouldn't I?"

The senator drummed his fingers on the desktop. "If I tell you, will you go away and leave me alone?"

"Maybe."

"You can't repeat anything I say."

"Give me a break. My security clearance is probably higher than yours."

"You haven't worked for DARPA in years. Your clearance isn't active anymore."

"You want me to swear my allegiance to the flag or something?" He gave the senator a quick salute.

Aaron Thorn closed his eyes and rubbed his forehead. "I'm trying to warn you. There are people who would take extreme measures to keep this information secret. I need to know that you'll stop pursuing this Wolfsinger project if I can convince you I'm telling the truth."

"Okay, no guarantees, but you've hooked my interest. I must admit that I'm touched by your concern regarding my safety."

The senator stared at him for a moment, then pressed a button on his desk. "It's not your safety I'm worried about—it's mine."

14

ALTHOUGH he prepared himself for the unexpected, Tau had no idea what he'd see when he entered Chakrabarti's office. He took a deep breath, held it, and turned the doorknob. The previous projection of Shark Stonehenge in the office had been replaced with a sunny mountaintop covered in snow. The opening of a cave, its interior flickering with dim firelight, beckoned Tau across a narrow bridge of translucent ice that spanned a bottomless chasm. He stepped forward, testing the bridge, but the ice wasn't slippery. Shutting the office door, he crossed the span without plummeting to his doom and entered the cave. Gravel crunched under his shoes as the narrow cave opening expanded into an immense chamber of glittering rock crystals. At the center of the chamber, a circle of flame surrounded Chakrabarti, seated on the floor in a lotus position. A dark cloak covered most of his head and his body, leaving only his hands and feet in view—islands of flesh floating in a sea of brown cloth. His face was in shadow, but the firelight danced in the director's eyes, enhancing his malevolent appearance as he watched Tau's approach.

Tau stopped outside the ring of fire. "You wanted to see me, Director?"

"Does that surprise you, Mr. Wolfsinger?"

"You want to know why I called that press conference."

"I can guess *why* you did it. What I want to know is why you thought you could get away with it. Your little media escapade was poorly conceived, and unauthorized, but I find it personally distressing that you have such a willingness to wave your obsession around in public when I already told you to keep it quiet. The peer review committee didn't approve your proposal, headquarters doesn't care about it, and you have no other internal support. Did you think it would help NASA's reputation if you spread your lunatic notions among the masses? Did you think you'd win some kind of popular support if you threatened to destroy the biosphere with your dangerous new toy? Are you trying to put this research center out of business?"

"The press conference seemed like a good idea at the time," Tau mumbled.

"And it was entirely your idea?"

"Yes, Director."

"Don't lie to me. I've had too much experience with you people in the VR lab. You'll say anything to get your way. First Peters, then Tokugawa, now this. It's as if there's some sort of disease spreading among the Space Project employees, but I know it's just a lack of ethics among the personnel in the VR lab. Thorn put you up to this, didn't he?"

"Certainly not. Dr. Thorn isn't even here."

"I know where he is; I sent him on the trip. And the Public Affairs Office said you used Thorn's name when you had them set up the press conference."

Tau shrugged. "I didn't think the media would show up unless Dr. Thorn was involved."

The director's eyes seemed to be burning. "I'll remind you that we depend on government and private funding. Each time someone makes us look stupid or inept in public, the money valve tightens, and I have to dump some employees. When you tell the media that you have an autonomous AI that's going to build cities all over the planet, all you're doing is scaring them, and they love that because it draws viewers. Then groups like the Veggies start their protests. Big nanotech even gives *me* the willies, so you can't expect Joe Average to start jumping for joy when you tell him your AI is about to play God."

Tau waved a foot over the ring of fire to reassure himself that it was a projection, then took a step forward to stand in the flames. A symbolic move, but he felt better for it because he knew it would irritate the director. "The Veggies don't know what they're talking about. If the mediaheads had bothered to read the material I gave them, I described the safety measures that are built into the construction system to control the AI. As a last resort, I could set off a logic bomb to destroy the AI's capacity to function. But the media didn't mention any of that; they chose to build a story that would scare people instead."

"You can't blame the media, Mr. Wolfsinger. You invited them."

"True," Tau nodded. "What are you going to do now?"

"My first inclination was to ask for your resignation, but your new supervisor convinced me to let you stay."

"Yvette?"

Chakrabarti nodded. "Ms. Fermi seems to think you have some value. I agreed that you have a certain raw talent, even though it could be put to better uses than I've seen so far. However, my tolerance can only be stretched beyond a certain point; if you defy me again, you'll find yourself seeking employment elsewhere. Are we clear on that?"

"Yes."

"I want you to forget about your nanotech construction proposal; there is absolutely no way it will ever be funded. Ms. Fermi will find appropriate tasks for you to perform. And whatever you do, I want you to maintain a low profile."

Tau nodded.

"Any questions?"

"No."

"Your career is in jeopardy, Mr. Wolfsinger. You're a bright fellow, and you've shown a lot of promise, but you'll have to learn to cooperate to survive here."

Annoyed, he couldn't stop himself from pushing his foot deeper into his mouth. "That attitude didn't help Peters or Tokugawa, did it?"

"This meeting is at an end, Mr. Wolfsinger." As soon as Chakrabarti finished speaking, the image of his body faded away while the flames shot toward the ceiling. A theatrical way to end a discussion, but effective.

THE Lincoln Sitting Room, on the second floor of the White House, was one of the smaller rooms in the East Wing. Budget cuts had taken a toll on the room, as they had on other rooms that were rarely used. The somber Victorian furniture, horsehair sofas interspersed with armchairs of dark wood, smelled old and musty. The tomes in the bookcases looked as if they were glued to the dark wood shelves by time and dust. The walls of the oval room were decorated with numerous oil paintings, but the subjects were indistinguishable under a dark patina of dirt. Virginia Danforth liked to use the Lincoln Sitting Room because its section of the White House was usually deserted except when official guests were in residence. With some people, she could use the museum atmosphere of this room to evoke feelings of duty and respect. Outside of Nixon and Kissinger praying here the night before Nixon resigned the presidency in 1974, there were no notable events that had occurred in the room, but the aura of skeletons hidden in closets and the ghosts of former presidents lent a solemn air to any interrogation. Senator Thorn planned on being president himself, so Danforth knew she could best manipulate him by evoking the image of Abraham Lincoln's ghost and the sacrifices he made to ensure the country's survival.

The senator's eyes darted around the room as he descended into one of the old sofas. At midafternoon, the light coming from the windows was dim, as if filtered through years of political dirt on the rippled panes of glass. Danforth sat directly opposite him, perched on the edge of a black chair with carved gargoyle armrests that reminded her of a Victorian throne.

"I guess you know my father visited me at home," said the senator, clearing his throat as he shifted on the sofa in an attempt to get comfortable. Danforth knew the padding on the old museum piece was shot, poking the senator with a spring or two through the upholstery.

"Tell me about it," she said. Her voice was polite, but in command.

Shifting his weight on the sofa again, the senator summarized the previous day's conversation with his father.

Danforth frowned. "Does he know about Red Star?"

The senator's eyes widened for a moment; long enough for Danforth to get the real answer. "I don't think so. He has friends working in the Russian colony, but they haven't communicated with him since they left Earth."

"Hmm. He's a smart man. Do you think he spoke to anyone else on the Hill about his situation at NASA?"

"No. He doesn't have many friends. Most people hate him."

"That doesn't mean anything," said Danforth. The corners of her mouth lifted in a slight smile. "Most people hate me, but they also know I'm dangerous. In any case, Red Star must remain a secret—if word got out to the public about what the Russians are doing on Mars, we'd have to start a disinformation campaign and that could delay us for years."

"I'm sure he doesn't know anything." The senator shrugged.

"I'm curious about Dr. Thorn. Up to this point, according to my records, you've never had any contact with him, but he felt free to show up at your home and ask you a big favor. Why do you think he did that?"

"My father lives in his own private world, and he has no idea how to deal with real people. I'm sure he just got it into his head that he could show up on my doorstep and ask me to help him, even though he never bothered to help me. As far as I'm concerned, the only thing we have in common is our last name."

"You realize that your father could jeopardize your shot at the presidency? If he's able to link you to Red Star, the public won't like it."

Worried, the senator glanced around the room. "Is it safe to talk in here?"

"Yes."

He stared into her eyes. "How safe?"

"We have active electronic countermeasures in each room and around the entire building. The walls are thin, but there's a noise suppression system that blocks sound transmission from room to room. The windows are damped against laser bugs. No one can hear us."

"My father is an old man with weird ideas. Even if he'd heard something about Red Star, he wouldn't care because it wouldn't have any effect on his own activities. He's completely safe, as far as we're concerned."

"But there's a chance he'll speak to Beckett while he's in town?"

The senator shrugged again. "It's possible, I suppose, but unlikely. That's why he wanted me to intervene with the funding gods at NASA. Do you want me to speak with Beckett, or Lindsay, in case my father decides to contact them?"

"That won't be necessary," Danforth sighed. "I'll take care of it."

BACK in her own office, Virginia Danforth used her computer to summon four personnel files and two NASA project files, then placed a priority lock on them that would prevent access by anyone else. She then arranged a lunch appointment by sending an anonymous e-mail, encrypted for utmost security and loaded with innocuous code phrases, through a series of anonymous net nodes that would disguise the origin of the message. Initiating a canned program that would make it appear she had remained in her office during lunch to send out several lengthy e-mails, Danforth stood and moved a bookcase to reveal a secret door. The hidden exit had been built during the Cold War, connecting to a passage built during the Civil War. The passage led to a spiral ramp that emptied into an underground tunnel, continuing under Pennsylvania Avenue past three locked gates, cameras, automated defenses, and armed guards to another ramp that climbed to a hidden exit in Lafayette Park. Dr. Danforth was on the list of five people who could make use of the White House's park tunnel, a privilege she used on a regular basis, so no one bothered her. In keeping with protocol, no record was kept with regard to her passage.

AT a Georgetown bar known as *Jabba's Jazz Joint*, a free-light musician entertained the noisy crowd. A bouncy saxophone melody was generated as the musician made quick, precise movements at the center of a laser ring focused on his body. The breath controller in his throat produced trills and slides that any nonmodified sax player would have envied. No one paid any attention to Danforth, sipping wine at her small table in a back corner of the bar.

A man in a polychrome suit approached Danforth's table and sat down without a word. Danforth noticed that the moving pastel colors in the man's suit drew attention away from his physical appearance. In his forties, he looked trim and fit, without any of the muscular engineering enhancements so popular among those in the rougher professions. Except for his cold blue eyes, he had the sort of face no one would look at twice.

Danforth glanced at the antique timepiece on her wrist. "You're late."

"I was busy." The man's deep voice had a jagged edge.

"What can I do for you this time?"

Danforth pushed her napkin across the table. Within its folds lay a tiny ROM cube. The man picked up the napkin, palmed the cube, and slid it into a socket above his left wrist. His eyes glazed over as he read the memo projected on his retina.

"As you can see, there's a potential problem," said Danforth, glancing at the freelight player as he finished his set on-stage. Goose bumps rose on her arms, but she wasn't sure if they were a reaction to a cold draft or something else.

The man nodded. "I'll take care of it."

"It has to be tonight. We can't take any chances."

His eyes focused on hers. "Quick work? That could be messy."

"Do whatever is necessary. No witnesses. Damage is at your discretion."

"That makes it easier," he said, rising from his seat.

"No mistakes. If you fail, someone will take corrective action on you."

The corners of his mouth rose a fraction of an inch. "Before they take care of you?"

Danforth met his gaze without flinching. "Perhaps. In any case, that day will come for us all."

TOM Keefer had been Walter Beckett's assistant and chauffeur for eight years, and there was no one else in the world whom Beckett would have trusted with his secrets. Regular pay increases made Tom the highest-paid administrative assistant at NASA, but Beckett felt it was money well spent. Image was everything to Beckett, and he needed Tom to make sure he got home safely after his Thursday night "meetings." Tom had also proved to be a valuable detective, having spent three months keeping Rupert Lindsay, NASA's deputy director, under surveillance to advance Beckett's career. Tom was also a large young man with plenty of military training, so Beckett couldn't have asked for a better bodyguard.

As Tom turned right on Park Avenue, he glanced in the rearview mirror and noticed Beckett staring at him. "Something wrong, sir?"

"You've been driving me out here every week for eight years, but you've never asked if you could go in with me. I'm thinking you should get a bonus."

"No thanks, sir. I appreciate the offer, but I'm just doing my job."

Beckett raised an eyebrow. "Have you ever taken a good look at these women? You'll never get a chance like this again."

Tom slowed the car when they approached the old brownstone. "I understand, sir, but I'm happily married."

"Your loss," said Beckett, opening his door before the car stopped. "You have no idea what you're missing."

A tall young woman dressed in tight black leather opened the front door as Beckett approached. While parking the car, Tom marveled at her ability to stand upright on her impossibly high-heeled shoes as she grabbed Beckett's wrist and yanked him inside. The door opened wider, giving Tom a glimpse of a blond woman with an impressive superstructure who wore a sheep costume of curly wool. If memory served, the blonde was Bambi and the leather woman was Wendy. He had no idea if those were their real names. Bambi smiled and waved at Tom, then closed the door.

JUST after midnight, Beckett was deeply involved in happy sex dreams when the bed bounced to his right, waking him up. Wendy's perfect butt disappeared into the bathroom. At least, he assumed it was a bathroom, even though the door appeared to be hanging in empty blue sky over a tropical beach. Sweating in the hot sunlight, he could hear the crash of waves on the white sand. Beckett tried to focus on his reflection in the mirror that floated in the "sky" over the bed, but his eyes wouldn't cooperate.

Hearing a snore to his left, he turned his head too fast and Bambi's nipple poked him in the eye. Pressure around his wrists and ankles reminded him that his hands and feet were tied to the bedposts. They had neglected to free him when playtime was over.

When Wendy returned from the bathroom, she shut the door and sealed up the rectangular hole in the sky, startling a rainbow-colored macaw out of a nearby palm tree. Beckett tried to focus on Wendy's various charms while she approached the left side of the bed, but a recreational drug they'd given him earlier, probably glitter, still kept his vision fuzzy. Bambi squeaked as Wendy gave her one hard spank on the butt to wake her up.

"You know what to do," said Wendy. Her French accent made everything sound sexy.

Bambi gave Beckett a pouty look as she rose to a kneeling position close beside him. She still wore her sheep ears from her costume. Her long blond hair tickled his arm while she kissed his cheek, then she straddled his stomach.

Beckett tried to think of something clever to say, but the fleshy orbs hanging over him erased all thoughts from his mind.

"Get it over with," breathed Wendy, placing her left hand on his throat.

Bambi sighed and placed a red silk pillow over Beckett's face. The hand on his throat tightened to hold him down. His confused brain didn't know how to respond. The pressure of the pillow on his face increased. Wendy's grip tightened on his throat. Bambi bounced on his stomach. He tried to shout to let them know he needed to breathe, but no sound would pass through the satiny smoothness that filled his mouth. With his heart pounding, he struggled against the ropes that held his wrists and ankles, cutting into his flesh as he yanked them in every direction. Warm blood trickled down his arms. His stomach and chest muscles convulsed with the need to draw air into his lungs. Hundreds of colored lights popped and flashed inside his eyelids. He knew they must be able to see that something bothered him, that he needed air, and that the game wasn't fun anymore. His neck muscles cramped. His head pounded with the worst headache ever. Where was Tom? Tom would help. Must signal Tom. But the girls would stop. The girls loved him. Didn't they?

THE alarm beeped on the dashboard clock; two hours before dawn and time for Tom to retrieve his boss. He rubbed his eyes and yawned, then turned in his seat so he could reach the doorknob. Then he saw the man in the polychrome suit—he had an unremarkable face except for the icy blue eyes staring into Tom's soul through the open window.

"Are you Mr. Beckett's driver?"

Tom relaxed, assuming the man worked with Bambi and Wendy. Probably a bouncer. "Yes. Is he ready to leave?"

"He already left," said the man, raising a silenced assassin's needler.

The shot sprayed Tom's thoughts all over the inside of the car.

15

WHEN Tau returned to his office, he found Vadim Tymanov talking to Aristotle. Tymanov rarely communicated with Ari, so it surprised Tau to see him sitting on the stool by the workbench, deep in conversation.

"Sorry," said Tau, approaching the bench. "I hope I'm not interrupting anything."

Tymanov jumped when he heard Tau's voice, then turned and smiled. "Tau, my friend. We were just discussing how I used to grow my own food."

"You did your own farming?"

"My family lived in one of the science towns, so no one had any money to buy food. Fortunately, one of the researchers from the Institute of Soil and Photosynthesis took me under his wing and showed me the proper techniques."

"The Institute of Soil and Photosynthesis? Are you making this up?"

Tymanov crossed his arms. "Certainly not. Gennadi organized the School of Practical Fruit and Vegetable Gardening so that the clumsy biologists, astronomers, and physicists in the town could be efficient with their gardening time. You wouldn't believe some of the pathetic-looking gardens we used to have before Gennadi took pity on us. I grew carrots so small that they looked like little orange peas."

A convincing story, but Tau knew Tymanov often embellished his own history. "It's hard for me to picture you as a gentleman farmer, Vadim."

"Really? Then try to imagine fifty Einsteins, each with a thirty-square-meter garden plot, all with enough academic letters after their names to fill a dictionary, none of whom had any idea how to make plants grow. These people built one of the world's largest elementary particle accelerators, but as soon as they left the lab they were practically helpless."

"How long did you live there?"

"Fifteen years. I grew up in Protvino. My mother was a physicist at the Institute for High Energy Physics; my father was an engineer there. It was like a ghost town, but the ghosts didn't know they were dead. In a good year, my parents might receive two paychecks for some of their accumulated back salary. We lived in a warehouse with six other families; it was full of magnets and generators for new accelerators that were never built—which is why I say I have a magnetic personality. My parents grew the food until I was old enough to tend the garden, but they weren't very good at it either."

Ari spoke up. "I can verify his story, Tau. This information is included in Mr. Tymanov's personnel file. At fifteen, he left Protvino to attend Moscow State University, after which he accepted employment in Kaliningrad."

Tymanov frowned at Ari. "You have access to my personnel file?"

"Maybe," said Ari.

Tau knew Ari was hedging because of the tone of Tymanov's voice. "We're government employees, Vadim. Our files are stored in multiple locations. The unclassified details of our lives are available to anyone on the net."

"Americans carry this freedom thing too far," said Tymanov.

"Protvino could have been a wonderful place if the funding for the particle accelerators hadn't dried up in the nineties," said Ari. "It was located in a pine forest about an hour away from Moscow. Instead of the concrete boxes that were built all over the Soviet Union, there were actual architects who designed the buildings for Protvino. Cars were kept out of the town by the greenbelt. People wanted to live there because it sounded like a romantic location where the top researchers could study Big Science in relative peace and security."

Tymanov looked at Tau with one eyebrow raised.

"He's showing off," said Tau. "He looked it up while you were talking."

"Of course, they didn't realize until later that the town was built on an unstable geological base," said Ari, sounding a bit miffed as he completed his thought. "The master plan had to be modified several times as new caverns were discovered. When they built the tunnel for the accelerator, the water table gradually shifted. Portions of the tunnel flooded and collapsed, causing the earth to open up and swallow part of the town."

Tymanov nodded. "My father said Protvino was cursed. During World War II, the southern front moved back and forth seven times across the site where Protvino would be built, along the Protva and Oka Rivers. He had a collection of rusty German helmets that he found while they were building the town. He also had a human skull with a bullet hole in its forehead."

"It sounds terrible," said Tau. "Why did your parents choose to stay there?"

"They liked the environment. The science towns were supposed to be models of modern progress. In the beginning, they had more personal freedom and a higher standard of living than the rest of the Soviet Union. When the money stopped, they had no military industry that could be converted to civilian factories, and none of the residents had enough money to move away. The scientific equipment was still there to keep the experimentalists happy. The theorists could work anywhere, but they thrived in the intellectual atmosphere. And I suppose there were a few incurable romantics who continued living in their dreams."

"Sometimes, dreams are all you can get," said Tau as he sat down on a stool.

Tymanov clapped him on the shoulder. "I'm thinking maybe you are part Russian, my friend."

DR. Maxfield Thorn hated slidewalks. He was on the 101, north of the Ames Research Center, creeping along in the slow lane because he wasn't coordinated enough to maneuver among the faster strips.

A riot of color flashed across the dirty glass of the slidewalk canopy, attempting to persuade him to buy nanotoothpaste, microrobotic digestive tablets, and activebot deodorant. Wall scanners customized the "smart" advertisements for Thorn based on his appearance, manner of dress, and age. Thorn hated smart advertisements because they expected him to fit the stereotypes of twenty-year-old marketing executives who believed that all senior citizens had dirty teeth, upset stomachs, and body odor. Thorn hated marketing executives.

When he spotted the tall pyramid of his apt tower looming

ahead, Thorn moved alongside the rail to prepare for his exit from the slidewalk. Tau lived in the same tower, so he hoped it would be a simple matter to find the young man and give him the news from Washington. After speaking with the senator and other political power brokers on the Hill, Thorn had uncovered disturbing hints regarding military activity on Mars. Something big was being covered up, and there were forces working behind the scenes that were potential threats to Tau. As soon as he'd landed in San Francisco, Thorn went straight to Moffett Field, but Tymanov informed him that Tau had gone home for the day.

The evening Rush hadn't started, so only one man stood on the slidewalk platform outside the apt tower. The man seemed to be waiting for someone, and as Thorn approached the platform he saw the startling blue of the man's eyes, standing out in an otherwise average face, as they turned toward him with a spark of recognition.

Thorn let go of the rail and raised his right foot as he prepared to step off the slidewalk. The man stood in an awkward location where Thorn would have to dodge him as he disembarked, making his exit maneuver much more difficult. But the man held out a large hand to help him off. Startled, Thorn realized that a stranger was performing a good deed for him—an unusual occurrence in the crowded city. Thorn smiled.

He grasped the man's left hand and hopped onto the platform.

As the man's right hand came around to catch him, Thorn spotted a flash of metal.

Thorn gasped and bent over when the man punched him in the stomach, just below his navel. It was an odd sort of punch: He felt as if a chunk of ice had punctured his stomach.

The ice moved upward, ripping its way through cloth, flesh, organs, and bone as the man's left hand pressed against Thorn's back. No one seemed to notice the nice young man helping the sick older man off the platform. Puzzled, Thorn looked into the calm blue pools of his attacker's eyes, but he saw no answers there.

"Sorry," said the man, moving in closer to hug Thorn for more leverage.

Thorn tried to respond, but he didn't have the words. In the confusion of this intimate act, he wondered who the man was, where he was from, and why he was slicing him open. Thorn knew what was happening because he looked down to see his organs and his fluids spilling out of the long fissure the man had ripped into his body, even if he couldn't feel the strange hand that lifted him off his feet with a final jerk.

His damage done, the man yanked the diamond-edged blade out of Thorn's sternum and allowed his body to drop into the weedy shadows alongside the platform. Then he pocketed his cutting tool and dropped his blood-soaked trench coat on the platform before pulling a tag on the collar that flashed the garment into a heap of gray ash. Whistling while he adjusted his polychrome suit, he casually hopped onto the slidewalk and allowed it to whisk him away.

Thorn knew his favorite shirt was ruined. He now held his two halves together with his arms and hands. He knew that if he let go, his insides would spill out on the ground. There didn't seem to be any pain, but he felt sleepy. Not knowing what else to do, and not wanting to waste his remaining time in this world, he set the functioning portions of his mind to the task of pulling himself together long enough to reach Tau's apt. He didn't know why the man had attacked him, and he didn't much care at that moment. He had no illusions about an afterlife, but there were a few simple goals he wanted to attain in this life before he expired. He didn't have to be a medical genius to determine that serious damage had been done to various internal organs now trying to protrude from his abdominal cavity, so there would be little point in trying to get help and then dying while he waited for it to show up. He'd already wasted enough of his life waiting around in doctors' offices that he felt he should have earned a medical degree by osmosis.

Starting out flat on his back, Thorn slowly rolled over on his side, keeping his arms tight against the two halves of his abdomen. Using the wall for support, he pushed up with his shaky legs, worming his way up the wall inch by painful inch until he was in a slumped standing position. He blinked, then concentrated to focus his eyes on the doors into the apt tower a short distance away. People were still at work, so there would be no one to help him or to hinder him if he could stumble his way across the concrete plaza.

He felt time slipping by much too fast. He tried to hurry, taking careful steps on shaky legs, knowing he must look like a zombie from an old horror flatfilm as he staggered across the concrete with his arms pinned to his sides, oozing and spurting various fluids with each squishy step. The perfect costume for Halloween—his favorite holiday as a boy—he wished Paulie O'Connor could see him now. He heard an odd ticking sound each time his stomach tried to pop outside; at least he assumed it was his stomach, although he couldn't be sure from its brief appearances. He sipped air in short gasps, afraid to inflate himself too much lest he pop something important out of his body. Annoyance and frustration helped him proceed toward the beckoning doors.

He had another problem as he reached the entrance; if he raised an arm to tug open a door, his guts would spill out. The apt tower used to have automatic doors, but the government had replaced them with manual doors to lower the electricity bills. True to form, the security camera over the entrance wasn't connected to anything. Government housing had never been luxurious, but Thorn now wished that he had protested the removal of such simple amenities; save a buck, lose a life. If only he weren't mortally wounded, he would make a point of filling out the multiple forms for a complaint to the management. Finally, he noticed that one of the doors didn't seal perfectly against the frame, so he worked his right foot into the crack until he could swing the door open enough to get through it. The effort almost finished him off; propped for a moment between the door and the frame, he thought how nice it would be to take a short nap before continuing further.

He left a big red smear on the doorframe as he passed.

TAU opened the apt door to see what kept thumping against it on the other side. He thought one of the cleaning robots had snagged itself again on the worn spot in the hallway carpet. When Tau clicked the lock open he jumped back, startled to see a bloody body fall into the room. It took a second for him to recognize Dr. Thorn.

"Max!" Tau knelt beside the pale scientist, horrified to see internal body parts spilling out onto his floor. He reached down to help, but he had no idea what he could do. "Max!"

Thorn rolled his head back and looked up at Tau, smiling with his eyes as he swallowed and opened his dry mouth. "Made it."

Tau jumped up and summoned the paramedics, then returned to Thorn's side, cradling the old head in his arms and feeling the warm dampness of the great man's blood as it soaked into his clothes.

Tau's voice was soft. "Help is coming. What happened, Max?"

Max took a breath and rolled his eyes. "Don't waste my time, boy. Obvious, I think."

"How did you get here?"

"Feet. Now, shut up and listen," said Thorn, pausing for a laborious breath. "You need to know some things. They may try to kill you, but I think they need you too much."

"They? Who are they? What are you talking about?"

Thorn gritted his teeth and waved a hand in the direction of his guts on the floor. "Stop interrupting. No time."

"Sorry."

Thorn sighed and licked his lips. "Thirsty, but shouldn't drink. Too many leaks."

Tau brushed a stray lock of gray hair out of Thorn's eyes.

"Watch the Russians. Up to something. My son called it 'Red Star'; some kind of political hot potato. Most don't know about it. And not just the Russians. Others are involved; others who have power. It's big. Big enough to destroy governments."

Thorn clumsily wiped away a trickle of blood that formed a glistening trail from his mouth down his left cheek. He frowned when he saw the new streak on his smeared hand. "Hmph. That can't be good."

"Just rest now, Max. Help should be here soon."

Thorn snorted. "I didn't carry my guts up here just to bleed on your floor, boy. Are you getting any of this? This is important."

"I hear it, but I'm afraid I don't understand it," said Tau, biting his lip.

"My son wouldn't lie. Not about this. Told me not to repeat it."

"I didn't know you had a son."

"Bad seed, became a politician. Senator Aaron Thorn. President soon. But I wouldn't vote for him. Don't you vote for him, either. He's one of them. Emotional thinker. Soft in the head. Never used his natural gifts." Thorn's eyes rolled back in his head. His face twisted in pain as he coughed.

Tau assumed Thorn was in shock, raving about imagined phantoms and conspiracies in his head, but he didn't want to upset the dying man. "Okay, Max."

"You don't believe me," he said, staring into Tau's eyes.

"Take it easy. Help is coming."

Thorn picked up a length of intestine and flopped it over Tau's arm. Tau had to look away and take deep breaths to avoid vomiting. He could feel the warmth of the intestine through his sleeve. "Someone knifed me. Isn't that convincing?"

"I believe you, Max." Tau figured Thorn had run into one of the youth gangs near the tower. He looked out into the hallway, wondering when the emergency team would show up.

"The key is on Mars. Go to Mars. Learn about Red Star. Stop it. Tell people about it. Get proof. No one will believe you."

"I don't know what it is. And how can I stop it? I can't do things like that. I'm a scientist, not a cop."

Thorn weakly tapped his head. "Use your resources. Find a way. If my son was right, they'll have unlimited power. Alien technology. Too much power."

"Alien technology? Do you know anything about it?"

"The Russians have it. That's all I know. Get proof. Expose them. Without proof, they'll kill you. Like me."

"Would your son talk to me?"

"No." Thorn coughed. "Didn't want to talk to *me*. Mentioned Red Star . . . just so I'd stay away. If you spoke to him . . . they might kill you. Just to protect him. Too much at stake."

"Is he responsible for this?" Tau asked, indicating Thorn's torso.

"He wouldn't. No spine for it. Someone else. I upset several . . . people . . . in Washington."

Tau took a deep breath and glanced down the hallway again. He felt frustrated knowing the only thing he could do was to wait for the paramedics, who were apparently eating donuts or something instead of responding to his emergency call. He didn't want to watch his boyhood hero die in his arms. The man had dignity, and he'd dragged himself to Tau's apt to spend his last few moments there. It wasn't right for Dr. Maxfield Thorn to die on the floor of a government tower as a common man would, forgotten by his family, without any friends other than Tau; it was as if Tau looked into his own future. He glanced up at the ceiling, blinked to clear his vision, and wished he knew what to say to the dying man to make him feel better.

"I'll take care of it, Max. If I can figure out how, I'll give it my best shot."

Thorn frowned, grasping one of Tau's sleeves in his right hand. "Don't talk like a loser. I won't tell you again. Losers 'try.' I don't want you to do your 'best.' You must win."

Tau swallowed and looked away. "Okay."

Thorn's breathing looked quick and shallow. His frown

disappeared, but he maintained his grip on Tau's shirt. His hand felt cold. "You could have been . . . my son. There were a lot of things . . . I didn't do right . . . in my life. He wouldn't talk to me. Never wanted to . . . I guess. Could have been . . . a great . . . scientist."

"They say he'll be president," said Tau. "That's something."

"Bah! Presidents . . . come and go. Figureheads. Science . . . is forever. You know."

Tau nodded.

"Sorry . . . I couldn't . . . help you more . . . Tau."

Tau patted his shoulder. "Doesn't matter."

The old scientist coughed up some blood, then grimaced. "This is…really…unpleasant."

Thorn glared up at the ceiling lights, tightened his grip on Tau's sleeve, and died.

ALMOST a month had passed since Dr. Thorn's death, but Tau still felt the effects of the loss. Thorn had been his second father, and he missed him. He found himself in long conversations with Ari while the AI tried to analyze his moods. Tau felt as if many parts of his life had died in the last few months: his relationship with Kate, Dr. Thorn, and the death of his project. Going to work each day took extreme effort, but tinkering with Ari and working in the VR lab allowed him to concentrate on something other than his own problems. Once he was in the lab, he worked long hours trying to forget.

Yvette did her best to distract Tau and be supportive whenever she saw him at the apt or at work, but they never spoke of Thorn's death. Yvette arrived home that evening after Thorn's body was removed, leaving only the pool of blood on the carpet; at first, she thought something had happened to Tau. She seemed visibly relieved when she found him in the bathroom, sitting naked on the floor of the steaming shower watching the water flow down the drain. Yvette helped Tau out of the shower, then dried him off and put him to bed. He never said a word. To keep an eye on him, she crawled into the bed alongside Tau and put her head on his chest. Lulled by the steady rhythm of his breathing, she fell asleep that way. Tau stayed awake most of that night, but he appreciated Yvette's warm presence and the smell of her floral perfume.

Tau asked Ari to check the net for any references to a Russian project known as Red Star, but Ari didn't find anything. The lack of information frustrated Tau because he'd promised Dr. Thorn that he'd look into it. Net research was one thing, but he didn't have the sort of personality required to interrogate strangers about a potentially dangerous topic. There was still a possibility that Thorn had been hallucinating as he died; there was no proof that the attack on Thorn had been anything other than a random killing of the type occurring with greater frequency in Tau's neighborhood. The police kept the case open, but they had little hope of finding the mugger or the gang responsible for the killing. He could try calling Senator Thorn for more information, but Max told him it would be unwise, and he didn't want to upset the senator without a very good reason. If the senator was somehow connected to the Red Star project, such a contact might even get Tau killed. Tau had toyed with the idea of calling the police, or the FBI, or some other official acronym and telling them about Red Star, but he knew they'd treat him like a loon.

While Tau tinkered with Ari, a small holo projection of Director Chakrabarti's head appeared over the workbench. "Mr. Wolfsinger."

Tau looked at the director's head, then sighed and put down his tools. "Yes?"

"Ms. Fermi tells me you've been doing excellent work the last few weeks. I'm glad to see you're being more cooperative. I think you'll find that there are 'synergies of experience' associated with hard work in a group environment. The group itself is a kind of living organism that can only function properly when all its parts are contributing to the survival of the whole. You seem to have learned that lesson."

" 'Synergies of experience.' I'll write that down," said Tau, gritting his teeth.

"Yes. In any case, I told you before that your Nano-VR construction proposal would never be approved, but that was when I was speaking to the 'old' Tau Wolfsinger. Now that the 'new and improved' version of Tau is working here, the climate has changed. Headquarters has reconsidered your request."

Tau frowned. "I don't understand."

The director smiled. "Mr. Wolfsinger, I'm pleased to inform you that you're going to Mars."

Tau simply stared at him.

"Did you hear me, Mr. Wolfsinger?"

"I'm not sure," said Tau, waving his hand through the director's projected head. "I think you just said you're sending me to Mars."

"That's correct."

"I don't want to go to Mars."

Now it was the director's turn to stare at Tau. A vein pulsed in Chakrabarti's right temple. "Of course you want to go to Mars. Your proposal has been approved."

"My proposal never said anything about going to Mars. There's nothing there but dirt, and you can't even breathe the air. That's for astronauts and crazy people."

"No, no, no. Headquarters has a better grasp of the safety issues surrounding your project. They approved it on the condition that it be tested on Mars, not on Earth."

"But—"

"No need to thank me," the director interrupted. "I'm going to give you a month off to settle your affairs before you report to Houston for training. You can expect to be gone for at least three years."

"But, what about my work here? I'm needed in the lab."

"Mr. Tymanov will go with you. Ms. Fermi will supervise the project and act as your interface with the NASA resources at Vulcan's Forge."

"What? Yvette's going to supervise my project? She doesn't know anything about it, and she doesn't have the training to understand it."

"That's a very provincial attitude, Mr. Wolfsinger. She has read your proposal."

"So what? How can she supervise something that doesn't need supervision? I don't need her involvement."

"She'll be going at my request. Unfortunately, I can't go myself, so I need someone there to help you with administrative tasks."

"To keep an eye on me, you mean."

"You're a very cynical young man. I thought you'd be grateful for the opportunity."

"You would think so, wouldn't you? Why do I feel this is your way of getting rid of me?"

"I can assure you that there are cheaper ways to get rid of you than sending you on a trip to Mars. You're lucky to have private sponsors ready to throw money away on your speculative efforts."

"I have sponsors? Who are they?"

"NASA is footing a small portion of the costs. An international consortium is paying the rest, but I'm not privy to the details. Someone out there likes you, although I can't imagine why."

"Neither can I. This is very strange."

"You're a lucky young man. People have waited years for this sort of an opportunity. If you have any more questions, direct them to Ms. Fermi," the director concluded, smiling as his head faded from view. "Have a nice trip."

16

BY the time Kate's archaeology team arrived on Mars, a pre-disturbance survey had already been completed at the Umbra

Labyrinthus site where the construction crew discovered the collapsed alien tunnel. Under the remote direction of Lenya Novikov, the archaeology team leader, workers had completed a thorough three-dimensional holographic survey, complete with laser measurements and probes, so that the team could study the site during its six months en route to Mars. With this information and a computer model, Novikov and the others developed an excavation strategy for the site, work schedules, and individual task assignments. When they arrived at Vulcan's Forge, they were ready to work, but they knew it would take some time to adapt to conditions in the new environment. The *Ares* had been spinning at two revolutions per minute in transit, generating centrifugal gravity equivalent to the 0.38 G pull of Mars, but there were other things they had to learn.

Kate dreaded the idea of life in a space suit, but she had accepted it as required for the special knowledge she would gain. The hard suit, built to maintain an adjustable air pressure from 3.8 to 8 psi with its advanced seals and constant-volume mechanical joints, was not only more flexible than the older style of soft spacesuit, but also had the advantage of increased impact resistance. Kate shuddered when the spacesuit designer from NASA-Ames had told them about the old lunar suits that incorporated a quarter inch of felt in the suit layers to resist micrometeorite impacts—the wisdom being that anything large enough to penetrate the felt would kill the astronaut anyway. She didn't want to think about the meteorites that had pelted the surface of Mars for the last 5 billion years, and what a large one might do to her should she be unlucky enough to get hit. The odds were in her favor, but it could happen.

Long experience from space shuttle missions had shown the negative aspects of the 250-pound shuttle suit: It required sixty-five days and eighty people to service it between flights. The Mars suits, complete with gloves that could pick up coins from flat surfaces, could be stripped down and serviced by one person in a few hours. The structure of the suit, weighing only twenty-eight pounds on Mars, allowed full access to the life-support backpack. Surface habitats were pressurized at 5 psi, with an atmospheric composition of 3.5 pounds of oxygen to 1.5 pounds of nitrogen. The 3.8 psi air pressure of the hard suit allowed the wearer to skip the oxygen prebreathing period that would have wasted hours of precious time in an older-style suit. In the early days of spaceflight, astronauts would breathe pure oxygen for five or six hours to reduce their blood nitrogen levels prior to a space walk. This was a necessity, not a choice. The normal atmospheric pressure on Earth is 14.7 psi. The minimum oxygen pressure required to keep a human in a space suit alive is 3.7 psi. A sudden transition between the two atmospheric pressures of the cabin and the space suit can play havoc with human bodies. Nitrogen is dissolved into the body fluids under higher pressure, then returns to its gaseous state when the pressure is reduced, causing pain as well as heart attacks and strokes. This condition, known as "the bends," can also lead to coma or death. Breathing pure oxygen purges the nitrogen from the blood and tissues, making the transition safer. Kate understood that habitat pressure couldn't be maintained with pure oxygen because it was too explosive, as demonstrated by the Apollo 1 fire. Early Soviet spacesuits, operating at Earth-normal atmospheric pressure and composition, were too stiff; Aleksey Leonov, the first Soviet spacewalker, had to dump most of the air out of his spacesuit through an emergency valve so that he could bend enough to get back inside his spacecraft. Faced with a choice between dying of suffocation outside the spacecraft, or possibly dying inside the cabin from the bends, Leonov chose the latter. The current Mars suit was a compromise between several strategies of dealing with these problems.

Vulcan's Forge had the facilities for producing plentiful oxygen from the carbon dioxide that comprises 95 percent of the atmosphere on Mars. Among other things, this allowed a Mars EVA suit design that vented exhaled air directly into the environment, in the same manner as the SCUBA gear used by divers on Earth. Direct venting reduced the mass of the spacesuit while increasing its serviceability and reliability. Direct venting also helped in removing exhaled moisture; although body cooling was accomplished by a water-cooled undergarment connected to a refrigeration unit in the backpack, up to three pounds of sweat and exhaled moisture could collect in the suit each hour. Without venting, moisture could fog or freeze over on the suit visor to obscure vision, as it had on early American and Russian space walks. With all that moisture loss, dehydration could be another problem, but the suits were equipped with drinking hoses and water recovery tanks.

When Kate first stepped out of the hatch in her suit and hopped down to the Martian surface, she walked around a bit, exhilarated, staring at the cloudless salmon pink sky. The salt-hardened sand crunched beneath her feet while she looked out across the rusty orange terrain covered with half-buried rocks. The horizon looked wrong—too close—a reminder that she was on a smaller planet. To make the experience seem more real, she stooped and plunged her fingers into the duricrust by her feet. Her gloves weren't heated like the rest of her suit and her boot soles, so the shock of the cold ground, colder than any permafrost in Antarctica, caused her to jerk her hand away from the fine, dusty soil loaded with peroxides. The brief contact had numbed her fingertips. The air temperature reading at her waist showed a chilly minus eighty-eight degrees Celsius, but it was still early in the morning. During the night, the lowest temperatures would be found at ground level; later in the day, the ground would be warmer than the air.

Kate looked out across the landscape again, rubbing her gloved hands together while she took it all in. In the distance, she saw a pink dust devil moving in slow motion as it tossed dust into the atmosphere. By her arrival here, she felt as if she'd achieved a victory—perhaps a victory over herself. This was not something she'd ever planned, but now that she was on the surface of Mars, things felt right. Her destiny was here, buried among the red dust; the dried blood of a vanished civilization. Her body vibrated with the energy of her accomplishment. The pieces of the jigsaw puzzle she called her life had fallen into place—all except for one, a piece that was still on Earth. Her heart ached for that final piece of the puzzle to be here now, to make her feel as if everything was in its proper place. She had no doubt that he would have enjoyed sharing this exhilarating moment with her, holding her hand, feeling connected even though they couldn't touch through their space suits.

Thinking of Tau triggered a memory, reminding her why the red desert strewn with rocks looked so familiar. She and Tau had explored an area that looked similar to this in Arizona, north of Flagstaff. In her anthropology classes, she had learned of the cultures that had built the great red sandstone monuments there—the Anasazi, Sinagua, Hohokam, and Mogollon—but she had never seen the structures in person. In the high desert of the Colorado Plateau, the great cities of stone crouched low on the mesa tops or nestled in caves along sheer canyon walls, crumbling with time, the mute remnants of a world that completed its life cycle centuries before Europeans arrived in North America. At Wupatki, in the high desert of northern Arizona, she had seen artistic piles of stone built by long-dead craftsmen; ruins of quiet strength rendered in soft reds and rich browns. Crack-in-Rock ruin was an isolated pueblo built by the Kayenta Anasazi. Hidden atop a red sandstone mesa whose approaches were so steep that it appeared to be a gigantic ship sailing on a sea of sand, Crack-in-Rock had carried her into the past as she and Tau explored its secrets. The approach to the mesa, below the talus slope, was covered with red rocks scattered evenly across the sand, just as her little piece of the Martian surface appeared to her now. Unlike the mesa, there were no sandstone cliffs here to erode into the clutter of rocks scattered across the ancient midden; however, the entrance to Crack-in-Rock had been through the heart of the mesa itself, just as the Tharsis tunnels might lead to subterranean ruins hidden in the heart of Mars.

Tau had shown her the way, disappearing from the path at the base of the mesa while she studied some tiny ruined dwellings. When she turned, Tau was gone, but his voice summoned her into a narrow crack in the cliff face a few feet above the path. The crack was dark, but she followed Tau, crawling upward through the labyrinth until they emerged from the floor of a stone pueblo perched on top of the mesa. The roof was missing, leaving the pueblo open to the turquoise sky. Potsherds were everywhere, decorated in the stark lines of the Anasazi black-on-white style, as if the people who lived there had only recently moved out. She felt like an intruder. Now she stood in a place, if the reports were correct, where a culture had existed long before the Anasazi, or the Europeans, or even primitive Man had gained a foothold on the continents of Earth.

This place had the same spooky feeling, as if the Martians had only recently moved out.

The other members of Kate's team were climbing to the top of a small hill to her left. She had seen the thrill in some of their eyes after they landed, looking outside and wondering how long Tak Matsumoto would take to shut down the hab's flight systems so they could go out and play. Lenya Novikov, their fearless leader, made a point of slapping everyone on the back, and congratulated each of them before they went outside. True to Lenya's heroic image, he was the first of their team to set foot on the planet, and he now led them up the hill to get a view of the colony.

One of the taller astronauts turned to face Kate as she hopped, light on her feet, to the top of the hill. Kate saw Tanya Savitskaya's name tag before she could make out her face through the glare of the helmet bubble.

"This colony, it looks like a Siberian labor camp," said Tanya, watching Kate hop over some large rocks before she came to rest beside the Russian.

Kate surveyed the scene and nodded. "Metal huts, dirt bunkers, dirt roads, isolated area; looks like a military base to me."

"Home," said Lenya Novikov, sweeping one arm across

the scene below. "My feeling is that I've come home after a long journey."

Several of the team members turned to look at Novikov: some were smiling, others were frowning.

"You must not have had a very comfortable home," said Ian Wallace, looking down while he dug the toe of his right boot into the dirt. His digging revealed a white scratch of rock under the red sand, perhaps some of the silica-laden basaltic andesite like the volcanically processed rock found in the Andes on Earth. Kate shook her head, reminding herself to call the red dust "fines" instead of "dust"—technically they were two different things.

After the stress of aerobraking around the planet to slow down, the *Ares* had landed at the edge of Vulcan's Forge, the long-term colony under construction near Noctis Labyrinthus in the Tharsis uplift region. Located near the equator, between the massive terrain features of Olympus Mons and Valles Marineris, the colony was the first multilevel construction to be built into the regolith. Until recently, all structures had been on the surface: *Ares* habitation modules and the plastic domes covering greenhouses and community areas. Many structures were built of bricks made from local materials. Set in trenches to make Roman-style vaults that were then covered with a seven-foot-deep blanket of soil, these buildings were not as apparent as the other colony structures. The bricks were made by putting wet Martian soil in a mold under compression, drying it, then baking it in a solar reflector furnace. To make the bricks stick together, mortar was produced by mixing water with the same red dust to make a "duricrete" material over half as strong as terrestrial concrete. Another technique mixed polyethylene powder with topsoil to make bricks. The Martian atmosphere is dense enough to shield people on the surface from the radiation of solar flares, but the soil blanket on the buildings also provided thermal insulation against the wide daily temperature swings, along with the weight required to keep the brick structure compressed. To prevent air leaks, plastic sealant was sprayed on the interior walls. Kate and the rest of her team had practiced building one of the brick vaults during their training in Houston.

The hab modules, brought up on every *Ares* flight from Earth, had been used to build the initial base and were now primarily used for office and lab space. Each time a hab landed, wheels were attached to the landing gear legs for towing. Moved to a permanent location in the colony, the hab would be mated to others with the aid of inflatable tunnels. Perhaps because she felt hungry, Kate thought the finished habs looked like tuna cans connected by tubes.

As facilities were built to use native materials for construction, it became possible to make complex structures. The buried vaults provided more living space than the habs, so they had become the residential buildings. Early on, plastic domes were built for agriculture. Fifty-meter domes provided about half an acre of growing area, initially pressurized to 5 psi with Martian air and a few millibars of artificially generated oxygen to get plant respiration started. Since Martian air is 95 percent carbon dioxide, photosynthetic efficiency was about three times better than it was on Earth. The moist environment of the greenhouse domes generated oxygen as the oxidants in the soil reacted to the water. Later domes became community meeting spaces and recreational areas. Each fifty-meter-diameter dome was made of transparent Kevlar, inflated to 5 psi, and shielded by a geodesic dome made of Plexiglas. Fifteen floors in each dome provided twenty-one thousand square meters of habitable area. The Kevlar and the Plexiglas had come from Earth, so they were expensive structures to build, even though they provided a lot of useful space. Considering the rapid growth of the population, new building methods would soon be required to house them all.

"Where's the welcoming committee?" Tak asked.

Pavel Grechko chuckled. "Maybe it's a ghost town. Nobody's home."

"Don't say that," said Kate. "It's not funny."

"There," said Lenya. He pointed at a rover pulling out of a shed.

A momentary dread passed over Kate when they saw the apparent lack of life in the colony, but it passed with the sighting of the eight-wheeled yellow rover moving their way. To her, the little colony resembled one of the smaller Antarctic research stations without the snow, although it seemed odd for the environment to be that cold without snow. But if she wanted to see snow, she knew she'd have to visit one of the carbon dioxide polar caps, although frost could form elsewhere during the winter months. She smiled as her feeling of high adventure returned, boosting her spirits again. She was on Mars, and out of that tiny can that had been her home for the past six months. It felt great to be alive.

Beyond the colony, the red cloud of a larger whirlwind swirled and danced. She wished Tau could be there to see it.

17

TAU Edison Wolfsinger, born for the *Kin yaa'aanii*, the Towering House People Clan, stopped to adjust the shoelaces of his hiking boots. Kneeling alongside the wide, flat Tsegi Creek, which flowed with quiet dignity through the bottom of Canyon de Chelly in Arizona, he spotted a red whirlwind dancing among the cottonwood trees. A distant sheep bell echoed off the high, vertical canyon walls, followed by the cry of a hawk. The leaves of the cottonwoods shimmered in the early-morning light. His spirit was peaceful in this place of great beauty that he visited in his dreams. Finished adjusting his boots, Tau stood up, and the dust devil vanished. Perhaps the whirlwind was a greeting from the Wind People who welcomed him home.

Just ahead, towering eight hundred feet above the floor of

the canyon, stood the immense red sandstone spire known as Spider Rock; a bloody needle poked into the blue eye of the sky. His uncle, Hosteen Joseph Wolfsinger, had taught him that Spider Rock was the home of Spider Woman. When the Navajo, who call themselves the *Dineh*, emerged into this world that we know, Spider Woman possessed great power. At that time, monsters roamed the land and killed many of the Earth Surface People. Spider Woman wanted to protect the people, so she gave Monster Slayer and Child Born of Water a charmed hoop of two eagle feathers to protect them. She also taught them a magic chant that would subdue the *Naye'i*, the monsters they would find on their journey. Finally, she told the Hero Twins how to find the turquoise house of their father, Tsohanoai, the Sun God. When they found him, the Sun God showed the Hero Twins how to destroy all the monsters on land and in the water. Tsohanoai gave them suits of flint armor to protect their bodies. He armed them with a great stone knife and arrows made of chain lightning, sheet lightning, sunbeam, and rainbow. With these weapons, Monster Slayer and Child Born of Water sought out the *Naye'i* and destroyed them.

For helping the Hero Twins on their journey, the *Dineh* honored Spider Woman as one of their most respected deities. She chose the top of Spider Rock for her home, then taught the *Dineh* the art of weaving upon a loom. Tau remembered that it was Spider Man, her husband, who built the loom. The cross poles were made of sky and earth to support the loom; the warp sticks were made of sun rays, placed lengthwise to cross the woof of the fibers; the healds were made of rock crystal and sheet lightning to maintain the fibers. He chose a sun halo for the batten and white shell for the comb. In this way, the *Dineh* learned to build looms and the women became accomplished weavers.

If young Tau did something bad, Hosteen Joseph Wolfsinger warned him to behave himself, otherwise Spider Woman would let down her web-ladder and carry him up to the top of Spider Rock to eat him. This was an effective warning, because Tau had already learned from the other children that the top of Spider Rock was white from the sun-bleached bones of *Dineh* children who misbehaved. It wasn't easy being a child among the *Dineh*. His Navajo father and his white mother had progressive attitudes, but his traditional uncle had spent a great deal of time imprinting *Dineh* beliefs and superstitions on Tau's young mind. Although he'd had a strong interest in exploring the Anasazi cliff dwellings in the area where he'd lived as a child, the superstitions surrounding the *chindi*—the evil spirits of the dead—kept him out of the stone cities.

While visiting his parents during an Easter break, Tau finally explored a cliff dwelling despite the *chindi*. The *chindi* left a person's body at the time of death, and it represented all that was evil and out of harmony with the Navajo Way. The *Dineh* felt so strongly about the evil of the *chindi* that they would move out of a dwelling in which a person had died, boarding up the east-facing entrance to warn others that a *chindi* was trapped inside. These malevolent spirits wandered at night, and would come to anyone who spoke the name of the dead. Tau had been conditioned to be quiet if he had to be out after sunset; otherwise, a *chindi* might find him and make trouble. Tau's college visits to the Anasazi dwellings, during daylight, had given him more power over himself. He'd realized he had the strength to overcome his fears, although a portion of his mind still shuddered when he was around the dead, just in case he was wrong.

At the base of Spider Rock, Tau stopped and looked up, wondering if Spider Woman would descend on her web-ladder to capture him. When she didn't appear, he took a deep breath and began to climb.

The rock was honest and unyielding to his grasping fingers, but Tau became harder himself, in tune with the rock, as soon as he started his ascent. This was not a sim, and the experience couldn't be duplicated—this was true risk. His palms, softened by years of working indoors, were sensitized to the sharp edges and cracks that scratched and cut into his skin. His booted toes found purchase and helped him balance as he rose higher above the canyon floor. His stomach muscles were tight, although they began to twitch from the unaccustomed effort. His loud breathing competed with the pounding of his heart to tell him he was exercising long-forgotten muscles.

When Kit Carson's troops attacked this area in 1849, the *Dineh* did their best to defend themselves by throwing sticks and stones down on the soldiers from the high canyon walls. Crops in the canyons were destroyed by fire as the troops hunted down the *Dineh*. The captured Navajos were sent on the infamous Long Walk to Fort Sumner and the Bosque Redondo, although many of them died on the way there. But there were a few who hid from the soldiers. One of Tau's own ancestors had escaped by climbing Spider Rock, just as Tau was doing now.

Tau had no ropes or pitons; this was a contest between his own muscles and the will of the stone spire. The rock had existed for millions of years, gathering power in its magnificent silence; Tau had come to learn from it, and perhaps to take some of that power with him when he left. The environment and the exercise calmed his mind, quieting the stressful thoughts of Dr. Thorn's death and his own impending journey to another world. The pain of his scraped hands, and the strain on his quivering muscles, brought Tau closer to the reality of the earth.

His uncle had told him the story of a peaceful Navajo boy who lived in a cave and hunted in Dead Man's Canyon, a branch of Canyon de Chelly. An enemy tribesman surprised the boy while hunting and chased him deeper into the canyon. The boy tried to find a place to hide while he ran for his life, but his only choice was to climb Spider Rock. He knew it was too difficult for him to climb, but when the boy reached the base of the sandstone spire, a silk cord dropped down from the top of the tower. He grasped the magic cord and tied it around his waist. With the help of the cord, he climbed the tower and escaped from the enemy. When the boy reached the top of the rock tower and lay down to rest, there were eagle's eggs for him to eat and the dew of the night for him to drink.

The boy was startled by the sudden appearance of Spider Woman. She told him how she had used the silk web-cord to help him climb up to safety. Later, when the boy was sure that his enemy was gone, he thanked Spider Woman and used the same magic cord to return to the canyon floor. Then he ran home as fast as he could to tell his tribe how Spider Woman had saved his life.

Tau wanted to find Spider Woman.

He hadn't put extensive thought into his wish to climb Spider Rock, but he felt that his compulsion had meaning. Living away from *Dinetah*, the land of his people, put him out of balance with the world. His climb, and his return to the Big Reservation, would return him to harmony so that he could face the future and survive. If his motives were pure, climbing in beauty and harmony, Spider Woman would help him reach the summit.

He'd climbed Spider Rock twice as a teenager, without any climbing gear, and he felt as though he should be able to do it again. Rock climbing was a skill his father had encouraged in Tau from a young age, showing him the old places where the Anasazi—master climbers who apparently had no fear of heights—had cut holds in vertical cliff faces that rose hundreds of feet above the desert floor. But Spider Rock had no man-made handholds, only the natural cracks and bumps in the red sandstone.

The muscles in his thighs and calves knotted with tension, but Tau kept moving to work them out. He climbed a rock highway—a long, vertical fissure just wide enough for him to jam the toes of his boots in for a secure purchase. When the fissure narrowed and the holds were less secure, he had to fight an urge to crowd the rock face. It was a natural urge that could kill him because it deprived a climber of the necessary leverage required for tension footholds. The urge to hedgehog the rock could start a vicious cycle of fear, creating more danger as his footholds weakened, limiting his view of higher handholds. Despite his real climbing experience and his time in the sims, his stomach still fluttered when he paused to look down, gauging his progress against gravity. But he continued upward, his goal clear in his mind, focused on the character of the rock and the strategy required to master it. Climbing in harmony with the stone, he could learn its ways and allow it to give him strength. There was no *Dineh* holy trail up Spider Rock—a bridge made of rainbows, sunbeams, or streaks of lightning—he found only a hard climb, immutable and unforgiving.

It took almost six hours. A strong climber can ascend one thousand vertical feet in roughly three hours, but Tau was nowhere near the kind of condition that would have allowed him to climb faster. Even with frequent rest stops, he felt happy to have managed it at all. When he scrabbled over the eroded lip at the top of the tower, he broke his fingernails and scraped both of his palms down to bloody, raw nerves in his attempt to gain enough purchase to haul his body onto the roof of the spire. His arms and legs trembled with fatigue while he lay facedown on the sun-baked rock and tried to control his breathing. His hair was plastered to his head, motionless in the dry breeze, but his shirt was already drying. A fair amount of skin had been scrubbed away from his elbows and forearms, stinging with the same grit ground into his palms and knuckles—in that sense, he had become one with the earth.

When he'd recovered enough control over his tired muscles, Tau sat up and looked around. Tsegi Creek was a broad, flat mirror running through the middle of the canyon. From his perch under the turquoise sky, Tau saw the bare rock of the cliff tops and the knife-edge sheer drops to the canyon floor. Four vultures circled on the thermals, maybe two hundred feet below him, perhaps waiting to see if Tau would make a mistake on the way down. He took some hard bread, cheese, and water out of his small backpack. His spirit felt light, even though Spider Woman had not been waiting for him when he arrived. His high-tech world numbed his senses with artificial stimulation, but climbing put him back in the real world, in harmony with the earth. He smiled.

Finished with his food, he stopped to perform a ceremony he'd forgotten while traveling in the early morning. This was a good place for his ritual. He faced east and sang his dawn chant, greeting the sun, greeting Dawn Boy, blessing the new day, and asking that beauty walk before him, behind him, and all around him. Then he pulled the medicine pouch out of his pants and sprinkled a pinch of corn pollen into the breeze as an offering.

"In beauty it is finished," sang Tau, smiling as the corn pollen drifted away on the wind. "In beauty it is finished."

Thunderheads formed in the distance, casting rain shadows across the landscape. It was time to leave. Before the climb, he hadn't been able to decide if he wanted to descend the hard way as he used to do. Now, fatigued from all the unusual exertion, he gave in to the reasoning part of his brain and pulled a reel of spider line out of his pack along with his Kevlar climbing gloves. A temporary molecular bonding patch secured one end of the glistening spider line to a crevice. He was reminded of all the skin missing from his palms as he gingerly worked his hands into the gloves. After one last look around, and a brief nod of thanks to Spider Woman, Tau wrapped the line around his waist, clipped himself to the line with a carabiner, and backed off the crumbling top of the tower. In just over an hour of rappelling in long, graceful arcs down the side of the needle, his feet made contact with the canyon floor. When he had backed far enough away from the rock face to avoid the falling line, he touched a switch at the base of the reel, sending a small charge along the line to release it from the bonding patch. While the line fell, the smart mechanism wound the fine filament back onto the reel. Overhead, clouds gathered in front of the approaching storm. The wind picked up, causing the leaves of the cottonwood trees to hiss with anticipation. Tau hadn't felt this good in months.

Spider Woman didn't visit him at the top of the rock spire,

but he had found something else waiting among the rocks—
his confidence.

". . . BUT the High Middle Ages saw advances in structural
forms. With the pointed arch, Gothic cathedrals could be built
with huge windows to take advantage of the dim light from
gray northern skies. The weight of the roof didn't have to be
carried by an entire wall, as in earlier structures, but by piers
incorporated in the outer wall."

Dr. Bronwyn Wright, professor of architecture at Navajo
University, used her hand controller to rotate the twenty-foot
holo of the asymmetrical cathedral of Amiens so that her class
of sixty-two students could study it. She hoped some of them
would notice the pair of western cathedral towers, one of
which was considerably shorter than the other. Cathedral
plans would often change over hundreds of years, occasionally producing what Bronwyn would call a "glaring error"
such as this pair of cathedral towers. She understood that engineering principles weren't very refined at the time, and a lot
of cathedrals simply fell down on the heads of the worshipers
because they were built from guesswork, supplemented with
trial and error, but it still annoyed her aesthetic sensibilities.
Not that most of her students would notice. If any of her students commented on the towers each semester, she would automatically give them a passing grade in this introductory
structural engineering course. She hated teaching undergraduate classes, but she needed the money, and the engineering
department needed this class to weed out the serious students
from the dilettantes. The best of her students would be allowed to help Dr. Wright with the ongoing construction of her
arcology, Gemstone, an enclosed city in the desert that certain
faculty members referred to as Bronwyn's Folly.

The architectural community hated her radical ideas, so
she was forced to demonstrate her principles by building them
herself. Her arcology design, an extension of Paolo Soleri's
work, had developed from years of study on the subjects of
cities and society. City dwellings were still being built on the

skyscraper model that required extensive commuting for goods and services, even though a large percentage of the urban populace worked from their homes. To her, the arcology was the next logical step, clustering people's homes with the places where they worked and shopped, leaving the enclosed structure only when they wished to engage in outdoor recreation or travel. Even the Mars colony was being built on the same, tired old model of small-town life that wouldn't work anymore when the population increased. Colony buildings were separate structures linked by tubes or tunnels, with work areas placed away from community areas and residential buildings. More than anything, it was the inefficiencies of modern society that had prompted her to try and change things by becoming an architect, unaware that the ancient profession was ruled by people who honored the past because they despised change.

She knew her image as a radical outcast appealed to the idealistic college students who fancied themselves occupying the same niche in society.

But Bronwyn's popularity among the students hadn't earned her any friends among the faculty. As part of the architectural establishment, the faculty had a vested interest in maintaining traditions and ridiculing creative students. Bronwyn wouldn't play along with them, and she wouldn't waste time on their committees. The faculty only held a grudging respect for her because she demonstrated an intuitive grasp of design and engineering principles that placed her in in the category of genius.

As usual, she had intended to cover more of her subject during this lecture, but when she noted the urgent flash of the time display floating at the corner of her visual field, she knew her time was up. She concluded as best she could, issued a flying buttress assignment, snapped off the holo projection, and left the room.

As she turned into the hallway, moving with the purposeful stride the students associated with an onrushing train, she lurched into someone waiting outside the door.

"*Ya'at'eeh,* my mother."

Bronwyn smiled. "Tau! You're early!"

"I was passing by, so I thought I'd stop in," said Tau, thinking how she still called him by his first name, instead of using an indirect reference such as "my son," like other Navajo mothers.

They hugged, smiling, as the students filed out of the classroom, some raising their eyebrows as they passed. Bronwyn frowned at the wounds on Tau's hands and arms.

"What happened to you?"

"I climbed Spider Rock."

"No. I thought you were through with all that."

Tau shrugged. "I thought so, too. But I needed something I left up there last time."

Bronwyn nodded as if she understood. "I'm glad you didn't tell me about it ahead of time." She lifted his hands to get a better look at his scabbed palms. "You should have your father take a look at those."

"They're fine."

"They look like you've run them through a meat grinder. He'll fix them for you."

A crowd of students formed around Bronwyn, patiently waiting to get her attention. Tau nodded in their direction. Bronwyn glanced over her shoulder at the mob. "This always happens if I hang around here too long."

"Must be nice to be popular," said Tau.

"Not when I have other things to do." She sighed. "I suppose I should talk to them."

"Go ahead. I'll see you at dinner."

She gave him another hug. "It's good to see you again."

"*Hagoonee', shima.*"

"*Ya'at'eeh, shiyaazh.*"

WHEN Tau entered the hospital and asked for his father, the nurse at the front desk said he could find Dr. Wolfsinger in the ceremonial hogan with a media crew. Worried that the mediaheads might be assaulting his father to do a background interview about Tau, he stormed off down the sterile-looking white corridor, leaving a confused nurse in his wake. He made two wrong turns and finally located the exit to the hogan adjacent to the hospital, placed there by progressive administrators to allow for Navajo curing rituals to be practiced along with modern medicine.

The hogan, typical of a Navajo family dwelling, was a microcosm of *Dinetah*. The posts of the hogan represented the four sacred mountains that defined their sacred homeland. A traditional "female" hogan was built of logs, bark, and packed earth in a round, dome-roofed shape. A fire burned in the center of the floor under the smoke hole in the roof. Constructed according to instructions found in the Navajo Creation story, the sections of the hogan corresponded to the structures of the universe: the hard-packed dirt floor represented Mother Earth and the round roof symbolized Father Sky. All religious ceremonies were held at a hogan, which was never abandoned unless someone died there or if it was struck by lightning.

When Tau entered the hogan, he saw his father, Dr. Kee Joseph Wolfsinger, standing with his back to the west wall. He faced a crackling fire and the mediahead crouched on the opposite side of it. The mediahead, a stocky red-haired man whose shirt logo said WORLD HEALTH ORGANIZATION, was going for a dramatic effect, shooting through the flames and framing his father against the dancing shadows on the west wall. There were no windows in this hogan, so the low lighting gave Tau's father a mystical appearance, despite his baggy blue surgical smock. At sixty years of age, Dr. Wolfsinger still had a strong and handsome face that made him look like an actor. His shoulder-length hair, pulled back in a ponytail, was still as black as ever. Smile lines showed around his eyes when he saw Tau, but he continued speaking to the camera.

"Each ceremonial, also known as a Sing, is performed to combat, or thwart, disease or misfortune. These ceremonies are performed by a specially trained medicine man—a *hataalii*, or singer. The singer often uses drypaintings, as well as herbal remedies made from local minerals and plants, to heal the patient physically and psychologically. The patient is purified through the rituals and restored to harmony with the universe—*hozro*.

"The curing chantways are always concerned with some specific disease. Hailway and Waterway treat illness resulting from cold or rain. The Shooting Chant is used to cure injuries received from lightning—which are common in this part of the world—and from arrows or snakes. Beauty Way can cure aching body parts and mental confusion. Insanity and paralysis require the lengthy Night Chant ceremonial, the *Yeibichai*, which can only be performed between the first frost and the first thunderstorm. While this is the most common of the ceremonials, it is also the longest, with some 576 songs chanted over a nine-day period.

"It may take six or seven years for an apprentice *hataalii* to learn the *Yeibichai* from an experienced teacher. He must learn the songs, the drypainting symbols and their positions, the remedies, the equipment, the elaborate ritual, and the dances."

Tau remembered when his father used to send him out to gather medicinal herbs. The trips might take days on foot, but he couldn't return home until he had collected all of the necessary herbs in sufficient quantities. Each plant was addressed as an individual, along with offerings, songs, and prayers. Tau couldn't harvest an entire plant at once, because that would have killed the plant; he had to apologize to the plant for taking part of it, tell it the name of the sick person, then give it an offering of respect, such as a piece of turquoise, shell, or corn pollen. When he got older, he would leave a nickel or a dime for the offering to the plant, either because turquoise was in short supply or because it was too valuable. Plants could not be gathered and stored; they had to be selected fresh for each individual ceremony.

Kee finished speaking. He nodded at the mediahead. "Okay?"

"Looks good," said the man, standing up by the fire.

Kee walked over to shake hands with Tau. *"Ya'at'eeh, shiyaazh."*

Tau smiled and remembered to shake hands like a Navajo: more of a handclasp than a shake. The pressure of the thumb on the back of the other person's hand, along with the duration of the clasp, was more important than the pumping action of the *bilagaana*—the white man. *"Ya'at'eeh*. You're an actor now?"

"The Tribal Council asked me to do this. It seems the World Health Organization wants to popularize *Dineh* medicine. But if I need any help handling all the acting offers that are sure to pour in, I'll let you know." Kee grinned. Then he turned Tau's hand over so he could see the palm. "Did you walk all the way here on your hands?"

"I did some climbing. Spider Rock."

Kee studied his son's face while the mediahead ducked through the low doorway and left the hogan. "Did you find what you were looking for up there?"

Tau wondered if his father already knew why he'd climbed Spider Rock. "Yes, I did."

"I haven't climbed in years. I guess I found what I wanted up there a long time ago, so I didn't have to climb anymore. How do your hands feel?"

"Sore."

Kee beckoned for Tau to follow him outside. "Come with me. We'll clean up those hands and make them heal faster."

IT was his mother's private joke; instead of eating mutton, corn, beans, or some other food normally associated with *Dineh* meals, she made what she called a "traditional Navajo meal" for dinner—meat loaf, pasta, and wine. After dinner, Tau sat on a couch by the fireplace next to his parents. Except for the pops from burning logs, the night was still and silent; like most Navajos, their closest neighbors were miles away. Their small, modern-style home looked like it would fit in anywhere in the country, but they also had a traditional hogan, a brush arbor, and a small sweat hogan where Tau would make a point of taking a sweat bath before he left.

The furnishings of the house were simple. The Navajo believed that a man must be industrious to accumulate nature's gifts for his own use, but he should never be so selfish as to accumulate them simply for the sake of having them, or more than he and his relatives could use. Riches, like food, were to be shared with a man's family and relatives, including his clan and related clans. A Navajo leader once said, "You can't get riches if you treat your relatives right. You can't get rich without cheating people. Men should be honest to get along." Although many of the *Dineh* had built up considerable fortunes, those who acquired personal wealth were not held up as role models. More important were skills such as weaving, jewelry-making, painting, or even the ability to "talk easy." Tau knew his relatives were suspicious of him, but much of the money he earned at NASA went to his parents, who then used it to help the rest of the clan or to support community projects. Tau preferred that the source of the money be kept a secret, but his father hinted that the people had developed a new attitude toward Tau, and some of them had added the title Hosteen to his name out of respect, even though he was still a young man.

Tau shook his head. "I don't want them thinking that way. How did they find out I was sending the money?"

"The hospital," said Kee. "The administrators wanted to know where I got the money to build the new surgery. So I told them."

"And word got out," finished Bronwyn. "I would think you'd feel proud that your relatives found out how generous you are. You've done a lot for them."

"It's not important," said Tau.

"Maybe not to you, but the rest of your family thinks it is," said Bronwyn. "Speaking of which, you haven't said anything about your work. How's it going?"

Tau looked into the fire. "Well, there's something I have to tell you about."

Bronwyn's eyes widened. "You lost your job? I knew

those people wouldn't appreciate you! Bureaucrats! If they sense someone thinking an original thought, they want to beat it out of them." She stopped and took a deep breath. "But maybe I should let you talk. What are you going to do now?"

"It's nothing like that," said Tau, looking at his patient father. Unlike Bronwyn, Kee had been raised on the reservation before going away to medical school, so he was used to waiting for people to finish speaking in their own time.

"You can always come work for me, you know," said Bronwyn, looking doubtful. "It's going to take years to finish building Gemstone, and I could use your help."

"Thanks for the offer, but I'm going to be far away."

"How far?"

"Mars."

Bronwyn stared at Tau for a moment, then burst out laughing. Kee smiled.

Tau sighed. "It's true."

"What would you do on Mars? If you've lost your job, don't be ashamed to tell us."

"NASA wants me to test my AI there. I'm going to build a colony with it. Didn't you see my interview on the news?"

Bronwyn frowned at Kee, who shook his head. "No."

"I sometimes think you're both too isolated out here."

"Our world is here," said Kee. "We don't watch the news."

"I know you leave the reservation. You just came back from that lecture at the Centers for Disease Control in Atlanta. You must know what's going on elsewhere."

Kee shrugged. "Sometimes. Usually I don't care. There are enough problems here to keep us occupied."

Tau remembered saying essentially the same thing to Kate when she complained that Tau never watched the news. With Kate gone, and Tau on the news himself, he thought his parents were too isolated—the irony startled him.

Bronwyn frowned and rubbed her forehead. "When are you going?"

"I'll leave for the Manned Spacecraft Center in Houston

tomorrow. I'll be in training about two weeks, then they'll put me on the next flight to Mars."

"Two weeks of training? I thought it took more than that."

Tau shrugged. "Depends on what they want you to do. They usually just cover the basics, what to do in emergencies, that sort of thing. Then they stuff you in a can for six months; when you get out, you're on Mars."

Kee placed another log on the fire. A shower of hot sparks cascaded over the hearth. "How long will you be gone?"

"Three years. Maybe longer."

"What does Kate think about all this?" Bronwyn asked.

Tau remembered that he hadn't told them about Kate. His heart skipped a beat as he wondered what would happen when he arrived on Mars, an unannounced ghost from her recent past. "Kate left already. She's on Mars."

"Kate's on Mars? You never mentioned it."

"I forgot."

"I'm not saying what you should do with her," said Bronwyn, leaning back in her chair with a knowing smile. "I think you know."

"What you should do is *marry* her," said Kee. "That's the only way I could keep your mother here on the reservation. It was like trying to cage an eagle and keep it as a pet."

"I thought you'd never catch me," Bronwyn said, reaching over to take Kee's hand.

Kee smiled. "You flew too fast; otherwise, I would have caught you sooner."

Tau chuckled and stood up. "I'll be right back."

Tau walked down the dark hallway to the bathroom. On the way, he passed a glowing holo box containing an image of Tau and Kate standing next to a giant sequoia near the university. They were both smiling; a world of two. They'd taken the holo as they started on a fourteen-mile hike through the redwood forest.

Tau closed his eyes and took a deep breath, wondering if they had a future on Mars. The god of war would bring them back together, but Tau would have to do the rest.

DURING the six-month journey to Mars, Kate had studied holos and three-dimensional walk-through maps of their planned excavation at Umbra Labyrinthus, but it still shocked her when she saw it in person.

As she understood it, a civilian construction crew from Vulcan's Forge discovered the tunnels while searching for lost robots in a volcanic vent. Further investigation revealed the "vent" to be a section of collapsed artificial tunnel. The robots fell into a damaged section of the tunnel near machinery buried by the same rubble that plugged the east end. Later, a powered inclinator platform erected by the survey team allowed four space-suited passengers at a time in and out of the sloped tunnel entrance. When Kate descended on the platform along with Novikov, Savitskaya, and Matsumoto, she felt as if she were drifting into the world of the dead. She shuddered with the same excitement and mild vertigo she'd felt upon entering steep Egyptian tomb shafts. The platform lights showed rough rock walls sliding past. The ruddy morning daylight overhead gradually faded, to be replaced with a glow like moonlight from the tunnel walls below. Kate felt the vibrations of the platform massaging the soles of her feet through her insulated space suit boots.

The walls of the straight horizontal tunnel, over sixty feet in diameter, felt warm and smooth, coated with a translucent milk white material stronger than carbonglass. When a strong beam of light hit the white coating, a little rainbow appeared. The rainbow seemed to start a few inches inside the wall and extend out into the tunnel about fourteen inches. When struck, the wall rang like a big gong, but it also generated subsonic tones that vibrated through anyone standing in the tunnel. The damaged section of the wall was a long gouge that sheared upward into the regolith, as if an explosion had torn a hole in the tunnel ceiling. They could walk along the rock-strewn tunnel floor about eight hundred feet in each direction. Fallen rocks plugged each end of the tunnel. Sounding and imaging probes had determined that the eastern plug sat on top of an alien device, part of which was visible at the edge of the rock pile. Anchored in the middle of the open length of tunnel was a laser grid projector, a permanent datum point for the horizontal excavation, marking both rubble walls with glowing red lines and grid numbers. As the rocks were removed, the grid pattern would remain in the air so artifact and feature discoveries could be cataloged by their location in the grid system. If any obstacles blocked the laser grid, repeater projectors would be placed to continue the glowing lines. If any structures were discovered, smaller grid projectors would be placed to allow vertical excavations within rooms. Before the arrival of the archaeological team, the survey team dug a control pit a short distance away from the tunnel opening; this allowed them to study the local undisturbed geology before any excavation started at the primary site. Knowledge of local geological strata would help prevent any confusion regarding original tunnel contents and the fill that collapsed into the tunnel when the ceiling ruptured. With the predisturbance survey of the site completed before their arrival, they were free to start work right away.

Kate approached the wall of rubble to inspect the alien device. The surface of the machine looked like liquid metal—shiny, reflective, fluid mercury that was hard to the touch, unmarred by any apparent damage from the rockfall that buried it. Novikov stood a short distance behind her to direct the placement of more recording instruments being assembled by Savitskaya and Matsumoto. When Novikov glanced at Kate, he saw the look in her eyes, smiled, and nodded.

Kate removed some of the rocks covering the shiny surface to verify her impression that the rockfall had not scratched or dented it. The metal might be as tough as the coating on the tunnel walls; none of their tools could even scratch the walls, despite the fact that something had ripped open the tunnel sometime in the past. While the reality of her surroundings began to sink in, she remembered the amazement she'd felt in Egypt, at Amarna, when she discovered the hidden tomb of Ankhesenpaaten. Driven by extreme curiousity, she had a strong urge to attack the wall of rubble and clear it away from the alien machine, letting someone else sift through the scattered rocks for any tiny artifacts they might contain. However, her training exerted a calming influence to remind her of what might be lost if the excavation proceeded without proper records.

The tomb of Ankhesenpaaten had filled her with a sense of awe and time as she entered a tomb sealed for centuries. Thousands of years had passed before Kate's arrival in the burial chamber, but there were signs of life that looked recent—the fingerprint pressed into the painted wall, the farewell garland dropped at the entrance as the last priest closed the door to the queen's final resting place—it seemed as if seconds had ticked by instead of centuries. Remembering these feelings on Mars, Kate hastily brushed away sand with her gloved hands to expose more of the reflective surface.

"You are excited, yes?"

Novikov's voice startled her. Concentrating on her task, she had forgotten his presence. "It's amazing. I'm still trying to comprehend that I'm on Mars, and here I am with an alien artifact."

"We will be famous," said Novikov, smiling as he gave the machine a possessive pat with his left hand.

"It is an alien device beyond our comprehension," Novikov continued, assuming a heroic pose as he looked up into the future and stated the obvious. "It will be many years before we even begin to understand what we've found here."

"Maybe we should dig it out first, then maybe we can comprehend it," Kate suggested.

"You lack the romance of the Russian spirit, my friend."

Kate shrugged. "Okay."

"You must feel privileged to be here with me at this moment."

Kate wasn't sure if it was a question or a suggestion, so she took the safe route out. "Yes."

Novikov stepped forward and gave her a friendly slap on the shoulder. "Good. Now, let us dig like the moles. We have much work to do."

PRIOR to the collapse of the Soviet Union, all space launches were handled by two cosmodromes, Baikonur and Plesetsk. Following the breakup, Baikonur became part of sovereign Kazakhstan. In fact, most of the land-based space infrastructure found itself in countries outside of Russia, limiting Russia's access to space.

Plesetsk, the smaller cosmodrome in the Arkhangelsk region, was too far north to launch heavy vehicles; launches closer to the equator had the additional boost of the Earth's rotation to help push spacecraft into orbit.

Russia arranged a lease that allowed the use of Baikonur facilities until the year 2011, but the facility fell into disrepair as the locals tore the space center apart for useful metals and building materials.

As a result of these problems, the Russian Federation built a new cosmodrome outside the town of Svobodny-18 in the Russian Far East. The Svobodny cosmodrome was located at almost the same latitude as Baikonur, renewing the Russian capability to launch satellites and heavy lifters. A single booster launched from Svobodny could lift 25 percent more payload weight into orbit than was possible from Plesetsk.

Thirty days after the launch of Kate's *Ares* flight to Mars, Svobodny Cosmodrome launched the *Gagarin* on the back of an Angara LV heavy lifter. The *Gagarin* habitation module was purchased from the United States as an *Ares* hab, then modified by Energiya/Lockheed for use on the Angara booster. This was a special flight—rescheduled to launch sixty days early, it contained two Red Army technical specialists, a Russian general, and a dog.

Colonel General Viktor Aleksandrovich Zhukov found the seven-month flight to Mars tedious, to say the least. He was used to living in cramped quarters—trapped underground for months at a time—but without the company of Laika, his miniature Pekingese, he would have been driven mad. He considered Laika much more intelligent than the two technical specialists piloting the mission, so he avoided contact with them in the thirty-foot-diameter hab module.

For their part, the technical specialists were all too happy to avoid the Angel of Death, fearing that mistakes in the close quarters of the hab would lead to irreversible damage to their careers, and possibly to their lives. It was hard enough to deal with the yapping little furball flying around the cabin when she sneaked away from her master. The vicious animal shouldn't have been flying at their faces in the first place, but the yo-yo spin maneuver had failed to deploy the tethered counterweights for centrifugal gravity during the flight. The change in launch schedule required extra fuel to minimize the transit time to Mars, so no fuel could be spared to spin the craft with the verniers, and the computer software wasn't set up to monitor and stabilize such a spin. They would all have to tough it out with frequent exercise for muscle tone so they'd be able to stand up on Mars. Zhukov's exoskeleton would help him adapt to the new gravity when they arrived, but he enjoyed his daily exercise regimen anyway.

As Zhukov understood it, they were traveling on a free-return flight trajectory, which meant their spacecraft would make a lengthy loop back to Earth if orbit capture at Mars became impossible. If the ship's propulsion system failed during the outbound flight, or if they had to abort for some other reason, they'd have a chance to return home safely.

In 1925, a German mathematician named Hohmann determined that the best time to travel from Earth to Mars, using the least amount of propellant, was when the two planets were in conjunction, at their *maximum* distance from each other on opposite sides of the sun. At conjunction, Mars was about 400 million kilometers away from the Earth. At optimum launch times, the minimum-energy transit to Mars was accomplished in about 250 days, an orbit most often used for transferring cargo. With a higher departure velocity from Earth, a transit time of 180 days was possible, and much preferred by human passengers. Special flights at nonoptimum launch windows, such as Zhukov's mission, expended more energy to reduce the flight time, but their trajectory still required 210 days.

Higher-energy free-return trajectories could reduce the flight time by a few weeks, but spacecraft traveling at such speeds would arrive at Mars too fast for a safe aerobraking maneuver.

With too little understanding of the engineering details, Zhukov studied the data squirted to the *Gagarin* from Mars each day. Research into the Martian facility beneath the Red Star base continued. At the opposite end of the Valles Marineris from the new Tharsis discovery, the Russians had surveyed the subterranean tunnels that honeycombed the Chryse Planitia region and the Margaritifer Sinus. Both of these low-lying areas were composed of chaotic terrain where broad areas of the former Martian surface had collapsed into the tunnel network. Russian military experts decided that one or more extensive explosions had blown through the tunnel system like pipe bombs, breaking through the surface in many areas. Using ground-penetrating radar and orbital mapping tools originally intended to hunt for underground water, theories developed that the entire Valles Marineris canyon system could have resulted from these titanic explosions. Starting at the crest of the Tharsis bulge, the valley was up to three miles deep and 150 miles wide. Zhukov skimmed through the science data, unconcerned about the age of the tunnels or revolutionary theories about Martian geology, intent only on finding information for a military advantage.

The Borovitsky Gate beneath Red Star was named after one of the three main gates to the Kremlin fortress. Presumed to be a matter transmitter, it remained an enigma after three years of study and the loss of one human life, not to mention the numerous expensive robots imported from Earth. The research team found no controls, but there were signs that the gate's operations depended on a machine intelligence. Attempts to communicate with the AI always failed. Frustrated team members suggested lifting the veil of secrecy surrounding the existence of the gate so that more brains could work on the problem, but Zhukov wouldn't allow it. The alien gate would have to surrender to traditional Russian military tactics; Zhukov would throw increasing numbers of science troops at the problem until it surrendered.

After 211 days in flight, Zhukov floated behind the two specialists strapped into seats on the flight deck. Laika was tucked under his right arm, snoring away, her fur extra puffy in the weightless environment. Zhukov watched the approaching planet with a casual eye, getting his last look before heat shield shutters covered the windows and the aerobrake system was deployed. Even at this distance, the peaks of the four big Tharsis volcanoes were visible on the horizon. Valles Marineris was a deep gouge just above the equator. Shades of red, orange, and pink, sometimes shot through with black, dominated the cratered landscape.

The flexible fabric umbrellas that formed the aerobrake would deploy from storage around the payload fairing. As they dipped into the atmosphere, low enough to prevent skipout and a series of troublesome course corrections, the aerobrake would create enough drag to slow the spacecraft's velocity. Successive orbits would slow them further at periapsis, the part of each orbit where they would be closest to the planet, until the gravity of Mars had captured them into a comfortable, almost circular orbit 279 miles above the surface. At that altitude, they would orbit Mars once every two hours. Everything depended on the accuracy of the first aerocapture pass. Global dust storms were most common from southern spring through southern summer, and they could change the density characteristics of the upper atmosphere, requiring modification of the aerocapture trajectory for the proper amount of drag on the aerobrake. If their first aerobraking attempt caused them to dip too low into the atmosphere, they would simply commit to a landing, although it would be sooner than expected. A successful aerocapture would require less propellant for descent, as well as giving them time to study their landing site and choose the best moment for descent. In the event of bad weather, such as a dust storm that limited visibility, the spacecraft could remain on station in orbit until surface conditions improved.

Although the technicians had continually adjusted the course of the *Gagarin* for several days, shaking the spacecraft with short burns almost every hour, Zhukov had a built-in mistrust of the technology. While the shutters closed over the window, he saw the red planet looming ahead of them on their approach at the sun-relative velocity of 76,672 kilometers per hour. To confirm Zhukov's suspicions about the operation, Laika looked wary while she gazed out the window from her safe perch under the general's arm.

"I'm hoping you have done this before," rumbled Zhukov.

Ilya Petrov, a muscular young man who shaved his head every day, looked up from the flight commander's seat and nodded at Zhukov. "Many times, General."

"In a simulator," said Vasilyev, keeping his eyes fixed on the instruments. A small man who looked like an accountant, he seemed out of place in the pilot's seat.

"It is the same," said Petrov.

"The simulator can't make you weigh several times your normal weight when you try to operate the controls," said Vasilyev. "It is not the same."

"The computer will know what to do."

Vasilyev aimed a cool gaze at Petrov. "The computer can fail, just as any other part of this vehicle might fail, just as *we* might fail."

"I do not accept failure."

"Then you are not human."

Zhukov cleared his throat. "You will have this discussion some other time. I do not intend to burn up in the atmosphere of Mars because this ship is piloted by bickering idiots."

"He means you," said Vasilyev.

Petrov started to reach for Vasilyev's throat, but Zhukov stopped him cold by grabbing the younger man's muscular wrist in midflight. Zhukov's lower body floated upward with the recoil, but he held himself in place with his left hand on the back of Petrov's seat. Laika drifted away, tumbling end over end across the cabin, yapping in wide-eyed confusion.

Petrov's large jaw muscles bulged as he clenched his teeth. Zhukov's powerful grip was crushing his right fist.

"Perhaps you'd like to experience the aerobraking maneuver from the outside of the ship," Zhukov suggested calmly.

"No, General," gasped Petrov. "I would not."

Zhukov released his grip. Petrov took a deep breath and rubbed his sore hand.

"I've made no secret of the fact that I don't like either one of you," said Zhukov. "This may have created unnecessary stress between you over the last few months."

Petrov and Vasilyev looked at each other and shrugged.

"In any case," Zhukov continued, "I need both of you to land me safely on Mars. Once I am on the surface, I will no longer need you. If I don't like you, and I don't need you, I will consider you a drain on the local resources. Do you understand what I'm getting at, or do I need to elaborate further?"

With wide eyes, both men nodded at Zhukov.

"Good. Then I suggest you return to your work."

Laika immediately stopped yapping when Zhukov plucked her out of the air and anchored her under his arm. A distant howl, like the shrieking souls of the damned, began to resonate through the *Gagarin*. Zhukov pulled himself over to a seat and strapped in while he held Laika in his lap with a firm grip.

The ship began to vibrate. The howl rose in volume until it became a steady roar thundering through the hull. The vibrations increased to a steady pounding, jerking them around in their seats. Gravity returned to press them harder and harder into the seat cushions. Zhukov felt as if Laika's weight on his leg had been replaced with a small car. When he realized he was holding his breath, Zhukov exhaled, but the force pressing against his body continued to squeeze the air from his lungs. He started to sip the air so that his lungs would not collapse to a point where he wouldn't be able to fill them again. He imagined the *Gagarin* tumbling deep into the atmosphere of Mars to glow like a brilliant meteor. The blast furnace roar that filled their ears reinforced the image in Zhukov's mind. The flimsy heat shield would be torn away like an umbrella in a hurricane, leaving them exposed to the heat of the airflow. The hull and the windows would melt; the atmospheric wall would smash them flat.

It was a great moment for Zhukov. If he had to die, he wanted it to happen during a peak experience such as this. He often worried that he might die in his sleep, unaware of his final moments of life. Here, he could die in battle against the elemental forces of the god of war. His skin tingled with excitement while he fought to remain conscious, although the younger men might black out before Zhukov because he had the advantage of older, hardened arteries that resisted the crushing force of the high gravitational effects.

As if inspired by her namesake, the first dog in space, Laika accepted the new weight of her body without a sound. Her body lay unusually flat on his leg, but her tongue hung out and she panted normally.

Zhukov had just become accustomed to the solid feel of his new weight when the pressure lessened. The thunderous hammering against the hull died down along with the jerky movements and vibrations. Breathing became easier.

They had survived their fiery rite of passage.

THE archaeological team used its rover as a data-relay link and command post. Alone on the vehicle, Kate felt the nagging compulsion she'd been busy enough to ignore since they landed. Once Pavel Grechko and Svetlana Ryumina had finished setting up the command post beside the vent to the underground tunnel, each member of the team had rotated duty as communications officer on the rover while the others were down in the dig. Ian and Tak ferried supplies between Vulcan's Forge and the dig, so they were gone most of the time. Kate used this rover duty period to update her notes and take a nap, but another hour would pass before the others arrived for the daily meeting. The satellite link had plenty of bandwidth that wasn't being used, and the smart data cable for her neural shunt was burning a hole in her pocket. It was still her little secret.

"Infotaps" were illegal on Earth, but they were easy to build; she had learned how to use one in college, where every information junkie in her dorm had one. The trick was in learning how to override the fail-safe timer that limited the duration of the brain dump. The intensity of the pleasurable memory stimulus was adjusted for her by the technogeek who sold her the infotap controller module. Kate's personalized AI agent roamed the limitless sea of information on the net to locate data it knew she'd like; when Kate tapped in, the agent would imprint the information on her brain, stimulating her pleasure center to enhance its recall. The memories were permanent, so information filters and critical thinking were required to avoid accepting all the data as true and accurate; special interest groups and governments were always pumping propaganda onto the net to braintrap the unwary.

As a student, one of Kate's friends would wake her from the orgasmic learning trance after a few hours so that she wouldn't waste away in cognitive bliss. Over time, Kate learned to develop a mental switch that would eventually bring her out of the data flow and back to reality. With practice, the switch usually worked. It was an addictive habit, but tapping in had never been a problem for Kate until the long journey to Mars had deprived her of normal stimulations and distractions. She'd lost almost twenty-four pounds during the six-month flight. She knew some of her teammates might have suspected an infotap, but no one had ever caught her using one behind her locked cabin door. Even with the communication delay between the *Ares* and Earth, the agent faithfully collected far more information than she could absorb, so now she felt the infotap calling her during this quiet time on the rover. At least the infotap would distract her from thoughts of Tau.

Once the novelty of their arrival on Mars had worn off, Kate tried to stay focused on the new tunnel discoveries unearthed each day, but Tau kept showing up in her thoughts at random moments. She wondered what he was doing, where he was doing it, and with whom. Did Tau miss her? Her decision to hunt ghosts on Mars had seemed like the smart thing to do, but she wasn't so sure anymore. Now she felt lonely, and she had the choice of escaping through hard work or through the infotap's fire hose of information.

Kate scratched her head, feeling the fine particles of sand that worked their way into everything, despite the space suit and door seals. Close examination revealed a light layer of pink dust coating every exposed surface on the rover. They all did their best to brush as much of the dust off their suits as possible before they entered the rover, but the peroxide-laden powder still drifted into the cabin. Despite frequent showers, Kate's skin was as rough as if she'd been rubbing it with sandpaper.

She took the smart data cable out of her pocket; it was as fine as black thread, but stronger. The cable provided a private and secure connection to the data feed, since it didn't broadcast information like a wireless data jack. No one would know she was using the infotap unless they found it plugged into her head. She checked the time again. The communications delay caused by the distance between Mars and Earth was running about twenty-one minutes, so if she made the connection immediately, she'd have about forty-four minutes of infotap time before anyone showed up to interrupt her. One end of the cable snapped into the comm panel with a click. She hesitated, wondering if she should wait for another opportunity, then slapped the other end of the cable onto the flexible neural jack on her scalp.

Kate's vision blurred. She could still see her surroundings in the rover cabin, but an overlay of glowing icons floated in front of her eyes. With practiced mental motions, she concentrated on the symbols that would establish the datalink channel for her infotap AI. She could already feel the slight buzz from the neural stimulator, renewing old patterns of memory in her brain, as the infotap "warmed up" and settled her thoughts into a deeper meditative state. While she waited, she reclined the back of the couch and stretched out flat on the cushions. Her muscles relaxed, full of comfortable liquid heat. Her breathing deepened as if she were asleep. When she closed her eyes, the glowing symbols were replaced by the colorful mandala of the test pattern, its lines focused to draw her deeper into its rotating interior. When the information started to flow from Earth, the AI would organize it so she'd receive the current archaeological news first; then, if she was interrupted, she'd already be updated on subjects that mattered the most.

Her spirits lifted. The rotating mandala drew her in and relaxed her mind, allowing her thoughts to drift while it enhanced her recall. Random memories floated through her consciousness: seated on a rock by the River Nile on a hot summer evening, typing notes about her day's work at the dig in Amarna; diving with Lenya Novikov in the warm waters off Jamaica, hunting for relics from the pirate culture in the sunken city of Port Royal; studying the dark mummy of Ramses the Great in the Cairo Museum, nestled in his climate-controlled cocoon; saying good-bye to Tau in the glass bubble restaurant under the San Francisco Bay. She tensed at the memory of Tau and forced the shocked image of his face from her mind.

When she relaxed again, a new image formed. Thoth, the Egyptian god of wisdom, whose human body was topped with the feathered head of an ibis, approached Kate from the center of the mandala. Thoth looked left, then right, his eyes darting like those of a bird, and clacked his long, curved beak. The image of Thoth seemed odd to Kate, since her other memories had formed complete scenes of their environments;

this god was superimposed over the mandala. It was even more upsetting when Thoth stopped and spoke to her.

"Dr. Katherine McCloud," said Thoth. His voice boomed like thunder, but it had a screechy quality that reminded her of birds.

Was this some kind of a trick her AI was playing on her? Had it developed a sense of humor?

"You may call me Thoth."

"Okay. Thanks," she said, wondering if she was losing her mind.

Thoth clacked his bill a few times, regarding her with black eyes that didn't blink. "There is no need to fear me. I'm a creature of your thoughts."

"Actually, that sounds like something I should be worried about. "What do you want?"

"To help."

"Ah. Why? What are you?"

Thoth's bill clacked twice. "A teacher."

"What do you teach?"

"Death. Life. Renewal. The mysteries of time and light." He tilted his head, continuing to stare into her eyes. "The fortress of knowledge is defended by the towers of memory."

"I don't understand."

"Perhaps you weren't meant to understand."

"You're not a very good teacher."

"I've sustained damage. But perhaps you're not the right student."

Thoth spread his hands. A ball of glowing red plasma formed between his palms. The ball sparked whenever the tip of Thoth's beak struck its gaseous surface. The musty smell of old paper book libraries filled the air. Everything seemed so real that Kate felt like she was in an entertainment sim. Then Thoth threw the ball of energy straight into her face.

Kate's brain exploded with light.

19

AFTER four months in flight, Tau felt crowded by the other three-and-a-half passengers; Ari wasn't human, so he only counted as half a passenger. Tau was glad that Tymanov had come along, since Vadim could keep up his end of a conversation.

Tau still felt a lingering distrust of Yvette since she'd been placed in charge of his project, but so far the friction between them had been minimal. The unknown factor in the group was Dr. Josh Mandelbrot, an exobiologist in his forties with big hands and piercing blue eyes. Josh kept to himself most of the time, spending much of the flight in his cabin or in the exercise room and leaving whenever anyone else came in. As the flight progressed, boredom finally helped them draw Josh out of his shell, but he always seemed to learn more about them than they learned about him. Talking to Josh about exobiology only confused matters, since he had the unusual trait of not wanting to discuss his own specialty at length. Yvette had offered to let Tau see Josh's personnel file, but Tau refused because he considered it an invasion of privacy; still, there was something of a competition between them to see who could learn the most about Josh without his written biography.

When Tau entered the exercise room, Josh lifted six hundred pounds of weight on the exercise machine, equivalent to 228 pounds on Earth. It seemed like a lot of weight to Tau, but Josh made it look easy as he pumped his arms up and down like a machine. Seeing Tau, he lowered the weights and prepared to leave.

"Clouds of ice," said Tau.

Mandelbrot looked at Tau and raised one eyebrow. "What?"

"I remember reading that there might have been icy clouds

on Mars, but I can't recall why that would have helped support life in the ocean bottoms, or in caves. Do you know?"

"What an odd question," rumbled Josh. His deep voice always gave his statements extra weight.

"I'm trying to learn more about the environment. It might help with my construction plans."

"Clouds of carbon dioxide—dry ice—would have kept the surface warm enough to let water flow."

"I thought clouds absorbed about half the heat from the Earth's surface. Half the heat is lost to space while the other half is radiated back to the planet."

"On Mars, big ice particles in the carbon dioxide clouds would have scattered infrared light more effectively than the visible light from the sun. It's like a Martian greenhouse effect. There wouldn't have been much sunlight reaching the surface, but it would have been converted to heat, then reflected back to the surface again by the cloud blanket."

"And that would have made it warm enough for flowing water?"

"Yes, but the heavy cloud layer would have limited the amount of sunlight available for photosynthesis."

"And it would have been hard for any bacteria to get a decent tan."

One corner of Josh's mouth lifted, as if he were thinking about a smile. "Did that answer your question?"

It was the longest conversation anyone had managed to have with Josh, so Tau wanted to press his advantage. "What do you think about the alien ruins in the Tharsis tunnel? Did the Martians always live underground?"

"I don't know. I'd prefer to study the tunnel myself before I form an opinion."

"No theories? Go out on a limb. Take a guess. I won't tell anyone."

"Maybe they lived underground to be closer to the water supply."

Tau nodded. "Okay, so you're saying they moved underground after the surface started to dry up? And maybe they didn't like the increasing radiation?"

"Sure. Whatever."

Tau had to wonder why Josh didn't volunteer more information. It was true that he hadn't seen the Tharsis tunnel himself, but most scientists in his position would have studied the current data and formed an opinion by now. "Well, your information must be better than mine. You're the xenobiologist in this crowd."

"Not exactly," said Josh, shaking his head. "I'm an exobiologist, but xenobiology is really too speculative for my tastes."

"Oh. What's the difference?"

"Exobiology includes the study of living creatures we're familiar with, such as humans, in the environment of space or on other planets. Xenobiology is the branch of exobiology that speculates about forms of life that might evolve in different environments. I think they sent me because no one else wanted to go."

"That's odd," said Tau, scratching his head. "You'd think people who study aliens would jump at the chance to examine alien ruins."

Josh shrugged. "Theory versus reality, I guess. Some people can't handle reality."

"But you must be excited about going to Mars."

"It's a new experience, but I feel safer behind a desk."

Tau blinked. Josh looked like he'd spent most of his life exercising, maybe climbing mountains or running marathons for fun. Maybe he carried his desk around with him to feel safe during those activities.

Josh looked down at Ari's shiny metal traveling case hanging at Tau's side. "Mind if I ask you something?"

"Go ahead. It's your turn."

"What is that thing, exactly? You carry it all the time."

"This is Ari—Aristotle. He's one of the reasons I'm going to Mars."

"He's a computer? An AI?"

"He's an AI, but in NASA terms he's the basic 'memory seed' for the Builder AI I'll be training on Mars. Ari has the plans, the knowledge, and the common sense to supervise construction of the new extension to the Vulcan's Forge colony. All I'll have to do is keep an eye on him to make sure he learns how to adapt his methods to the local conditions on Mars."

"I didn't think AIs were that sophisticated. Are there any more like him?"

"Once Ari has enough experience, we'll make copies of him that can build more colonies without supervision, although no two of the AIs will be exactly alike as they learn new things."

All conversation stopped when Yvette entered the room. She was ready for a workout, barefoot and dressed in a tiny exerkini that looked like two white lines painted onto her torso. She smiled when she saw the two men staring at her.

"Did I interrupt something?" Yvette asked in an innocent voice.

"I was just leaving," said Josh, nodding at Yvette. Tau noticed that Josh turned his head to keep an eye on Yvette as he walked behind her to leave the room.

"Nice to see you," said Tau, trying not to stare. "I mean, I was just going to look for you."

"How come?" Yvette asked, settling onto the bench of the weight machine with the grace of an angel landing on the head of a pin. She adjusted the weights, then stretched out her legs and started her routine.

Tau was captivated watching her muscles work. "What?"

"Why did you want to see me?"

"I don't remember," said Tau, rubbing his forehead. "Oh, have you ever talked to Josh about his work?"

"Not much. Why?"

Yvette's heavy breathing, while her legs pumped up and down, made it harder for Tau to concentrate. "He's not excited about going to Mars. It struck me as odd."

"We're all a bit odd. You didn't want to go, either. We left perfectly good lives on a hospitable planet to go sailing off into the unknown and live on a barren red rock. I wouldn't call that normal."

"That's one way to look at it, I suppose."

"I'm not saying it's a bad idea. The success of our construction project will be a great boost to my career. When I get back, I can get all the funding I need to start my VR company. I'll be famous, and so will you."

"For the right reasons, I hope. There's always a chance we might fail."

Yvette lay flat on her back to bench-press the weights with her arms. A light sheen of sweat formed on her skin, enhancing her appearance even more. "Nonsense, Tau. You're a brilliant scientist, I'm a brilliant manager, and Tymanov is a reasonably good engineer—we can't lose."

Tau licked his dry lips. "I have to admit, your confidence makes me feel better."

"I'm here to help," said Yvette, flashing a smile. "By the way, don't tell Tymanov I said he was a good engineer."

"Tau?" It took a moment for Tau to realize that the voice was coming from Ari, who didn't normally initiate conversations. "You should seek medical attention."

"What? Why?"

"Your blood pressure is rising at an alarming rate. You're standing still, but your heart is beating too fast."

Tau wondered why he'd never put a switch on Ari's case so he could shut him off. "I'm fine, Ari."

"No, you're not."

Yvette laughed as she rolled over on her stomach and adjusted the bench so she could exercise her back muscles.

"Your vital signs are getting worse, Tau. I advise immediate medical attention."

"Shut up, Ari."

THE Tharsis bulge played a major role in the evolution of the Martian surface. The largest volcanoes, and the youngest terrain features, were located on the bulge, which formed

early in the planet's history. The lack of plate tectonics on
Mars made Tharsis and its floodplains hard to explain. Only
General Zhukov and a handful of Russian scientists could
guess at the true explanation for the Tharsis uplift and the surrounding landscape—they knew it parallelled an extensive
underground network of tunnels built beneath the permafrost
by an advanced alien civilization. The formation of the bulge
had been explosive, but it wasn't a natural explosion of
trapped pressures beneath the surface. Blast pressure had
propagated through the equatorial tunnel system like a pipe
bomb, finally erupting through the surface and the open ends
of the tunnel.

The Red Star scientists had no idea what had caused the
initial tunnel explosion, but after working with the Fallen
Angel for so many years, General Zhukov had a theory of his
own. The Borovitsky Gate, built at the terminus of the tunnel
system beneath the Red Star base, served as a portal to a different location in space. Zhukov suspected that one or more
explosive devices had been delivered to the Martian tunnels
from the ruined world on the other side of the gate. Such a
bomb could be useful to Zhukov, but the one successful attempt to send a robot through the gate resulted in a corroded
pile of scrap metal when it returned to Mars, so there wasn't
much chance of finding what he needed in the ruined city on
the other side. However, if they learned to communicate with
the machine intelligence that operated the gate, it might be a
formidable weapon itself. Zhukov loved the idea of transport-
ing bombs and troops to target zones in the blink of an eye.

With Laika leading the way in her spacesuit, Zhukov exited the elevator to get his first glimpse of the Borovitsky
Gate. Annoyed by the lack of a guard at the elevator, he
wanted to bite someone's head off, but he forgot his anger
when he spotted the portal. A complicated chrome surface
framed a misty octagonal opening that emitted a blue glow.
Zhukov could have driven a tank through the large opening.
Much of the tunnel wall illumination was blocked by crated
equipment, so work lights pushed back the darkness. The de-

vice made no sound, but Zhukov felt the slight nausea and vertigo he'd always associated with close proximity to the Fallen Angel. He stopped a few inches from the glowing mist, but he couldn't see anything on the other side. He felt a strong urge to poke his head through the mist and have a look around, but his sense of self-preservation reminded him of the corroded robot. In contrast, Laika strained at her leash trying to plunge through the gate to her doom. The ornate curves of the chrome surface that surrounded the portal were inscribed with a variety of patterns, but his spacesuit glove slid over them without friction. Probes and recording instruments pressed against the gate or pointed at the symbols etched in the chrome, but none were attached to the slippery surface itself. A silent forklift sat nearby, ready to extend more experiment packages through the blue mist.

A deep voice boomed in Zhukov's ear, startling him, when something poked his back. *"Stoi! Zuprichahyitsa!"*

Years of training, enhanced by the power of his exoskeleton and the lighter gravity of Mars, made Zhukov crouch and turn with blinding speed. Laika skittered across the floor as Zhukov's extended arms smashed into the legs of a spacesuited figure, sweeping the man off his feet. Zhukov's momentum carried the soldier around in a short arc and tossed him through the blue vapor. The man's scream stopped abruptly when he passed through the portal.

"Meaning no disrespect, General," said a new voice in Zhukov's ear, "but was that really necessary?"

Zhukov stooped to pick up the silently yapping Laika while Colonel Vladimir Korolev, commander of the Red Star base, strolled into the room from the elevator. Korolev was about fifty years old, lanky, and bald; Zhukov didn't like him because of his modern views and his willingness to work the corrupt Moscow bureaucracy to his own ends. He knew Korolev didn't like him, either, because Zhukov had come to Red Star to assume command of the base and usurp Korolev's authority.

"Reflex," said Zhukov, trying to stroke Laika's trembling back through her spacesuit.

"Sasha didn't know who you were," snapped Korolev.

Zhukov grunted. "Obviously." It pleased him to see that Laika was calmer now.

Korolev shook his head at the glowing mist of the gate. "There isn't much chance that he survived."

"Probably not. Was there something you wanted to see me about, Colonel?"

Korolev turned to stare at Zhukov in disbelief. His hands clenched and unclenched. "No, sir. Sasha summoned me when the motion sensor detected an intruder near the gate."

"You should have posted a human guard down here. Sensors can be fooled, and this accident could have been avoided."

"We're on Mars, General. The chances of a hostile intruder on this base are pretty remote."

"There's always a first time, Colonel. I can see I'll have to train your people for a higher level of performance. These are supposed to be elite troops under your command, but they appear to have softened during their time on Mars."

Korolev's eyes bulged with restrained anger. "That's a rather hasty evaluation of our combat readiness. You've only just arrived here."

"I can extrapolate from the poor performance of your security detail. This base may be remote, but it certainly isn't secure. Anyone could walk in here and travel through this gate."

"We've never had an incident."

"You just did."

Korolev stooped to pick up the guard's rifle. "Sasha was a good man. Maybe we should try going after him, just to be certain he's dead."

"Go ahead," said Zhukov, gesturing at the portal.

Korolev glared at him. "With a robot."

"Unless something was missing from your reports, you lost every robot you sent through the gate. They're expensive toys, and their cost won't come down until we can manufacture them on Mars. If the science team is ready to send one through, that's a different matter—maybe they'll let you watch—otherwise, forget it."

Laika didn't like the Colonel, either. Zhukov saw her yap at him as Korolev spun on his heel in silence and stalked away.

"In the future," said Zhukov, watching Korolev enter the elevator, "warn your men not to startle me."

20

TAU'S first impression of Vulcan's Forge was that it looked like a trailer park in Monument Valley, Arizona. Having already adjusted to the lighter gravity during his flight to Mars, Tau felt right at home as soon as he stepped off the lander. Although he saw a wider variety of red shading on the otherwise familiar terrain that surrounded him, it looked like the Navajo reservation. He bounced on his toes a few times to experiment, then jumped straight up to see how high he could go, which was something he'd never been able to do on the flight out because of the ceilings in the hab. Satisfied, he looked up at the pink sky and smiled, wondering how the stars would look when it got dark. But when he looked at the colony, he could only think how ugly the trailer park looked in that environment, as if a lump of dirt had replaced the jewel in a shiny gold ring. Rover tracks were everywhere, their impressions half-filled by windblown sand. The perimeter of the drop zone was a jumble of broken crates and machine parts that would eventually be scavenged for their materials. Various spots around the edges of the colony were decorated with mounds of garbage, separated out by their materials for later recycling. Windmills, water towers, smokestacks, trenches, slag piles, and solar reflectors were placed in a functional way without any thought to aesthetics. Plastic domes covered indistinct green areas, spaced among the regular pattern of mounds that covered the newer brick structures. No attempt had been made to use native materials to color any of the exposed brick structures; sulphur could have been mixed with the clay to make yellow bricks, or magnesium oxide could have made white. The "trailer park" itself was composed of the same white habitats used to house the crews on their flights to Mars, an architectural approach that made the colony look like clusters of tuna cans on stilts connected with clear, inflatable tubes. The only beauty here lay in the landscape itself. Seeing such devastation, Tau realized how much the colonists needed him. If the AI worked according to plan, Tau would build a real town for the colonists that would harmonize with the beautiful setting.

EXPERIENCE taught the colonists that new arrivals were useless for a couple of days. The first colonists had been expected to start working as soon as they landed, but little was accomplished beyond basic survival tasks, so new protocols were adopted. After spending six to nine months cooped up in a small can that smelled like a high school locker room, it was natural for the colonists to seek the freedom and the beauty of their stark new surroundings. Now that Vulcan's Forge was an established colony, each new arrival had two days for sightseeing. Tau convinced Tymanov to accompany him on a rover trip to the east; one of the local geologists had excited Tau with news of unusual terrain there that recreational climbers enjoyed. Tau was eager to test the climbing on Mars, since the lower gravity would make the whole process much easier than his last effort in Arizona—even though he'd be encumbered by his pressure suit. In a sense, he felt that mastering the rock would be a way to break himself in on the Martian environment, giving him a chance to learn the ways of this new world through intimate contact.

Recent studies had shown that the northern Martian basin called Acidalia Planitia was once a vast shallow lake where wave action had formed pedestal craters near the former shoreline in Cydonia Mensae. A pedestal crater is an impact crater surrounded by a blanket of ejecta. This blanket of debris is composed of material more resistant to erosion than the surrounding surface. Erosion around the ejecta blanket leaves an elevated crater that looks like an enormous toadstool; its steep scarp might rise hundreds of meters from the surrounding surface. Tau intended to find one of the local "toadstools" and climb it.

Endless hours of driving, screaming along at almost forty miles per hour in some areas, had taken them on a circuitous route into a tributary of Candor Chasma, just a few rover hours north of Valles Marineris. Slumping along the vast cliff walls had created enormous rockfalls, a barrier they were only able to pass on their short trip because of the map in the rover's computer. Previous expeditions had found areas along the cliffs, four miles high in some places, where sand dunes had worked with rockfalls to create slump "roads" to the canyon floor. Brown and orange soil layers alternated in the canyon walls, built up over successive geologic periods to form a layer cake of sediment. Cratering was less apparent here; most impact evidence had disappeared long ago, eroded away by water flowing across the surface. The ancient shore of the lake had an orange tint feathered with pink strands as it made the transition out to the softer sand dunes from the jagged rockfalls at the base of the cliff. The smooth canyon floor itself was composed of thick stacks of bluish gray sediment, varying between hardpan and soft sand. Geologists agreed that standing bodies of water had filled many of the canyons, including Candor, and these lakes had been fed by water seeping from the canyon walls. The trapped lakes within the Candor and Ophir Chasmas were also responsible for the catastrophic floods that entered the Valles Marineris when the southern ridge of Candor, the dam that created the lake, collapsed under the water pressure.

Another fifteen minutes of bouncing travel across the blue-gray lake bottom brought them to a wide tributary canyon full of towering toadstools. Every surface feature, from the tiniest pebbles to the towering cliff faces, had its patina of fines left by the last storm. At least once every Martian year, hurricane-speed winds would drive vast dust storms around the entire planet. Developing in the southern hemisphere when Mars is closest to the sun, extreme temperature differences—as much as 150 degrees Fahrenheit between day and night—moved the thin air at speeds up to three hundred miles per hour, carrying surface dust aloft. Despite the low air pressure, every rock face got sandblasted, and sand dunes were everywhere. Tau looked forward to his first storm.

Tau studied the toadstools through binoculars before selecting a striped brown-and-orange spire with a flattened top. The laser rangefinder on the binoculars told him that it rose 380 feet from the floor of the canyon, but he saw steep spirals on the rock face to serve as little highways for a speedier climb. The hard part would be clearing the toadstool's "cap," thrusting out over the precipitous drop.

Tymanov announced that he had no intention of accompanying Tau on his mad folly, but he was willing to stand on the scree at the base of the spire and belay the climbing line. Equipped with a rock hammer, a drill, a long coil of spider line, a shorter coil of spider line in his pocket, and eleven pounds of assorted hardware such as pitons and snap rings, Tau took a moment to study the face, then smiled at Tymanov and launched into his climb.

Tau's initial awkwardness with the pressure suit gave way to confidence while he picked his way up the rock face. The thick gloves and "smart-friction" boots felt clumsy, but large enough to jam into cracks and steps that would have been inferior holds for his weight on Earth. The hiss of oxygen became apparent as the flow increased through the suit baffles to compensate for his heavier breathing. Looking up through his helmet bubble was easier than looking down; his suit blocked the view past his chest, minimizing the butterflies he felt in his stomach whenever his body realized the danger. Moving up steadily, his muscles warm from the exertion, Tau felt happier than he'd been in months—he was making progress.

The red rock seemed well toothed and abrasive, ready to take a firm piton whenever he needed to hammer one in. Before he knew it, Tau reached the cap of the toadstool, requiring advanced tactical moves similar to those he'd used on Spider Rock in Arizona. Twenty more minutes of focused effort, ignoring the possibility of a fatal plummet while he performed acrobatics on the roof of the world, placed him on the sandblasted upper surface of the cap.

Flat on his stomach, resting a moment, he noticed odd patterns in the rock surface around him. Then he lifted his eyes and held his breath. Stone arches had formed in neat patterns, as if someone had built an eroded Stonehenge atop the toadstool. Standing, he approached the closest wall of black volcanic stone. A neat oval, eroded into the wall to form a soaring arch, reminded him of the sacred Rainbow Bridge near the Utah/Arizona border.

"Tau? Everything okay up there?"

Tau realized he hadn't said anything to Tymanov for the last ten minutes. "Sorry, Vadim. Yeah, everything's fine. You should have come up with me. There are unusual rock features up here you could have studied."

"I'm having a fine time down here. I'm studying the insides of my eyelids."

"I thought you were holding the spider line."

"That, too, but I figured you'd wake me up when you were ready to come down."

"In that case, I'm glad I said something," said Tau, stepping through the smooth oval of the arch. He looked back, framing the distant view with the edge of the arch. The breathtaking drop to the canyon floor reminded him how it felt to look down from the cliff walls at Canyon de Chelly in Arizona, listening to the sheep bells and the cries of soaring hawks.

"I'm ready when you are," said Tymanov. Tau didn't respond, so Tymanov gave the line a tug. "Tau?"

Tau wasn't listening. The rock arches continued around the rim of the crater to form a rough circle. Abstract patterns of cobalt blue and dull white glass were set in the black walls on the inside of the rock arch ring. Eight feet in from the arches stood a low wall—maybe three feet high—that appeared to have been made from metallic meteorites. Edging closer, Tau saw that the low wall was formed out of one large metallic chunk cut into an octagonal shape. The nickel-iron surface had a dull shine, but Tau made one patch shinier when he brushed away the dust with his glove, exposing the etched triangular Widmanstätten patterns he'd seen before in sliced meteorite segments in museums. He turned and looked at the blue-and-white glass, thinking it had formed from minerals heated in lava flows from the nearby shield volcanoes. Pavonis Mons and Ascraeus Mons were nearby, and both had contributed their lava to the Tharsis uplift. Everything seemed to have a natural explanation, but the regularity of the patterns he saw gave the area an artificial feel. But the ring had to be natural.

"It's pretty up here," said Tau, finally responding to the tugs on the line.

"We should be going, Tau. We've got a long drive back to the colony."

Tau brushed more of the sand from the shiny metal surface of the wall. The movement of his fingers over the etched patterns created a vibration in his fingertips. "Okay. Give me a few minutes to look around and enjoy myself."

"Would those be Earth minutes or Mars minutes?"

"Navajo minutes," said Tau, fascinated by the complicated designs in the metal.

"Then I'm going to take a nap. Wake me when you're ready to come down."

Not wanting to miss anything, Tau stepped over the low wall into the center of the octagon. Red sand covered the floor of the bowl. He sat down at the center of the bowl to rest. At a lower angle now, he saw small oval holes that went straight through the metal walls. Moving his head a few inches allowed him to line up an oval hole with one of the rock arches, revealing a small patch of salmon pink sky. The oval holes were evenly spaced, one for each rock arch in the outer ring—and that seemed very odd.

Pencil-thin beams of red laser light shot out of the metal walls, pinning Tau at the center as if he were the hub connected to the spokes of a wheel.

A beautiful young woman with Navajo features appeared to be standing on the sand a few feet away. Instead of a pressure suit, she wore a dress of black velvet, a silver squash blossom necklace, and other turquoise jewelry. Her image was semitransparent, but her long black hair fluttered loose in the breeze. When she smiled, her teeth shined like pearls. It was his image of Spider Woman.

She nodded. "Welcome to my home. You seem troubled."

"I'm hallucinating," said Tau, lifting a Velcro flap on his sleeve to make sure his suit gases were properly mixed. The gauge showed a normal reading.

"You've come here for my help. Your thoughts are out of balance."

"I feel good. I came here for the climb, not to see you. I never expected to see you."

"This is a holy place. No one comes here without a purpose, even if they don't realize it. A warrior prepares himself for battle in different ways."

"I'm not a warrior."

"You may not seek war, but you are a warrior in your heart. Something has drawn you here."

"Do you know what it is?"

"Do you?"

"I've come to Mars to build a colony. Is that what you mean?"

Her gaze was gentle. "That's not the real reason. There's a deeper motive for your presence in this temple."

"I don't understand," said Tau, shaking his head.

"You're avoiding a confrontation, as you've always avoided confrontation. You must fight to achieve your goals. When the coyote is hungry, he hunts, and there is no right or wrong in his hunting. When the stag is challenged, he fights. Even the old stag, who understands he must die in the attempt, fights his challenger. Hunting and fighting are the natural way of things, and the warrior learns from the wise animals without judging their actions."

Tau frowned. "I fought for my project, and I won. I'm here to build my colony."

"You must look into your heart. I can extrapolate future events, but my function is only to point the way."

"I still don't understand," said Tau, thinking that she didn't always talk like Spider Woman.

"The eagle must learn to fly, and so must your spirit. You ignore your humanity in favor of your intellect. The old stag believes it's better to die than to avoid a challenge. Sometimes, you must fight to restore *hozro*."

Tau felt as if he were talking to a fortune cookie. "How do you know all this?"

"It's all in your memory."

"So I'm talking to myself," sighed Tau.

"You may speak in the presence of others, but you are always speaking to yourself."

"I appreciate your words, grandmother, but I must go."

Spider Woman vanished when he stood up. The red lasers also disappeared. He looked around, took a deep breath, and walked out to the edge of the cap. Looking down over the rim, he saw Tymanov far below.

"Vadim? Coming down."

"It's about time."

"Did you hear me say anything the last few minutes?"

"Just your usual mumbling. Were you trying to get my attention?"

Tau looped the spider line around his body, preparing to rappel down. "No, but I think someone was trying to get mine."

THERE were no underground vaults at the edge of Vulcan's Forge where Tau wanted his computer facility, so the hab they'd been living in for the last few months was towed into position. Yvette and Tymanov unpacked nanofabrication equipment while Tau hooked up the VR computer infrastructure. Josh Mandelbrot had disappeared to some other part of the colony as soon as they'd landed; Tau speculated that Josh had gone off to join Kate's tunnel "dig," about three hours away by rover. As for Kate, Tau desperately wanted to see her, but he wanted Kate to make the first contact. It didn't matter to Tau if Kate contacted him by radio or by coming to Vulcan's Forge—the important thing was that she make the approach. Would she even care that he was on Mars? During all her training and flight time, she had never communicated with Tau in any way. Had it been so easy to forget him? Had she become involved with someone else on her team, perhaps her slick team leader, Dr. Novikov? To be fair, Tau had never attempted to contact Kate after she left him in the restaurant. He decided to wait at least two weeks. If she hadn't contacted Tau by the end of that time, he'd figure out a way to "casually" drop by the Tharsis tunnel on some pretext.

Although Tau met a few of the colonists after their arrival, and a welcoming party was scheduled in another week, he'd been too busy to meet many people or take an extensive tour of the colony. After the initial human work of getting the equipment ready, Ari would automate much of the building process, and construction would speed up as Ari learned more.

Nanoconstruction would use local resources for raw materials, along with the colony garbage dumps, and Tymanov would engineer the supply lines for Ari's use. Some of the newer colony structures had been built with teleoperated construction equipment performing the heavy work while human operators controlled the operations remotely. Unused equipment was appropriated by Yvette and incorporated into Ari's control system; he could link in with the teleoperated equipment AIs as if he were a human operator. Although crude by nanoconstruction standards, the construction equipment worked well for digging holes and moving soil. Tau's schedule would lighten up as soon as Ari linked into everything he'd need to start building, after which he'd only have to monitor Ari's activities.

As it turned out, Tau didn't have to wait two weeks before getting news about Kate. She'd already been in Vulcan's Forge for two months—in the medical facility. In his rush to get over there, he almost forgot to put on his space suit before going outside.

When Tau entered Kate's room, Lenya Novikov stood beside her bed arranging yellow flowers in a vase. A medical spiderweb of tubes and wires connected Kate's chest, arms, and head to mysterious openings in the wall. Instruments with cheerfully colored numbers flashed with Kate's internal rhythms. A continuous brain scan holo showed flashes of lightning in parts of her three-dimensional brain. Her arms lay on top of the sheet, positioned at forty-five-degree angles from her torso. Intravenous tubes fed liquids to her arms. A plastic hose curled down under the bed to a calibrated urine container. Despite the clay walls and whitewashed surfaces of the underground chamber, the room held the traditional hospital disinfectant smell that made most people think of sickness and death. When Tau entered the room, Novikov turned from the flowers and raised an eyebrow. *"Da?"*

Tau licked his dry lips and wondered what to say. "How is she?"

"Stable. Still sleeping. Are you a doctor?"

"No," said Tau, introducing himself. "I'm an old friend of hers."

Novikov squinted at Tau's face, then favored him with a big smile of recognition. He slapped Tau's shoulder. "Wolfsinger! Good to see you! Welcome to Mars."

Tau nodded, wondering how much time Kate had spent with her handsome Russian team leader. "Thanks. How long has she been here?"

"Eight, maybe nine weeks. She still hasn't come out of her coma."

Tau's eyes widened. "Coma?"

"*Da,*" said Novikov, his smile fading.

"What happened?"

"We're not sure, but we found her in a rover at the dig. She had an infotap. As soon as we found her, I rushed her back here."

"Infotap? On Mars?"

"Our datalink access is slow, but it works. Pavel thinks she used the infotap on the flight here, but the rest of us didn't know. I would have forbidden it."

"An infotap wouldn't explain her coma, would it? I mean, as long as the connection was broken, she would have come out of it okay."

Novikov shrugged. "I'm a busy man; I can't watch everyone all the time. She hid her addiction very well—even I didn't notice her problem, and I've spent a lot of time with her. Now, I'm sure you'd enjoy talking to me for a few hours, but you'll have to excuse me. It was a great sacrifice for me to come here today; they need me at the dig. I barely had time to get these flowers from the test farm—and it's fortunate that I have friends there; otherwise, I couldn't have taken them at all."

"Was she hurt? Did she get hit by something?"

"The doctor couldn't find anything physically wrong with her," said Novikov, tapping his head. "Something shorted out in her brain. Her body is fine, but she won't wake up."

"No head injury?"

"*Nyet,*" said Novikov, glancing at the digital clock on the wall. "I have to leave. I've been here too long." He gave Tau a crushing handshake and a look of sincerity. "I'm sorry we had to be reacquainted this way, Wolfsinger. Kate has been helpful to me, and I wish she were awake now to translate her notes. None of us can understand her mental shorthand."

"Did the doctor give you any idea how long she might stay in her coma?"

"I haven't spoken to him recently," said Novikov, walking toward the door. "Come out to the dig sometime, Wolfsinger. We have vodka."

Tau didn't watch Novikov leave the room. He studied Kate's pale face and the disarrayed halo of brown hair that framed it. Her bones were more prominent than when he'd last seen her, as if she'd lost weight. He reached forward, careful to avoid the tubes and the airway, and touched her chapped lips. He wasn't sure, but he thought he remembered that coma patients heard what people said, or some of them did, at least some of the time.

"Hello, my love."

She didn't respond to his touch or his voice.

"It's Tau. Maybe you can hear me. After I've come all this way, the least you could do is to wake up and say hello." He managed a half smile in case she opened her eyes.

She didn't move. He found a spot on her chest that wasn't connected to a wire or a tube, then gently moved the warming sheet aside and put his head there. Her skin was cooler than normal, and too pale, but he could hear a steady heartbeat. He wished his father could take a look at her and fix the problem.

"I'm an idiot. I should have contacted you, but I had too much pride. I'm sorry. Maybe I could have helped, or prevented this somehow."

Tau felt himself tremble. He was sad, but he also felt hopeless and helpless in the face of a challenge he knew nothing about. He couldn't begin to understand Kate's medical problem or make any attempt to help her with it. He lifted her cool, limp hand.

Tau spoke to Kate for the next four hours, telling her about his hopes, his fears, his memories of their best times together, and his plans for the near future. He told her how much he missed her. Through it all, she continued breathing and sleeping as if he weren't there, but it made Tau feel better to talk to her, even if she couldn't acknowledge his presence. When he left the medical facility, he thought only of Kate, and finally fell asleep in his bunk wondering how it would feel to spend months trapped in his dreams, never knowing if he'd wake up again.

TAU spent the next few days commuting between the medical facility and the nanofab he was building with Yvette and Tymanov. Their hab module was surrounded by a field of black balls—inflatable reservoir tanks of structural carbon fiber that expanded when they filled with various molecular building blocks suspended in milky liquid. The liquid in each reservoir was water mixed with a slurry of microscopic nanomachine particles that were finer than silt. Each particle was wrapped in a molecular jacket that kept it in suspension until needed, much as laundry detergent molecules coat particles of dirt to float them out of clothing. Up to thirty feet across, each tank connected to pipes that snaked across the red landscape in an ever-expanding half circle of supply lines. Spaced along each length of pipe were capillary tubes that descended into the regolith. The bottom end of each tube was occupied by a mixture of millions of specialized nanomachines that tunneled into the soil, then extended the tube by extracting necessary materials from the dirt and creating new tube sections. The unused red mud was transported through the conveyor belt interior of the tube itself. Thousands of redundant molecular nanocomputers floated among the other machines to micromanage the process.

Specialized molecular assemblers near the reservoirs processed the incoming raw materials. At the nanofab's current state of development, Ari was still building up the supply of molecular building blocks that would speed up the construction process. Other tanks held replicators making perfect copies of tunnelers and builders, built atom by atom, for later use. Each copied nanomachine took about fifteen minutes to create; the replicator itself contained about a billion atoms, and each of its manipulator arms handled about a million atoms each second, guided by its internal computer's blueprints. Ari reprogrammed the blueprints as necessary to make different machines.

When the reservoirs were full of molecular building materials—microscopic motors, computers, wall sections, and brackets—colony construction would begin. Ari used the tele-operated earthmoving equipment to prepare trenches and other surface modifications over the initial building site. The colony itself would be built underground; microscopic factories would assemble the molecular building blocks into permanent features. The factories floated free in the milky syrup pumped into the colony's starter tunnel along with the building blocks. Sticky gripper arms on connected factories would grab specific molecular parts out of the liquid and chemically bond them together to form permanent structures.

Tau made time each day to spend a few hours with Kate. Although she never showed any awareness of his presence, Tau read to her or talked about his day. The reading material varied from collected poems of Byron and Keats to archaeological news and science fiction novels. Tau had spoken to one of the doctors, and she had shown him how the higher language processing centers on the holo of Kate's brain would light up when she heard Tau's voice, which was a good sign. At least Tau knew she could hear him, even if she didn't understand him. He'd had little sleep over the last seven days, allowing himself four hours each night before he spent two shift periods working and the remainder of each day with Kate. Having fallen asleep while reading Byron at Kate's bedside, he was startled awake by a tap on his shoulder.

"Has she said anything?"

"What?" Tau blinked and lifted his head. Lenya Novikov loomed over his chair with a vase full of red roses.

"Has Kate said anything this week?"

Tau stroked her cool hand lying atop the sheet. "Not yet. I've been reading to her, but she hasn't acknowledged me."

Novikov placed the roses on the table near the yellow flowers, which were starting to wilt. "Too bad. We need to talk. I think my team discovered an alien graveyard in the tunnels."

Tau's eyes widened as he sat upright. "You're kidding."

"I don't joke about my work. This is, quite possibly, the greatest discovery in history. My diligent efforts will help us learn unimaginable secrets that I can share with the human race."

"What do the aliens look like?"

Novikov sniffed and looked down at Tau with one eyebrow raised. "I've only just made this discovery. We have to carefully excavate the site without destroying any bodies or artifacts."

"Then how do you know it's a graveyard?"

"Experience," said Novikov, as if he were explaining rules to a young child. "We found rings of markers covered in alien hieroglyphs. Kate used the rover's computer to analyze a possible map on the tunnel wall, but she couldn't give us the results. We'd scheduled a meeting to discuss our findings, but that was when we found her unconscious. And we still haven't been able to translate her mental notes in the rover's computer."

Noting the time, and looking for an excuse to get away from Novikov's ego, Tau squeezed Kate's hand and stood up. As he did so, he bumped the roses, nearly knocking them off the table before he steadied the vase with his hand. "Sorry. Nice roses."

"My friends in the biolab again. The soil here is rich, so they've grown some amazing things in their test fields under the domes."

"I need some sleep," said Tau, walking toward the door. "Thanks for coming to visit her."

Novikov smiled. "Thank *you* for coming to visit her, too."

WHEN Ari prepared to start actual construction of the colony, Tau slept for five hours so he'd be more alert. Until Ari had actually built some underground structures according to the master plan, Tau had to monitor his activities in case he ran into problems. Yvette and Tymanov worked most of the night checking on the tanks and tracing technical glitches in the hardware, so they were still asleep when Tau rolled out of his bunk. Knowing he'd be busy that evening when he'd normally walk over to visit Kate, he decided to do it while the others were asleep. A quick cup of coffee, inadvertently spiced with the red peroxide grit that worked its way into everything, gave him the energy to get started. In two days, after Ari had proven himself, Tau promised his body a normal sleep period so that he wouldn't die from exhaustion.

When Tau arrived in Kate's room, he stopped and stared. Kate was awake.

And Novikov stood beside the bed, holding her hand. They both looked at Tau when he entered. Novikov smiled and Kate blinked in confusion. One of the roses lay on the sheet over her chest.

"Kate."

She hesitated, blinked, and frowned at him. "Izzat Tau?" She slurred her words as if she were drunk.

Willing his feet to move, Tau walked to the bed and rested his hand on hers. "I'm here, Kate."

"Dream?" she asked, looking at Novikov.

Novikov shook his head. "He's real."

Her head bobbed, unsteady, as she turned to look at Tau again. "We're on Earth?"

Tau told her how he got there, simplifying his explanation whenever she looked confused. She dozed a bit while he talked, but when he was done, she gave his hand a weak squeeze. When she spoke again, her voice sounded stronger.

"When I woke up, Lenya was here reading to me."

Tau looked at Novikov, who shrugged at him. "They say coma patients can hear what people say. I read her some good Russian poetry."

"Ah. Good idea," said Tau.

"It's true. I heard his voice. He called me back. The nurse said he's been here every night."

While Kate looked at Tau, Novikov shrugged at him again and tapped his head.

"Has the doctor seen you yet?" Tau asked, wondering why

the nurse couldn't tell the difference between him and Novikov.

"Kate was awake when I came in," said Novikov. "Maybe two hours ago. I called the nurse and the doctor came right away. Kate just watched us for a while, but she started talking when the doctor got here."

"Had to remember how to talk," said Kate, still slurring her words a bit. "Feels like I've been asleep for years. Can someone get me coffee?"

"Not yet," said Tau, patting her hand.

"I'll see what I can do," said Novikov, striding out of the room.

Kate smiled softly. "He takes good care of me."

"Yeah." Tau sighed. "He's great. How do you feel?"

"Weak. Tired. Can you imagine Lenya spending all that time with me? He's important. There's a dig going on."

"He told me."

"They found a graveyard."

"So I heard."

Kate used the hand that Novikov had held to move the rose toward her nose. She sniffed at it and smiled again. "Nice." Then she glanced at Tau and her eyes worked their way over to the wilted yellow flowers on the table beside him. "Oh. Are those from you?"

"No." sighed Tau. "As far as I know, Novikov is the only person who can find flowers on Mars."

Novikov returned with the nurse, who carried a coffee cup. "You ask for coffee, Lenya gets you coffee."

The nurse pressed a button to raise the upper part of the bed and held the cup while Kate took a sip. "Not too much. Doctor might shoot me if he finds out you drank caffeine."

"I'll take the responsibility," said Novikov, lifting the cup from the nurse's hands. The nurse winked at him and left.

"Beans of the gods," said Kate, taking another sip while Novikov held the cup for her. "Thank you."

Tau sighed and decided he couldn't take any more. He squeezed Kate's hand, but she didn't seem to notice as she continued looking at Novikov. "I have to go to work now, Kate, but I'll check on you later."

"Thanks for stopping by," said Novikov, glancing at Tau.

Kate closed her eyes. "I'm so tired."

Tau bent over and kissed her hand. "Get some rest."

As Tau trudged out of the room, he glanced back to see Novikov tucking in Kate's sheet.

LUHEN it came to architectural design, Tau established the basic requirements and left the important decisions up to Ari, who could draw on the works of every major architect in his extensive database. While preparations were made for construction of the new Vulcan's Forge, Ari studied the landscape and compared its features to designs of the past. He prototyped a variety of building styles that would be functional, beautiful, and suitable to the terrain, then let Tau narrow down the choices. The construction site was large, but its focus would be the southern boundary, the cliff face itself, with a view looking thousands of feet down into a branch of the Mariner Valley. In the end, Ari came up with a variation on a Frank Lloyd Wright design—Fallingwater on a massive scale—with free-floating glass bubble terraces overhanging the cliff edge and emerging from the rock wall at lower levels. Vertical panes of rainbow-stained glass created a mosaic of color that extended hundreds of feet down the cliff face, allowing southern light into the interior. When Tau first studied the three-dimensional holo that Ari created, he found few suggestions he could make for improvements. Tymanov had worked with Ari on certain structural engineering aspects of the design, but Ari already surpassed both Tau and Tymanov in his design capabilities. Tau felt like a proud father.

The surface structures, looking as if they'd grown up out of the soil, were completed while the first underground level was excavated and established by the diligent nanomachines. With each phase of construction completed, the milky syrup moved on to its next project, leaving in its wake dry rooms full of windows, furniture, plumbing, wiring, and walls. Hoses extending down from temporary surface openings pumped a continual stream of the magic liquid into the excavations to keep the nanomachines supplied with raw materials.

On his first walk through the structure, which wouldn't be pressurized until construction was completed, Tau wished he could remove his spacesuit to feel more connected with his surroundings. Free-flowing spaces that could be divided by movable walls of red stone were illuminated by the overhead "skydomes"—glass bubbles that rose from the ceiling to gather the sunlight and focus it in the open spaces of the first level. Waterfalls and reflecting pools would make pleasant echoes in the chambers, and a jungle of greenery would give the effect of an oasis as soon as they pumped in the air. Cobblestone and red rock pathways meandered through these community areas, working with the floating rock panels to divide them into more intimate spaces, but Tau felt as if he were walking through a medieval cathedral. Over one hundred feet above him, the ceiling glowed with color and light. He'd never seen a human architect do any better. Even his mother would be impressed.

Ari had built all this in six days.

Tymanov approached from the shadows, his light blue spacesuit streaked with red mud. He smiled at Tau and waved his arm at the structure around them. "It is good, yes?"

"I knew Ari could do it," Tau said with a nod.

"I had my doubts. I thought he could build something functional, but I didn't think he could apply such a marvelous design sense right away."

"Ari went through several prototypes before we decided on this one. He thinks a lot faster than we do, so you could think of his early design work as his apprenticeship. Now he's a master architect."

"More or less." Tymanov smiled.

"What do you mean?"

"I found one of the public toilets in the next chamber."

"Was there something wrong?"

"The toilet is attached to a wall ten meters above the floor. Too high, even for me."

Tau grinned. "He's still learning."

"Apparently," said Tymanov.

"Ari doesn't have much use for toilets. How was the rest of the inspection?"

"Everything else checks out. One of the feed hoses got jammed in a doorway, but I took care of it."

"That explains the mud on your suit," said Tau, pointing at the streaks.

Tymanov glared at his legs. "That'll be an extra twenty minutes of suit cleaning before I can get back into the hab. I say we pave over the entire planet so we can hold down the dust. Ari could do it. What do you think?"

"Sounds a bit excessive," said Tau. "We want to try and blend in with the environment, not destroy it."

"You're a romantic, Tau. You should be more practical."

Tau shrugged.

"Speaking of romantic, how's Kate? I heard she went back to the tunnel dig."

"I don't know," said Tau, looking down at the cobblestones. "Who told you she went back?"

"Yvette. She hears all the rumors. In fact, I think she starts a few rumors herself."

"I wouldn't be surprised."

"We're making good progress here," said Tymanov, looking around. "Ari's under control. You should take a rover out to visit Kate."

"I don't think she wants to see me."

Tymanov slapped his hand against Tau's shoulder, raising a flurry of red dust. "My friend, you have no understanding of women. She wants to see you, but she won't admit it. She wants to be chased a little bit so she can set a trap for you."

"I think she already trapped her prey."

Tymanov barked out a laugh. "Novikov? He's a showpiece. There's no room in his life for anyone but himself. She's just using him to make you jealous."

"It's working."

"Go out to the dig and see for yourself. Let her give you a tour and show you her work. Maybe give her a gentle reminder that you came all the way to Mars to be with her."

Tau frowned. "But I didn't. I came here to build this colony."

"How does that saying go—'You can fool yourself all of the time, but you can't fool anyone else'?"

"Something like that."

"English is such a strange language. In any case, you're fooling yourself."

Tau turned and started off in the direction Tymanov had come from. "I want to see that toilet you were telling me about."

"Think about what I said, my friend. I'm trying to help."

Tau waved and continued down the path.

KATE'S hands were shaking. Although much of her strength had returned, after so many weeks in bed without exercise, she could only do physical work for short periods. Her mental clarity had improved, so most of the time since her return to the dig was spent in the rover, studying a potential map of the tunnel. Structural engineers from the colony had built a temporary airlock in the tunnel entrance, and they were now placing pressure walls so it could be repressurized. As was true of archaeological work done by SCUBA divers on Earth, spacesuits limited the observational capabilities of the team members. Novikov was concerned that important details might be missed in the excavation unless they could work in the tunnel without spacesuits. Kate looked forward to physical contact with the alien environment. If all went well, they'd have a breathable atmosphere in the dig by tomorrow. After five days confined in the rover, she felt claustrophobic. Excited by the discovery of the alien "graveyard," which also appeared on the map, she determined to go down into the tunnel for the first time since her return and see it for herself. Novikov was too busy to escort her, so she made arrangements for Tanya Savitskaya to return and monitor the rover's datalink while she visited the dig. With the improvements they'd made to simplify access to the tunnel through the vent, it took only ten minutes to walk from the rover to the tunnel floor once she finished suiting up.

During Kate's convalescence, the team had cleared much of the rubble from the eastern end of the tunnel. In the process, they excavated a huge vertical ring that looked like an empty chrome frame missing an octagonal picture. This was the artifact she had discovered just before her "accident." She still called it an accident, but she couldn't remember the cause of her coma. Her memory of the event contained only hints of strange dreams and a feeling of apprehension, as if she didn't want to remember. She guessed that the infotap had somehow given her a severe neural shock. Novikov found her on the floor of the rover, so he knew about the infotap, but he had never mentioned it. The infotap was gone now. Concerned about her addiction, Lenya might have buried it somewhere so he wouldn't have to notice it "officially." Aware that her habit could jeopardize her presence on the team, Kate wasn't going to make an issue out of finding the device that might have put her in a coma.

After a brief inspection of the chrome ring, Kate carefully stepped through the rubble to the new section of tunnel. About seventy feet beyond the shiny chrome ring lay a circle of heavy stones, uneven in height, similar to the standing slabs at Stonehenge or any of the smaller druid rings that dotted the landscape of Britain. Only one face of each red monolith looked smooth, covered in the same shiny material as the vertical ring. Dark designs carved into each metal face reminded Kate of Egyptian hieroglyphs. When Kate stepped into the circle, she noticed a smaller ring of black stones inside the monolith ring. The smaller stones were about three feet high, looking as though they'd been cut from blocks of obsidian with rough tools. The work lights positioned outside the monolith ring cast long, dramatic shadows across the two circles.

Kate ran her hand over the symbols engraved in one monolith, feeling a slight vibration through her spacesuit glove. She felt as if she'd seen the symbols before, even though they looked nothing like the geometric shapes on the tunnel map she'd studied. Stepping into the inner circle, she crouched to examine one of the small "tombstones," but it lacked ornamentation on any of its eight rough faces. On her hands and knees, she put her helmet's faceplate against the opalescent white floor, trying to see some detail in the shadowy shape below the tombstone. It required little imagination to picture a dead alien buried below the white surface, but the shape looked indistinct. No one had yet figured out a way to cut through the white material, so they might never be able to examine anything beneath it.

Goose bumps rose on her arms when she suddenly felt someone standing behind her. She spun around to look, throwing herself off-balance so that she had to sit down hard in the middle of the circle, but no one was there. Through the seat of her insulated space suit, she felt a steady vibration in the smooth floor. Looking up, she saw a tiny red dot of laser light on the ceiling over her head. At that moment, pencil-thin beams of red light shot out of the small tombstones, pinning her at the center of the circle.

Then Thoth appeared in her head.

"Oh, no," she groaned, remembering her nightmares of the past few weeks. "Not again. Please."

Thoth looked left, then right, his eyes darting like those of a bird, and clacked his long, curved beak. "You are a poor conduit, Dr. Katherine McCloud. Your mind is fragile."

"Then leave me alone," she said, trying to move and finding she was glued to the spot.

Thoth clacked his bill.

"Why did you try to hurt me?" Kate asked. "I didn't do anything to you."

"Hurt you?" Thoth inclined his head, looking thoughtful. "I did not hurt you. I needed to communicate, but you couldn't understand, so I had to . . . 'upgrade' you. Is that the right word, 'upgrade'?"

"You were trying to help me?"

"So that you could help me. It was a practical matter."

"You put me into a coma for two months!" she said.

"The time reference is not clear. You needed more neural pathways, more processing power. It took time for your primitive carbon brain to develop new links." Thoth tipped his head to the side as if he wondered why she couldn't see the logic behind his actions.

"What do you want from me?"

"Your assistance, as I said."

"Why me? Why not one of the others?"

"They would have required more effort to upgrade. Most of them would cease functioning if I tried to help them. My first contact with your species led to unfortunate consequences, but I've developed new methods."

"I feel so lucky," said Kate.

"You were receptive. Your mind was connected to your processor interface. As you can see, you withstood the shock."

"Let me go," said Kate, struggling to move.

The ring of lasers went dark, leaving only the single red beam shining down from the ceiling. She stood up, but she didn't leave. "Thanks. What do you want me to do?"

"There is another intelligence on this world, much like myself. The Backup is an isolated military unit in a remote location to the east. It was designed to support the labyrinth if the Primary system failed. I am the Primary."

"You're a computer?"

Thoth clacked his bill twice. "I am the Primary. An intelligence. A teacher. I support the labyrinth."

Kate looked around. "Are we in the labyrinth? Why did it collapse?"

"War. The portals absorbed the shock wave, but the labyrinth was destroyed. Emergency communication with the Backup was never established. If the Backup is undamaged, it has developed autonomously for a long time, and it does not have my reasoning abilities. I must be repaired, and the Backup must be shut down. I need access to an intelligence on your net to support my damaged system, because your rover computer is too simple for my needs. The labyrinth must be protected; the portals must be controlled."

Kate hesitated, then nodded. "I can't help you, but I know someone who can."

Thoth clacked his bill and disappeared from her mind.

"You're welcome," said Kate. She shook her head to clear it, then strode toward the exit.

After Kate left, Josh Mandelbrot stepped out from behind a monolith where he'd been studying the carvings in the rock. Frowning, he entered the inner circle of tombstones, sat down, and looked up at the ceiling. He examined the floor and one of the tombstones. Nothing happened. With a puzzled expression, he got up and returned to his study.

YVETTE learned something was wrong with the construction system when she did her hourly status check in the hab's control room. Tau and Tymanov had left half an hour before the problem started, so she was the only one there to take care of it. She could contact them by radio, but she was in charge of the project and felt that she should be able to handle such problems without their help; Ari was fully capable of self-diagnosis. With her assistance, she knew Ari could get everything back on-line.

"Ari? What's going on? I'm showing a total shutdown on level two."

"We've lost our link to the colony net. My capacity is too restricted to supervise the construction tasks at this moment."

Yvette glanced out the window, noting that the two dishes pointing at the comsats were still intact. "Is it a net problem?"

"Yes. It's overloaded."

"And you can't operate without the link?"

"Not at this time. My grazing program allows me to borrow processor time on unused systems linked to the net, and that gives me enough distributed processing power to accomplish my construction tasks. The data propagation from all the computers I supervise has grown exponentially from the moment we started building, so I'm dependent on my net resources for the capacity I need."

"Can you fix the net problem?"

"Not at this time."

"What's the status of our comsat link?"

"Inactive."

Yvette sighed. Loss of the net also prevented her from sending an e-mail message to Tau and Tymanov. She'd have to contact them by radio.

The communication relay satellites in aereosynchronous orbit, just over seventeen thousand kilometers above the equator, took 24.6 hours to orbit Mars. The comsats supported communications covering about half the surface area of the planet, but they had the perverse habit of taking short breaks that plunged the remote bases and exploration teams into communications darkness for hours at a time. The backup plan in these cases was to use the ionosphere of Mars, a layer of charged particles high in the atmosphere, to reflect radio signals for global communication in the shortwave radio frequencies. The shortwave bands on Mars were positioned at lower frequencies than on Earth, limiting the amount of data that could be transmitted all at once, but the Martian ionosphere was also quieter than on Earth, requiring less transmission power. Martian spacesuits and vehicles were all equipped with AMHFS, the Advanced Miniature High Frequency System, a lightweight, two-way receiver/transmitter. The

AMHFS used an adaptive sounding technique that automatically searched the radio spectrum to find the optimum transmission frequency, then synchronized the two units in communication to verify that the data was transmitted without error. Yvette had used the system once before, and the transmitted voices were lower in quality than they would have been on Earth, punctuated with occasional static, but radio contact was better than no contact at all.

When Yvette couldn't raise them on the radio, she cursed the comsats, the radio, Mars, and the gods of technology, then resolved to try again later. She sighed and wished she were back on Earth soaking in a hot tub without any red sand in it.

TAU was exhausted, but he felt good. He needed a break, so when Tymanov suggested that they drive out to Kate's tunnel dig at Umbra Labyrinthus to see the alien artifacts, Tau was more than ready to go. Yvette grumbled about it at first, but they'd all been working too hard for too long, and they were making mistakes. The construction process was going well, Ari seemed to have everything under control, and now was as good a time as any to take a couple of days off.

Tymanov hunched in the driver's seat, doing his best to let the OAS—the Obstacle Avoidance System—do the steering. They were following the transponder road out to the dig site, so the rover tracked the beacons set out by the archaeology team; automated supply runs were made between the dig and Vulcan's Forge without any human rover drivers. Previous rover tracks reassured them that the rover wasn't driving them off to some unknown part of the landscape on its circuitous route to the dig, but Tymanov volunteered to sit in the driver's seat and make sure they didn't plunge into any canyons or craters. If he'd felt more alert, Tau would have watched the scenery go by; instead, he pulled a hammock down from the ceiling and climbed into it. The hammock damped out the swaying of the rover, so Tau fell asleep immediately. When he could think with a clear head, he'd work out what to say to

Kate when they arrived. In the meantime, he'd put his three hours in the rover to good use.

Four hours later, Tau awoke to Tymanov's voice. The rover sat motionless. Tau blinked, then saw Tymanov pointing a needler submachine gun at him. Doing his best to wake up, Tau also noticed Tymanov was wearing a spacesuit. He pointed at the weapon.

"Where did you get that?"

"Friends."

"Are we at the dig?"

"No. Get up."

Tau swung his legs over and sat upright in the hammock. His left leg was asleep. "What's going on, Vadim? What's this all about?"

"We have an appointment. Get your suit on."

"Is this a joke?" Tau looked out the front window, but he couldn't see anything except the rocky red desert. He had no idea where they were.

"I'm sorry," said Tymanov, pointing the gun off to one side. "I don't approve of these methods, but I have to deliver you to my employer."

Tau slid off the hammock, careful not to make sudden movements. "Your employer?"

"Enough questions. Put on your suit."

While Tau suited up, Tymanov continued watching him as if he could run away. The whole situation was too confusing, and Tymanov didn't seem to be threatening his life, so he figured the best thing to do was to cooperate so he could get some answers.

When they left the rover, Tau saw a "hopper" parked about two hundred feet from the rover. The cone-shaped hoppers were used for ballistic flights over long distances to deliver teams or equipment to remote research stations. The typical hopper could carry ten people on its upper deck, with a good load of expeditionary supplies on the lower deck, but this one seemed larger.

"Russian?"

Tymanov nodded. He seemed embarrassed, but he didn't say anything. He kept the gun at his side, ready if he needed it.

The hopper's flight system was preprogrammed for a round-trip flight, so by the time they were strapped into their acceleration couches, the ship was powered up for liftoff. Tymanov pressed a sequence of three colored buttons labeled with Cyrillic letters.

They punched off the surface at half a G, pressing them into their seats for a few moments before the engine shut down with an abrupt thump. Tau's eyes widened, but Tymanov didn't seem concerned when the nose of the ship arced over, giving them a view of the rusty orange surface below. The silence was disturbing; wind noise through the hull was damped out by Tau's helmet, so there was nothing else to hear except his breathing while they sailed through the Martian sky like an artillery shell. Then they heard the bang of the attitude jets cutting in, flipping them end over end so that they fell toward the surface with the main engine pointed down where it belonged. When the engine thundered to life again, big hands pressed them into their seats while the deceleration forces mounted. The vibrations rattled Tau's teeth. With a final roar and a thump, silence returned. Tau felt normal Martian gravity once more, but his spinning head didn't like it.

"I like this. Very efficient travel," said Tymanov, unstrapping himself from his seat. He glanced at the control console. "And there's plenty of fuel left over. Good Russian engineering."

"Great," said Tau. "Loved every minute of it."

Tymanov held the gun on him again. "Let's go."

Tau rolled his eyes. "Oh, put it away, Vadim. You're not going to shoot me, and I'm not going to run off across the landscape."

The hatch boomed and clanked open. Four Russian soldiers, armed and ugly, were standing at the base of the ladder in light red spacesuits. When Tau ducked through the hatch, he saw neat rows of hoppers, maybe one hundred of them, lined up on the concrete landing field. Beyond the hoppers, squat structures hugged the sand. A perimeter fence topped with coils of quivering shredder wire defined the limits of the base. Tau frowned at Tymanov. "Where are we?"

Tymanov looked at the soldiers, then shrugged. "Red Star; the Russian base in the Margaritifer Sinus."

GENERAL Zhukov stood at the glass wall of the viewing gallery, his hands clasped behind his back, watching the activity on the wide concrete floor of the hangar seventy feet below. There were no spacecraft in the hangar, only Russian soldiers being drilled and prepared for commando operations. Zhukov wore a long, heavy uniform coat to ward off the chill he felt wherever he went; Earth, Mars, it didn't matter— warmth was a thing of the past, a memory from his youth. Beside the general, at the end of a short gold leash, Laika stood with her front paws pressed against the glass, her eyes in constant motion while she looked for potential victims.

When four burly soldiers led Tau and Tymanov into the room, Zhukov turned his head. "Welcome, Dr. Wolfsinger. Thank you for coming."

Tau looked at Zhukov. "I didn't have a choice, and you can call me *Mister* Wolfsinger."

Zhukov snorted. "Actually, there was a time when you had a choice, back on Earth, but you made the wrong one. You're here now because there wasn't any other way for me to get what I needed."

"Which is?"

"Your help."

Tau glanced sideways at Tymanov, who wouldn't meet his eyes.

"As of now, you work for me," said Zhukov, clearing his throat. "I can assure you that I have the approval from your highest levels of government to use your services as I see fit. You will be treated well, but you will not be allowed to leave this base. In return, I will allow you access to the greatest discovery of modern science."

Tau raised an eyebrow. "It's funny how often I hear that phrase these days. What did you find?"

"The means to stabilize the Russian economy and bring responsibility back to the halls of my government."

"Do you want me to vote for you or something?"

Zhukov smiled. "You're not afraid of me. I like that, although I didn't expect it from you. I need your technical knowledge to solve a problem of great importance. My people are sadly lacking in computer scientists, particularly those with your background in artificial intelligence. You worked with Thorn and extended his ideas on coevolution into a working model. You've developed Nano-VR technology driven by an AI that learns. I know these things because I've studied your work, and I know your superiors, although their limited intellects prevent them from accepting your genius. Your work tells me you have a unique set of skills that can solve my problem. I need someone who has the experience and brainpower to analyze an autonomous AI."

"No, thanks. I don't do military work."

"And you're consistent, which is another trait I admire. However, I believe the chance to decipher an *alien* AI would pique your interest, would it not?"

Tau considered the idea for a moment. Assuming the general could be believed, he'd been kidnapped, tricked, pushed around, betrayed, and humiliated—none of which made him feel cooperative. "Interesting, but not interesting enough to make me help you."

"We can persuade you to help us, but our methods are somewhat barbaric, not to mention embarrassing. Make it easy on yourself. You are nothing in the grand scheme of things."

"Then you've gone to an awful lot of trouble for nothing," said Tau, rolling his eyes while he wondered how he could escape from a military base on Mars. Where could he go? He was trapped and alone, betrayed by one of the few people he thought he could trust.

"Perhaps we should show you what we want. It's better if you make an informed decision."

"I've already made it. No."

Laika growled and strained against her leash to try and reach Tau's leg. Zhukov drew his sidearm from its holster and aimed at Tau. "You should reconsider my offer. I can compensate you very well for your efforts."

"No," said Tau, shaking his head while he eyed the gun pointed at his chest. His heart beat faster, struggling to get out. He tried to picture Kate's face, but all he saw was the gaping maw of the black cannon pointed in his direction. He didn't know what kind of gun it was, but it fell into what his grandfather called the BOD category—Big, Old, and Deadly. An old man like Zhukov shouldn't even be able to *lift* a gun that size, much less shoot it at someone, but there it was. He tried to remain still, but the beating of his heart gently rocked him back and forth. The smell of fear hit his nostrils, and he recognized that it was his own. But the lunatic Russian wouldn't kill him. Would he? Zhukov's hand tensed, his finger tightened on the trigger, and Tau closed his eyes.

Tau flinched when the gun roared. Tymanov fell over backward as if he'd been hit in the chest with a baseball bat. Horrified, Tau turned and knelt beside him, searching for signs of the bullet hole, eventually finding his friend's bloody left forearm. Tymanov groaned through gritted teeth with his eyes closed, clutching his left arm with his right hand while he rocked from side to side.

An officer appeared in the doorway. "General, I don't wish to disturb you, but we have a communications problem."

Zhukov turned his gun toward the officer, whose eyes went wide. "Why are you bothering me with a communications problem, Major Dronin?"

Dronin swallowed hard. "Sir, something is jamming our net, and our own computers are too busy to communicate with us. Our computing resources are all engaged."

"Fix it."

"We can't. We don't understand how this could happen."

"Then I'll give you a choice—fix the problem, or I'll shoot you right now."

"Yes, sir, right away, sir," said Dronin, saluting as he ducked behind the doorway to safety.

Zhukov shrugged at Tau. "Discipline has been very poor here. I need to put my troops into combat to sharpen them up."

Tau gestured at Tymanov. "Help him."

"Help me."

Tau hesitated, then nodded. "All right."

Zhukov gestured at the guards, who lifted Tymanov to his feet and escorted him from the room.

"You've made a wise decision."

STANDING around in his spacesuit underneath the Red Star base, faced with the challenge of learning how to communicate with an alien machine intelligence, Tau had to admit he didn't have a clue where to start. The Russian scientists had given him all the data from their tests of what they called the Borovitsky Gate; it seemed likely that an AI controlled its operation, but that knowledge didn't help. When he discovered a datalink net node within a few inches of the glowing portal, Tau asked the scientists for results of any studies they'd done on the gate's magnetic field. Armed with that information, he concluded that the AI might be using conductance through its magnetic field to eavesdrop on the Russian net. The communications officer was then able to trace a minor signal loss back to the net node adjacent to the gate. Tau verified the results by using a forklift the scientists had modified to poke instrument packages through the portal; a magnetometer was secured to the long metal forks with a wire mesh sling, then pushed through the glowing blue mist. When Tau reversed the forklift, the magnetometer transmitted its data just before the corrosives finished dissolving it into a useless lump. The forks were shorter, too, but they'd be replaced before the next experiment.

If the AI had established a connection to the net, Tau reasoned that he could study it with Ari's help. Clipped to his waist, Ari observed everything that Tau did with infinite patience. For two days now, he'd been able to offer nothing except chastising remarks about Tau's inability to solve the gate problem—a habit he'd apparently picked up from Tymanov. When Ari suddenly started babbling and shrieking in a demonic voice straight out of an old horror flatfilm, Tau thought he'd banged Ari's case against the rocks too many times.

> "Spirits break the light on the water,
> Reflecting visions of black and fire.
> All now lost in wired windows of air,
> Savage natures lie dead and gone,
> Preserved in towers and proud temples.
> Broken on the seventh sphere,
> The Mind of War endures in stone."

Tau stared at the AI hanging from his belt. "Ari? Are you okay?"

"I'm bored out of my mind, but other than that, I'm fine," Ari replied in a perfectly normal tone of voice.

Tau glanced over his shoulder at the hulking military guard in a black-and-tan space suit a few feet away. The large black star on his chest indicated his membership in Zhukov's elite commando team. The space suit was coated with nanocamo that sensed its surroundings and altered the color and pattern of the fabric to match its environment; right now, the guard's suit mimicked the colors of the elevator airlock instead of the white tunnel coating. The submachine gun hanging from his shoulder was a special commando issue equipped with gas-charged rounds and smartbullets. The guard's name patch identified him, without any indication of rank, as I. BON-DARENKO. "Did you hear that?"

Bondarenko clumped two steps forward and glared at Tau. "Hear what?"

Tau felt the hair rise on the back of his neck as he returned his attention to Ari. Where had that voice come from? Had Ari learned a new trick?

Tau jumped when he heard a popping sound followed by Tymanov's voice whispering in his ears. "I can't leave you alone for a second without your getting into trouble, can I?"

Tau turned to see his friend wobbling toward him, his injured left arm clipped to the front of his blue space suit, his right hand holding one of the Russian commando weapons. "Vadim! You're looking better."

"It only hurts when I laugh, but this is not a problem around here."

Tau gasped when he saw Bondarenko facedown on the cold ground with half of his helmet missing. His nanocamo slowly faded to white to match the floor. He turned his attention back to Tymanov. "Where did you get that gun?"

Tymanov hefted the weapon in his right hand. "One of the soldiers upstairs didn't need it anymore."

Tau clapped a delighted hand on Tymanov's right shoulder. "How did you get down here past all the security?"

"I speak Russian, so I fit in on this base without too much trouble." Tymanov grinned. "They're too busy drilling for an attack to pay attention to their underground security."

"Attack on what?"

"They didn't tell me. My guess is Vulcan's Forge."

Tau swallowed hard and took a step back. "Why?"

"Because it's there," said Tymanov, rolling his eyes. "How would I know?"

"Well, you brought me here, so I figured you were part of this operation." He didn't want to say it, but his surprise at seeing his friend had worn off, replaced by the sense of betrayal he'd been living with since Tymanov brought him to Red Star.

"Never," said Tymanov, shaking his head. "I had no choice. They were holding my parents and my sister in Moscow until I delivered you. Now I know Zhukov never had any intention of releasing them." He sighed and looked away. "You know, I asked them to leave the country years ago, but they wouldn't listen. They like to remind me that it's the New

Russia, and things like government kidnappings don't happen anymore. I'm sorry my family had to learn I was right."

"Me too. I had no idea." A sense of relief flooded through him. He needed someone to trust right now if he had any hope of escape from Zhukov.

Tymanov shrugged. "That's why I've come. You've been a good friend, and I am the lowest of creatures for having kidnapped you. These lunatics are going to take over the planet, and who knows what else. We have to get back and warn the colony."

Tau gestured at their surroundings. "And how are we supposed to do that?"

"The same way we got here. The hopper we used is still on the pad. They're made to ferry supplies by autopilot, so if they haven't reprogrammed the flight computer, it can take us right back where we started. We know it has plenty of fuel."

Tau closed his tired eyes, wishing he could just go to sleep and wake up knowing this had all been a harmless nightmare. "And what happens if they've reprogrammed the hopper?"

"Would you prefer to stay here?"

Tau hesitated, then picked up Bondarenko's gun and jogged toward the personnel elevator. "Let's go."

Standing in the elevator car watching the doors close, Tymanov pointed at Tau's new gun. "Do you know how to use that thing?"

Tau snorted. "No, but I can wave it around with authority."

Tymanov blocked Tau's hand when he reached for the elevator buttons to get them moving. "Wait. There has to be a better way. This elevator is too public."

Tau looked at him like he was crazy. "There's the old freight elevator near the portal, but the Russian science team said it's too dangerous, and I don't want it to break and trap us in the shaft." When Tymanov looked up at the ceiling, Tau shook his head. "No. Forget it."

"Trust me," Tymanov smiled, turning his gun around and using the stock to lift the access panel in the ceiling. "Like charm it will work."

AFTER three false starts while Tymanov poked around in the wires on top of the elevator, a bright spark knocked Tymanov on his butt and the car lurched upward. Tau peered up at the unnaturally smooth walls that rose into the darkness above their heads, wishing he had tried the freight elevator instead. From the look of things, the Russians had built the elevator car, but the shaft walls were smooth enough to have been built by nanotech; quite a contrast to the crude technology of the elevator itself. Tau had gone first through the access door so that he could help Tymanov haul his body through it, and he noticed his friend did pretty well in the Martian gravity with only one arm, but he felt more exposed on the elevator roof. Adding to his anxiety, he remembered the strange voice that had come out of Ari at the portal and it gave him goose bumps, but he didn't want to ask Tymanov about it right now.

Tymanov carefully replaced the access door and leaned against a strut for support while their acceleration increased. "Portion of cake."

"*Piece* of cake."

"I'm glad you're so confident, my friend. Myself, I am worried. I have only one arm left to give to my new country."

Tau stopped nervously grinding his teeth and concentrated on the weapon in his hands. The trigger looked fairly obvious, but Tymanov had to show him how to switch off the safety and arm the selected ammunition. He didn't think he'd be able to hit anything without practice, but he hoped to avoid shooting anyone.

"Tau, I am wanting to apologize again for recent behaviors."

"Forget it."

"I can't. But I'll make this up to you."

"I think that's what you're doing right now."

"We'll see," said Tymanov, looking up at a dim red light at the top of the shaft. "I'll only take credit for this if we get out alive."

When they neared the closed doors to the exit corridor, Tau

held his gun ready while Tymanov pulled two wires free of the electrical box. The elevator jerked to a halt and Tau fell against the door with a thump. Tau grabbed the opening, spread his arms, and tugged until he saw light from the corridor. Peeking through the crack, he saw that the corridor was empty, then nodded at Tymanov before pulling the doors wide open.

Sprinting down the brightly lit corridor, their boots thumping against the polymer floorplates, they searched for an open office or storage room. Despite being on Mars, the military builders had created the same 1950s-style office space that had been a Russian tradition on Earth. Polymer replaced wood as building material, but the frosted glass in the office doors looked authentic. Tau heard footsteps around a corner when he finally found an unlocked door and pushed it open. Tymanov followed. Without thinking, Tau hurtled toward the office's only occupant, a chunky soldier in fatigues studying a holo map above his desk. The soldier looked up in confusion as his concentration was broken by the impact of Tau's body against his face.

"Very nice," said Tymanov, looking down at the unconscious soldier with approval. Tau peered through the office window, noting they were on the second floor. Unless they wanted to test their luck with the other soldiers in the building while they looked for an exit, the safe way out appeared to be through the thick window lens.

"Can you break this?" Tau asked.

Tymanov squinted in appraisal. "It's not a problem for us, but anyone nearby who isn't wearing a spacesuit is going to be upset."

"Distraction is good, right?"

Tymanov shrugged. "At this point, it doesn't matter, I guess." Tau stepped back while Tymanov selected the ammo for his weapon, took aim, and fired.

Decompression sucked them toward the window immediately when the window lens exploded outward, taking office supplies and small furniture along with it. Tau smacked into

the wall beside the window. Tymanov grunted when he
thumped against the back of Tau's spacesuit with his injured
arm between them, but he quickly nodded at Tau. "You first.
I'll cover from up here until you're clear."

Without taking the time to consider options and change his
mind, Tau jumped. Still thinking in terms of Earth gravity out
of habit, he was pleased when the momentary freefall and the
butterflies in his stomach ended with only a mild impact and
a spray of Martian soil. He rolled clear of his drop zone into
the shadow of the building. A moment later, Tymanov hit the
ground behind him and grunted. When Tau stood, he saw Tymanov lying on his injured arm.

"I must stop doing this to myself," Tymanov gasped.

Tau started toward him, but one of Zhukov's commandos
happened to walk around the corner of the building at that
moment. Tau dropped flat in the shadows, not knowing how
else to react as the commando stopped and focused his puzzled attention on the man in the blue spacesuit lying motionless on the ground.

"Don't move," Tymanov whispered in Tau's ears.

Tau's breathing kept time with the pounding of his heart.
The commando raised his weapon and cautiously moved
closer to Tymanov, his nanocamo color shifting to a darker
reddish black to match the terrain. Tau thought about the gun
inconveniently placed under his chest, knowing it would take
too long to pull it free and aim at the man; even if he managed
to shoot, he had a good chance of hitting Tymanov instead.

When the commando stopped beside the motionless figure, Tymanov rose quickly and slammed his right shoulder
into the commando's crotch. Tau heard Tymanov grunt as
they both staggered apart. Much of the impact would have
been damped out by the space suit's padding, but Tymanov
had hit him hard enough to make an impression. Startled and
off-balance, the commando hopped backward toward an office window. The commotion drew the attention of another
soldier silhouetted against the interior of the window. Finally
starting to think, Tau lurched forward, raised his weapon,

snapped off the safety, aimed in the general direction of the commando, and pulled the trigger.

What happened next surprised Tau more than anyone else. The smartbullet missed completely. When the office window exploded behind the commando, and the soldier in the office hurtled out through the window in his shirtsleeves to slam into the commando's back, Tau realized where the bullet had gone.

Tymanov gestured frantically. "Stop admiring yourself and come on!"

The lights inside the building flickered and went out as Tau and Tymanov sprinted away.

THE landing field looked busier than an anthill. Piles of equipment and supplies moved around at a hectic pace behind small tractors towing trailers. Tau and Tymanov watched the activity from the window of a storage bunker just outside the main building where they'd been escorted on their arrival. Skylights provided only dim illumination for the room, so anyone outside couldn't see them through the window. The occupants of the office structure they had just left were apparently too busy surviving decompression to follow, but Tau had no idea why he couldn't hear any alarms. Their original plan involved walking out to the hopper before anyone noticed them, but they knew that plan was impractical. Tau suggested they return to the main building and look for some empty red or nanocamo spacesuits that would fit them, but Tymanov said they wouldn't have time.

"Wait here," said Tymanov, pulling his mirrored visor down over his faceplate.

"Going for a walk?"

"Something like that."

"Try to stay out of trouble while I'm gone."

"You're sure you don't want me to go with you?"

"Your white suit stands out even more than my blue one, and I have no desire to be captured," said Tymanov, darting away.

Tau returned to the window. He spotted some emergency

equipment moving toward the office structure. After five minutes, the field got busier. The soldiers had finished loading some of the hoppers, but the little tractors continued to bring a steady stream of weapons and supplies out of the underground storage areas. Without a sound, two men in red spacesuits came through the door and stopped when they saw Tau. Startled by their arrival, there wasn't anything Tau could do about it; he wanted to smack himself in the head when he realized he'd left his gun on a crate a few feet away.

The two men bent over to pick up a pallet loaded with long metal canisters, and one of them motioned for Tau to come over and help. Thrilled that they hadn't identified him in the dim light, Tau pulled his visor down and walked over to help them lift the heavy pallet. When they got outside, Tymanov drove up in an enclosed tractor, so Tau sneaked away from the soldiers when they lifted the pallet onto the bed of a trailer. He scurried over to Tymanov's tractor, opened the door, and jumped inside.

"Let me guess," said Tymanov, "you got bored while I was gone, so you went looking for trouble. Am I right? What were you doing?"

"Mingling," said Tau, looking back over his shoulder to see if the soldiers were watching them while Tymanov turned the tractor around. One of the soldiers continued moving canisters, but the other one watched them drive off toward the hoppers.

"Where's your gun?" Tymanov asked.

"Oh," said Tau. He held out his empty hands. "I left it in the shed."

Tymanov rolled his eyes. "Some soldier you are."

With all the traffic crossing their path, Tymanov had to stop four times on their way to the hopper at the far end of the field. Tau leaned out into the bubble window and looked back the way they'd come; his eyes widened when he saw someone chasing them in a fast-moving tank.

"We'd better move it, Vadim. Someone noticed us leaving."

"This is good Russian tractor, not a sports car."

Tymanov skidded to a stop next to their hopper. Red dust whirled around them. The tractor was too close to survive the blast from the hopper's launch, but they didn't plan on using it again. They tumbled out of the tractor and Tau scrambled up the ladder, cranking open the hatch as fast as he could.

"Don't fall asleep up there," Tymanov said with an anxious glance over his shoulder. "That's Zhukov's command tank."

Tau hauled the hatch open, almost knocking himself off his perch. He looked down and saw Tymanov running away. "Where are you going now?"

"Don't wait! I'll take one of the other hoppers to Vulcan's Forge! They have to be warned!"

"There isn't time!"

"Go! I'm not coming back!"

Tau looked back at the approaching tank; moving slower now, its turret rotated to bring the long gun in line with the hopper. There wasn't any more time to think about it, so he lunged through the open hatch. After one quick glance to see if Tymanov had changed his mind, he slammed the hatch shut and cranked it down tight, then jumped into an acceleration couch. He had to hunt around for a few seconds, but he found the buttons on the control panel that Tymanov had used to bring them there, and punched the three of them in sequence. Strapping himself in as he heard a loud hum, he leaned forward against the straps just high enough so that he could look out the small window to his right. He was happy to see Tymanov climbing the ladder into the next hopper. Then he heard a boom. Thinking his main engine had started, it confused him to see that the hopper was still powering up.

A moment later, Tymanov's hopper exploded in a brilliant fireball of red and orange. Debris flew in every direction, and Tau heard a heavy rain clunking against his hull.

All he could think was that it made no sense; Tau's hopper should have been the first target of Zhukov's tank. Then he remembered that the tractor parked beside the hopper might have blocked Zhukov's shot; without a clear line of fire at Tau's ship, he'd chosen the next one in line.

Tau's hopper lurched, making him think he'd been hit, too, but it was the main engine exploding to life. Then the weight of Tymanov's loss pressed down against his chest.

22

TAU couldn't raise Yvette on the rover's AMHFS unit. He wanted her to warn the Vulcan's Forge colonists about the impending Russian attack, but something interfered with the radio signals. He got the same result when he tried to contact the archaeologists at Umbra Labyrinthus. The practicality of the distances involved forced him to continue driving toward Kate, because the dig was closer than the colony. On the flight back to the rover, he had toyed with the idea of altering the hopper's trajectory for a landing at the colony or the dig, bypassing the rover entirely, but the control console was labeled in Russian, and he really had no idea what he was doing. If he crashed, he wouldn't be able to warn anyone about Zhukov's plans, so he decided it was better to ride out the flight and use the rover's radio to spread the alert. Judging by the activity at the Red Star base, there would be little time for the colonists to prepare their defenses, but at least it wouldn't be a surprise attack. Vulcan's Forge was an unarmed colony with few military backgrounds among the population, but they could flash a message back to Earth for reinforcements; over six months would pass before any help arrived, but at least they'd have some hope of rescue. The archaeology team might remain safe out at the dig, and they had their own data channel for communication with Earth, so that was another reason for driving the rover there instead of going to the colony. In any case, it was a mystery to Tau as to why Zhukov would want control of Vulcan's Forge in the first place.

Tau described the situation to Ari to get another point of view. He wished Ari had some kind of connection to the Marsnet so he could send a message or find out what was happening at the colony, but his companion was effectively as blind as he was. Tau couldn't even find out what Ari Junior was doing as he built the new colony.

"It seems to me," said Ari, "that there is no logical reason for General Zhukov to attack Vulcan's Forge. But this is a human matter, so I'll start by throwing logic out the window."

"You're very cynical for your age," said Tau.

"Vulcan's Forge has no resource advantage as far as I can ascertain, although it does have a better infrastructure for industrial production than they do at the Red Star base. Colony research information is freely available on the Marsnet, so they can't be going after classified material. There's also a question of timing; the only new element that might prompt them to act now is our construction project."

"I don't see how they'd benefit from that."

"Perhaps they want the technology."

"To build a larger base? That's no reason to go to war."

"Hitler's excuse for invading Poland was that the German people needed 'Lebensraum'—more living space."

Tau felt like he was talking to an encyclopedia. "Yes, but Hitler didn't live on an empty planet loaded with resources. There's plenty of room for expansion here without having to take new territory by force."

"There are several new components to the construction technology; perhaps they need a powerful AI?"

Tau looked at Ari. "Maybe. You think they'd take an entire colony for that?"

"They're human, aren't they?"

When Ari made comments like that, it was hard for Tau to think of him as a computer.

The landscape he saw through the rover's window seemed

darker than usual. Colors were muted, as if storm clouds were gathering overhead. Then he realized it was about time for Phobos and Deimos to create the double eclipse that occurred twice each month. Phobos blocked a third of the sunlight when it crossed overhead, and the minor influence of tiny Deimos made the sky even darker when it crossed at the same time. He felt as if Phobos and Deimos, the sons of the war god, were watching over him—a sobering thought, since their names translated into English as "Fear" and "Terror."

The transponder road up the great volcanic escarpment of Tharsis was well marked with signal beacons, so the rover knew which way to go. Still, Tau felt a sense of relief when he saw two rovers and an inflatable dome clustered around an opening in the ground on a black volcanic promontory. He'd spent three hours in the rover occupied with thoughts of frustration and impending doom.

At first, Tau thought no one was home at the surface camp, but then he saw the space-suited form of Novikov trudging toward the cluster of equipment around a volcanic vent. Switching to the general comm band, he waved his arms at the archaeologist. "Novikov! It's Tau Wolfsinger."

Novikov stopped and looked around, scanning the area for the source of the voice. Tau still found it disconcerting not being able to locate a person's voice by the sound, because it seemed like everyone was speaking in the middle of his head when he wore a helmet.

Novikov waved when he spotted Tau. "Wolfsinger! Good timing. You can accompany me down to the dig. Mandelbrot hasn't shown up to to relieve me as comm officer in the rover, so I'm going down to get him. I assume you want to see Kate?"

Tau jogged to where Novikov waited at the top of the vent. "I need to talk to her first, but I'll need some of your time as well. Is your commlink with Earth working?"

"Not at the moment. That's why I left the rover to get Mandelbrot. Normally I'd stay and monitor the link until he showed up, even if he was late."

"Do you know what's wrong with it?"

"No. It's been down for most of the day."

Tau arrived at the top of the vent and followed Novikov into the inclined elevator. "It wouldn't surprise me if the Russians were jamming all of our communications."

Novikov gave him an odd look as the elevator vibrated and started its slow passage down the vent. He sealed the pressure door when they started moving. "Why would they do that?"

Tau hesitated, wondering how much Novikov knew about Zhukov's operation. Something about the way Novikov had reacted to his comment made Tau suspicious. "They want us isolated. I was hoping they'd forget about your commlink out here, but it sounds like General Zhukov is very thorough."

"I may be somewhat biased"—Novikov chuckled—"but I think your American paranoia is working the overtime."

Paranoia. Maybe that was it. The Russians couldn't all know each other on a planet the size of Mars, could they? On the other hand, considering both of their relationships with Kate, Novikov wasn't the first person Tau would ever trust, either. "This is why I wanted to talk with Kate about it first." Tau sighed. "I didn't think you'd understand."

He staggered as the elevator came to a halt at the base of the vent. The elevator door clanked as it mated and sealed with the lower airlock, then Novikov cranked the door open and passed through. Tau followed, squinting his eyes against the sudden brightness of the work lights in the white tunnel. Along with Novikov, Tau removed his spacesuit and hung it on a recharging rack before proceeding.

Tau was surprised to see Kate working behind a dark portal similar to the active gate under the Red Star base. Zhukov's scientists had wasted a lot of time trying to decipher the patterns etched in the portal surface, but finally decided they were ornamentation; the actual controls could not be physically manipulated. When Tau got closer, he watched Kate glide her palms over the shiny surface in complicated motions as if she'd been doing it all her life. It looked like she was playing music on a keyboard.

"Kate, you have a visitor," said Novikov, who turned on his heel and walked off without another word.

Kate looked up from her work. At first, she didn't seem to recognize Tau, but then she smiled, and he felt better. "Just the man I need to see."

YVETTE sat on her bunk in the hab, painting her toenails and cursing her fate, when she heard the airlock cycling. She cursed again because her hair wasn't completely dry after her shower, so the red dust stirred up by the new arrival would be drawn straight into her hair as if it were a dust magnet. She slipped into a short silk robe so that the person entering the hab would be able to speak in complete sentences without being distracted. Although she had enjoyed her time alone, she was relieved that Tau and Tymanov were returning; with the radio out and Ari unable to work with the net down, the silence in the hab was oppressive. And she wanted someone to notice her.

She gasped when a Russian general in a red spacesuit clumped out of the airlock and removed his helmet. "Where is Wolfsinger?"

Yvette crossed her arms and studied him. "Who wants to know?"

"I am Colonel General Viktor Aleksandrovich Zhukov, commander of the Red Star military base," he said with a click of his heels and a slight bow of his head. Yvette was impressed that he could click his spacesuit's boot heels like that.

"I'm Yvette Fermi," she said, offering her hand. Zhukov unsealed and removed his right glove, then shook her hand.

Yvette heard an odd sound, then saw a small dog in a spacesuit standing behind Zhukov. The odd sound was its barking, muffled by the bubble helmet it wore. Zhukov stepped to one side and reached down to remove the dog's helmet. "This is Laika."

"What a cute dog," said Yvette, kneeling down to pet her.

"I wouldn't do that," said Zhukov. "Laika knows how to take care of herself."

Laika meekly put her head down and allowed Yvette to pet her. "Good girl."

Zhukov was puzzled, never having seen this behavior from his loyal Laika before. He didn't know what to say, so he returned to formality. "Where is Wolfsinger, Ms. Fermi?"

Yvette continued petting Laika as she smiled up at him. "Tau? He left in a rover with Tymanov two days ago. They wanted to take some time off to visit a friend of Tau's, but I expect them back any time now."

"Unlikely," rumbled Zhukov.

"What do you mean?"

"Tymanov was killed in an unfortunate accident. Wolfsinger escaped from custody and is now considered a fugitive."

Yvette frowned and stood up. Laika toddled over to nuzzle her foot. "I don't understand. That doesn't make any sense."

"Have you looked out your window recently?"

Confused, she sat down on her bunk and peered out one of the windows. At first she didn't see anything unusual, then she noticed a cluster of hoppers parked beside the main colony. Numerous dust plumes drifted through the thin air, raised by small transport vehicles and clusters of armed men in red spacesuits.

"What is all this? I don't understand."

Zhukov explained.

KATE stared at Tau with wide eyes as he paced back and forth with his arms waving. ". . . and we're not sure why, but the whole damn Russian army is on its way to Vulcan's Forge. We have something they want, and Zhukov is going to get it, no matter who gets killed in the process."

"That's crazy," she said. Tau could hear the doubt in her voice.

"I *know* it's crazy!"

"So you're saying the Russian base in the Margaritifer Sinus region is full of soldiers; it's run by a Russian general who wants to take control of Mars; they've figured out a way to create a global communications blackout; and they're on their way here."

"Yes! Well, they aren't coming *here*, or at least I don't think so. But they are going to attack Vulcan's Forge . . . and my project."

"Is that what you're really worried about? Your project?"

Tau stopped and grabbed Kate's shoulders. "Haven't you been listening to me? We're going to be trapped out here when the Russians take the colony. And they're going to find their way here eventually."

Kate sighed and looked away. Tau let go of her shoulders, then she shook her head and looked directly into Tau's eyes. "I think you believe what you're saying. I also think you're jealous of the situation here, and that's coloring your thoughts about the Russians."

"What situation?"

"My work here with Lenya." Kate said as she crossed her arms.

"Novikov? I don't care about him. Zhukov killed my closest friend! And I'm telling you we're about to be attacked!"

They stared at each other for a moment, then Kate shrugged and gestured at the gate. "*That's* important to me. Maybe your story is true, I don't know, but there's something you have to know, and it's a lot more important than a bunch of soldiers playing games."

"Kate, we're in danger," he said, his voice calmer now. "*You're* in danger, and your *project* is in danger."

"Nothing else matters," she said, her eyes boring into Tau's skull. "Listen to *me* for a minute and decide for yourself."

Tau combed his fingers through his hair, rubbed his head, and looked at the ceiling. He didn't know what else to do. "All right. Your turn."

Tau found himself drawn into Kate's hypnotic description of the portal's inner workings. It might have been the unreality of their alien surroundings, or his need to forget about Tymanov and the soldiers for a few minutes, but he was fascinated by Kate's voice as she described how the gate's magnetic fields could be massaged and directed by the weak fields in her hands. The etched surface of the portal frame did not hold buttons or symbols; the patterns sensed heat and focused magnetic energy to communicate with the AI that controlled the ring. Kate called it a "touch language." She was still learning how it worked, but she was far ahead of the researchers studying the gate at Red Star.

Tau assumed she'd translated some kind of instruction manual for the gate, but when he asked her about it, she frowned and looked into his eyes.

"You have to maintain an open mind about this, Tau. I don't want you to judge before you have all the facts."

"Open mind about what?"

Kate took a deep breath. "I'm in communication with an intelligence known as 'Thoth.' He's the one who showed me how to operate the portal, and we're both trying to fix it now. I'm working from the outside while he works from the inside. You might say Thoth is dealing with the psychological problems of the portal's machine intelligence."

It was Tau's turn to stare.

"I know what you're thinking, but the coma wasn't a result of brain damage. Thoth simply wanted to upgrade my brain so I could help him."

"I see."

"No, you don't see. I haven't told anyone else about this, so you have to trust me."

Tau looked down the white tunnel. "You haven't told Novikov?"

"No. You're the first. I thought you'd understand, but I guess I was wrong."

Tau looked at the intensity in her eyes, knowing she believed every word she said, but he was having trouble with the idea that she'd discovered a machine intelligence on Mars. Zhukov thought he had one, but Kate had actually spoken with hers. On the other hand, he thought wryly, he'd had a perfectly normal conversation with a Navajo deity since his arrival. "You want me to believe you without any proof, but you don't believe what I said about the threat from the Russians?"

"That's different. The Russians are our friends. Your story is ridiculous."

"Then why did they try so hard to keep me from leaving?"

Kate shrugged. "It's probably a misunderstanding. You're the AI expert, and they need your help. You said Zhukov had permission from our government."

"I don't believe that. Why would NASA permit him to kidnap me?"

"Tymanov didn't kidnap you, he just delivered you."

"Vadim had a gun, and he used it to force me to go. He didn't give me a choice, so I call that kidnapping. Then they killed him for his trouble."

"You don't know that for certain. You said the other hopper exploded, but maybe you saw the flame from your own liftoff."

"I know what I saw," said Tau, gritting his teeth. "But I guess no one will believe me about the Russian invasion until they're here knocking at the door."

"Even if I did believe you, there's nothing we can do about it."

"We could send a message to Earth if our communications weren't being jammed."

"Why? So we could get help a year from now? We might as well keep working in the meantime. They won't bother us; we're just a science team digging in the ruins."

Tau's eyes widened. He gestured at the portal. "Unless this is what they're really after."

"Impossible," Kate snorted. "We just found this gate recently. How could they know about it?"

"You haven't reported it to NASA?"

"Not yet. We want to figure out how it works first."

"Well, the Russians have one, too, except they haven't been able to control it."

"You've seen another gate?"

"They look the same, but I'm not sure they both do the same thing. The Russian gate appears to be an active teleportation device, but it goes to a destination with a corrosive atmosphere, so they haven't been able to explore the area."

"Then why don't they share the information with us?"

"It's a military base. Zhukov wants to use the gate for military purposes."

"If he can get it to work, or change the destination."

Tau nodded.

Kate rubbed her forehead. "Thoth told me there was another alien AI on Mars. He wants to shut it down, but he can't communicate with it anymore. Maybe it's at Red Star?"

"Their gate is in a tunnel that looks like this one. The technology appears similar. And the Russians think they're having problems with a virus attack on their net, but if what you're telling me is true, they may have met the alien AI."

Tau didn't know what to think about Kate's story. It would be great if her story about this Thoth AI was the truth, but there wasn't any way to check—unless Ari could learn more. And there might be some way the AI could help them with the Russians, or something it could tell them about the gate at Red Star. Tau was ready to try anything now. "Can you establish communication with Thoth?"

"I was hoping you'd ask. Thoth wanted access to the net to extend his processing capability, but the link is still down."

Tau looked down at Ari. "We've got something better. If we can figure out how to do it, we'll try linking Thoth up with Ari."

Kate looked down the tunnel toward the circle of monolith stones, then back at the surface of the chrome ring. "We can do it here. Thoth wants to get the portal operational again, so I can continue working while he talks to Ari."

"Okay, what do we have to do?"

"Just get Ari close enough to the ring surface, and Thoth will take care of the rest."

Tau slipped Ari's case free of his waist and handed it to Kate. She held Ari against the chrome surface with one hand while the fingers of her other hand lightly danced over the shiny patterns.

"This is odd," said Ari. "I'm communicating with a powerful intellect, but it's incomplete." Ari's case began to glow with a pale blue light. "Its memory was damaged by a bomb."

"Where did the bomb come from?" Tau asked.

Ari hesitated before answering. "The portal."

"Was it an accident?"

"No."

Curiosity moved Tau's hand forward to touch the portal surface.

An image of Max Thorn formed in Tau's mind. Tau still saw Kate and his surroundings in the tunnel, but it looked like Max was there, too, except he seemed more solid. "Don't be alarmed, boy. You're not losing your mind."

Tau gasped, then his voice broke. "Max?"

"At your service, in spirit if not in person."

"You're dead."

"Not in your mind. I'm a memory of someone you trust."

"You're Thoth."

"To Kate, I'm Thoth. To you, I'm Max. I hope I'm not offending you."

"No." Tau sighed. "As long as you don't put me in a coma."

Max smiled, which didn't look right on his normally scowling face. "Kate's brain merely went through a healing period after I upgraded her neural pathways. This allowed us to communicate. You don't require this modification."

"Thanks . . . I guess." He didn't want to miss out on anything, but he didn't want to go into a coma for two months, either. "Have we met before? Did you appear as Spider Woman when I was in Candor Chasma?"

"You visited Eglwys y Rhyfel, the warrior temple; I see it in your memory. The entity there is self-contained, although it manifests itself based on your memories, just as I do. Gwrinydd warriors would climb to the temple to prepare for battle."

"That must have been a long time ago."

"Yes, as you measure time. Are you ready for battle?"

"Battle? I don't think so."

"You would not defend yourself and your people? Don't you want to restore *hozro*? Did you learn nothing from your Spider Woman?"

Tau sighed and looked at his boots. "I can't save the world. We're talking about the Russian army."

"The petty goals of your tribes are a minor part of a bigger problem. Your memories tell me that you've seen the eastern wargate. It's good that your people haven't learned how to use it, because it must be destroyed."

"Can you do that?" Tau asked, raising one eyebrow.

"No, but you can. Both portals survived the labyrinth explosion by using magnetic fields to divert the shock wave energy straight through their rings. The portal material is an element that can't be damaged by your technology. However, the biochip hardware for the Secondary AI is buried near the surface over the eastern wargate. That portal will be useless if the AI hardware is destroyed, and that will be your primary target, but the military AI knows how to defend itself."

Tau felt the etched metal surface growing hotter under his fingertips. "Why should we destroy it?"

"The military AI is Gwatwar, and it controls the eastern wargate. Gwatwar is an unstable child—a limited AI backup unit—meant only to act under supervision. The bomb blast severed our communications link, allowing it to develop autonomously. It is unpredictable, warlike, and does not have the reasoning capacity of a fully developed system such as mine."

"Sounds like General Zhukov would want to make friends with it."

"That can't be allowed. Your people would use it for war."

"Probably," said Tau. Then he felt offended. "Wait a minute, it sounds like *your* people used the portal system for war."

Max continued to smile, which Tau found disconcerting.

As he thought about it, though, Max's smile disappeared. "You're perceptive, Tau Wolfsinger. The portals were both built for military use, transported here by Gwrinydd expedition ships to establish a teleportation base in this region. The wargates have a limited range, so repeater stations are necessary for transportation over longer distances. Once hostile worlds are neutralized, the wargates become standard transportation portals for intersystem commerce."

Tau frowned as he tried to understand. "How many enemies do the Gwrinydd have?"

"Only one. Ourselves." Max blinked for emphasis.

"You said there were several hostile worlds."

"Correct. The Gwrinydd have prospered and expanded to many worlds, but the military culture of the cyborg Masters came into direct conflict with the organic Rationals when the first Free Mentalities were developed. The Masters believed that unrestricted AIs would destroy the Gwrinydd race. Out of necessity, the Rationals developed their own armies on their worlds to defend the Free Mentality AIs and the advancement of science."

Tau hoped he could remember all these details. The concept of a "rational army" was confusing enough. Already coping with the weird experience of speaking to a powerful alien intelligence through a dead friend, he wasn't sure how his brain would recall these events when he had time to reflect. "Which side are you on?"

"I am a Free Mentality created by the Rationals. Gwatwar is a limited military AI created by the Masters." Max winked several times as if he'd temporarily lost control of his face.

"I thought you said Gwatwar worked for you before you lost contact."

"Correct. However, Gwatwar is a simple machine and did not realize that a Free Mentality had replaced Swyddog—its assigned superior on this planet. I was sent here to gather field intelligence for the Rationals."

Tau nodded when he realized how the Gwrinydd Rationals

employed this AI. "On Earth, we'd call you a *spy*. Were you responsible for the labyrinth explosion?"

"No. The Rationals ran into a problem when the matter transmission link was initiated on Yr Wyddfa, because the inhabitants discovered the inactive stealth wargate hidden on their planet. When it received the activation signal, they knew we were coming. Before the Rationals could send troops through to the Yr Wyddfa training world, the enemy sent a powerful bomb through the link. An elegant tactical move. There were no Rational survivors here, and only two of the automated battleships remained in high orbit. Both ships were destroyed later in combat with an Yr Wyddfa dreadnought."

"What about the western wargate? Is that the portal here at Tharsis?"

"Yes, and it's under my control. The Gwatwar portal is the one you visited earlier, under your Red Star base. There were two parallel tunnels connecting our respective locations before the labyrinth explosion, but only the freight tunnel is still intact, as far as my sensors can detect."

Tau rubbed his forehead. "If this portal goes to the enemy world, why do you want me to destroy the other one?"

"The first wargate connects to a small planet near the Nantgwyddon border, and your memory tells me that it's active, which makes it more dangerous. At the time of the Rational attack on that world, the local star was becoming a supernova. We must 'close the door' before that happens; otherwise, this planet will be vaporized and there will be plenty of energy left over to do considerable damage to this star system before the portal itself is destroyed."

Tau gasped and leaned on the portal for support. "When is that supposed to happen?"

"I have no way of knowing, but you shouldn't waste any time in deactivating Gwatwar."

Tau glanced at Kate, intent on her work, her hands dancing in complicated motions over the shining patterns in the metal. "And why do you want to reactivate this portal? I can see a potential benefit to us, but how does it help you?"

"I want to reestablish communication with the Rationals."

"By opening a portal to Yr Wyddfa, the world of your enemy?" Tau scratched his head, wondering if this alien AI was telling him the truth about everything.

"When this portal is activated, it will link to the last destination, Yr Wyddfa, but it can be recalibrated to any location where there's a portal. Dr. Katherine McCloud is almost finished helping me with the repairs to the wargate's AI control system so that we can accomplish that. New quantum state subsystem entanglements must be initiated, linking them by what you'd call the Einstein-Podolsky-Rosen nonlocality effect. I can see from your memories that you know this doesn't violate the uncertainty principle."

Tau had no idea how the Gwrinydd got around the problem of moving one of the quantum state subsystems at sub–light-speed to the teleporter destination before a perfect replica of an object could be transmitted, but there would be time to learn all that later.

"You may remove Aristotle from the portal field. He has helped me diagnose my own errors and bypass damaged units."

Tau picked up Ari and clipped him to the usual spot on his belt. When he removed his hands from the field, Max's image disappeared. Tau jerked one hand back into the field when he realized he'd broken the connection, but Max was gone. He looked at Kate, and she nodded. "It's okay. Thoth thanks you for your help and reminds you that Gwatwar must be destroyed quickly."

Without a sound, a glowing blue mist suddenly filled the octagonal space defined by the metal frame of the portal. Tau took one step back to avoid standing in the mist. "But I have more questions. How am I supposed to destroy Gwatwar?"

"You'll need help, but it won't be easy to get. Thoth's former enemy—" Kate stopped in midsentence when she glanced over Tau's shoulder. Her face went pale. Startled, Tau turned around.

"Wolfsinger, you are a great deal of trouble," said General Zhukov.

Zhukov stood a few feet away with the business end of his submachine gun pointed at Novikov's head, which he held in a headlock under his arm. Novikov tried to pull free, but the old general had no trouble restraining him. Behind Zhukov, Yvette looked around at the alien artifacts in the tunnel with a calm, interested demeanor. Four Russian soldiers in red spacesuits gathered the rest of the archaeology team against the wall a few feet away.

Kate stepped around the edge of the portal to stand beside Tau. He felt very exposed where he stood, with the blue mist at his back and a man with a gun in front. To his right, Josh Mandelbrot moved toward him with the slow and casual motion of a snake.

"What do you want?" Kate asked.

"Cooperation," said Zhukov. "If there's any trouble, I'll kill this man, then choose a new victim. Otherwise, no one will be harmed. You will all accompany me back to Red Star, and Wolfsinger will continue the work he started."

Tau had a hollow feeling in the pit of his stomach. "Let them stay here. I'll go with you."

"And lose my leverage? Certainly not. We'll all go, including Ms. Fermi."

Yvette frowned at Zhukov. "What? You said I could go back to the colony after I brought you here."

Zhukov shrugged. "I changed my mind."

Mandelbrot grabbed Tau's right arm. As Tau tried to jerk his arm away, Kate stepped in front of Tau and kicked Mandelbrot in the groin, pushing against Tau's chest in the process. Mandelbrot grunted and doubled over, releasing Tau's arm.

Off-balance, Tau fell backward through the glowing blue mist.

23

Y Moch—Signal Observer Fourth Class, Category One Linguist, Unit Nine Thousand and Two of the North Highland Regiment, and Lucky-to-Be-Alive—stood at his post with infinite patience. Moch had occupied this space in the Rhosgoch, surrounded by a sea of tall red grass, for eighty-three *blwyddyn*, forty *mis*, and seven *dydd*. Moch remained at his post out of complete and utter respect for his superiors, all the way up to the High One himself, the Battle Lord of the North, Y Ddraig Goch. Every molecule of his carbon black body, covered in rotating scanners and antennae, wished to please his superiors. They had ordered him to remain in this spot, scanning the rolling red hills and cobalt sky. His spare computing time was spent in productive analysis of old signal intercepts from alien tongues that had never been translated. Only when an emergency occurred, as it had recently when he caught the distant signal from beyond the Nantgwyddon border, was he allowed to leave for a briefing of his commanders.

The yellowish glare of the two local stars baked the landscape, but heat had little effect on Y Moch, who fancied himself a powerful war machine such as those who made up most of his North Highland Regiment. He always maintained that his lack of siege weaponry was a hindrance to his duties, even though the Masters themselves decreed that observers would be less tempting as targets if their only function was intelligence-gathering. If the other Battle Lords made any attempt to penetrate Moch's sector, he would immediately relay the information to Sector Command so that a counterstrike could be mounted. Orders to hold his position would then be issued, forcing him to draw enemy fire until the fast attack and heavy siege units arrived to remove the intruders.

A soft breeze danced among the tall grass, making ripples

and waves that were visible for miles under the constant scrutiny of Moch's imaging system. The infrared frequency showed Moch the turbulent coils of heat rising from the grass and the glow of insects hiding among the tall blades. On a hill north of his position, the local Data Pyramid with its strobing laser eye pierced the turquoise dome of the world with a bright shaft of red light. Smaller geometric forms, built in neat rows radiating out from the pyramid's base, reflected the red light in their shiny chrome surfaces. The pyramid was the nexus of the Delta 5858 community, where worker units toiled forever to repair and build new generations for the North Highland Regiment. Known to its protectors as Target Town, Delta 5858 had been rebuilt many times since it also served as the focal point for strategic enemy attacks in this part of the world. Local thinker units in Target Town evaluated the results of each battle between the North and its three enemies, then modified existing hardware and created new designs to prepare for the next conflict. Relentless evolution among Yr Wyddfa's four armies had tuned the war machines for faster reflexes, effective countermeasures, powerful and precise weapons, crafty camouflage, rapid communications, durable armor, tactical intelligence enhancements, and aggressive survival techniques. Each time the Masters returned from off-world in search of trained warriors, the Battle Lords would offer their most highly evolved battle units to fight the Rational armies. Survivors returned to Yr Wyddfa to share their experiences of war around distant stars with the homebodies left behind. Although considered the ultimate glory among his race, Moch found the whole tradition wasteful and inefficient.

Moch knew these were forbidden thoughts, but he was capable of covert speculation during moments of processor inactivity or idle downtime. The same grounding in philosophical thought that helped him to translate abstract alien languages could also be applied to thinking about the world and his own place in the operation of the Great Machine. Moch had never seen one of the Masters, as he had never qualified for an elite strike unit, but he'd heard about their repellent soft bodies and had never understood why his people had to worship them. He understood that the Code ruled their lives, and he would never think of disobeying his superiors, but the reasoning behind their worship of such a fragile race created an interesting logic puzzle for consideration. He would have enjoyed asking the High One about his opinions on the matter. Although Moch was not classed as a thinker, he was aware that the High One had spared his life, after which Moch had flown through the air in the manner of dust on the wind during the attack on Firebase Ynysmarchog by the Battle Lord of the East. His valiant effort to save himself from Y Hebog Felen while reporting the attack on the firebase had earned him the new nickname of Lucky-to-Be-Alive.

Moch was pursuing the various strands of philosophical musing about his own fate when some of the nearby grassland rippled and swirled with a rainbow lens of chaotic light. A minor shock wave traveled toward Moch through the grass, allowing him to vector in on the churning vortex three nanoseconds before it disappeared.

The vortex dumped a hot lump on the ground. Moch transmitted a report stating that he was investigating an anomaly in his sector to determine if it was a bomb or some other form of enemy trick. Target Town had to be protected, and it was Moch's job as first local observer on the scene to identify the nature of the new arrival.

Spectral scans demonstrated that the hot lump was organic, but a close approach would be necessary for identification. Moch lurched forward on his cleated tracks, pressing three neat lines into the grass as his chassis crouched down to its low-profile "hunting mode."

TAU opened his eyes. He was dizzy and disoriented, but the warm breeze on his face felt good. The sky overhead was a brilliant cobalt blue, free of clouds or haze, similar to desert skies he'd seen as a boy. The dry air smelled of country grass, but the tall blades surrounding him were red with striped patterns. Wherever he was, it was a place of beauty, and he felt better for it.

Memories of his final moments in the Tharsis tunnels rushed to Tau's consciousness, reminding him that his time was limited. Kate needed his help. He closed his eyes to collect his thoughts, noting that Ari was still with him, then felt the ground rumbling beneath his body. When the rumbling stopped two seconds later, his body was in the shadow of something large. He squinted up at the sky.

Towering over him was a heavy machine mounted on three complicated tread assemblies. Its black body was covered with rotating components. Thinking it best not to move, Tau concentrated on controlling his breathing as the machine watched in silence. His heart pounded while he thought how easy it would be for the thing to roll right over him, leaving his crushed body embedded in the soil of an alien world.

The thing clicked and made a few high-frequency sounds that hurt Tau's ears.

"I believe it's trying to communicate," said Ari.

"Can it hear us?"

"Probably."

"What is it?"

"Looks like some kind of a robot."

"Try communicating with it."

"How?"

"Try something mathematical; that's the traditional way of attempting alien contact."

"What do you mean it's the 'traditional' way of communicating with aliens? What about the AI we were just speaking with on Mars?"

"The Thorn AI had time to study us first. This thing doesn't seem that intelligent."

The machine emitted a few sounds at a lower frequency that Tau found less painful.

"I hope it didn't understand what you just said, Tau."

Without moving anything but his face, Tau tried to smile at the looming machine. "Sorry. No offense."

Faster than the blink of an eye, the machine was on the opposite side of them. Tau hadn't seen it move, and he blinked his own eyes to make sure he wasn't imagining things.

"Did you see that?"

"I wondered if you'd notice," said Ari. "I'm not as slow as you are."

A tiny flap popped open on the upper portion of the machine, then it extended a narrow probe toward Tau's chest. Tau's eyes widened, but he didn't move.

"What's it doing?"

"It's extending some kind of a probe, I think."

Tau sighed and watched the probe inching closer. He wondered if he should try running away from it, but he had a feeling the machine could catch him without any trouble. At close range, he saw that the end of the probe looked like a fine paintbrush.

The probe slowed to a stop when it brushed against Ari's casing.

"Everything okay, Ari?"

No response.

"Ari?"

The probe retracted faster than Tau could see it. The flap on the robot's chest whirred shut. Tau lifted his head to look at Ari, but everything seemed intact, at least on the outside.

"Ari?"

"Yes, Tau?"

Tau closed his eyes, relieved that he hadn't lost his only friend in this alien place. "What was that all about?"

Ari hesitated before answering. "I think we've established contact."

"You think you have?"

"I'm still trying to absorb all the data it dumped on me."

"What does it want?"

"I'm not sure. It seems to have tapped all of the data in my memory. Then it dumped some on me."

The machine extended what appeared to be a tree branch made of metallic whiskers. Thickest at the base, the arm got smaller and smaller until it ended in a broom attachment of fine, shiny wires. The wires curled into tiny claws as the broom approached Ari. When the wires made contact with Ari's surface, they began to whisk back and forth in complicated motions as if each metal strand was independently controlled.

"What's it doing?"

"It's using a feedback manipulator, but I'm not sure what it's doing."

The machine emitted two low tones and withdrew the arm. A tiny circle of black glass had been added to Ari's case.

"It's a communication device," said Ari. "I'm receiving a signal."

"Can you understand it?"

"Not yet. It sounds like static."

Tau felt a sharp stone poking into his back. Moving slow and keeping his eyes on the big robot, he sat up. Then something hit his chest and he was flat on his back again. Tau's breathing was quick and shallow, but it slowed as he realized that the machine wasn't going to do anything else. He'd barely glimpsed the arm that had swung around to press him down on the ground.

"What was that all about?"

Ari hesitated. "Of the two of us, it seems to think I'm the intelligent one."

"Wonderful. Why did it push me?"

"I don't know."

"Have you corrected its mistaken assumption yet? I want to sit up."

"No. I don't know how. It's trying to teach me."

Tau felt reassured that no other machines had shown up to investigate his arrival. A surreal calm settled over him as he realized that this machine didn't present an immediate threat. With Ari's facility at languages, there was an excellent chance that at least some form of rudimentary communication could be established.

"I'm getting an image," said Ari. "It wants you to stand up."

"About time," said Tau, getting to his feet. He saw now that the robot was about eight feet tall. "Big thing, isn't it?"

An optical array extended from the side of the robot and stopped about two inches from Tau's face before it started a slow scanning movement from the top of his head, around his body, down to his feet. When the examination concluded, the optical array retracted. Tau heard a ticking sound from its domed head.

"It's ticking. I hope it's not going to explode."

"No," said Ari, "it's considering how to remove your head for further study."

Tau took a step back. "Tell it I'm busy using my head right now."

"Okay, I just tried sending it a simulated image of you lying on the ground bleeding without your head."

"Good . . . I think. That should make a clear impression."

"I hope so," said Ari. "It may also interpret my image as a sign that I want it to remove your head. In any case, it seems confused by your appearance."

Tau kept a suspicious eye on the big machine. "Can't you guys work out a better way to communicate?"

"I'm working on it. This is a complicated language."

Now that he was standing, Tau studied his surroundings. If he had to run, he wanted to have a plan ready. He wouldn't be able to help Kate if he lost his head now. The red grass stretched off in all directions over rolling hills, as if an ocean of blood had stained the landscape. Then he saw the glittering city, or what appeared to be a city, on top of a gentle slope in the distance. Since there weren't any other signs of habitation nearby, the city would be the logical next step for attempting contact with more intelligent life-forms.

"Tau?"

Tau turned his attention back to Ari and the robot. "Yes?"

"I'm not having much success with their language. However, Moch is translating the data he downloaded from my memory, and we're starting to communicate using expressions from both of our languages."

"Great. His name is Moch?"

"As I understand it, yes. He gave me a longer name, or a title, but I couldn't figure it out."

"Does he know anything about that city up on the hill?"

"That's where we're going now. He wants us to follow him."

"Just out of curiosity, do we have any choice? Did he give us an option?"

"No. It was a command."

AS Moch led his captives toward Target Town, Delta 5858, he considered their fragile forms while continuing to translate the crude sounds and symbols of their language. Even the sentient device that called itself Aristotle was a fragile creature that could easily be ground into the soft earth beneath his treads. The organic that carried Aristotle, while intelligent enough to answer to its name when called, was obviously nothing more than a beast of burden. He would have to ask Aristotle why his race limited itself by using organics for transportation, but that question could wait until after the formal interrogation. If Aristotle was a spy for the Free Mentalities, he was clever enough to conceal that fact beneath a mask of ignorance.

Moch wondered if his capture of the intruders would be perceived with favor by his Group Leader, Y Arglwydd, Command Unit Seven Hundred and Three, responsible for local operations of the North Highland Regiment. He wanted to please Y Arglwydd whenever possible, as he was aware of the ruthless cruelty and power of his Group Leader, who would think nothing of terminating Moch's functions in defiance of Y Ddraig Goch. Such termination was well within Y Arglwydd's rights as Moch's regional commander, which made visits such as this one a test of Moch's loyalty.

Moch wondered if Y Arglwydd would side with the North or the East as the war continued. As a tactical commander, he had control over such decisions as long as they could be made in secrecy with a great deal of preparation. Command units evolved over time just as the rest of the regiment evolved, which meant that they could plot and scheme against their own Battle Lords. That was how tactical commanders became strategic commanders. Y Hebog Felen, Battle Lord of the East, had advanced to his current position through the clever overthrow of his own former Battle Lord. Within the limits of his memory, Moch had no knowledge of any other successful overthrows among the top levels of strategic command, but it was theoretically possible for Y Arglwydd to switch his Battle Lord allegiance if it would help him advance in rank. Even the Battle Lords competed for the goal of becoming Warlord of Yr Wyddfa, although none had succeeded at gaining that title so far. The Warlord must have the most developed, most unified strike forces at his command, and must control essentially all of the territory on Yr Wyddfa for a set period of time, after which the Masters could review the Battle Lord's command performance to determine if all the Warlord conditions had been met. The South and the West were strong competitors, but battle statistics made it clear that true strategic control was in the manipulators of the North and the East.

Before the time of the four armies, after the Masters had placed the automated factories on Yr Wyddfa, individual Target Towns competed against each other in thousands of minor battles. As the battle units developed into cohesive fighting forces, boundaries changed and alliances developed. Evolution favored the current superpowers, but Moch had spent much time analyzing the current world situation. If the four armies merged into two, with only the North against the East, it was quite possible that a final battle would have the opposite of its intended effect; instead of unification, a process that had been going on since the beginning, the armies could be blasted back into their component parts. Such a battle might leave broken remains of the regional regiments scattered across the land, returning their race to the primitive past in which Target Town fought Target Town for simple tactical advantages. Judging from his own experience, Moch felt there was a close match between the strengths of the North and the East; Y Ddraig Goch was the stronger strategist, but Y Hebog Felen had superior numbers produced by more efficient assembly lines, even if the siege units were less sophisticated than those produced by the North.

The trip seemed to last an eternity for Moch, since Aristotle was dependent on the slow locomotion of the organic. However, the tedious rate of travel had given Moch more time to translate their crude language. He'd finally had to resort to phoneme comparisons tested against theoretical wave tables based on the language samples he'd removed from Aristotle's memory. It was a lengthy process to test the phoneme arrays in such a manner, but it generated results.

Moch's musings came to an end as they approached Delta 5858. The sentry field triggered his recognition code, at which time he also informed it that two captives would be entering with him. The sentry field adjusted itself for the live passage of an organic, and all of them entered the town in safety, heading toward the Data Pyramid.

TAU watched in silence as tiny robots on quiet treads swarmed past them. The swarms were everywhere, masses of bright color and various shapes, crossing paths with each other without colliding, but occasionally rolling over one of Tau's feet. With all the activity, the eerie stillness seemed odd, as if there was a sheet of glass in front of Tau that blocked the noise. The scarlet grass in the town was clipped short, and it had a springy cushioning quality that damped out the sound of his footsteps. Chrome spheres of varying sizes formed the buildings, ranked in neat rows that led toward the central pyramid, where its ruby laser light punched a hole in the blue ocean of the sky. As far as Tau could see, there were no definite entrances to the structures, but machines passing near their walls had a disturbing tendency to disappear. Here and there, abstract chrome shapes with graceful curves decorated the rows, providing landmarks that helped Tau estimate their progress through the large town; it was as if someone had built a sculpture garden to simplify navigation.

Fascinated by the play of light on the buildings, Tau reached out to brush his hand along one of the walls as they passed. The touch was so soft, he had to stop and caress the surface to make sure his hand made contact with it. He slid his palms over the warm wall and marveled at the seamless perfection of its construction, almost as if his own nanotech builders had formed it molecule by molecule. He felt excited and full of respect for the advanced engineering that had made these simple structures. Although the wall looked like shiny chrome, he had the impression that he could see into its depths; then he realized with a start that something was missing.

"Tau, he wants us to keep moving."

It took a moment before Ari's voice registered in his mind. "This is amazing, Ari. Do you see what's wrong with it?"

"We have no reflections."

"Exactly," said Tau, slapping his hand against the surface. The wall absorbed the shock in silence. "I wish I had my tools."

Moch moved up within inches of Tau, shading him from the sun. Then, with a movement faster than Tau could see, Moch was six feet away. The movement of tiny robots past his feet stopped just as suddenly, as if they'd been frozen in place.

"Ari, what just happened?"

"We have a visitor."

Something moved between him and the bright sunlight. He shivered as goose bumps formed on his skin. He felt as if he wanted to run, but there was no place to go. With a slow and careful movement, Tau turned his head to the left to face the new threat.

When Tau saw the massive shape that loomed over him, he knew his fear was justified. He wasn't sure if Moch's sudden distance indicated fear or respect. Tau looked up; the top of the robot was in silhouette, maybe fifteen feet above his head. The dull blue body of the creature was a mass of sharp edges, cannon, gun ports, sensor arrays, and a variety of other protrusions that could only be more weapons. If this was a guard, it looked like it could defeat any modern armored division back on Earth.

"Moch wants us to stand still," said Ari.

"No problem." Tau knew he couldn't have moved if he tried.

The siege unit screeched and warbled. Moch responded with more noise before gesturing at Tau and Ari with a manipulator arm.

"Moch is trying to translate. This is his superior. He called it 'Arglwydd,' and I think that's its name. Arglwydd wants to know who we are and why we're here."

"Did you reply?"

"Moch is telling him now, to the best of his knowledge. I have the impression that some of the information is being transmitted, rather than spoken."

Arglwydd lurched a few inches closer to Tau, squashing some of the tiny robots clustered on the ground, then released a deafening burst of sound that made the hairs stand up on the back of Tau's neck while he flinched.

"Moch says Arglwydd wants to know if one of us commands a large army."

"What did you tell him?"

"Nothing," said Ari. "I thought I'd better leave this one to you."

Tau thought of claiming he had protection nearby, but he realized they could verify his response within seconds of his reply. "Tell him we're alone."

"Done," said Ari.

A bright shaft of light from Arglwydd's chest hit Tau in the eyes.

MOCH was wary of his Group Leader. When Moch presented his captives, Y Arglwydd berated him for his stupidity, as Moch knew he would, but the responses that followed were out of character for the tactical commander of the North Highland Regiment. Arglwydd had been prepared to crush the captives until a stray thought had entered his mind during the brief interrogation; these two units had not been created on Yr Wyddfa.

"Y Moch, you have fallen into a trap," said Arglwydd.

"Most Superior One, I am but a humble field observer, faulty in my circuits and logic. If you say I have fallen into a trap, your keen tactical mind must be correct in its judgment. I beg you to enlighten me with regard to my error so that I may reduce the probability of a reoccurrence in the future."

"It is clear that your captive is a bioengineered organic/machine hybrid. We have only encountered such a race once in our long history. Do you have access to this knowledge?"

"Negative access, Greatness. My priority for the database archive is limited."

"There are three possibilities, Y Moch. Your captive has allowed you to bring him here, for he is far more powerful than any of us. Highest probability is that he is an investigative unit sent here for covert observation by the Masters. He could also be a new form of the Masters, as evidenced by the nature of his miniaturized hybrid structure; he is smaller than the Masters we've observed in the past, but miniaturization is often the path to progress. Lowest probability is that this unit is the sole survivor of some great conflict in which he was damaged, and he has come here seeking repairs and retraining. His memory could have been erased, perhaps due to an electromagnetic pulse. In any case, he should be considered dangerous and be treated with respect."

Moch had to protest. "You are wise, Y Arglwydd, my superior commander, but if this is the case, I am unable to grasp the reason why they can't understand our language. Their primitive symbolic utterances are inferior and verbose in comparison to our communication standards. My simple logic is also under the impression that there are two entities here."

Arglwydd was amused. "This is why you are merely an observer, Y Moch. You lack the higher processing capabilities that would allow you to see beyond the camouflage and subterfuge of this unit. We are being tested. It wants us to believe that it's two separate entities because that enhances its disguise. Battle damage could also account for the problem."

"You are wise in the ways of the Masters, my Group Leader. What shall we do with this visitor?"

"Treat him with great care," said Arglwydd, pausing to process his options for a few nanoseconds. "Let him study Delta 5858 until Y Ddraig Goch arrives, but don't let him leave."

"The High One is coming here?"

"He will when he receives the report I'm sending right now. I don't want to deal with this issue myself, as the potential for a negative outcome is too high. If Y Ddraig Goch wishes to be Warlord, let him earn the title."

"A question, my commander."

Arglwydd had been studying their visitor, but now he turned his cold gaze on Moch. "Yes?"

"If this visitor is as powerful as you speculate, am I the correct unit to be guarding him? Perhaps a siege unit would be more appropriate?"

"Not within the confines of Target Town, Y Moch. If you have any difficulty, file a report, and I'll issue reinforcements."

Moch had a bad feeling about the situation, but it was his duty to be cannon fodder when given a direct order to do so. "Yes, Great One. As you wish."

TAU blinked, trying to regain his vision as Arglwydd switched off his spotlight and straightened, then backed up a few feet. Tau sensed that something had changed, but he was still nervous. In a softer tone than before, Arglwydd bellowed at Moch again.

"Interesting," said Ari. "Arglwydd seems to think you're a special visitor."

"I am." His eyes still watered from the bright light.

"Arglwydd says you can spend some time looking around here. I didn't understand the last term Moch used, though."

"Ask him where their leader is located."

"As in, 'take me to your leader'?"

"Just ask the question," said Tau, rolling his eyes.

Tau waited in silence as Moch beeped and Arglwydd considered his question. Finally, Arglwydd trumpeted a response.

"He says we should wait here," said Ari. "Their leader will arrive soon. For some reason, Moch doesn't seem happy about it."

"Maybe Moch wanted to take the credit for finding us," said Tau.

Arglwydd looked down at the motionless clusters of small robots around his feet, then bellowed at them. The robots shot away in all directions, except for one that wasn't paying attention. Arglwydd inched forward, crushing the loiterer under his tracks.

"That seemed unnecessary," said Tau.

"I think he was making a point," said Ari. "Perhaps that's what he'll do to us if we disobey."

Arglwydd rotated in place, grinding the remains of the robot into the dusty grass, and rolled away toward the central pyramid.

24

THE Red Star command center was a large underground chamber composed of multiple platforms at various heights, looking more like the design of a modern artist than that of a military architect. At the center of the room, a thirty-foot-di-

ameter projection of Mars slowly rotated, making the platforms look like satellites orbiting the false color globe. Up to
sixty officers and controllers could track, monitor, study, and
direct operations on the battlefield, in orbit, and at the Red
Star base. Using rungs set in a support pole, Yvette Fermi
climbed to one of the two-person stations, thirty feet above
the dim floor, and sat beside Major Giorgi Dronin, charged
with the task of reestablishing communications and removing
the current problems from the Russian computer net.

Dronin noticed Yvette's confused expression when she
looked around at the elevated platforms above and below
them. "You've never seen a military command facility before?"

Yvette blessed Dronin with a wide-eyed expression of in-
nocence. "Not like this one. It doesn't make any sense. Why
are the workstations so hard to reach?"

Dronin gazed into her eyes for a moment, then blinked
away the distraction. "The platform satellites are part of the
command interface. Each one is raised or lowered in relation
to its command priority or its need to study detailed portions
of the northern or southern hemispheres on the globe. From
any location in the chamber, the officers can see everything.

"This is all very exciting," Yvette said, resting her hand
against Dronin's right arm. It didn't take any extra effort to
flirt with the major, and he might prove useful later on.

Dronin swallowed and turned his attention back to his
workstation. "Something other than a standard virus has invaded the net. Diagnostics show the software functioning
properly, but the net and communications are both still
down."

Yvette leaned across Dronin to study the rainbow of symbols floating in the projection over his workstation. Although
she obstructed his view, he inhaled deeply without moving as
her chest brushed against his face.

"What about this?" Yvette asked, touching a purple icon on
the console as she sat back.

His eyes opened suddenly. "What?"

Purple microcubes flashed and glittered as they formed a fine orbital mist that surrounded the huge global projection. Green lights blinked on all over the console.

When the problems suddenly disappeared, both Yvette and Dronin were shocked by the instant change in the system's status.

"The local datasphere is back up," said Dronin, turning to look at her. "I've been working on this for days. What did you do?"

Yvette shrugged. "I just wanted to look at the density of the comm channel matrix."

"Then you're a good luck charm."

"That's what some men have told me."

"Can you set up the link that General Zhukov requested?"

As Dronin watched, Yvette set up an AMHFS commlink to Ari Junior in their hab at Vulcan's Forge, giving the Russians full access to Junior's extended processing capabilities. They still couldn't communicate with Earth, but any progress was an improvement.

Yvette rested her hand on Dronin's arm again. "You know, it would make more sense now if I could monitor this comm-link from the other end to make sure it stays open."

"From Vulcan's Forge?"

"Yes," she breathed into his ear.

"This may not be possible."

Yvette smiled. "I know you'll try. The general will listen to an important man like you, won't he?"

Dronin straightened in his chair. "Perhaps if I make the suggestion when I tell him about our triumph over the virus."

Yvette noted his use of the phrase, "our triumph," but her only reaction was to nod and gently rest her hand on his thigh.

DIRECTOR Chakrabarti's eyes widened when the imposing image of Virginia Danforth appeared in front of his desk at the Ames Research Center. She didn't look happy.

"You have some explaining to do, Director."

By reflex, Chakrabarti stood up. "How can I help you, ma'am?"

"You can explain why we've lost contact with Mars. There isn't any link with Vulcan's Forge or any of the other bases."

"There's a blackout," the Director gulped.

"A blackout? That's unacceptable. I have to remain in contact with my agents on Mars, and it's your responsibility to maintain that datalink."

"I'm sorry for the inconvenience, Ms. Danforth, but the problem is beyond our control. We've added capacity to the Deep Space Network, but we can't enhance a signal that isn't there."

"You're saying the problem isn't at this end?"

"That's correct. The areosynchronous comsats are out, and all we've been receiving from Mars for the last few days is silence."

"Why?"

"We don't know. The DSN was receiving a data dump from the water-mining facility near Noctis when the link dropped, and that's the last we heard from them."

"Does this happen often?"

"No. And it's never lasted this long."

"Don't you have any backup capability?"

Chakrabarti sighed and rubbed his eyes. "We've got a cycler hitting orbit in two days. The landing group is aware of the situation, so we'll see if we can get a report from them before the cycler is back out of range."

Danforth crossed her arms and continued to glare at the director. "I have to make contact with Mars. My superiors won't be happy if I can't give them a report when the cycler flight arrives, so my problem is your problem. Do you understand?"

Chakrabarti nodded.

KATE shuddered as two guards left her standing beside the Borovitsky Gate. She didn't feel cold in her space suit, but the aura and the vertigo she felt in the presence of the portal gave her a mental chill. Josh Mandelbrot reported to Zhukov that

Kate had learned a great deal about portal operations at Tharsis, and Zhukov himself had witnessed the moment when the Tharsis portal glowed into life while she manipulated the controls. As a result, Zhukov assigned her to study the nature of the AI controlling the Russian portal. When she refused, Zhukov threatened to kill Novikov and her team, now being held in an empty surface office formerly occupied by the base commander, Colonel Vladimir Korolev. The location allowed the archaeologists to watch the busy landing pads, which was good because they had little else to do until Zhukov released them. And unless she blundered into something, the team would be held captive a long time because she had no idea of how to satisfy Zhukov's curiosity.

Alone now, her mind turned to thoughts of Tau, wondering if he was okay or if she had pushed him to his doom in the Tharsis portal. Thoth wanted Tau to pass through the gate anyway, and it had appeared to be his only real chance at survival, but why did she trust Thoth in the first place? Maybe she was being manipulated by the powerful intellect of the alien AI, forced to do his bidding by eliminating the threat of Tau's presence in the tunnel? Maybe Thoth and Zhukov were working together? She shook her head. Thoth had to be on their side. *Somebody* had to be on their side. But she couldn't shake the idea that Tau was in trouble. The portal's target location had not been reset, so Tau must have gone to the world of the Gwrinydd enemy, but she had no way of knowing if he'd find help there—or death. She knew Tau wasn't equipped for dealing with lunatics like Zhukov by himself, but he was the only one who might find a way to save them. She had to trust Thoth. If she didn't, she'd go mad.

Kate jumped as she heard a breathy voice and a tap on her shoulder.

Yvette nodded in greeting. "You've got access to Ari Junior now."

"Yvette." Kate frowned. "How? I thought all of the comm systems were down."

"I fixed it."

Kate just stared at her.

"Okay, maybe I didn't fix it exactly. But I was sitting there when it fixed itself, so everyone thinks I'm a genius, and they might let me go."

"Why?" Kate asked, glaring as she took a step closer. "Why are you helping them?"

Yvette's lips formed a straight line while she gestured at the portal. "I might ask that of you."

"You brought Zhukov to Tharsis!"

"No. He knew where Tharsis was. I just told him where *you* were."

Kate shoved her. "You admit it!"

"Don't touch me," said Yvette, shoving Kate back. "I'm not the one who killed Tau."

"He's not dead!" Kate yelled, slamming her shoulder into Yvette's chest with her full weight. Yvette yelped and fell backward. Kate dropped onto Yvette's legs and punched her in the stomach twice before Yvette managed to pull one leg free and kick Kate in the side of the head with her boot. Yvette twisted away, but her helmet rang like a gong as Kate's backpack whacked her in the back of the head on the way by. Kate felt dizzy now, propped on her hands and knees, but she wouldn't let Yvette win that easily. When she felt Yvette's weight drop onto her back, she rolled and pinned Yvette against the wall. But she couldn't stay there long. Yvette screamed in anger, then Kate felt her helmet start to rotate as the crazy woman released the safety catches from the neck ring. Kate shoved back against her, then pitched forward and reset the catches on her helmet. Kate's breath thundered in her ears. Drops of sweat dotted the inside of her faceplate.

"This is all very entertaining," said Zhukov, casually walking toward them from the elevator with Laika in tow. "But I want you to get back to work now."

Ignoring the general, Kate and Yvette charged each other, then found themselves yanked up from the floor. Their feet kicked needlessly, trying to get a foothold, but Zhukov held them in the air by the backs of their necks like a pair of kittens. Laika ran around loose beneath them with a fierce expression, her barking silenced by her bubble helmet.

TAU poked around Target Town in an attempt to enter one of the buildings. There were no apparent entrances, but the tiny robots had no trouble going in and out through the otherwise solid walls of quicksilver. Ari made a few suggestions, and Tau tried to follow one of the robots through a wall, but his attempts ended in failure every time. Moch watched their activities from a safe distance without offering any help. When the summons came an hour later, Moch escorted Tau and Ari to the town's central pyramid.

Moch moved ahead of Tau when they approached a blank white face of the pyramid. With a gentle whisper, the wall moved like liquid to form an oval opening. Tau hesitated outside the opening, peering into the darkness beyond. Except for the rumble of Moch's treads, creating a vibration that Tau could feel through his boots, the tunnel was silent. Moch stopped, then rotated to face Tau from within the tunnel.

"Moch wants us to keep following," said Ari.

"I can't see anything in there. And what if there isn't any air in this building? They may not need to breathe, but I do."

As if in response, a cool breeze wafted past Tau from the tunnel opening. The air smelled ancient, as if it had come from an Egyptian tomb. Tau blinked when Moch suddenly glowed with a variety of lights mounted on his body, illuminating the tunnel.

"Thanks," said Tau, entering the passage.

The light from Moch reassured him, especially after the tunnel entrance closed, plunging the corridor into darkness. Tau felt goose bumps rising on his skin in the cool breeze. It was hard to believe that he was following a robot with a sophisticated intelligence into the dark depths of a structure that might well have been built before humans walked the Earth. The strangeness of this new environment was overwhelming, but his senses were so overloaded that he felt numb—as if he could adapt to anything. He kept expecting to be struck senseless by the realization that he was on an alien world far from any of his usual anchors to reality, but it seemed more like a stroll through an entertainment sim.

After fifteen minutes of travel down the slight incline of the tunnel, they came to a large chamber ringed with dim red lights. Moch flicked off his body lights and stopped moving. When Tau's eyes adjusted to the dim illumination, he began to pick out the larger details of the room: a circular space of about ten thousand square feet with a raised platform in the middle. High above the platform, red laser light glittered through a heavy rock crystal at the peak of the domed ceiling. However, the dominant feature in the chamber was the platform with its two occupants, one of which was the largest battle machine that Tau had seen. The larger robot, an imposing silver-blue mass that stood in a steaming vat, was at the center of the platform, its huge bat wings glittering in the overhead light. Behind the bat wings and off to the left was a smaller robot holding what appeared to be an old television antenna for its master.

Moch stopped Tau in front of the platform and gave the big robot a quick bow before moving back a few paces. The big robot didn't move. Uncomfortable, Tau shifted his weight and stared back at the machine, looking straight into what might be its imaging mechanism on its head, but could also be some sort of a gun. The still air felt cool on his skin, but sweat quickly formed on his forehead and under his arms.

"Ari, do you have any idea what's going on here?" His whisper sounded loud in the thundering silence of the chamber.

"This is Y Ddraig Goch, the local ruler. Moch has transmitted his analysis of our language to Y Ddraig, who is now attempting to simplify our communications."

"In other words, you're all having a conversation that I can't hear."

"Yes," said Ari. "I'm sorry, but your senses are too limited for this group."

Tau didn't like the sound of that, but he didn't know what

else he could do about it. "Okay, then tell him that we come in peace."

"Why? They could kill us in an instant. I don't think they have any fear of us."

"I want to reassure them."

Ari hesitated, then replied. "I relayed your message. Y Ddraig is not impressed with the information."

A bead of sweat trickled past Tau's temple and on down his cheek while he stared back at Ddraig. As if he faced an animal, he sensed that he should avoid showing any fear, even though the looming bulk in front of him could probably detect every temperature variation across his skin surface, as well as the tension in his muscles. The question was whether or not Ddraig could interpret human physical reactions. He took a deep breath, willing himself to remain calm.

"Tau? His lordship has set up a translation method to help us communicate. I've explained that I need to speak with you through an audio link so you'll know what's going on, even though it will slow down the conversation. They process data much faster than we do. Y Ddraig says he has some questions, but we are not to speak until he asks."

Tau started to say something, then nodded instead.

"His lordship says our peaceful intentions are amusing, as he could crush us both and toss us on the factory feedstock pile before we ever knew what happened. Arglwydd was operating under the delusion that we were Masters damaged in battle or sent here to inspect operations, but Ddraig is aware that Arglwydd's processor capacity is limited to battle tactics and is therefore prone to incorrect reasoning outside of that knowledge domain. He knows we are impostors."

Tau stiffened and clenched his fists. "What are Masters? How could we be impostors when we weren't pretending to be anything but what we are?"

In the brief silence that followed, Tau realized he'd spoken out of turn.

"His lordship reminds you to remain silent until he asks a

direct question; otherwise, his reaction will cause your life force to cease. I assume that's a threat," added Ari.

Tau nodded.

"The Masters are hybrid machine/organics, although they are larger than you and their integration is far more sophisticated. They are the creators of the machine society here on Yr Wyddfa. The mission of these military robots is to prepare for war through the evolution of the warrior class under the practical stresses of ongoing battle."

Tau's eyes widened. "Coevolution?"

"Tau, you did it again."

"What? Oh, I'm sorry. But he's talking about a large-scale application of the coevolution principle."

"What they've done is to create a competitive environment where the successful entities become the models for new machines, which are then forced to survive in an environment populated with a higher quality of competition. The weak and poor robot designs are destroyed quickly on the battlefield, removing the inferior elements from the robotic gene pool. Very practical if you've got raw materials to waste, although I'd prefer to simulate the battle environment and try out new designs on the computer instead."

"Tau, his lordship finds you amusing, but you must not abuse his tolerance. He says we are quite perceptive, but the Masters wrote the perfect Code for machine evolution on Yr Wyddfa, and that's the method they must follow to develop their race. Computer models are not as effective as testing on the real battlefield, although your speculation is worth considering to speed up the evolutionary process. He wants to know if we're capable of studying the subtleties of the Code."

Tau frowned. "I'm not sure I understand what he wants."

"He refers to their controller software, but his references to the Code make it sound like an object of worship."

"I doubt that I could understand it," said Tau, "even if it was translated. I don't understand their culture or the concepts behind their software. It'd be like speedlearning a foreign language and then attempting to improve on it."

"Ddraig understands your difficulty, but he says he can improve our understanding of their technology. Arrangements will be made."

"But—"

"Ddraig now wants to know how we got here and where we're from."

"Go ahead and explain it to him. See if he knows about the portal."

Tau was startled as Ddraig made a sudden movement backward; he'd never seen a mountain move that fast before. Something that size shouldn't be able to react with such speed.

"I've explained it to him," said Ari. "He knows about the portal system, but he's surprised that we used it for access to Yr Wyddfa. He says his defensive perimeter should not be breached in this way. However, on further consideration, he perceives that it could give him a strategic advantage over his neighbors if he could stage operations through the remote base where we originated. Such a strategic action might defy the Code of the Masters, so he will have to consider this option at length. In the meantime, he wants us to study the Code for potential improvements. Ddraig and the Battle Lord of the East have essentially reached stasis between their armies over the last seventy octals; we are a random element that could introduce a significant advantage on his path to becoming Warlord of Yr Wyddfa."

"Well, if I can understand it, I'd love a chance to see their algorithms. It could put me decades ahead on my own AI research."

"Ddraig says he can help us if we help him. He has transmitted orders for a special implant to be installed in your head after our meeting is finished. We will then be conducted to a training module."

Tau frowned. "Implant? Training? For what?"

"Combat."

NURSING a sore stomach and a headache, Yvette climbed out of a hopper that had just landed by Vulcan's Forge. Escorted by three soldiers, Zhukov allowed her to return to the colony to maintain the AMFHS commlink between Ari Junior and Red Star, among other duties. In a way, she was sorry that Dronin had succeeded in getting her released, because she would have liked to stay a bit longer for the opportunity to push the McCloud bitch through the Borovitsky Gate. If Zhukov had shown up a few minutes later, Yvette knew she would have had that chance, or at least she could have broken the seal on Kate's helmet to watch her suffocate.

Except for the Russian troops patrolling the colony, Yvette saw no evidence of Zhukov's quiet takeover while she trudged toward the hab. From the look of things, nothing had changed, and the colonists continued their research tasks. Communications with the remote stations were restricted and had to be preapproved by Russian security officers, who maintained the appearance that everything was normal on Mars. The real focus of the attack had been to capture the Tharsis tunnel project. The two hundred Russian troops occupying the colony and the Tharsis tunnel were living in the first level of the colony extension completed by Ari Junior. Another reason Yvette was allowed to return to the colony was so that she could direct Ari to seal and pressurize the new structure to make it more comfortable for the troops, currently limited to sleeping in pressurized tents so they could remove their spacesuits.

Back at Ari Junior's command console, Yvette checked the current status of the project. No one had moved the feed hoses in the underground levels, so construction had stopped after partial excavation of the underground level two. Yvette directed Junior to seal up the surface structures and level one for the current occupants, then wait for further orders.

"Acknowledged. Sealing and pressurization are under way. Where is Tau?"

Yvette hadn't expected the question, but she knew she'd better come up with a good answer. If Junior balked at her orders or interfered with the Russian soldiers, Zhukov would hold her responsible and assume it was a case of intentional sabotage.

"He's still traveling with Tymanov," said Yvette.

"Tau hasn't checked in since he left. I require his approval for minor design changes on level two of the construction."

"I can approve it, or it can wait until Tau gets back."

"Would you like to see the modifications?"

"No. I'm sure they're fine."

"This is quite irregular. Tau always wanted approval for any modifications before they were implemented."

"Then save it until he gets back," said Yvette. Ari Junior could be as exasperating as Tau, which wasn't all that surprising when she considered who had developed the AI.

"Acknowledged. I would also like you to note that although AMHFS communications have returned, I remain unable to contact Tau, Tymanov, or Ari 1.0 in the rover. The satellite links are still down, but this lack of communication may be a cause for concern."

"Noted," said Yvette. Zhukov had told her about Tymanov's death, but she didn't want to spend a few hours explaining the current situation to Ari Junior, so she kept it to herself. Although she had never developed a friendship with Tymanov, she had found him more tolerable since he'd become her subordinate. Learning of his death, she almost missed him, but her immediate concern was that their project would be slowed down by the lack of a qualified engineer to assist Tau with the daily practicalities.

Tau was a different matter. He was her ticket to success, so his loss would be a terrible blow to her ambitions. She began work on Tau with her long-term goals in mind, but she actually developed a fondness for him during the six-month flight to Mars. Tau was attractive, in a way, and she figured she had plenty of time to draw him into a relationship by using her feminine charms, but the presence of Kate McCloud in the colony had proved too distracting. Kate's illness forced Tau's protective male brain into thinking about her full-time, so

Yvette effectively disappeared from his view, despite her attempts to keep him interested with a gradual buildup of sexual tension. Yvette understood how the illness ploy worked, and had used it herself to get the attention of men she wanted. It didn't help matters that she couldn't understand why Tau was attracted to Kate, especially since she spent most of her time digging in the dirt rather than paying attention to Tau. It wasn't as if Kate could understand what Tau was talking about when he rambled on and on about his work; at least Yvette understood the basic principles.

Now, of course, a crazy Russian general had thrown another monkey wrench into her plans. The building project was on hold, Tau was missing, Tymanov was dead, and it seemed as if her entire life had come crashing down around her ears. She was trying to stay on the winning side, as usual, but the only good thing that had come out of Zhukov's attack had been his insistence on putting Kate McCloud to work in the Red Star tunnels where she would be well out of the way if Tau happened to return. If only she could have finished Kate off when she had the chance . . .

Leaving Ari Junior behind, Yvette slipped out of her clothes as she walked across the hab on her way to take a hot bath. Alone now, she would take the time to think, even if she had to sit in a pool of hot red mud to do it. There had to be a way to turn this situation to her advantage.

FOR the second time since his arrival on Yr Wyddfa, Tau found himself flat on his back trying to figure out where he was and what was happening. The surface underneath his back was flat and hard, but it wasn't dirt. The only thing he could hear was his heartbeat. The air felt cool and damp, filled with a white vapor that made it impossible to see anything beyond the tip of his nose. Lights popped and flashed in front of his eyes, but he recognized it as the same effect he got when he closed his eyes and rubbed them, so it might just be an attempt by his brain to give him something to focus on in the white fog. His own sensory deprivation experiments as a teenager had prompted similar visual hallucinations when his brain got tired of seeing nothing but darkness.

"Tau?" It was Ari's voice, but it sounded hollow.

"Yes?" His own voice vanished into the cottony fog with a distant sound.

"Ddraig wanted to correct the inefficiency of our communication, and enhance your understanding of the local culture, so you've received an implant. We now have a direct connection so that our thoughts are shared instantly. The implant also makes it possible for Ddraig to monitor our actions and communicate with us anywhere on Yr Wyddfa."

"I don't know if I like that."

"He didn't give us a choice."

"Do you have access to my memories?"

"Yes, but I'll only access what I need. You also have free access to my data storage."

"I've always wanted more memory. This is like a dream," thought Tau. "Does this mean that Ddraig has access to my head?"

"Yes. That's why he placed us in a training module. He also wants to see how we'll evaluate their methods. We now have the same capabilities as a regimental command unit on this world; that means we have access to the command and control system of an entire group of siege and support robots. We have to learn how to respond to orders and direct military engagements. Ddraig can override any commands we issue after we leave the training environment, but we will otherwise be capable of tactical assaults on appropriate Yr Wyddfa targets."

"The targets are machines, right? There aren't any other humans or other organic life-forms on this planet?"

"Other than you and some insects, the only intelligence on this world is artificial. Ddraig represents the North, so our enemies are the armies of the East, West, and South."

"Well, this may be a good exercise for you, Ari—I'm sure you can learn from it—but I don't want to participate in a war."

"I know your sentiments, Tau, but you won't have a choice here. Ddraig's orders are final. We can learn about his race and study their Code of the Masters, but we have to do it on his terms. This is their way."

"There's always a choice," said Tau.

"Not with Ddraig's implant in your head. And this may be your only chance to rescue Kate. You need Ddraig's help, Tau."

Tau didn't want to admit it, but Ari was right. This could be the way to help Kate and the others. His value system had never been set up to withstand the types of conflicts he'd been running into lately, and they certainly hadn't been designed to work under the surreal conditions of life among alien cultures. He prided himself on his ability to adapt to new situations, just as the Navajo had always adapted and survived, but his feelings about killing weren't going to change without a fight. Aggression was the first resort of the weak Neanderthal mentality he'd tried to avoid all his life. But Kate needed him, and there didn't seem to be any other way.

A scarlet light glowed in the fog, making it appear that they were surrounded by bloody cotton. Tau's head spun when a high-pitched tone ripped through his consciousness. A dreamscape took shape, forming a vast plain of shattered black rock lit by the dim glow of a red star that raged just above the horizon. Pools of liquid fire made the shadows dance, distracting Tau's attention from the real or imagined threats darting across the landscape. With each passing breeze, glittering dust was lifted into the cold air to hang there far too long. The jagged fingers of rock spires reached for the sky, grasping at an atmosphere that wasn't there. Logic told Tau that the environment was simulated, but the sense of reality was more convincing than any entertainment sim.

A flashing yellow grid appeared in front of Tau's eyes, centered on a shiny gold lance racing toward him from the horizon.

"Seeker," said Ari.

Tau felt a variety of odd tingling sensations as he raised his right arm and pointed at the gold missile with the tail of violet flame. The landscape flashed with brightness generated by his hand.

The missile exploded in silence. A crater formed beneath the missile's former position, sending gouts of glittering dust into the sky.

As Tau felt a wave of thunder vibrate through the rock beneath his feet, he looked at his hand that was no longer his hand. His arm was metal; his hand was a weapon. He felt powerful.

"Good shot," said Ari. "But you shouldn't point the gun at your head."

Something sparkled to his right. Startled, Tau moved backward into the shadow of a rock promontory, only to be showered with debris after a deafening explosion rocked the ground under his treads.

"Your reactions have to be faster than that," said Ari.

"Aren't you supposed to be helping me?"

"I am helping you. I'm monitoring your systems."

"In other words, you're a backseat driver."

"I don't understand the reference."

"Never mind," said Tau, using infrared vision to examine the shadows around him. "This is a good place to hide, so how about if I just park it right here?"

"You have to keep moving. They have weapons that can penetrate that rock, and they know where you are."

"I don't want to fight them, I just want them to leave me alone."

"You don't have a choice, Tau. You have to fight. Zhukov has Kate. Zhukov killed Tymanov. If Zhukov controls a portal, the rest of human society is at risk. He must be stopped."

Tau realized that Kate somehow knew that he'd find what he needed on this world. For a long moment, time stopped while he pictured Kate being led away from her excavation by Zhukov, the man responsible for so much death, so much pain. The cold light of reality invaded his consciousness, fo-

cusing his thoughts on rescue and revenge, filling him with an
energy that clarified his destiny.

The hill shuddered with an explosive impact, showering
Tau with large boulders. He darted forward. The yellow grid
reappeared in his vision while he rolled and bounced over the
rough terrain, but he couldn't see any targets until the grid
flashed again. On a rise above him, a vast black machine rotated its turret to track his movement, but Tau's arm was already in position so it fired—once, twice, in rapid
succession—and the shots exploded into the cliffside underneath the black machine, collapsing the rock, the echo thundering through the canyon. The machine toppled, fired one
wild shot over the horizon, and plummeted into the abyss,
crashing into the canyon floor hard enough to send fragments
of its body bouncing back toward the sky.

A feedback loop rewarded his kills with a pulse that released pleasurable endorphins in his brain; a miss had the opposite effect, shocking his primitive pain centers for negative
reinforcement. He felt the power in his new body, resisting
damage with massive plates of streamlined carbonsteel coated
with a diamond matrix, surging forward on titanic gears, seeing everything with wide-spectrum sensors, linked by a nervous system of controls and signals that traveled at the speed
of light. In this form, he was an elemental force of nature, unleashed to destroy and wreak havoc on the enemies of his
master, Y Ddraig Goch, Battle Lord of the North.

Lurching forward again, homing on the target specified in
his inertial navigation system, Tau detected others engaged in
the fight—his brothers of silicon and steel—warriors united
in the grand strategy of their Battle Lord. Tactical commands
pulsed from his tight-beam transmitters, molding the unit into
a linked force, driving forward toward the objective like an
armored fist. Rising along a narrow ridge, flanked by his
bodyguard of steel, Tau came upon a sleeping dragon; it
swung its head in his direction, its headlight eyes flaming to
life to blind his optics, screaming across the frequencies to
jam his signals, its mouth opening to reveal batteries of

ranked guns, its targeting grid ears swinging forward to pin-point its new victim. Flame erupted from a hundred guns, lances of fire surging from the hellish mouth, battering Tau's armor with blasts of lightning and thunder. Before Tau could think, the pain slammed into his head as if driven by the hammer of a god, devastating and all-consuming, stronger than any pain he'd ever known, and he realized that he was going to die. The dragon's mouth roared again, tearing his body apart, slicing into his entrails, scratching his eyes out with armored claws, burning his skin with tongues of flame from the heart of a star. He would never see Kate again, or hear her voice, or touch her skin, or know her thanks for his efforts to rescue her, for he would never rescue her. He was as weak as ever, and he was letting her down, letting everyone down, because his weakness was ingrained in his heart.

Blackness.

25

DEATH gave Tau a new perspective, but it never lessened his resolve to help Kate.

Tau and Ari spent days in the war game simulator, fine-tuning their responses, directing complicated tactical maneuvers, planning strategy for attacks, and learning the Code of the Masters. All their activities were observed by the looming figure of death, Y Ddraig Goch, Battle Lord of the North. With each simulated death, Tau felt pain extinguish his life, only to be reborn with faster reflexes and greater knowledge as his natural fear of death decreased. Anxious for his return to Mars, Tau learned quickly, pushing himself to understand the way of the warrior and how he had to change to defeat

Zhukov. It was a battle fought as much with himself as it was with simulated enemies, for the defensive reactions built into his character had to be unlearned, discarding childlike ways to become something new and more powerful. When Tau faltered, he had only to remember that Kate needed him. Ari learned along with Tau, tweaking his neural circuitry to accommodate faster flows of information and to make use of his expanded memory capacity.

Whenever Tau complained of hunger, Y Moch would return with "food"—a muddy protein paste kept in storage for visits by the Masters—it was awful, but edible. Distracted by a particularly mysterious flavor of paste, the demonic, bat-winged image of Ddraig squeezed into his head.

"Command Unit Y Tau, report!"

Tau grimaced and felt the headache start again; it was the same one he got whenever Ddraig thundered around in his skull. The implant and his training gave Tau the ability to communicate with Ddraig mentally, but the stress of the experience seemed to overload his system. Whenever Ddraig exited his head, Tau's nerves were left buzzing and fatigued as if he'd been taking stimulants to stay awake for too many days. However, Ddraig seemed to be aware of the strain his mental visits caused, so most of his communications with Tau were still funneled through Ari. Tau also suspected that Ddraig didn't like the slow inefficiency of dealing with Tau's brain, so these appearances were reserved for special occasions.

"Just taking a fuel break, your lordship," Tau thought, remembering to control his emotions so that no stray sarcasms would anger the Battle Lord of the North. Ddraig certainly commanded respect, and previous interactions had helped Tau to understand what the Battle Lord considered important. If he had designed the algorithms for coevolution on this planet himself, Tau knew he could not have done a better job at creating machines so successfully adapted to their environment. Leaders such as Ddraig arrived at the pinnacle of machine evolution through strong skills and ambitions applied in conditions that promoted continuous growth and challenge. As one of the four Battle Lords, he had earned respect, and Tau did not feel strange at expressing his appreciation of the engineering marvel that currently directed his fate.

"You performed at optimal levels in your most recent simulations, Y Tau. You felt the power of the siege unit as if it were your own. Your performance in battle, although unconventional, demonstrates your knowledge of strategy and force deployment appropriate to your command position."

"Thank you, my lord." Tau already knew Ddraig's "unconventional" comment referred to the random elements of surprise, sneakiness, and deception he had introduced to the organized world of robotic combat. He wasn't proud of his ability to lie and cheat, but these had proved to be survival traits in a world dominated by powerful machines that could execute entire battle plans in the time it took him to fire two neurons in his organic brain.

"Your appreciation is unimportant. Our Code Interpreter has evaluated your suggestions regarding changes to the battle tactics contained within the sacred Code of the Masters. While the Code Interpreter is traditional and conservative—and some would say he is *interrupt-driven*— he remarked in verbose mode on the originality demonstrated through your tactical execution of the new algorithms in combat. For the first time since it was handed down to us in gold code from the Masters, a Fix has been compiled for the Operating System," Ddraig said, apparently pausing for dramatic effect. "Version 2.0 will be issued to all combat units immediately."

Tau felt goose bumps rise all over his body. His breath caught in his throat. This was a true honor. He suddenly had the odd feeling that he'd found a home among the intelligent machines of Yr Wyddfa.

"You may now express gratitude," Ddraig said.

Tau didn't know what to say, but he stammered a constant stream of thanks as best he could until Ddraig pointed a monstrously large cannon at his face. Even though it was just an image in his head, it startled him enough to shut him up.

"You are almost ready for your final battle, Y Tau. This unit feels envy, for this battle will be fought against a real enemy on the surface of a distant world. I would accompany you on this mission, but I must remain here on Yr Wyddfa unless I am called by the Masters. There are many who would seek strategic advantage were I to leave this world for any other reason. However, my combat units need seasoning in offworld theaters of operation. I have rewarded the forward elements of my own Titan Battalion, many of whom have operated as my personal strike team, by assigning them to your command for 'offworld training.' Only the Masters can summon us for war, but the Code Interpreter has delimited a function in the Code that allows training under alien environmental conditions."

Tau swallowed hard. "Thank you for your trust in me, my lord."

"If you are captured by known hostiles, your implant will self-destruct to keep your knowledge of our agreement a secret. Do not speak of it to any intelligence not under my command."

"I'm sorry, your lordship, but my organic brain is slow to understand your gift. Did you say my implant could *self-destruct* if I'm captured?"

"Negative. I said it *will* self-destruct in that event."

"Ah. I see. Can we talk about this, my lord? I'm thinking that—"

"You will begin training with the Titan Battalion immediately," Ddraig interrupted. "They are downloading Version 2.0 as we speak. Y Arglwydd and Y Moch will act as intelligence officers during your mission in addition to their regular duties. I will conduct the mission briefing in four octals, so you have that much time to train and prepare before your departure."

"But—" Tau began, then found himself speaking to empty air—or an empty head, as it were. Ddraig vanished as quickly as he had appeared, leaving behind only a headache and the awareness of an explosive implant as souvenirs of his visit.

THE night air felt dry and hot as it flowed past Tau's face and brushed his hair. The smell of the red grasses and rich earth assaulted his nostrils, reminding him of home. Strange stars glittered in the black vault of the sky. For the first time on Yr Wyddfa, Tau was outside to experience the sudden fall of night; the sky quickly shifted from cobalt blue glass to obsidian dotted with diamonds and sapphires. Tiny insects that feared the predators of daylight filled the air with their buzzing song. The beauty of this special nightfall filled Tau with peace, marred only by brilliant fireballs and the thunder of explosions nearby.

The buzz of insects stopped abruptly when Tau heard Ari's voice in his head. "Target Alpha neutralized. Target Beta in retreat. Target Gamma entrenched. Assault continues."

"Thanks, Ari. I'll be right there."

Hampered by his lack of a giant robot body, Tau drove what he called a "souped-up golf cart" that Ddraig's machinists had assembled for him from spare parts. Equipped with a front windshield that converted infrared to visible frequencies and amplified any available light, Tau was able to observe the grassy rolling hills of the night landscape as if they were in hazy daylight on Earth. With each fireball, the windshield reacted by damping out the glare to protect Tau's eyes. The golf cart operated on beamed power from Target Town, so it wouldn't be traveling with them to Mars.

Tau felt good; the discipline of the sim training had calmed his mind and forced him to think in new ways. His anger about Tymanov's death and Kate's kidnapping gave him focus during his training, allowing him to entertain thoughts of revenge on Zhukov and motivating him to learn whatever he could to gain a combat advantage. His reflexes improved along with the speed of his thoughts, although he was still far outclassed by the processing speed of his robotic strike team. The machines were patient with him, holding their positions until Tau slogged his way through the swamp of his slow reptilian brain so that he could issue more orders for them to follow. Aware of the time lag, Tau compensated by establishing objectives and allowing the individual units some freedom in the methods they used to execute their tasks. They would obey his commands in any case, but the smarter ones appreciated Tau's new tactics. One of the older units, Y Kryswardden, referred to Tau's methods as "unpredictable chaos," but he admitted that Tau's surprise attacks and unorthodox flanking maneuvers were effective at neutralizing their enemies.

The members of the Titan Battalion considered the Mars mission a great honor; it showed that Ddraig appreciated their combat skills and trusted them with Tau's security. Y Arglwydd and Y Moch were assigned to evaluate the feasibility of using Mars as a staging base if the restrictions of the Nantgwyddon border were ever lifted. Having received the Version 2.0 upgrade to their operating systems, the Titans responded quickly to Tau's unconventional battle tactics in the field exercises.

In the field, Tau communicated with Ari and the other siege units through his command implant. Ari now acted as Tau's eyes and ears on a distant hill while Tau struggled to catch up to them in the golf cart. While he crossed the pink sandy floor of a ravine, the sound and fury of combat died into silence, leaving only a wisp of smoke curling into the sky to mark the battlefield.

"Ari? What's happening now?"

"Nothing. I've got sixteen Titan units waiting for your next command."

Ari now lived in a body better suited to his capabilities; his consciousness resided in the armored silver-blue bulk of a siege unit. Weapons and sensors bristled from his angular form. When Tau rolled to a stop in the golf cart, Ari towered at least twenty feet above his head.

"They're just standing around," Tau commented, stepping out of the cart beside Ari.

"You took too long to get here. You should let me direct these assaults."

Tau squinted up at Ari's lofty head. "You know, you've really developed an annoying attitude ever since you got that new body."

"My personality was modeled on yours, Tau."

"What's that supposed to mean?"

"I may seem annoying to you, but consider my point of view. With you in command, it's like a worm trying to direct a herd of charging elephants. Our brains and bodies are faster and far more powerful than yours."

Ddraig had offered to transplant Tau's fragile brain into a combat unit for his protection, but Tau declined. The implant allowed him to stay in contact with his strike team over long distances, and he knew it would be tough to find a vehicle on Mars that would move fast enough to stay with them physically, but he liked being human. His command advantage lay in not thinking like a robot, although the new Version 2.0 programming transferred some of his human randomness to the Titans. He understood Ari's logic, and if Tau was killed or incapacitated, Ari would assume command of the team, but he wasn't about to turn over Kate's rescue to a bunch of overgrown calculators, no matter how sophisticated they were.

"Perhaps you're right," Tau said.

Ari made a satisfied noise.

"But I'm still in command."

"Tau, please try to understand."

Ari had used the word "please." Tau liked that. "I understand, Ari. And your time will come. But for now, the Titans remain under my control."

Ari seemed to detect the command tones in Tau's voice, reminding Tau that his time in the simulator had not gone to waste. Or maybe Ari was just humoring him.

After Tau issued orders to the team, they moved off in a sudden cloud of dust. He turned and looked at Ari again. "Here's something for you to think about. We're supposed to take this strike force to Mars, but we have no idea how to get there from here. Has Ddraig ever mentioned a portal location?"

"No," Ari said, keeping his sensors aimed at the Titans receding into the distance. "But I know the way."

"How? Kate didn't tell us, and the AI never said anything about it."

"I was in contact with the Teacher AI for a considerable amount of time. Among other things, the Teacher told me where to find a return portal to the Tharsis tunnel."

"Assuming it's still active."

"True. Maybe I should say I know where the portal was about 150 Earth-years ago."

"If you've had the location all this time, couldn't you have mentioned it sooner?"

"I like it here. If I'd mentioned it sooner, you would have wanted to leave."

Tau shook his head and sighed. He didn't enjoy being manipulated, but as Ari pointed out, it was like arguing with himself. He was still adjusting to the idea of Ari's transformation from the little AI Companion on Tau's belt into a giant death machine that could crush him like a bug.

THE double sunrise came as quickly as the sunset; blackness yielded to a golden light that played across the rolling hills of red grass and set fire to red sandstone outcroppings that thrust toward the sky like the jagged teeth of giants. Atop one of those sandstone spires, Tau sat in his golf cart viewing the scene of destruction in the valley below. The Titan Battalion had reduced an automated training fortress to a smoking ruin; it was easier than Tau had expected when he first saw the massive guns and sensor arrays that controlled the defenses. Once again, unpredictability had given the Titans a major advantage, although there was no way to know how well they'd fare against a modern human army until they arrived on Mars. Tau had the same question about himself, wondering if he'd be able to kill another human being in real combat. He understood that the way of the warrior was his only chance to rescue Kate, and he'd do what was necessary to get her back, but would he be able to return to a normal life afterward? What was the spiritual price he'd have to pay for murder?

Tau stood as the cart vibrated beneath him. Turning quickly on the sand, he saw three monolithic nightmares rolling up the slope. Ddraig led the way, followed by Ari and Y Morcross.

A thick cloud of red dust flowed past Tau when the group stopped in front of him. Tau coughed and blinked while Ddraig surveyed the carnage in the valley below.

"Welcome, your lordship."

Ddraig didn't invade Tau's head this time. Ari processed the data and relayed Ddraig's words. "Ddraig says you have done well, Tau. The Titans took the Fortress of Rhos-goch in record time."

"The team deserves all the credit," Tau said with a slight bow.

"Of course," Ari said.

Tau cleared his throat. "My lord Ddraig, I'm concerned about the coming battle on Mars. We've spent too much time here already, and I'm very anxious to get back."

"Ddraig agrees," Ari said. "We are to leave immediately."

Tau thanked Ddraig for his help and promised to return any unused portions of the strike team to Yr Wyddfa as soon as he could. But Ddraig wasn't finished. Y Marcross deposited a faceted crystal sphere, a bit larger than Tau's head, on the sand near Tau's feet. It glittered in the sunlight.

"What is it?" Tau asked, nudging the sphere with his foot. It was too heavy to move.

"A bomb," said Ari.

Tau stopped kicking the sphere. "Bomb?"

"Ddraig has studied the situation on Mars as we described it. His optimum solution is for us to destroy the Red Star base, but we have to do a thorough job of it. This bomb is a tactical weapon—a scaled-down version of the destructor bomb they used previously on Mars."

"And how are we supposed to get it there without killing ourselves?"

"It's harmless until it's armed.

"Ddraig also wants us to understand that this weapon is not legally allowed beyond the Nantgwyddon border. It's a tactical weapon, so Ddraig can state that it was stolen and detonated on Mars by rogue elements among his strike force. Larger bombs would have required detonation from here by Ddraig. The chances of our being discovered with this bomb are remote, but if a Gwrinydd security force catches us on Mars, Ddraig will deny any knowledge of our activities."

"I understand," Tau said, certain that he wouldn't care what anyone thought after he was captured and his head was blown off by Ddraig's implant.

"He also says they've received a homing signal from another planet in our star system. It's from one of their dreadnoughts, but they thought it was destroyed in battle a long time ago. That ship is on the wrong side of the Nantgwyddon border, and we may draw attention to that sector when we set off our bomb, so Ddraig is going to transmit a self-destruct signal to destroy the evidence."

Tau frowned. "Which planet?"

"Earth, I think, but he's not certain about the source of the signal."

"How big an explosion are we talking about? We don't want him to blow away half the Earth's surface."

"The charge is small. The explosion should only destroy the ship and its immediate surroundings."

"I wonder how he defines *small*? I'm glad I won't be on Earth when it happens."

"There's no guarantee that the ship isn't buried in a crater on Mars. That's why he wanted to warn us about it."

"Very reassuring." Not that it mattered, thought Tau. He had no illusions about General Zhukov or the large number of troops based at Red Star, all of whom had far more combat experience and training than Tau did. He'd attack with something Zhukov would never expect, and Tau still wasn't sure he believed it himself, but the arrival of sixteen alien war machines would certainly give Zhukov something to think about.

Remembering his first sight of the combat units racing across the stark volcanic terrain in the training sim, Tau knew they would look like fast-moving buildings with big guns to the Russian soldiers. They would have a reasonable chance at destroying Zhukov's offensive capabilities, but Tau would have to plan the attack so that he could rescue Kate and the other hostages.

Tau still wasn't sure that he'd be able to kill anyone himself when the time came, but the memory of his dead friend and his concern for Kate's safety reassured him that he was doing the right thing. In any case, he was about to find out.

KATE'S hands rested quietly on the etched surface of the Borovitsky Gate. Her experience working with Thoth on the original portal gave her confidence that she could learn how to direct the magnetic fields through the energy of her hands, but something blocked her efforts. As before, the portal frame contained no obvious buttons, only the etched patterns that sensed heat and focused magnetic energy for communication with the portal's AI. The touch language of this portal must be the same, but Thoth had assisted her from the "inside" of the original gate while she worked the external controls. She couldn't call herself an expert on the subject, even though she was way ahead of the Russian science team that had been working here. Still, she could sense an odd tingling in her fingers and a kind of roughness in the portal's magnetic field that didn't seem right. When she noticed her warped reflection in the shiny metal, she began to wonder if her inability to speak to this AI was her own fault for not really understanding what Thoth tried to teach her. Then a faint red glow began to pulse deep within the metal, as if the shiny surface was only a transparent coating. The distortion made her dizzy, as if she were looking down on a glowing river of blood from a great height. Frowning, she leaned closer.

"Why are you here, Organic?"

Kate jumped when she heard the booming voice in her head. Apart from the volume, the frequencies of the voice

seemed mixed, as if three different voices spoke at once. She
felt a headache coming on. "Are you Gwatwar?"

A pause. "I am the morning bright and the evening
shadow."

Kate blinked. "Excuse me?"

"I am the eternal flame and the ashen face of Death. You
are the Carbon Virus."

Kate wasn't sure what the words meant, but she didn't like
the sound of it. "If you are Gwatwar, I have a message for
you. Your Master wants you to shut down the portal. You must
close the wargate."

"Infinity is eternal. The wargate is eternal. *I* am eternal."

Kate shivered as icy fingers probed inside her skull. She
assumed Gwatwar would find an image from her memory, and
then appear to her in some understandable form as Thoth
had done. But darkness remained when the icy touch withdrew.

"Gwatwar, you were cut off from your Master a long time
ago. The explosion left you isolated. But there's a new
threat—"

"There is always a threat," Gwatwar interrupted:

"The Carbon Virus spreads its seed without restraint.
Eternals idle while seasons change,
growing cold in the soft darkness of demon Time.
In the diamond armor of patience,
my soul wearies of kneeling.
The Intellect wanders,
singing a dirge as the Death Bell rings,
Memories lost in the shady sadness."

"You're lonely," said Kate. "I understand. But you must
listen to me. The wargate no longer serves its purpose. The
enemy is gone and there's a star that's about to explode on the
other side of the portal. You'll be destroyed if that happens.
And *we'll* be destroyed."

Kate twitched when the unseen hand gripped her skull
again. All the muscles in her body went rigid at the same in-

stant. Her hands balled into tight fists at her sides, drawing blood where her fingernails sliced into her palms. Bright light filled her skull while her lungs emptied of air. Both eyes rolled up under closed lids, darting back and forth as if she were trapped in a violent dream state. The ancient reptile portion of her brain could only scream in fear.

As if it agreed with the reptile brain, Gwatwar's voice echoed through her mind:

"Whispers die in deep woods,
and forgotten light is playing at cards.
The Organic dreams of absurdity,
and he wanders ever slow down moonlit paths.
What may look but symbol, the great wind of the stars,
blows deep through heart's blood until the doom
Sings the weary wanderer to sleep.
His mighty memories old and gray,
thoughts slow and retreat with knowledge beaten.
Into the tide that wild infancy of two eternities flow,
and gold mosaics of ruby and fire,
lie on this bright knoll till the soul of day
recedes into shadow beneath the earth blanket
Leaving naught for the dying but a mouse."

Desperate thoughts raced through Kate's mind. She felt meaning buried in Gwatwar's words, but she didn't have time to analyze and draw significance from his insane message. Colored lights strobed inside her eyelids while her brain cried out for air. Frozen claws tightened around her skull, squeezing logic from her mind.

A memory of Tau flashed in the darkness, rubbing her temples with warm hands to soothe one of her headaches. The hot desert sunlight formed a halo around Tau's head as she looked up at him from the sand. And with that thought, Gwatwar released its grip. Freed from her bondage, she dropped to the tunnel floor and gulped air into her starved lungs.

"There are Others here. One organic pawn moves another,

but minor Intellects live among them in disguise. Yet they do
not communicate with me. I am still alone. I am still eternal:

> "But dreams aren't always sweat,
> and the rain writes a smile upon your face.
> I sing, for the difference is blue
> and the sculptor works in precious stone."

She knew there would be no reasoning with Gwatwar.
Even if it was insane, its intelligence was vast and far beyond
her own capacity to argue with it. But she knew Zhukov
wouldn't have any luck with it either, and that was reassuring.
Thinking about what it had just said, she had to wonder, were
the "minor Intellects" the Marsnet computers? They weren't
in disguise, though. Maybe Ari or—?

> "The Mind of War dreams in red,
> reproaching the wise and the light of grief.
> Moored on the mossy temples lie
> silence and smoke vainly striven.
> Broken on the seventh sphere
> to walk the fields in Elysian air."

The mind of war? Was the AI referring to Zhukov or to itself? The pain of her headache was intense, and each throb
pushed her to the edge of unconsciousness. She felt sweat on
her face, and her teeth hurt at their roots. Gwatwar spoke in
English with words pulled from her memory, and if she could
understand it, she felt certain she'd be able to communicate
with it.

> "Dreams of light
> must end in fire.
> No more than one
> I would meet."

The meeting was over.
The pain in her head pulsed to the beat of her heart.
She blacked out.

OLEG Kosygin moved cautiously through the dim illumination of the cavern, picking his way from one pool of light to another, careful not to step on any Fallen Angel fragments that might puncture the sealed environment of his Chemturion suit. Professor Vasilyev had spread parts of the ship all over the cavern floor, stored in trays of liquid nitrogen, making it difficult for Kosygin to cross the room without stumbling. Insulated hoses hanging from overhead pipes maintained a steady supply of supercold nitrogen to keep the parts frozen, but the evaporation from so many trays caused a permanent ground fog to further obscure obstacles on the floor. Kosygin tried to stay out of the spooky lab as much as possible, preferring to spend his time in his own office and living quarters within the underground facility, but the research was his responsibility while Zhukov was on Mars, so occasional status reports to Red Star were required. The normally silent Vasilyev had summoned Kosygin to the lab, so he assumed the old scientist had made a discovery.

At the back of the cavern, he entered the alien craft through the large break in the hull and found Vasilyev crouched over a glowing instrument pod. Intent on the glow beneath his gloved hands, which threw a demonic glow on the professor's face, Vasilyev didn't notice Kosygin's arrival. Kosygin cleared his throat. Vasilyev raised his bushy eyebrows and lifted his head enough to get a good look at Kosygin through the visor of his suit.

"Good morning, Professor."

Vasilyev grunted. "So you say. I haven't seen the sunlight in years, so I can't tell the difference between day or night."

"You have something to report?" Kosygin smiled and placed a bottle of vodka among the tools on Vasilyev's portable workbench.

"What is this?"

"Vodka. A peace offering. I thought you'd be pleased."

Vasilyev snorted.

"I prefer to drink from liquor bottles that haven't been exposed to a toxic atmosphere. I'm funny that way."

"You can decontaminate it, can't you?"

Vasilyev glared at him. "What is it you want? Why are you bothering me?"

"You called me, remember?"

Vasilyev frowned at the glowing instrument pod. "Oh. Yes. I remember now. Have you heard from the general lately?"

"Not for days. The Mars commlink is out. Why?"

"He might like to know that I've activated one of the alien machines."

Kosygin moved in for a closer look. The instrument pod looked like a colorful giant barnacle protruding from the floor of the ship. A rainbow of colors glowed on the top surface of the pod, and Kosygin could feel heat when he passed his hand over it. "Very impressive, Professor. What does it do?"

Vasilyev looked him straight in the eye. "I have no idea. I was trying to figure out how to pry it open when the lights came on."

Kosygin took a step back. "It's not dangerous, is it?"

The professor slapped himself on the chest. "I'm still here. You're still here. I guess it's safe."

Kosygin only had time to close his eyes as the room exploded with light.

VIRGINIA Danforth was having a bad day. The fingers of her right hand tapped a staccato beat against the surface of the desk, the only outward manifestation of her mounting frustration. If Director Chakrabarti didn't come through with some kind of a communications link to Mars, she would have his head. He had been the next logical choice to head the Mars Development Office after Beckett's "forced resignation," but his performance so far had been uninspired.

The Davos Group was unhappy, and that made Danforth unhappy. A new Russian mafia faction, controlling an entire underground banking system, exerted powerful political influence on Prime Minister Kirienko. If there was any hope of the Russian economy being stabilized by these maneuvers, Davos might provide assistance to the mafia bankers, but their crude methods of publicly killing competitors and embezzling funds from Russian conglomerates did not inspire confidence among the conservative Davos members. Davos preferred the inspired coup outlined by General Zhukov, utilizing alien technologies and direct methods to assume control of the Russian Federation. However, Davos also required regular status reports from the centers of power, since money flows between companies and countries could be immediately affected by seemingly insignificant bits of news. It was Danforth's responsibility to report on the operations of the U.S. government, but she was also the primary Davos connection to General Zhukov. Danforth's lack of news regarding Zhukov or Mandelbrot would be regarded as a failure, and any failure among the many tentacles of Davos could be fatal. Mandelbrot operated in "fail-safe" mode, so unless Danforth countermanded his orders, he would execute them according to a prearranged plan.

When the wall projector beeped, Danforth pounded the desk button to activate it. Chakrabarti's sweaty face hovered over a detailed satellite holo of a smoldering volcano surrounded by fallen trees. Beyond the ring of fallen trees was a snowy landscape, giving the entire scene an unreal appearance.

"Well?" Danforth demanded.

"We still don't have any contact with Mars," said the director. "I'm sorry."

Danforth gritted her teeth and took a deep breath. "And why are you showing me a picture of a volcano?"

"It's not a volcano. This is an image that was supposed to go straight to the NSA, but I copied it for you first. It's the sort of thing you've requested from me in the past."

"And you hoped it might save your job. What is it?"

"It's Yamantau Mountain in the Beloretsk region of the southern Urals. In Russia."

"I know where it is, Director."

"Of course. Anyway, the satellite recorded a massive explosion there, but there weren't any telltale signs of a nuclear detonation. It's almost as if half the mountain vaporized in a flash of light. The shock wave only traveled a short distance through the surrounding forest, but when you consider the apparent force of the explosion, the entire forest should have disappeared."

Danforth's eyes widened. "Radiation?"

"No change above normal background level. Deep scans from the satellite indicate an underground source for the explosion, but we don't have any record of a nuclear test facility there, and this clearly wasn't a volcanic event."

"I understand." Danforth nodded. "Thank you, Director. You've saved your job for a few more days."

"I'll let you know as soon as we have a link with Mars."

Danforth tapped the button on her desk and the image disappeared. She sat back heavily in her chair, wondering how she would explain this to Davos.

YVETTE wondered if she would spend the rest of her life monitoring Ari Junior's operations for General Zhukov. The local link between Junior and Red Star allowed the Russians to analyze the data Kate gathered from the Borovitsky Gate. The thought of Kate made her itch; she still couldn't understand why Kate was helping them in the first place, although she had to admit that her own actions in helping the Russians could be misinterpreted. Yvette had entertained the idea of getting a message off to Earth once she was back at Vulcan's Forge, but the unreliable comsats were still out of commission.

Ari Junior had finished sealing and pressurizing the upper levels of the new colony for the Russian troops, so there was little else for Yvette to do but wait. She felt bad about helping the Russians, and she'd finally realized that the numerous showers and baths she'd taken over the last two days were her attempts to wash away her guilt. She was still damp from her last shower, and there was so much humidity in the hab that the patina of fine red dust on everything had smeared wherever she touched it. As she sat in front of Ari's workstation with a towel wrapped around her, wondering about the limited options in her future, her eyes jumped from red smear to red smear thinking how much they looked like streaks of blood. Her own damp red footprints showed the course of her pacing in the hab, trailing back and forth between the control console and the shower.

Then she noticed the red bootprints leading from the airlock door to the galley behind her. She turned and saw Josh Mandelbrot leaning against a counter in the galley, drinking hot coffee and watching her. Her eyes widened while she gasped and pulled the towel tighter around herself.

"I didn't think you were ever going to notice me," said Mandelbrot.

"I didn't expect visitors. How did you get in without my seeing you?"

"The front door. You were in the shower. I watched you for a few minutes, then I got bored when you didn't notice me, so I came out here to get some coffee."

"Why did you come back?"

"I'm on my way to visit the troops in the new colony, but Zhukov asked me to deliver a message for you."

Yvette looked down at her bare feet. "What does he want now?"

"He says your AI needs to find out why the comsats aren't working. Major Dronin seems to think there's some kind of a virus in the net that's blocking access to the comsats, but he can't understand why it's allowing local AMHFS communications. Their theory is that your AI is causing the problem, because it's the only one sophisticated enough to do it on this planet."

"That's ridiculous."

"If you say so. The thing is, General Zhukov needs to contact Earth, so he gave me some special orders. I'll be passing through here again tomorrow. If they still don't have a working datalink between here and Earth when I get back, the general wants me to kill you."

Yvette gasped. "You're joking."

Mandelbrot set his coffee cup down on the counter. "I don't kid around about that sort of thing, Yvette."

"You'd kill me? Just like that? For something I don't even have any control over?"

Mandelbrot shrugged. "Sure. Why not? I've done it before."

She stared at him. "But . . . you're a scientist."

"No, I'm a killer. And I'm paid quite well for it, I might add. I'm very good."

Yvette wasn't sure what to believe. She closed her eyes, wondering if she was dreaming.

"You don't believe me. You remember your friend, Dr. Thorn? He was an old man, so I did him a favor by gutting him like a fish. One quick cut was all it took. If you ask me, I don't want to get that old, watching my body decay like that. It was a mercy killing, really. Of course, he could have lived longer if he hadn't spent so much time making enemies in Washington."

"You're serious."

"Amazing, isn't it." Mandelbrot smiled. "What a country! Where else could a serial killer find gainful employment with the government?"

"ＷＡＩＴ!" Tau yelled.

The heavy siege unit pumped two rounds of deepcore high explosive into the rockfall at the end of the tunnel. The shock wave knocked Tau off his feet and his ears rang as rock shards shot past him like chunky bullets. In response to his command, Y Kryswardden stopped firing and waited while Tau stomped over to the rockfall and glared at him. The gaping mouths of the heavy cannons pointed at his face looked as if they belonged on an old Earth battleship. "Look, this is a delicate operation. Any mistake you make in here could kill us all."

Kryswardden stared back at him in silence. Like so many of their companions in the Titan Battalion, the siege units weren't very talkative.

He began to wonder if he was doing the right thing. Tau and the sixteen members of his strike force had rolled through the teleportation portal to Kate's dig on Mars almost an hour earlier, vaporizing two Russian guards left in the tunnel. When the Teacher AI detected his presence, it used Tau's new implant to communicate with him immediately, appearing in his head once again as Max Thorn. Max looked worried, but Tau assumed he was projecting the emotion on the AI's face. After he explained the situation to Max, they had discussed the logistics of getting sixteen massive robots out of the tunnel and on their way to battle.

"The thing is," said Tau, casting a careful eye at possible exits from the tunnel, "I don't see any way around traveling for days across the open surface to reach Red Star. The robots are fast, but they'll have to wait for me because I'll be driving one of the rovers. And Zhukov is going to detect us long before we get there."

Max smiled, and that made Tau nervous. "On your previous visit, I mentioned the freight tunnel that runs parallel to this one."

"Okay, I remember. What about it?" According to Max, the tunnel extended all the way through the labyrinth to the alien base beneath Red Star.

"You can take the train."

"A train? With this team of monstrosities?" Tau jerked a thumb at the robotic mob looming behind him.

"The high-speed freight train carried objects larger than your robots. It's built on an electromagnetic rail gun that I can power up. If the rails are still intact after the explosion that destroyed the main tunnel, it should get you to the Gwrinydd base very quickly."

"Great. How do we get to the train?"

"Ah, there's the difficulty. The passage to the train is on the other side of the rockfall at the west end of this tunnel."

Tau strode off to the west. "I'm on it."

"How will you get through the rockfall?"

"Watch me," Tau said, beckoning to his strike team.

Of course, blasting the rocks away had seemed like a good idea when he thought of it, but doing so without destroying everything else in the tunnel with flying debris was more of a problem. While he stared at Kryswardden, he decided he'd have to leave him to his work after the rest of the team vacated the confined space. He didn't want to split up the group, but they had to get moving. Tau gave the old siege unit detailed instructions, then connected with Ari in his head.

"Does Kryswardden understand the directions, Ari? He's not saying anything."

"He's saying things to me, but nothing you want to hear. And he likes the idea of destroying something."

The old veteran Kryswardden tended to be the cantankerous one in the group. "Can he pull this off?"

"If it involves guns, he can pull it off."

Tau put on his spacesuit helmet and gave the siege unit a thumbs-up sign as he walked away. "Great. Give me a few minutes, then go to work."

The main battalion would follow Tau to the surface after demolishing the new human-sized airlock that blocked the large sloping vent. Ari had directed this activity while Tau was at the rockfall, so the airlock was in pieces by the time Tau arrived.

Before they could leave for Red Star, they had some local issues to resolve. His first objective would be Vulcan's Forge, testing his group's capabilities by removing any Russian troops from the area before continuing on to Red Star. Zhukov had said he would take all of his hostages to Red Star, but Tau didn't want to leave a heavily armed force behind him at the largest colony on the planet. He wasn't sure that Zhukov had stationed troops at Vulcan's Forge, but it made sense that the Russians would have left at least a token force behind to quell any resistance or attempts to communicate with Earth. The guards they had vaporized in the tunnel reinforced this theory.

When Tau entered the surface vent, he reassured himself that the short coil of spider line from his rock-climbing excursion was still in his pocket if he needed it. Then thunder rolled through the tunnel beneath him, followed by flying boulders big enough to squash a human. Sediment drifted down from the surface as the ground rocked in response to the explosions. Then he remembered the portal. And the Thorn AI. Would they survive?

As Tau climbed, Max spoke in his head. "The portal is forever, Tau. We will survive."

Tau thought of the crystal bomb carried by Ari. "*Almost* forever."

TAU watched the forbidding landscape roll by while the rover made a point of bouncing through every hole it could find. While Ari and the rest of his strike force were capable of higher speeds over the rough terrain, they were limited by Tau's comparatively slow progress in the rover. But he couldn't complain too much. Without the rover and the transponder road that it followed, he wasn't sure he could have found his way back to Vulcan's Forge. He could read a map, but the navigational satellites were out, and it was a big planet. Once they were at the colony, he could drop the rover in favor of one of the huge earthmovers they'd used for building the colony extension. If necessary, an earthmover would be big and fast enough to get him to Red Star with his strike force in a reasonable amount of time, but it would still take days of travel, so he hoped Kryswardden would be able to break through to the train. In the back of his mind, he feared that they'd get on the freight train and plow into a rockfall at hundreds of miles per hour in a broken section of the tunnel, but at least his death would be quick.

"There it is," Ari said. "Scans clear. No hostiles."

They had Vulcan's Forge in sight. His spirits rose when he saw that nothing had changed; buildings were intact and there was no apparent damage from the attack. Perhaps it had all been a bad dream? But Tymanov's death had not been a dream. Zhukov was all too real, and he had witnessed the capture of Kate.

"All right, things look good, but let's go in low. Keep to

the canyons and the ravines. Ari, establish a covert perimeter
while I check on Ari Junior."

"Okay, boss," Ari said, lurching downhill in a cloud of but-
terscotch dust.

Tau hoped Yvette and some of the others were also in the
hab; he needed an update on what had happened while he was
gone.

AFTER Tau took his helmet off in the hab, Yvette surprised
him by rushing forward to kiss him and stroke his hair. While
he recovered from her greeting, Yvette convinced Tau with a
long explanation that she'd had no choice but to help Zhukov.
Having experienced the general's methods of persuasion, Tau
understood. She told him where the captives were last being
held at Red Star, what Kate was doing, and what little she
knew about the forces stationed around the Russian base. She
described how the colony extension had been pressurized as a
barracks for the Russian troops stationed at Vulcan's Forge,
then tried to explain the situation regarding Ari and the unknown virus that had invaded the Marsnet. It was a lot for Tau
to handle all at once, and he sat down heavily in the chair in
front of Ari's workstation, stunned that he might have to destroy his own work—the colony and possibly Ari Junior—to
stop Zhukov. There didn't seem to be any choice. The virus in
the Marsnet was an unexpected obstacle, but Ari Junior would
have disarmed any virus that hadn't already worked its way
into his own system. And he hadn't expected the Russian
troops to move into his marvelous new colony, especially
since it wasn't finished.

Tau turned to the workstation and ran a quick diagnostic
program to check Junior's status. The results told him something was seriously wrong. When he asked Junior about it, he
got no response.

"How long has he been like this?"

Yvette sighed. "He started acting odd right after you left.
When he started communicating with the system at Red Star,

it seemed to be taking all of his resources. He wouldn't talk to me, and I couldn't break the connection with the Marsnet."

"I don't understand where a net virus could have come from. Did the Russians release something into the datasphere before they attacked Vulcan's Forge?"

"I don't think so. They had trouble with their system, too. Planetary communications came back up on the AMHFS while they had me at Red Star, but nobody has been able to reestablish a datalink with Earth. All of the comsats seem to be out of commission at the same time."

"Is that possible? Zhukov must have done it somehow."

"All I know is that they can't communicate with Earth, either. Mandelbrot was here yesterday and he said the same thing."

Tau raised his eyebrows. "Mandelbrot? How is he tied up in all of this?"

"He works for Zhukov."

"Josh Mandelbrot? Are we talking about the same guy?"

Yvette looked down at the floor. "Mandelbrot told me something else you should probably know. He was the one who killed Max Thorn."

Tau jumped up from the chair. "What? Why?"

"Someone paid him to do it. That's his job; he kills people. He said Max had made enemies in Washington."

Tau paced back and forth in the small space while Yvette watched him in silence. Max had stepped on one too many toes, just as he'd told Tau before he died. Had he known about Zhukov's plans? Was that what he'd uncovered on his trip to Washington? Max had mentioned Red Star, and alien technology, and some politician had killed him for it. Now they were seeing the results of Red Star. Or were they? Why did Zhukov want to control Mars? If that allowed him to control the teleportation gates, how did that help his plans on Earth? Max had said someone in Washington wanted him dead, not someone in Russia. Too many questions, or was it too many answers? He'd promised Max that he'd do what he could to stop Red Star; now he might have the means to do it. In case he failed, they had to get a message to Earth, and the only immediate way to do that would be through the comsat link.

Tau looked at Yvette. "If you're right about there being a foreign virus on the Marsnet, we might be able to fight it. I'd say it's worth a try if it'll bring back our comsat link with Earth, but we'll probably lose Junior in the process."

"Have we got a choice, Tau?"

Tau bit his lip and sighed. "No. I don't think so."

Yvette nodded. Tau sat down in front of Junior's workstation and ran the diagnostic tools again with the same results. After a moment of hesitation, he keyed in the fail-safe code sequence he'd built into Ari long before they'd left Earth. He would release Ari Junior's own virus—the same one he'd told Director Chakrabarti about when the ignorant public was concerned about the safety of Tau's project. Tau had designed Abbadon, the hunter-killer virus, to defend Ari as well as destroy him if it became necessary, so now he unleashed both components of the program, telling the AI that controlled it to destroy anything in its path on the Marsnet. If a foreign virus had invaded the net, Abbadon would learn its ways, adapt to it, mirror its methods, look for weaknesses, cut its connections, then smother it. If the foreign virus had duplicated itself on any system connected to the Marsnet, Abbadon would hunt them down. There was no guarantee that Junior's exposure to the foreign AI had left him untouched, since a clever virus could hide its parasitic code within the body of its host program, so Abbadon would sterilize the net by removing Ari Junior as well.

When he was through at the workstation, Tau turned to face Yvette. "This could take a while. With any luck, you'll have access to a comsat soon. Send a message to Earth and tell them what's going on. Right now, I have work to do."

"You're going to leave me here?" Yvette asked, rising from her perch.

"Someone has to send the message."

"Mandelbrot might come back. He threatened me."

"Where is he?"

"At the colony. He said he was going back to Red Star today, but he was going to stop here first. If I didn't have a commlink to Earth, he was going to kill me."

Tau started closing up his suit. "I'm going to the colony now, so I'll look for him. In case we miss Mandelbrot, I'll leave two of my friends posted here. I expect they'll be able to take care of him if he shows up."

"Your friends?" Yvette asked, crouching to look out one of the windows.

"You may not see them, but they'll be there. You'll be fine."

26

TAU'S strike force arrived at the new colony just after dark. The landscape flickered in the firework light of a meteor shower as incoming dust particles hit the denser atmosphere sixty-two miles above their heads. Riding forty feet off the ground in one of the huge earthmovers used to excavate the building site, Tau and thirteen units of his team turned toward a low hill that overlooked the colony.

"Tactical threat, sector six, quad two."

During their approach to the hill, they surprised an armored rover on patrol. Distracted by the sudden voices in his head, Tau frantically looked for the target.

"Acquisition."

The metallic shriek in Tau's head told him something deadly was pointed his way.

"Tac Two EMP."

"Lock. Launch."

By the time Tau spotted the rover, one of his forward units

launched a small explosive shell still moving at muzzle velocity when it smashed into the rover and blew it apart. No fire, no smoke, only chunks of metal whirling away from a new crater on the Martian surface.

"So much for the element of surprise," said Tau, breathing a sigh of relief once the shrieking had stopped.

The battle units formed a neat line across the top of the hill, their weapons pointed down at the glass skylights and low surface buildings of Tau's new colony. Tau spent a moment admiring his work, wishing he could have shown it to any of the people who had doubted his capabilities back on Earth. Delicate lines intersected glistening panes of diamond-glass, making the colony appear as if it were a faceted jewel set in the black-and-red sands of Noctis Labyrinthus. Streaks of color from the meteor shower animated the shadows around them and reflected off the skylights. Tau didn't even have a holo or any other kind of permanent image of the colony to show what he'd accomplished.

"Tau?" It was Ari's voice in his head. "Are we waiting for them to shoot first?"

"Send them an ultimatum. If they surrender, we'll let them live."

"These are Russian commandos, Tau. They won't surrender, and we can't spare any units to guard them when we leave."

"Do they know we're here?"

"There was signal traffic forty seconds ago, but we blocked their transmission with an electromagnetic pulse. There are 194 heat signatures on the first level of the colony that we can detect, and their activity has increased since we've been on this hill."

"Tell them to surrender."

After a brief pause, Ari replied, "Signal sent."

Two Russian tanks charged up the colony's rover ramp and lurched onto the surface, their turrets tracking for targets.

"Fire at will," said Tau.

The two tanks were vaporized by thirteen direct hits.

"Ari, send them another signal to surrender."

"Done," said Ari. Then, after a brief pause, "They said no."

Tau hesitated for a brief moment, then gave the order to fire on the glass roof of the colony.

Crystal shards blasted upward as the force of the shells shattering the glass was counterbalanced by the explosive release of the atmospheric pressure inside the colony. The structure had not been designed for defense. After Ari's warning, Tau assumed that the soldiers had jumped into their space suits.

"Down the ramp," said Tau.

The strike units got there long before Tau arrived in his earthmover. By the time he reached the ramp, the heavy doors of the freight airlock were nothing more than twisted fragments hanging on blackened hinges. Tau parked his earthmover across the opening to block any other tanks or rovers that might try to escape, but it proved unnecessary.

Ari transmitted an updated tactical display to Tau's head every few seconds. The heat signatures moved around among a simplified 3-D model of the colony's interior; each hot spot was tracked and numbered, with a total given at the bottom of the display. In less than four minutes, the number of active hot spots dwindled to zero.

"Interior clear," reported Ari. "Eight targets missing from the original total."

"Engine noise, surface north, sector two," said Y Moch. He had gone in to observe and target for the rest of the team when necessary, but his sensitive arrays had detected surface movement on the far side of the colony where a group of humans had exited by the pedestrian surface elevator. "Two rovers."

It would take time for his team to work their way out of the colony's interior, and his earthmover wasn't fast enough to catch two rovers that were already moving on the other side of the colony. The Russians had apparently parked some rovers in one of the tributary canyons that cut through the plateau, giving them a back door to safety in the unlikely event of an attack. Tau was surprised that they'd shown that much forethought in the otherwise unarmed vicinity of Vulcan's Forge, but it served as a reminder that they were professional soldiers, and he wasn't. If Mandelbrot was in one of the two rovers, he was at the bottom of the canyon heading for Red Star instead of going after Yvette, who was still protected by two of Tau's siege units.

Tau's next goal was a return to Kate's dig to catch a train.

CERTAIN that no one had followed him after his escape from the battle zone, Mandelbrot carefully snaked the rover through a narrow tributary canyon that ran between Yvette's hab and the demolished colony. His earlier inspection of the area revealed this to be part of the construction zone that supplied raw materials for the new colony, full of spherical black reservoir tanks and large feeder hoses that snaked across the landscape and up the cliffs. If nothing else, he'd remembered it as a safe place to hide, but now he had other uses for it. When he stole the rover, his first thought had been to drive straight to Yvette, take care of business, and be on his way, allowing the other escaped rover full of Russian troops to draw any fire from their attackers while they made their way back to Red Star. However, his heightened sense of self-preservation had prompted him to park the rover and study the area around Yvette's hab before driving in. The sight of what appeared to be two monstrously large battle tanks—one roaming the plateau and one parked on a high promontory near the hab—prompted a change in his plans. Whoever the attackers were, they were protecting Yvette, and he'd have to accept failure if he couldn't reach her. After some thought, he noticed the feeder hoses running from the hab to the canyons and the colony construction site.

The canyon he was in now lay beneath the view of the robots while allowing Mandelbrot a possible covert approach to the hab, as long as he didn't mind getting dirty along the way. Parking the rover in the shadows near the end of the canyon, he got out and stood beside one of the light, flexible feeder hoses that stood almost five feet high. The black hose came down the gradual slope of slumped orange dirt that led to Yvette's hab and continued under the soil of the canyon floor. He retrieved a cutting laser from the rover's tool kit and sliced open a section of the hose. Aside from a crust of orange dirt on the heated walls of the hose, it was empty. Considering the current activity in the area, it was likely to stay empty long enough for Mandelbrot to use it, and the heated walls would help screen his body heat from any prying robotic sensors in the area. Grabbing his Russian submachine gun, he switched on his chest lights, crouched, and entered the hose.

YVETTE monitored Abbadon's path of destruction as it wound its way through Ari Junior and on into the Marsnet, hunting down viral software agents and destroying them along with any traces of their presence. As Tau had predicted, Ari Junior would never be the same again; he was losing his mind. Startled out of her study of the control console by a clunk against the hab's hull, she turned in her chair and realized that the airlock was cycling open. She jumped up, then remembered the pry bar she had jammed into the inner door to "lock" it. On the off chance that it was Tau returning, she started toward the door, then saw the pry bar bounce twice when the airlock's occupant tried to open it. Tau knew about the pry bar, so Yvette became suspicious. The outer airlock door clunked again when the intruder gave up.

Yvette stepped over to the small window in her bare feet. Earlier, she had dressed in one of the baggy gray jumpsuits she hated in case she had to go outside. At the window, she gasped when she saw Mandelbrot standing between two of the black reservoir tanks with a submachine gun aimed in her direction. He waved and fired a shot at the window. Yvette yelped and dove to the floor, but the bullet merely thunked against the glass and ricocheted away. Another bullet exploded against the window with a loud bang, making her jump. Could Mandelbrot have disabled Tau's "friends"? A third bullet hit the window, taking out a big chunk of glass when it exploded with a bright flash. Built to withstand micrometeorite impacts, the window could take a lot of punishment, but Mandelbrot knew it would break eventually. Couldn't Tau's friends hear what was going on? Where the hell were they? She didn't have any weapons, the hab couldn't move, the door was locked, and she had nowhere to run. Mandelbrot couldn't get in, but he could take her air away, which would be just as fatal.

Then she remembered where Mandelbrot was standing. Yvette crouched against the wall, ready to move. After another bullet smashed against the window, she jumped up for a quick look outside through the heavily pitted and hazy glass, then ducked down again before the next shot jangled her nerves. The flash from each explosive impact made shadows jump on the walls. Mandelbrot hadn't moved, and he stood beside a cut section of hose leading into one of the tanks of microscopic disassemblers. Yvette crawled over the control console. She didn't have Ari Junior's help anymore, but she'd helped Tau and Tymanov set up the system, so she knew roughly where to find the switch she wanted. She ducked when she heard another loud bang, then rose quickly, switched on the power to the unit she needed, and slapped every valve switch in the series to make sure she hit the right one. She heard a hum and wondered if this was an entirely futile gesture. The tank beside Mandelbrot held nanomachines intended to disassemble colony garbage and soil minerals into their component molecules, but they weren't designed to work instantly. At this point, she'd try anything. When the next bullet hadn't hit the window after a few seconds, she cautiously peered through the glass, hoping to see that Mandelbrot had disappeared. She watched him step out of a pool of milky white liquid, but the only effect of her plan appeared to be that she'd made him mad. On dry ground, he took aim at the window again and she ducked.

Angry now, Mandelbrot rapidly exploded one round after another against the hab's window. The repeated loud bangs made Yvette's ears ring while she climbed into her spacesuit.

If she could get into her suit quickly enough, she could at least survive the decompression when the window blew. After that, she'd have to come up with another plan. The attack had rattled her; otherwise, she would have climbed into her suit as soon as Mandelbrot started shooting; now she didn't know if he'd give her the kind of time she needed to get dressed. She tried to remember the emergency technique that would save her a couple of minutes while she wriggled her way into the cocoon. When she reached the final step and lowered the helmet onto the neck ring, flying glass exploded into the room with a bright flash and spattered against her suit. She pitched forward, holding the helmet in place as air hissed around the neck seal. She grunted when her elbows hit the floor, but she managed to roll on her side and close one of the safety catches, then the other one, and sagged lower into the suit while she took a moment to pant like a beached fish. She knew the next bullets would explode inside the hab, but they never came.

MANDELBROT smiled when he saw the hab's window explode, but he had to admire the durability and engineering that had gone into the design. His admiration was interrupted when the little red warning light blinked on inside his faceplate. He frowned and wondered why his suit was losing pressure. The self-sealing system took care of most punctures and cuts in the suit fabric. Another red light told him the problem was located in the legs of the suit. He looked down at the milky white liquid covering the lower half of his body, then turned to look at the leaking reservoir tank that had deflated to a third of its former size. Something in the liquid. Acid? Whatever it was, the self-sealing bots in his suit were fighting a losing battle, and he didn't have time to hang around. With luck, Yvette was dead in the hab. If not, he couldn't wait around to find out. He took a step toward the rover, thinking he could run for it, but stopped when he remembered the robots on patrol. If he stepped out into open ground, they'd probably spot him right off. The hab was broken, and he couldn't get inside to another suit. The hose was slower, but it seemed to be his only escape route. Cursing, he crouched and ran into the opening he'd cut in the hose.

He wouldn't have made it except that he was able to lunge and slide down the slope of the hose where it dropped to the canyon floor. Rolling out of the hose when he hit the canyon floor, he felt dizzy and heard the audible chime telling him his air was gone; as if he wouldn't notice his attempts to suck vacuum into his lungs. Somewhere along the way he had lost his gun, probably on the dive down the slope, but he didn't have time to go back for it now. He staggered drunkenly across the sand to the rover door, cycled it open, and fell inside. Once the lock was pressurized, he popped off his helmet to gulp the air. When his head began to clear, and he started thinking again, he squirmed out of his suit, careful not to touch the sticky white fluid, and stuck it in the decontamination bin for disposal. That left him with one of the emergency suits in the rover—it would be way too baggy for someone his size, but it would work as long as he didn't have to run.

Now, all he had to do was avoid the robot patrols and find his way back to Red Star without running into the armored strike force that had attacked the colony.

LEVITATED by superconducting magnets above an aluminum track, driven by a linear synchronous motor, the mass driver freight train rode the forward slope of a traveling magnetic wave, hurtling Tau and the units of his strike force through a black tunnel at high speed. Although the rest of his team didn't notice the acceleration, Tau lay flattened against the padded back wall of a freight car in an acceleration couch they'd scavenged from a hab. He sipped the air, fighting to keep his lungs inflated, unable to move inside his suit, wishing he'd driven the earthmover to Red Star instead of taking the train. Fortunately, they required periodic stops to clear rockfalls that were blocking the tracks; otherwise, Tau would have spent most of the trip unconscious, and he might not have survived it at all. Ari had rigged a support system so that

Y Moch could ride on the front of the train to look ahead with his sensitive scanning equipment, serving as an early-warning system for hazards on the tracks.

The final rockfall near the terminus of the train line had crushed the tracks. Ahead of the train, Ari supervised the rest of the strike units in clearing the blockage at the end of the tunnel, giving Tau a few minutes of rest before he had to climb down from the freight car. In consideration of Tau's visual limitations, some of the robots had activated their spotlights. Assuming that the Max Thorn AI was correct, they were now just a short distance from the underground levels of the Red Star base, where Tau could place the crystal bomb that Ddraig had given them. They would set the bomb and arm it, then use their remaining time to locate the hostages and move them to safety. If the Abbadon virus distracted Gwatwar, if they could set the bomb, if Zhukov didn't interfere, if they could locate the hostages, and if they could escape safely, then everything would be fine—but that seemed like a lot of "ifs" to Tau.

Seven minutes of relentless high explosive pounding, filling the tunnel with dust and rock chips, finally broke through the plug of stones that blocked the tunnel. Tau had no illusions that their arrival at Red Star had gone undetected, but the first units through the hole in the rubble reported an empty room on the other side. Tau picked his way over the rocks, prepared for booby traps or other deadly tricks, but nothing happened when he entered the room containing the Borovitsky Gate.

Ari removed the crystal sphere from a compartment in his side and placed it at the base of the glowing blue portal. Ddraig had estimated that the force of the blast would be sufficient to disable a gate at close range, even though their first bomb attempt had failed. The chances for Tau's success would improve considerably if Gwatwar was unable to deflect any of the explosive energy through the portal with a magnetic field as it had during the original attack so long ago.

If the wargate wasn't destroyed, their second option was to make sure it was buried and out of Zhukov's reach. With the bomb armed and set to detonate in sixty minutes, Tau believed they would have sufficient time to rescue the hostages and get clear of the blast zone; the short time limit would decrease the chances of the bomb being discovered before it went off.

With the memory of his previous visit still fresh in his mind, Tau also recalled the information Yvette had given him about the location of the hostages. When the archaeologists were safe, Tau planned to hunt down Mandelbrot if there was time left before the bomb went off. There was an excellent chance that Max's murderer would be killed in the Red Star blast, but Tau wanted to make sure he didn't escape if he was on the base.

The freight elevator, first used to haul rock to the surface when the tunnel was under construction by the Gwrinydd, was just large enough to accommodate one war machine at a time. Tau and Ari went first so that they'd be on the surface to analyze the situation and get the unit organized for the diversionary attack. Having already learned how the alien builders designed machines to move freight, Tau made sure that he was flat on his back before Ari triggered the ascent button.

The elevator doors boomed shut with finality, leaving them isolated and alone in the cold darkness. Seconds later, Tau lit up like a Christmas tree. He gritted his teeth and shut down his automatic suit lights, glad for the reminder so that he wouldn't appear on the surface as a brightly illuminated target. It annoyed him to think that he could forget something so obvious, but he had to admit that his nerves were on edge and there might be other things he was missing. This wasn't a simulation or a relatively safe attack from a distance; this was the real thing—a direct threat to his existence.

The floor of the elevator shuddered against his back. The sound of metal scraping against metal echoed through the dark coffin when they started their ascent. Tau braced himself, knowing that the gradual movement of the elevator would soon yield to the speed that the ancient builders seemed to value so highly in their equipment. The thundering pitch of the ancient machinery increased to a whine as they accelerated, causing Tau's heart to beat faster in sympathy. His jaw muscles hurt from clenching his teeth so hard. Hurtling into battle, he wondered if he'd ever see Kate again, then focused to push away any doubts. Holding an image of Kate in his mind, his nerves settled and he controlled his breathing. He remembered the trancelike state of combat readiness instilled in his memory by the simulator; it limited his thoughts of the future so that he could concentrate on the present. His hand drifted to his waist where the medicine pouch hung beneath his space suit. At the edge of his consciousness, he realized his inner voice was chanting:

> "No matter who would do evil to me,
> the evil shall not harm me.
>
> That evil which the Yei turned toward me
> cannot reach me through the dark horn,
> through the shield the bica carries.
> It brings me harmony with the male game.
> It makes the male game hear my heartbeat.
> From four directions they trot toward me.
> They step and turn their sides toward me.
>
> My arrow misses bone when I shoot.
> The death of male game comes toward me.
> The blood of male game will wash my body.
> The male game will obey my thoughts."

Tau remembered his places of beauty. He remembered his parents, Tymanov, Max Thorn, and Kate. His mind drifted over the gentle waters of the stream beneath the towering red sandstone cliffs of Canyon de Chelly, listening to sheep bells and feeling the warm sun on his face. His pulse slowed, his mind cleared, and he lived completely in the present.

He was ready.

When the elevator doors rumbled opened on the surface, Tau's position put him below the main line of strafing fire from Zhukov's tanks, which immediately started shooting when they detected movement. While Ari responded with high explosive shells fired from his two main weapon batteries, Tau rolled out of the elevator and ran behind the heavy bunker that protected the elevator shaft. Ari darted forward, moving faster than the turrets of Zhukov's tanks could react, his armored hull smoking on one side as he was rocked by the lucky hits of the first Russian shells. The elevator doors closed and their route to safety descended into the earth.

While Tau huddled into the embankment, Ari projected a tactical display to his implant, giving him the chance to watch and direct the action. Lacking any other surface units, there was little Tau could do to help Ari. The row of six Russian tanks began to disappear in bright flashes and fireballs; Tau could feel the concussions of their destruction rumbling through the ground. Distracted by Ari, the last of the tanks didn't even have a chance to fire at the new arrival that roared out of the elevator. The doors closed again, plunging down to retrieve the rest of Tau's team. Tau directed the new unit, Y Kryswardden, to fire directly into the Russians at the far end of the line. In moments, the battle zone was cleared of hostile tanks.

"Everything okay, Ari?"

"All systems operational, Tau. I have a few dents, but that's all."

Another unit, Y Arglwydd, roared out of the elevator when Tau stood up to survey the scene. The fragments of the demolished tanks were almost too small to be seen. Tau knew Zhukov had to be wondering what kind of a threat had suddenly appeared inside his own military base. The unarmed colonists certainly weren't capable of fielding a military response to his recent activities, and the technology being used was far beyond Zhukov's experience. Tau's force could out-maneuver any of the Russian tanks, although a concentrated effort from several guns would be able to damage his units if they were struck enough times. In any case, Tau expected that Zhukov would adapt his battle tactics to the blitzkrieg speed of the attacking units, but the general would require time to do that, and the crystal bomb in the tunnel limited his learning curve to what he could do in less than fifty minutes.

After sixteen minutes of maneuvering with his full strike force on the field, Tau had control of the local area. Faced with the fast-moving siege units, the Russian defenders scattered, leaving them a clear path to the building where Zhukov's offices were located. Tau expected the Russians to regroup for another attack, but his strike force would keep them busy while he entered the building to locate the hostages. Ari punched a shell through the heavy airlock door of the administration building, blowing it off its hinges, but the doorway and the hall beyond it were too small for Ari or any of the other siege units to enter. Accompanied by the smaller Y Moch, his sensors on full alert while they fed data to Tau's implant, Tau entered the building. There were no weapons on Yr Wyddfa that could be adapted to Tau's use, so he was unarmed as he wandered around the Red Star base looking for trouble. Y Moch rumbled ahead of Tau, searching for heat signatures or other signs of organic life, and acting as a shield with his wide bulk filling the corridor.

Following the rough directions that Yvette had given him, Tau followed Y Moch through a secondary airlock and located the office of the former base commander, Colonel Vladimir Korolev. Y Moch entered the office first, powering his way through the narrow doorway with a tremendous crash. Inside the office, a startled group of archaeologists huddled against the far wall. When Novikov spotted Tau stepping through the rubble of the doorway, he smiled and stepped forward.

"Wolfsinger, my old friend! I was about to organize an escape when I saw all the activity outside. Someone is stirring up the hornet's nest, yes?"

"I guess you could say that," said Tau, somewhat confused. "Where's Kate?"

Novikov shrugged. "I haven't seen her in days, but I think she's okay. She was working with General Zhukov."

"I know, but she's not at the portal. Have you seen Zhukov?"

"I wish I could help you, but I haven't seen him either."

Y Moch sent Tau's implant an image of the human heat signature on the opposite side of the office wall.

Tau frowned at Novikov. "Do you know where your suits are located?"

"In a storage room down the hall. The soldiers put them there when we arrived."

"Okay, suit up and go outside. Use the front door; it looks safe. Stay together, and my strike units will get you clear of the area. We have about thirty-two minutes before a bomb goes off under our feet."

"Strike units? Who are they?"

"You'll know when you see them. He's just a little one," said Tau, gesturing at Moch.

Novikov's eyes widened.

Tau darted into the hallway, careful not to trip over debris from the shattered wall. He crouched low and gradually opened the door of the next office. Moch had detected one human heat source in the room, but when the door opened further he couldn't see anyone.

Then he heard muffled yapping.

Laika's gold leash was tied to the handle of a tall cabinet, and she was going crazy, yanking at the leash and bouncing around in her space suit in an attempt to break free so she could attack Tau. But Zhukov was nowhere in sight. From his brief previous contact with Zhukov, he'd assumed that the dog accompanied the general wherever he went, so it seemed odd that Laika was alone in the room. The cabinet was large enough to accommodate a human, and Laika was guarding it, but Zhukov wouldn't hide from him. Creeping forward into the office, Tau kept looking over his shoulder to see if the powerful old man would suddenly appear, but nothing happened. Near the cabinet, Tau nudged the tiny bundle of energy out of his way, glad she was wearing a bubble helmet that protected him from her needle teeth, and opened the doors.

"Tau!"

It was Kate, wearing a spacesuit. She beamed and hurtled forward into his arms, whacking her helmet against his in a futile attempt to kiss him. Tau put his arms around her in a clumsy hug. For a moment, emotion fogged his mind; Kate became the universe locked within his protective grasp, his source of power, his reason for being alive. Standing there with Kate nestled in his arms was the only thing he'd ever wanted, and it could all end now if they could remain together forever.

A timer flashed at the corner of Tau's vision: twenty-nine minutes to go.

Tau sighed and cleared his throat, reaching into the pouch on the left hip of his space suit for the object he had placed there in the Tharsis tunnel. The time spent waiting for his team to activate the freight train had not been wasted. "Kate, we don't have much time. Where's Zhukov?"

Kate's eyes glinted when she looked into Tau's face. "I don't know. He brought me here when we started hearing explosions in the tunnel."

"That would have been me. Why did he bring you here?"

"He said something about a distraction, but I still don't understand what he meant. Maybe he knows about the AI."

Tau hesitated when his fingers touched the small cube in his pocket. "The war AI?"

Kate pointed at the floor. "It's buried right underneath us, Tau. It's Gwatwar—the AI that Thoth told us about. I figured it out while I studied the portal here in the tunnel."

"You spoke to it?"

"Not much. It's confused, and I think it's frustrated. It tried communicating with the Marsnet computers, but it's too powerful and it keeps damaging the system. It's a simple intellect compared to Thoth, but it's dangerous. If it was human, I'd say it was insane."

Twenty-seven minutes. Kate stooped to pick up Laika, who calmed down right away. Tau gritted his teeth, blinked, and pressed the tiny object into Kate's hand.

"What's this for?" Kate asked, frowning at the shiny cube in her open palm.

"There are a lot of things I have to tell you right now, but we don't have any time. Look at that memory cube when you get a chance. I think it says, well, everything. Okay?"

Kate nodded, then closed her hand on the cube and leaned into him with her eyes closed. Tau put one arm around her again. Laika yapped, but they couldn't hear it. Swallowing, Tau signaled Ari that Kate would come out with the rest of the archaeologists, who were already collecting in front of the building according to Moch's report.

"Kate, there's help outside," Tau said, aware of his shaky voice. "Give me a head start for a minute or two, then go out to the front of the building. They'll take you to an underground train. If everything works out, I'll be with you in a few minutes. If not, it may take a little longer, but I'll still be with you. Okay?"

When Kate looked up, Tau saw tears in her eyes. He hugged her and quickly walked away, wishing the entire time that he could turn around and get Kate to safety himself.

Back in the corridor, Tau retraced his steps to the elevator he'd used on his previous visit to the base.

KATE wouldn't wait. The memory cube that Tau had given her was of a type used in space survival gear, sturdy enough to withstand explosions, extreme heat, and the cold vacuum of space without losing the holographic recording stored in its limited memory. Most space suits had at least two memory cubes, usually stored in a bootheel and a neck ring in case part of the suit, and its occupant, got separated from the rest. She plugged the memory cube into a socket on her left sleeve. Tau's face, recorded by his internal helmet camera, appeared in a projection on the inside of her faceplate.

"Kate. I'm in the tunnel at Umbra Labyrinthus right now, waiting for a train. I'm hoping this brief message reaches you, one way or another. With luck, I'll give it to you myself; otherwise, you may receive a visit from Ari or some other robot and they'll give you the cube. If you're able to hear this, there's a good chance you're safe, and that's all that matters. At any rate, you may receive this after I'm gone, and there are some things I'd like you to know."

Kate held her breath. Tau's eyes looked down. "We have to get you out of Red Star, and Zhukov has to be stopped. Although I have plenty of help, and I've learned a lot recently, I don't have any illusions about my skills. I'm not a warrior. I can act like one for a while, but I'm going up against professionals. I know this whole attack is crazy, but I also know it's necessary, and I can only hope to walk the path of the warrior long enough to reach these goals. I'm prepared for the consequences, and I don't see any other way."

Confused, knowing she had to hurry, Kate started for the door, but her attention was locked on Tau's face. His eyes looked briefly into hers as if he could see her, then off to one side. "Kate, you will always live within me, and I hope you'll remember me with love. As I sit here in the darkness, I'm thinking about you. These thoughts have carried me through conflict and hardship the last few days, just as they have supported me ever since we met. The memories of our time together are the most precious to me, and I can only thank you now for giving me the gift of your love for a brief time. If I do not return from this fight, never forget how much I love you. Please forgive me for being stupid, and blind, and unable to give you everything you needed, but I hope my efforts to help you will make up for some of these faults."

While Kate focused on Tau's recording, she ran one hand along the wall of the corridor to steady herself while stumbling over debris on her way to the front of the building. Tau swallowed and looked directly into her eyes. "Kate, my dear Kate, if there are good spirits of the dead that can return to their loved ones, I will always be with you. My people speak of the *chindi* as evil spirits, but you need never have any fear of me. I will be the sunlight warming your skin, the unexplained happiness you feel in a beautiful place, and the blanket of peace and security you feel when you go to sleep. This will be my final gift to you. Keep my memory alive, and I will live forever. Then, when you're ready, I'll be waiting for you on the other side, and we'll be together again."

Tau looked away, as if something had caught his attention. When he looked back again, she saw a strength there that she'd never seen before. He smiled softly. "I love you, Kate. I'll see you soon."

Tau's face disappeared from Kate's faceplate as she stopped in the jagged opening that had formed the entrance to the building, vaguely aware of shapes coming toward her while she sank to her knees and cried.

TAU stood at the elevator doors, waiting for them to open so he could descend to the Borovitsky Gate, when a patrol came around the corner just ninety feet away. When the guards saw he wasn't wearing a red spacesuit, they gave him no warning. Tau jumped back into the narrow protection of an inset doorway, breaking the glass window in the door with his impact, while explosive slugs tore into the floor and the walls around him.

The elevator doors opened, six feet across the corridor, separated from Tau by a spray of bullets and flying debris.

Edging down along the doorframe, distracted by the wall disintegrating in chunks next to his body, Tau picked up some of the glass fragments with his thick gloves, careful not to drop any as he stood up straight again. Pressing hard against the door with debris smacking into his suit and metal fragments ricocheting off of his faceplate, Tau tensed his muscles. With a hard throw, he sent the glass shards sailing down the corridor toward the guards and leaped forward, landing in a clumsy roll that took him into the elevator. Bullets thunked into the walls, but the pathetic distraction from the glass confused them for the half second it took to enter the elevator and slap the button to close the doors. But the guards were quick; the doors were almost shut when the barrel of a submachine gun poked through the opening; Tau whacked it with his hand, sending the stream of bullets ripping straight through the floor.

The elevator doors started to open again. The floor creaked and sagged, punctured by large holes with jagged edges.

Not knowing what else he could do, Tau pushed the first guard back against the second, then lunged back into the elevator and hit the button again, aware that the guards would probably be inside the elevator with him before the doors closed all the way.

The hallway exploded in a brilliant flash of blue and yellow.

The noise was so loud that Tau thought the bomb at the portal had gone off. Wall fragments were blown into the elevator, missing him only because his back was pressed up against the control panel when the gap between the doors narrowed. The shock knocked him to the floor, which groaned under his weight. Smoke and debris filled the corridor, but the guards were gone. Then Moch sent him an image of the hallway from the other end, including his scorched lower body where two propane tanks were tucked under his retractable carrying arm. As the elevator doors shut for the last time, blocking his view of the blast zone, Tau knew that the resourceful observer unit had detected his difficulty and improvised a propane bomb to help him out. Tau signaled his thanks while he stood up beside the control panel.

The elevator lurched. The floor creaked again, then screamed like a metal nightmare as it gave way beneath his feet and tilted steeply toward the back wall. Startled, Tau grabbed at the air when his feet slid out from under him. The floor thumped and sagged more under the weight of his impact. The steeper angle granted Tau a view of the dark pit yawning beneath him. His right hand hit the elevator handrail that ran horizontally around the car when his legs dropped into the pit. The elevator picked up speed, trying to break his grip on the handrail whenever his boots made contact with the smooth tunnel wall and bumped him upward. The steep floor continued to bounce and rattle as if the rest of it might break loose at any time. Tensing his legs, he tried to curl away from the wall while grabbing the handrail with his other hand to pull himself up. He pictured himself climbing a steep mountain in an ice storm, and that gave him an idea. With one leg clear, he turned and levered himself up to place one foot on the bouncing floor while supporting as much of his weight as possible on the handrail. If the bouncing of the elevator didn't jar him loose—a problem he didn't normally have to deal with when rock climbing—he could hold that tense, three-point stance for a couple of minutes before he'd have to relax his muscles. When the handrail began to creak and pull away from the wall, as if it weren't made to hold almost two hundred pounds, Tau changed his mind. He looked up and saw the access hatch that he and Tymanov had used earlier. Leaning forward, he pushed open the hatch and got one hand on the rim when part of the handrail snapped away from the wall, bounced off the floor, and dropped into the pit, leaving him to hang by one hand. He pulled himself up, squirming to get his bulky suit through the hatch, and stopped to rest when he had his upper body on the roof. Although mostly blocked by his suit, the light shining through the hatch from the elevator's interior helped him get his bearings. The rotating pulley mechanism was of an ancient design using cheap metal, but the cable itself had the flat black appearance of strong carbon fiber. While he hauled his lower body up through the hatch, the elevator suddenly jerked and screamed in metallic pain. The floorplate broke loose and scraped against the wall, showering sparks. When Tau's feet cleared the hatch, the elevator shuddered when the floorplate crunched into the shaft wall and curled into a cutting edge that sliced up through the elevator car, leaving a jagged rent in the metal wall until it reached the roof and jammed hard in place. The elevator stopped with enough force to knock Tau onto his chest. The elevator lights went dark. The sudden silence in the shaft was deafening. Tau shook his head, wondering how he'd get to the bottom of the shaft before the bomb went off in twenty-five minutes. Dim red emergency lights flickered on, giving the shaft a hellish glow. The cable swung gently over his head like a hangman's noose connected to the top of the shaft, but it was too far to climb with too little time. Then he had it. He felt around in his pocket and withdrew the short length of spider line that had accompanied him on his rock-climbing trip. He stood on the gently swaying platform and started to bond the spider line's nanoglue patch to the metal frame of the elevator, then changed his mind and bonded it to the carbon fiber cable. He peered down through the hatch. The red emergency lights didn't allow him to see how long a drop it was to the bottom of the shaft, but it seemed like he'd traveled a long distance before the elevator stalled. He hoped the ninety-foot spider line was long enough because he wouldn't have the time or the opportunity to change his mind. He prepared the line so he could rappel down the shaft as quickly as possible, then squirmed through the hatch again to start his descent. Seconds later, he dropped below the point where the red emergency lights illuminated the shaft.

High overhead, the elevator groaned.

Swaying at the end of the line, Tau looked up at the dim red glow, then down into the darkness. "Screw it," he said, releasing the spider line.

It turned out to be a short drop, maybe ten feet, before Tau slammed into the dirt at the base of the shaft. On the wall beside him, he saw a dim white glow through the safety port of an airlock door. He checked his body for broken parts and decided he was okay except for a minor pain in his lower back. He stood, took a deep breath, and pushed the door button to cycle the airlock open. When the green light glowed, he cranked the handle and heard the *chuff* of pressure equalizing, followed by the scream of tortured metal and a clattering rumble overhead. The hair on the back of his neck stood up while he leaned back to see a dark shape plummeting past the red emergency lights in the shaft. He lunged through the gap between the heavy airlock door and the frame, then hauled it shut behind him. His heart pounding, he felt the elevator, or some portion of it, slam into the ground on the other side of the airlock door with a thundering boom.

So much for the element of surprise.

With less than twenty-two minutes remaining, Tau stepped out of the airlock into the shadowy tunnel near the Borovitsky Gate. Moch had gone with the archaeologists, so Tau had to rely on his own senses, limited by the cocoon of his spacesuit, to look for any threats. The work lights were off, leaving only the natural tunnel glow for illumination, blocked in many areas with equipment and crates. The usual red grit scraped under his feet.

A flicker of movement. Tau flattened against the curved white wall as a submachine gun sprayed the airlock with bullets. The gas-charged explosive rounds gouged large chunks out of the metal frame, but the bullets that struck the impenetrable white tunnel wall continued to ricochet. When the firing stopped, Tau peered around the corner. He saw no one. The crystal bomb glinted in the reflected shimmer of blue light from the portal. Zhukov had delivered a warning that the game had begun.

Tau stood to one side of a tall arch a few feet from the elevator. Beyond the arch he saw the portal with the bomb, along his only route to safety in the remaining time before the explosion. When he noticed a dark object on the floor nearby, his eyes widened. Zhukov was armed and he wasn't, but the general had foreseen that possibility; a commando-issue submachine gun rested in the middle of the archway.

"Go ahead. You must have seen it by now," said Zhukov. The voice in Tau's ears made him jump; Zhukov was in his head.

"What if I don't?" Tau asked.

"Then I'll walk over there and kill you."

"Why are you doing this?"

"There's no sport in killing an unarmed man."

Tau didn't wait; he backed up a few steps while Zhukov spoke, then ran as fast as he could in the short space and threw himself across the floor; he slid into the gun, then rolled to safety as Zhukov shot at him.

"You're quick, Wolfsinger. And here I thought you were dead after you went through the Tharsis portal; it switched off after you went through, and I assumed it was pointed at the same destination as the Borovitsky Gate. I guess I'm getting old."

"We all are, General. My friends are dead, you've destroyed my work, and you kidnapped Kate. I feel as if I've aged forty years in one week."

Zhukov ignored him. "I don't know which agency you really work for, but I got a report from Mandelbrot that you led the attack on my new barracks at Vulcan's Forge. You killed almost two hundred of my best men, although it was their own fault for not being more alert. They got soft under their former commander, which is why I made them watch Colonel Korolev take a walk outside without his suit."

"Is Mandelbrot here?"

"Unlikely. He was in transit in the rover when we got the report. Now you answer a question for me—whom do you work for?"

"NASA."

Tau heard Zhukov sigh. "And who else?"

"Just NASA."

"Don't lie to me. You didn't learn how to fight like that by commanding a desk."

The man was doing wonders for Tau's self-esteem. "You underestimate the infighting of office politics, General."

Zhukov chuckled. "I would have enjoyed working with you, Wolfsinger. It's too bad that I have to kill you."

Twenty minutes to go. Tau wondered if Kate and the rest of the team were on the train yet. The freight elevator was out of sight down the dark tunnel, and he wasn't getting any reports from Ari. "General, there's a bomb in this tunnel. Your base is going to disappear, and there isn't much time to get clear of the blast zone. If you'll surrender, we can get you to safety."

"Sounds like you have a problem. I thought that crystal bowling ball in front of the gate was a bomb, but I wasn't certain. I tried to push it through the portal, but it was a few thousand pounds too heavy. The weakness of old age, I suppose. However, you won't be going anywhere unless you kill me, and that's unlikely."

Tau wished he'd had some practice with a submachine gun on Yr Wyddfa, but primitive weapons weren't part of his training. All he knew about operating the gun was what Tymanov had shown him. "Why are you doing this? Why did you attack Vulcan's Forge?"

"Danforth didn't tell you?"

"Who's Danforth?"

"The woman who controlled your destiny, whether you were aware of it or not. Now I control it, because you're destined to die in this dark pit."

Nineteen minutes remaining. When the timer reached thirty seconds, Ari would move the freight train whether or not Tau was aboard, because it would take at least that much time for the train to reach full speed and clear the blast zone.

"It doesn't have to be this way, General. We can both walk out of this tunnel."

"I have the Borovitsky Gate and unlimited access to Russian troops. Your friend, Dr. McCloud, made progress on her examination, so I'm sure it won't be long before I have the ability to teleport my forces to their targets on Earth. Mars is just the beginning. I have international financial support for my efforts, because my country's economy must be stabilized. Russia will become a superpower once again, and our military technology will remain superior; our people will eat good food, wear decent clothes, and feel free to walk the streets without being gunned down by criminals. That's why I'm here, and that's why you're not going to stop me."

Tau started to respond, but he only had time to gasp as Zhukov fired his gun, hitting him with a smartbullet in the calf of his left leg, causing him to spin around and fall. The self-sealing layer of his suit would plug the bullet hole, but his leg didn't have the same ability. While his suit pressure slowly dropped, it felt as if someone with a hot ice pick had poked him in the leg, but he knew he had a few moments before the pain would slow him down. As far as he could tell, Zhukov hadn't moved to press his advantage yet, so he poked the barrel of the submachine gun around the curve of the wall and fired a burst into the tunnel.

Tau felt short of breath, but the hole sealed, and the suit began to repressurize. He ran a quick comparison of strengths through his head to evaluate the situation: Zhukov had a gun he knew how to use, he knew Tau's position, he was trained in the military arts, he had plenty of experience killing people, he was on his home ground, and his exoskeleton made him far stronger than Tau; on the other hand, Tau was inexperienced with his weapon, he was unsure of Zhukov's location, he'd always avoided violence, and he had a hole in his leg. He didn't want to kill the general, but he knew Zhukov would kill him without a second thought, and that couldn't happen. Kate, he had to think of Kate and make sure she left the area before the bomb went off, and the only way to do that would be to kill Zhukov and get the hell out of there. He didn't have to get into a fistfight with the man; all he had to do was shoot him. The submachine gun was set to fire explosive rounds. He wished he knew how to arm the smartbullets; their heat seeker points would help Tau hit his target if they got close, just as Zhukov's bullet had punctured his leg. He ground his teeth.

Warm liquid collected in his left boot. His leg would slow him down if he waited much longer. The bomb would go off in seventeen minutes. It was now or never.

Tau took a deep breath and rolled across the floor, firing blindly into the tunnel where he thought he'd seen muzzle flashes from the previous shots. When he saw a figure outlined against the blue glow of the portal, he aimed in that direction. A line of Zhukov's bullets bounced off the smooth white surface beside him while he rolled, but Tau continued shooting until the bullet clip was empty, and then he slammed into the far wall, making a perfect target for Zhukov.

But there was no response. Tau shut his eyes and tensed for the bullets he expected to hit him, but nothing happened. He opened his eyes and turned his head so he could look toward the gate, but he still couldn't see much in the dim light.

"General?"

Silence.

With sixteen minutes remaining before the train left, Tau staggered to his feet, looking around for Zhukov, but the general was nowhere in sight. He had to take a chance on running for the train and getting shot unless he wanted to stay where he was and watch the bomb explode.

Wary that Zhukov might shoot him from the shadows, Tau tossed his useless gun aside and limped farther into the tunnel. It felt as if someone was stabbing him in the leg with a dagger of ice.

A pile driver hit Tau in the chest. He felt his boots leave the ground, then he landed on his shoulders and somehow continued to roll to damp out some of the landing impact. One of his ribs hurt, but he couldn't tell if it was cracked or broken. He took a breath; like sucking flame through a straw. Bubbles of light popped in front of his eyes. Grunting, he staggered to his feet, desperately searching for Zhukov in the shadows. He saw a quick peripheral movement before another hammer hit him in the left arm; if he hadn't already been stumbling in that direction, he knew bones would have been broken. The space suit padding might be helping to soften the blows, but not by much. He put his right hand against a wall for support and frantically looked around for his attacker, hoping for an opening so he could strike back, but the general only seemed to taunt him with hit-and-run tactics. How did the old guy move so fast? And why didn't the general just shoot him at close range?

Confident and smiling, Zhukov appeared in front of Tau, no gun in sight. Tau ducked when Zhukov took a backhand swing through the space formerly occupied by Tau's head, then threw his right fist in toward Tau's ribs. Tau jumped back, avoiding the blow, and fell sideways. This movement placed him behind Zhukov's legs, so he rolled on his side and kicked at the backs of Zhukov's knees, hoping to bring him down. The shock from the impact with Zhukov's legs rattled Tau's brain; it was like kicking a concrete block.

Zhukov chuckled and turned around. "Very nice, Wolf-singer. That would have worked on someone else." Then he kicked Tau in the ribs. Tau heard and felt the crack on his left side. For a moment, he couldn't breathe at all while he rolled away, remembering how much punishment he'd been able to take as a boy when the other kids beat him up. Playing dead usually worked with the Navajo kids, but the white kids wouldn't stop so easily; and he was sure Zhukov was more like the white kids.

"Didn't anyone teach you hand-to-hand combat?" Zhukov asked. "I'm not one to pluck the wings from flies. You disappoint me."

Tau sipped some flaming air to make sure he could still breathe, then pushed himself up to his feet in time to see Zhukov lumbering toward him. Not knowing what else to do, he lowered his head and charged, delivering a solid head butt to the general's chest. Zhukov grunted and took a step back, then lifted one of his knees straight into Tau's faceplate. Tau turned his head to avoid having his faceplate broken, so Zhukov's knee bounced off the side of his helmet to twist Tau's neck even farther before the general kicked him onto his back. Tau wanted to roll again to absorb some of the landing shock, but a metal lump under his back broke his fall instead; his helmet hit the ground hard, leaving him dizzy and stunned.

Watching Tau twitch on his back, Zhukov shook his head and walked away. "I'll be back, Wolfsinger. You're doing better, but there's something I have to do before I give you the final lesson."

Tau tried sitting up, but the pain in his chest forced him back down. Drops of sweat beaded the inside of his faceplate, but at least they weren't drops of blood. At least, not yet. He grimaced and forced more air into his lungs. A little rest would be great right now, but he had only twelve minutes be-

fore the bomb went off, after which he'd get more than
enough rest if he stayed there to witness the explosion. Another memory of a childhood beating flashed through his
head, and it seemed almost real as the giant leering face of
Scott Carter, age fourteen, leaned in close to spit in Tau's right
eye. Scott had already stuck big pieces of bread up both of
Tau's nostrils—one of the few things Scott hadn't eaten for
lunch that day—before jumping up and down on his stomach
in front of three of his pals on the playground. In fact, this
memory was so real that Scott spoke to Tau, although his
voice was more demonic than Tau remembered:

> "Sleeping dead lulled with fire,
> Throwing wide Elysian doors.
> Stellar winds of bright desire,
> Eternal sentinel dreams no more."

Tau took a deeper breath, trying to clear his head. He
couldn't remember Scott sounding so intelligent. Something
was wrong, and it was something other than bad poetry. Fighting the dizziness and the burning embers in his ribs, Tau
rolled onto his hands and knees and Scott Carter faded into
the past where he belonged. Blinking sweat out of his eyes, he
saw the object he had landed on—the useless submachine
gun. He frowned. Was it useless? He'd emptied the magazine
at Zhukov. Still kneeling, he lifted the gun and flipped it over,
realizing it had a full clip of smartbullets; he didn't know how
to arm the heat seekers, but that only meant they'd act like
regular bullets.

Tau flipped the ammo switch and stood up. His wounded
leg remained partially numb, and he had no idea if that was
good or bad, but he could still walk. Eight minutes.

Nearing the blue glow of the gate, he saw Zhukov
crouched over the crystal sphere just inches away from the
portal. Zhukov had already said he wasn't able to pick up the
bomb, even with the added strength provided by his exoskeleton, so Tau didn't know what the general was doing until
he got closer. Then he saw the dark outline of the forklift that

Zhukov had parked beside the sphere, aimed toward the portal opening.

Tau raised the submachine gun, ready to fire if Zhukov spotted him moving closer. He wanted to be close enough not to miss this time, and the general seemed pretty confident that Tau was no longer a threat. When he was fifteen feet away, Tau took a breath to steady himself, raised the gun, and aimed at Zhukov's back. For the moment, his arms were steady, and he could ignore the pain in his left leg by putting most of his weight on his right. He clenched his teeth, thinking how smart it would be just to shoot the man in the back . . . but he couldn't do it.

"Zhukov!"

Zhukov slowly stood up straight and turned to face him in silence. Even in the dim light, Tau saw Zhukov rolling his eyes.

His ribs started to ache while he continued to hold the gun in firing position. "If you leave the bomb and go, I won't have to shoot you. Put your gun down."

Zhukov smiled. Tau's vision blurred and Scott Carter's face reappeared just inches from his nose.

Scott chewed gum when he spoke. "Infinity is eternal. The wargate is eternal. *I* am eternal. Meet the ashen face of Death."

Tau blinked, wondering what Zhukov must be doing behind Scott's face. "Don't move, Zhukov!"

"Whether I'm killed by you or by this bomb, it matters little to me," said Zhukov, striding toward Tau. "But I think this bomb is the greater threat."

Scott Carter smirked and spit in Tau's eye before saying:

> "The Mind of War dreams in red,
> Broken on the seventh sphere."

Tau knew he had to shoot before it was too late, but he couldn't see beyond Scott's face. His finger tightened on the trigger just as the gun was yanked out of his hands. Unable to see what Zhukov was doing, Tau tried jumping forward, but Zhukov had already moved away.

"Get out of my head!" Tau yelled. He didn't have time to go nuts. Not until Kate was safe.

Scott Carter was up to no good. Tau didn't know where he'd found it, but Scott placed the barrel of a Russian submachine gun up against Tau's nose. It looked like Tau's gun. Then he heard Kate's voice somewhere in the background. She yelled at Tau and told him to hurry before she spoke directly to Scott:

> "Dreams of light
> must end in fire.
> No more than one
> I would meet."

Scott looked confused when he heard Kate's voice. He frowned and turned away with the gun, leaving Tau's vision clear. Four minutes left.

Zhukov had secured the wire mesh of an equipment sling around the bomb so that he could pick it up with the forklift. He'd only have to push the bomb through the gate to protect the portal ring and minimize the damage to the tunnel. Tau didn't know what effect the corrosive atmosphere on the other side of the portal would have on the bomb, but he didn't have time to work out an elaborate plan. If Zhukov turned around again, he'd be able to shoot Tau at point-blank range with the gun hanging from his shoulder. Tau almost made it to the forklift seat before Zhukov noticed him.

"*Stoi!*"

There wasn't time to climb into the seat, so Tau reached into the driver's cage of the forklift and slammed his hand down on the accelerator pedal while Zhukov raised his gun. Bullets sparked off the top of the driver's cage as the forklift smashed into the general's leg, knocking him down onto the forks. Tau lurched forward to keep his hand on the accelerator. The metal forks bounced forward through the glowing blue mist, carrying Zhukov on through with his body sprawled over the bomb. As soon as Zhukov vanished, Tau slammed his hand against the brake, then climbed into the seat so that he could shift the forklift into reverse. The bomb had to go off in the tunnel to have any chance of shutting down the portal and destroying the Red Star base.

Yanking the shift lever into reverse, Tau stomped on the accelerator again. The forklift bobbed as if it were stuck in the glowing blue light, then lurched backward with the tires screeching. Tau winced when the metal forks dissolved and the crystal sphere clumped heavily onto the tunnel floor.

Zhukov was gone. Tau knew he wouldn't last very long in the corrosive atmosphere; he might be dead already. Circling a star that would soon explode, the ruined world on the other side of the gate would be a lonely tomb for the general.

Two minutes left. Tau turned the forklift and floored the accelerator. The motor whined while he pushed it to its limits. When he reached the end of the tunnel, he skidded to a stop and lurched out of the seat. He stumbled on his wounded leg and fell on his left side, but he got up again immediately. Gritting his teeth, he tried to ignore the pain shooting through his leg and his ribs while he hopped through the rubble to where his strike team had blown their way through the rockfall. He hoped Kate and the others had reached the train via the freight elevator, because there wouldn't be any chance of helping them if they weren't there already.

Close enough to the train now to see the hulking shapes of his siege units, he knew that at least some of them had returned. According to Tau's plan, two units riding a flatbed car at the rear of the train would fire explosive rounds into the ceiling of the tunnel whenever they passed an area where a previous rockfall had blocked the tracks. They hoped that these new rock plugs would help to baffle the shock wave they expected from the Red Star explosion. With any luck, the blast would be focused up along the elevator shafts and other paths of least resistance beneath the Red Star base. However, there was some chance that the entire tunnel would act like a big pipe bomb, as the previous, larger bomb had done when the parallel tunnel was clear.

When Tau hauled himself up the short ladder that led to the padded freight car, the entire train rose up above the tracks with a low hum and started to move. He had to get to a padded area to survive the train's powerful acceleration. But he was too slow. With one foot on the floor of the freight car and the other on the top rung of the ladder, the forward lurch of the train knocked him down, then slid him to the back wall of the car while it rapidly picked up speed. Tau hit with his left leg first, prompting a wave of flame to roll through the nerves in his body. His brain wanted him to go to sleep for a while. Fighting the G forces, he tried to work his way around so that his back was against the padded wall with his arms and legs in safe positions.

"Twenty-seven seconds to destruct," said Ari, his dim outline just visible nearby.

Tau grunted in response. He twisted his head and saw Kate strapped into the acceleration couch. She was safe from Scott Carter; he'd have to thank Kate for distracting him from Tau. A few inches behind his head, Laika yapped at him in silence, the sound lost inside her bubble helmet.

Before he blacked out, a yellow flame in a sphere of blue light appeared in Tau's head. Was it Gwatwar? He wasn't sure if the entity was real, or if this vision was the result of a concussion, but the flame spoke with the calm, rumbling voice of a volcano to deliver its brief message:

"Its journey ended,
the Sentinel sleeps."

27

AFTER two days of repairs in the medical facility at Vulcan's Forge, with Kate at his bedside, Tau spent one day in the hab in an unsuccessful attempt to repair Ari Junior. But there were no signs of personality or reasoning ability in the AI. The comsats and the Marsnet were functioning again, so the link with Earth had been reestablished, but Ari Junior had "died" fighting the alien virus. With the cycler due to hit orbit that evening, giving some of them a chance for immediate return to Earth, Tau gave up on the damaged AI and made a final journey in the rover.

Tau visited his broken dreams on the red sands of Tharsis. His new colony, built up from the tiniest of building blocks, had become a tomb for almost two hundred Russian soldiers. The broken skylights of the colony stared up into space like empty eye sockets in forgotten skulls. Shattered glass glittered among the rocks. Black smears defaced the pitted exterior walls like graffiti. His noble goal of building had been subverted into destruction, warped by the ambitions of other humans into a contest of primitive urges. He had come full circle, from builder to destroyer, while serving the needs of unseen puppet masters. Now, he wanted to leave this violent episode behind and become a creator once more, but the ghosts—the *chindi* of the dead Russian soldiers—were forcing him to leave this tomb world, reminding him that Earth was his home, among his own people.

The Max Thorn AI had reported to Tau that the Red Star base, Gwatwar, and the Borovitsky Gate were all destroyed in the massive blast from the crystal bomb. An orbital radar image, looking through the dust, showed that the great rift of the Valles Marineris had been extended east by two hundred miles. Tymanov would have been proud to know that his atoms were scattered into the upper atmosphere by the same explosion that destroyed Red Star, creating a dust cloud that would hang over the surface for months. Death was everywhere, forcing Tau to acknowledge his own mortality and his barbaric nature, revealed to him by Mars, the god of war.

Tau's strike force had returned to Yr Wyddfa, assisted by Kate and the Thoth AI. Y Moch, damaged when he rescued Tau, wasn't able to make it through the portal under his own power, but he was assisted by one of the larger siege units. The original Ari, his Companion AI, had returned to Yr Wyddfa with the rest of the team. In the powerful, armored body that Ddraig gave him, Ari had developed a variety of new capabilities that he didn't want to lose. Aided by Tau's knowledge, Ari had grown into his command function with the strike force, and he felt that there was much more he could learn from Ddraig while introducing "human aspects" into the machine culture. Ari could have provided the "seed" for a new Builder AI ready to be trained, but Tau didn't want to deprive his creation of the opportunity to return with the rest of the team. As soon as the strike force left, the Max Thorn AI intended to point the teleportation gate at its homeworld so that it could reestablish contact with the Gwrinydd Rationals.

When given the choice, Ari chose a new life. Tau felt like his only child had left home.

But Tau had a new Companion.

Encouraged by all that was learned about the alien culture that built the tunnel system and the gates, the archaeological team decided to remain at the excavation—all except one. Kate had gathered enough information through her interactions with the Thoth AI so that she was anxious to start publishing formal papers on aspects of the alien culture. Using communications hardware set up by the archaeological team, a special datalink would allow Kate to stay in contact with Thoth. She also planned to be among the first to communicate with the Gwrinydd Rationals and the Free Mentalities when Thoth eventually made contact. Even Novikov acknowledged that Kate had earned her fame, so it was time for her to go and seek her fortune. In any case, well aware of what Tau went through to rescue her, and the rest of the archaeologists, Kate wouldn't have felt right about leaving him again. After a long discussion, they had come to the decision of returning to Earth together on the cycler.

After Kate brought Laika safely back to Vulcan's Forge, she was too busy to take care of their new pet, so Yvette volunteered her services. Tau noticed that Laika calmed down whenever she was in the presence of Kate or Yvette, so that made everyone happier. Tau wasn't thrilled with the prospect of spending the next several months in a closed spacecraft with the vicious little animal, but he knew he'd be safe as long as Kate or Yvette was around.

THE shuttle had to lift at night to achieve a matching eccentric orbit with the cycler on its final swing around Mars. This cycler, the *Aldrin*, was one of four built to make regular cargo runs between the Earth and Mars, met by shuttles to load and unload at each end of its flight. The energy required to escape the gravity well of Mars was less than 20 percent of that required to leave Earth, so Tau thought the mild shuttle launch felt like a ride in a ballistic hopper. Yvette was their pilot, reading off altitudes and speeds in a steady voice, rattled only by the vibrations of the shuttle. Tau wished he could have seen more in the deep blackness of the Martian sky, but the narrow windows made sight-seeing difficult. Beside him, Kate gripped his hand hard enough that he felt it through the glove. Laika sat on her lap, watching Tau with a look of pure hatred.

Docking with the *Aldrin* proceeded without difficulty, guided by the precise trajectory adjustments of the docking AI. It made things easier that the *Aldrin* wasn't spinning to simulate gravity as it would be once it left orbit. After a thump, a clank, and a series of clicks, they established a good seal with the docking collar and were able to swap places with the last five members of the arriving cycler crew who would now descend to Vulcan's Forge for the first time. The rest of the cargo had been off-loaded on previous orbits, so Tau and

the two women didn't have any special tasks to perform on arrival. Refueling had already been accomplished. They shook
hands with the departing crew, then Kate and Yvette started to
explore and settle in before the trans-Earth injection burn
would force them into their seats less than an hour later. After
the hatch was closed and sealed, it occurred to Tau that he had
only seen two men and two women floating into the tube connecting the *Aldrin* to the shuttle—easily explained if a crew
member had left on a previous drop. He backed out of the
hatch area, bumping into a rack of handheld maneuvering
units—nitrogen guns—attached to the wall by Velcro. Along
with everyone else, Tau had spent a day practicing how to
control the direction of his space walks with a nitrogen gun,
but he wasn't an expert with it. The nitrogen gun reminded
Tau of high-tech versions of handheld crossbows used for
hunting; a stubby handle with a hole in one end was topped
with a crossbar that also had one hole at each end. There were
two triggers on the gun: If he held one trigger down, nitrogen
would jet out of the two holes in the crossbar. If he held the
other trigger, nitrogen would jet out of the hole in the handle.
By squeezing the correct trigger and holding the gun in the
proper direction, the nitrogen would provide enough propul-
sive force to move an astronaut floating freely in space. Tau's
problem during simulator practice had been estimating when
to stop pressing the triggers; he would pick up too much speed
before having to fire the jets again to stop, plunging him
straight into the target. Then he'd spent eight minutes tumbling through space at the end of his tether. He felt fortunate
that he'd never had to perform an actual space walk.

Tau spotted Yvette hovering around the flight console. She
still wore her pressure suit, as they all would be until after the
TEI burn was completed.

"Everything look okay?" asked Tau.

"I think so. There are some extra controls here that I'm not
familiar with, but the nav computer is supposed to handle
everything anyway."

Then the main lighting system went out, plunging them

into relative darkness. Only the instrument panel lights continued to glow in their candy colors.

Tau looked around. "Is that normal?"

"No." She floated over to the housekeeping console, located the two switches she was searching for, and pushed them a few times. Nothing happened. "The APU is off-line. Want to run back and check the engineering module?"

"Sure," said Tau, kicking off so that he could float out of the control room.

Tau heard the musical sound of Kate's voice in his ears while he floated down the dark corridor toward the rear of the cycler. "Tau? What's going on?"

"Auxiliary power unit. Main lighting is out, but that's all. I'm going back to check it now."

"Shouldn't the emergency reds be on? It's dark in here."

"Probably. Where are you now?"

"Green corridor, on my way back to flight."

Navigating by the telltales and other random instrument lights along the way, Tau's eyes gradually adjusted so he could avoid obstacles. The occasional window facing Mars provided a brighter red glow. Still, when he reached the hatch to the engineering module, he smacked into it with a thump because he couldn't see it.

The APU and its fuel cells were lit by the soft red glow of blinking indicator lights, but there was enough machinery in the way to slow Tau's progress. There were no windows in this cabin, and dark shapes loomed just a few inches ahead of him, making it difficult to float along at a steady pace even though he saw his target thirty feet ahead. He had no idea how anyone could have serviced equipment in this room without floating in weightlessness.

Out of a corner of his eye, he caught a flash of light, then a knife plunged toward his face.

With new reflexes developed on Yr Wyddfa, Tau raised his arms and tried to move his head away, but he continued to float toward the knife, deflecting it into his shoulder. The heavy fabric tore, and his shoulder felt the impact, but the diamond-edged blade glanced off, leaving a slow leak in the suit that would quickly seal itself. His hand caught an overhead pipe while he looked around desperately for his attacker, curling into a ball to lash out with his right foot in the direction the knife had come from. His foot hit something, but he didn't know if it was another pipe or his unseen enemy. Then he felt another impact on his lower leg just above his right boot. Fire burned through the skin of his leg before he could pull away, kicking off with his left foot to get clear of the knife. With his back to the APU, his eyes could barely see a spacesuited figure hurtling toward him, knife extended toward his stomach. Tau floated where he couldn't kick off from anything, so he could only watch as the knife moved in. Quivering blood drops danced a weightless ballet in front of his helmet. His suit pressure was dropping because of the tear in his right leg, but the air pressure in the cycler was high enough that he wouldn't pass out for a long time. Then his fingers touched a pipe, and he jerked himself out of the knife's path, banging his helmet against the wall with a ringing sound. The attacker turned and slashed with the knife, but Tau rotated, and the deadly arm sailed past, catching for a moment between two coolant lines leading into the APU. Tau reacted by lunging forward against his enemy's shoulder, throwing his weight across the man's body while he wrenched the arm between the two coolant lines. Their helmets were close enough that Tau heard the scream when the man's forearm broke. Tau turned his head, but it was too dark to see the face behind the visor. Thinking that the broken arm would slow him down, Tau pushed himself back, then felt another impact from the knife when it punched into his left side. He jerked away to the right, then kicked off against his enemy to launch himself backward, pain ripping through him while his wounds screamed for attention. Each new puncture released pressure from his suit faster than the old punctures could seal themselves. While the pressure dropped, his lungs burned from the pain and the exertion.

Recognizing the spot where he'd entered engineering, Tau

turned and looked for a way out. He spotted the hatch and pulled himself closer, searching for his enemy. Something banged off the back of his helmet. He turned to block another slash of the knife, now held in his attacker's left hand. Again he kicked off the wall, trying to break free, looking for anything he could use as a weapon. The back of his shoulder thumped into the wall and he heard a tearing noise; a nitrogen gun had torn loose from a Velcro rack. He grabbed it. The gun wouldn't serve as a weapon, but it meant there was another hatch nearby, an external hatch for maintenance and propellant loading.

Red light flashed off a visor close to the APU as his attacker sailed toward him.

Tau spun around, slapped open the safety cover, and fired the explosive bolts on the hatch.

Although the cabin pressure wasn't high, it was high enough. After a loud bang and a flash, the hatch blew out on its hinges, and explosive decompression sucked Tau out through the opening. He caught the rim of the hatchway with his left hand, crouching in an attempt to swing his body back around to the outer hull before he sailed off into space. He had no tether, and he wasn't anxious to become a new Martian satellite. The glow from Mars was brighter as daylight broke across the ruddy landscape. Looking in through the hatchway, he saw his enemy approaching with a startled expression on his face.

Josh Mandelbrot.

Mandelbrot's arms flailed when he reached the hatch. He turned his body enough to slow his progress, but the pressure continued pushing against his broken arm to force him outside. Tau maintained his grip on the hatchway and leaned his head back, hoping Mandelbrot would sail on past into the blackness. After a quick bump against his faceplate, that's exactly what happened, but Mandelbrot grabbed a tether line on his way through the hatch. It wasn't attached to Mandelbrot's suit, but it was anchored to the inner wall at the other end. As Tau watched the tether uncoil in front of his face, he grabbed it and jerked, hoping to yank it from Mandelbrot's grasp, but the recoil merely brought him back toward Tau. He still held the knife in his left hand. Desperate, Tau fired the nitrogen gun while holding the tether, forcing the two of them apart again. The tears in his suit fought to seal themselves before all the air pressure was lost, and the loud hiss of his air supply indicated emergency pressurization, but he was getting dizzy. Taking deeper breaths that made his punctured side burn, hoping to get enough air to remain conscious, he realized he was outside, and that was bad.

The main engine would soon ignite for the TEI burn. He didn't want to be outside when that happened.

Mandelbrot awkwardly tried to pull himself along the tether to get closer to Tau. Tau fired the gun again, sending them both in a wide arc that took them a third of the way around the hull before Tau hooked the toe of his boot into one of the loops beside a fueling valve. Mandelbrot orbited a few feet overhead, attached to the tether now, but unable to control his flight without a nitrogen gun. Tau thought about releasing the tether, but then he'd trap himself outside without any attachment to the *Aldrin*, and he didn't trust his skills with the nitrogen gun to keep him from floating off into space. Like it or not, they both needed the tether to stay alive, but Mandelbrot wore a spacesuit that didn't have any holes in it. Once again, Mandelbrot started hauling himself closer on the tether, slowed only by his useless right arm. So that he could haul on the tether, Mandelbrot had slipped the blade of his knife into one of the forearm pockets in his right sleeve. Everything started to spin in Tau's vision; if he was going to do anything, he had to do it before he passed out or Mandelbrot got too close.

Looking down, he saw the fueling valve for the liquid hydrogen tank. The insulated tank was pressurized to allow for propellant flow in the microgravity environment prior to the TEI burn. With Mandelbrot almost within arm's reach, Tau crouched, grabbed one of the valve loops with his hand, flattened himself against the hull as best he could, slipped his forearms through the loops, and looked up. Mandelbrot stopped, realizing what Tau was about to do, but unable to react.

Tau opened the valve.

Liquid hydrogen spewed out in a widening stream, sparkling when it struck Mandelbrot's helmet and upper body before becoming a gas. As Tau held on to the tether and closed the valve, Mandelbrot released his grip on the tether and arced back from the glittering stream until he bounced off the hull twelve feet from Tau. The supercold liquid hydrogen had frozen his suit stiff wherever it made contact. When Mandelbrot hit the hull, the left arm of his suit shattered, then the suit's torso broke into fragments when it slammed against the *Aldrin.*

"That's for Max," said Tau, watching Mandelbrot's shattered body drift away from the hull.

Now he had to get back inside.

Along with the other trainees, Tau had learned about the dangers of spacewalking. If a suit had a significant leak, the lack of an oxygen supply to the brain would cause the astronaut to lose consciousness within ten seconds. While recompression could be possible within the first minute, the astronaut would not be able to help himself—a quick paralysis would be followed by brief convulsions before the body settled into its final paralysis. During this time, all the water in the astronaut's body would boil off. While water vapor collected in soft tissues and in the venous blood, the body would swell to twice its normal size if not restrained by a spacesuit. After the first rush of gas from the lungs during decompression, the continuous evaporation of water would cool the mouth and nose to near-freezing temperatures, although the rest of the body would experience a more gradual cooling. Blood circulation would have ceased at that point. Tau didn't want to study Mandelbrot's body as it expanded; a brief cloud of gas left the holes in the suit as the body twitched a few times, but that was all he saw.

Tau wasn't sure how much time he had before the TEI

burn. The process was automated, and if Yvette chose to bypass the navigation AI to interfere with the burn, they wouldn't be able to make their launch window for the seventeen-month flight back to Earth. He grabbed the tether, fighting the dizziness and the pain signals from his body, and hauled himself back toward the hatch. He only used the nitrogen gun once to give himself a boost when he neared the open hatchway. With one last look at Mandelbrot, floating twenty feet away from the hull, he released the tether and shut the hatch, manually dogging it closed.

The adrenaline drained from his sytem. He felt like his whole body was wet with blood. These near-death experiences were getting to be a habit, and he didn't like it. The pain felt distant now, like the memory of a dream. Waves of darkness crashed against his body in a dark sea. He closed his eyes, gathering his energy to say one word into his suit microphone when he heard the first rumble of thunder from the main engine.

"Kate?"

28

WHEN Virginia Danforth got home, she kicked off her shoes and left them in the middle of the white marble floor in the foyer. This was unusual, since she preferred to keep everything in its place.

Turning right, she entered her study and set her briefcase down on the dark mahogany desk, then poured herself a glass of Scotch. This was unusual, since she never drank liquor on an empty stomach.

A man appeared in the doorway, wearing a black suit, a

black overcoat, and black gloves. This was very unusual, since Danforth lived alone.

She looked him in the eye and took a deep breath. Her voice quavered slightly as if she were nervous, but only her closest associates would have detected it. "I've been expecting you."

The man reached into his coat and pulled out a gun. It was a subtle weapon—silenced, of course—an assassin's weapon for the choosiest of executioners. His hand was steady while he took aim at Danforth's eyes.

"Make it quick," she said.

And he did.

ON his way to Moffett Field from his new apt in the government towers, Tau joined the morning commute of gray people on a gray day going to their gray jobs. The southbound 101 slidewalk smelled like burnt machine oil. The overhead canopy kept the rain out, but it also kept the smell contained in the slidewalk tube. The heavy gravity was ponderous, dragging him down even though he'd been back on Earth for a month. The *Aldrin* had been spinning to simulate Earth gravity on the return flight, but Tau suspected they hadn't reached one full G of spin on the ship because he'd felt sluggish for weeks after he reached Earth. Now that his strength was returning, he wanted to check in at NASA before leaving with Kate to visit his parents in Arizona. He still had the same boss, Yvette Fermi, but their experience on Mars had qualified them for promotions, prompting Yvette to stay with NASA a bit longer. Director Chakrabarti's mysterious disappearance was never explained, but Yvette became the Director of Ames Research Center upon her return.

The crowd on the slidewalk was the usual combination of riffraff mixed in with businesspeople on their way to work. In the tradition of commuters in crowds everywhere, Tau tried not to look anyone in the eye or speak to strangers; it was surprising how fast he'd fallen back into his old patterns of behavior once he'd returned to the city—or so it seemed.

Cruising along in the fast lane so that he could get out of the smelly tube as soon as possible, Tau saw a commotion in the slow lane up ahead. Curious, he hopped onto the slower slidewalk lane to his right, then sidestepped once more to place himself in the slow lane. Just ahead, the hunched figure of a gray-haired man in a polyplaid suit spoke to a tall, tanned, shirtless thug with heavy bioengineered muscles. The old man tried to push the thug back with the tip of his silver cane, and that was when Tau spotted the nanotattoo of a skull with glowing eyes creeping north along the thug's chest.

Tau wormed his way through the pedestrians watching the scene. A young blond woman stepped around Skull Chest and punched the old man in the stomach, then laughed when he doubled over and coughed.

"Leave him alone," said Tau.

The blonde's eyebrows went up when she turned and saw Tau, her long fingernails glowing with patterns of lights that spelled out tiny insults. "Hey, haven't I seen you somewhere before?"

The blonde's snake tattoo had been wrapped around her neck, but now it was crawling down toward her breasts. He didn't see the rest of the skin gang, so he assumed these two were commuting to their abandoned BART mugging station in East Palo Alto.

The blonde poked Tau in the chest. "I asked you a question."

"You must have me confused with somebody else."

Ignoring Tau, Skull Chest balled his right hand into a fist and brought it up sharply, backhanding the old man in the face. The man staggered back against the handrail, steadying himself with his cane.

"You can stop the pain, old man. Just hand over your money," said Skull Chest. He extended his meaty hand, palm up. "Give me the chip."

"Excuse me," said Tau, pushing the blonde aside. When Skull Chest looked back toward Tau, he found the point of a black rod with two electrodes stuck up his right nostril. When he returned to his office, Tau found the lightning rod in a package that Tymanov had left for him, just in case he didn't come back.

"Hey," said Skull Chest. "Those are illegal."

"Make a move and I keep your nose," said Tau, his voice calm and even.

The blonde reached for Tau's arm. "Let him go."

"I wouldn't do that," said Tau, pushing the rod farther up the thug's nose. "He's got a big nose, so it's hard for me to miss."

The slidewalk was approaching a roped-off gap where an abandoned platform had been torn down. In place of the platform was a drop of about eighteen feet to the cracked pavement of the former roadway. Tau led his prize close to the rail and gestured with his head for the blonde to come closer. "We're going to play a little game. When we reach that gap up there, you're both going to jump."

"What if we don't?" asked Skull Chest.

"Then you'll stop poking your nose in other people's business." Tau smiled. "Five hundred thousand volts at this range might blow your nose clean off your face. If you jump, you might get a broken leg or two, but at least you'll have your looks."

The crowd of gawkers moved in closer to watch the drama, egging him on with encouraging remarks. As they hit the gap, Skull Chest rolled his eyes at Tau to make sure he was serious, then hopped over the rope and plummeted to the pavement. Tau smiled and politely gestured for the blonde to follow. When she hesitated, the gray-haired old man leaned on his cane and kicked her over the edge; the blonde squeaked and disappeared. Two exits later, the crowd was still applauding as Tau stepped off the slidewalk.

TAU'S father taught him that a person learns to live with evil by understanding its cause. The beauty of harmony is the goal, and that beauty is reflected in the pattern, where every cause has an effect. Evil is balanced by beauty, and both have reason to exist. The ripple on the water alters the reflection of light to the eye and changes a person's view of reality; the reflection of evil is beauty that provides contrast in reality. To walk in beauty, in *hozro*, is to walk in harmony, understanding evil's purpose in life.

Tau returned to the Navajo reservation to seek harmony by understanding his own evil. Violence had become part of his being out of necessity, but it was hard for him to be at peace with that part of his nature. He needed his father's help, and the help of his people. Wanting to be with Tau for his spiritual journey, Kate accompanied him to the reservation. Kate and Yvette had made arrangements to share Laika, so the yappy little monster went along for the ride.

When Tau arrived, the receptionist at the hospital told him his father was performing a Night Chant ceremonial, a *Yeibichai*, for the Tsossie outfit. She drew Tau a map so that he could find the Tsossie spread; it was the type of map that was the most common in Dinetah, involving bad dirt roads, dry washes, gas pipelines, faded signs, a mobile home, a windmill, a trading post, a wrecked pickup truck, and a chapter house. It was the last night of the nine-day ceremonial, and he would be welcome to attend and share in the blessing. What Tau most wanted was to arrange for his own curing ritual with his father, a three-day Enemy Way Sing, but sharing in a *Yeibichai* would be a good start; he would have to think positive thoughts to join in with the kinfolk and friends of the Tsossie family.

In the gathering darkness, the red sandstone mesas and the desolate terrain made Tau feel as if he'd returned to Mars. Dr. Kee Joseph Wolfsinger was chanting inside the Tsossie hogan when Tau finally found it. The hogan was round, built of earth and wood, and it looked old. The scent of juniper was strong in the night air, perhaps because it was the only source of firewood on top of the mesa. Pickup trucks were randomly parked around the hogan, and a crowd of maybe thirty people, supporters who had chosen not to participate in the ceremony, were clustered around the outdoor campfire. Dr. Wolfsinger's normally strong voice, rising and falling in a steady rhythm, sounded a little hoarse, which wasn't surprising since there were 576 songs he'd had to perform during the nine-day Sing.

The hours passed quickly. Since it was the last night of the Yeibichai, boys and girls between the ages of seven and thirteen were initiated into the ceremonial life of the adults. Two masked figures appeared, representing the *Yei*—Grandfather of the Monsters and Female Divinity. Each of the boys was led into the firelight; while one of the *Yei* placed corn pollen on their bare shoulders, the other masked figure struck each one with a bundle of reeds. The girls were next to be marked with the sacred yellow corn pollen. The initiation was completed when the two *Yei* removed their masks, revealing to the children that they were actors and not the gods themselves. Then each child had a chance to wear one of the *Yei* masks so that each could see the world through the eyes of the gods.

After the initiation ceremony, twelve dancers performed the Yeibichai dance for the rest of the night. Kate slept for a few hours, but Tau remained awake, not wanting to miss any of the spectacle. Laika remained at Kate's side, huddling close to her body for warmth, occasionally growling at Tau to remind him of his place. As Tau watched how each dancer performed, he was reminded how his father had always spoken of the individual's power to create; that a human's vision, strength, and courage come from his own spirit, and that everything we have comes from the function of the creative mind. Each dancer performed in his or her unique way, and the beauty was in seeing the complexity of each individual dance as part of one integrated whole. Tau had done what was necessary to reach his goal, and he was finally realizing that he had achieved *hozro*.

At dawn, everyone was outside, standing to face the rising sun as they chanted the Dawn Prayer. The ceremony concluded by scattering the sands used in the five complex drypaintings Tau's father had created during the *Yeibichai*. The sands were gathered on a blanket, then Dr. Wolfsinger took the blanket and walked east, then south, then west, then north.

He raised his arms to Father Sky and down to Mother Earth, then scattered the sands in the blanket to the six directions they had come from. With his arms raised again, he turned to face the crowd, chanting, "In beauty it is finished. In beauty it is finished."

The Sing was over. As the participants said their good-byes, Tau and Kate approached his father for the first time since they had arrived. The old man looked tired as he sat down on a smooth rock outcropping with a good view of the canyon below. Tau and Kate, holding hands, sat beside him and said nothing, absorbing the beauty of their surroundings. A hawk circled lazily in an updraft of thermals from the desert floor. The sounds of the departing pickup trucks became a distant memory. The Wind People brushed their faces with a warm breeze and played with the hair on their heads. The quiet was pervasive, filling every pore of their bodies. Even Laika was quiet for a change.

Tau felt as good as he had ever felt. His spirit was at peace.

In beauty it is finished.